Pay the Price

About the author

Sam Tobin was born in Recife, Brazil and ended up in Manchester, England. He's been a BAFTA nominated producer, worked in kebab shops and studied law. He's lived in Moss Side, Brixton and Hollywood.

PAY
THE
PRICE
SAM TOBIN

HODDER

First published in Great Britain in 2023 by Hodder & Stoughton
An Hachette UK company

This paperback edition published in 2023

1

A CIP catalogue record for this title is available from the British Library

Paperback ISBN 978 1 399 70174 7
eBook ISBN 978 1 399 70175 4

Typeset in Monotype Plantin by Manipal Technologies Limited

Printed and bound in Great Britain by Clays Ltd, Elcograf S.p.A.

Hodder & Stoughton policy is to use papers that are natural, renewable and
recyclable products and made from wood grown in sustainable forests. The
logging and manufacturing processes are expected to conform to the
environmental regulations of the country of origin.

Hodder & Stoughton Ltd
Carmelite House
50 Victoria Embankment
London EC4Y 0DZ

www.hodder.co.uk

To Dr Hughes

Prologue

Standing on the pavement, it was impossible to know the strongroom was even there.

The house itself was one of a row of large, Victorian semi-detached homes on the outskirts of Bolton town centre. To their rear were the densely packed terraces of Daubhill, home to Bolton's South Asian community. Ahead of them a patchwork of fields and houses slowly fell away as the land climbed up towards Winter Hill, the peak that towered over all of Bolton.

The strongroom lay deep within the footprint of the house. It had no windows facing the outside world, nothing to reveal its presence to the casual observer.

The walls, floor and ceiling of the strongroom had been specially constructed with steel-reinforced concrete. The kind used for bank vaults. It had cost tens of thousands of pounds but set against the value of what was inside the room it was a drop in the ocean.

There was a single way in and out: a heavy, metal door set into an equally sturdy metal frame. The door had no handle inside or out, and on either side of it was an inset keypad. Without the eight-digit combination there was no way to get in or out of the room short of industrial-strength explosives.

The formidable door lay wide open. Someone was inside.

Slow, deliberate footsteps pressed down into the thick, burgundy pile of the carpet as a young woman crept past the exquisitely crafted, bespoke cabinets that lined the room. Made from imported Brazilian hardwoods and finished with a genuine gold trim, each cabinet was glass-fronted to better display its contents.

Racks of solid gold jewellery. Necklaces, earrings and bangles. Hundreds of thousands of pounds' worth. Rows of Rolex watches, each larger and more ostentatious than the last, sitting proudly beside their boxes and certificates of authenticity. All glistening softly beneath spotlights recessed into the ceiling.

The young woman passed them without so much as a second glance. She had something far more valuable in mind.

She wore skinny blue jeans, white trainers and a crop top beneath her knee-length, black padded jacket. The standard uniform of a million northern teenage girls.

Her hair had been scraped atop her head into a tottering bun, which gave a clear view of her face. She had the determined, thickly applied make-up of someone well used to passing for much older than her young years. But beneath the foundation, contouring and darkly painted eyebrows, there was no mistaking that she was barely older than a child.

She had only been in the room once before but it was just as she remembered it. She could never forget the smell. A strong, solvent-clean stink of the brand new. Trapped in the airless room it was overpowering.

Passing through the room something caught her eye. She stopped dead in her tracks.

There on the wall hung a painting. The girl didn't have to look at the signature to know who painted it. Back before she was permanently excluded, Art was the only subject to ever hold her desperately divided attention. It was an L.S. Lowry. A *genuine* L.S. Lowry.

She held her breath, in awe to be so close to true genius.

Absent were the painter's iconic, scratchy figures and crowded terraces. This painting depicted a hillside view across Bolton. A dark church nestled between smoking mills with the city stretching away into a grey horizon broken only by chimney stacks. Bolton had changed immeasurably from when Lowry had sat atop a hill to paint it. The mills and chimneys were long gone. The churches deserted or converted into mosques. But the girl instantly recognised the endless, grey horizon. Some things never change.

Overwhelmed by the beauty of it she reached out, brushing her fingers against the frame, eager to somehow be closer to what she saw.

A noise came from outside. The distinctive sound of Punjabi spoken with a thick Bolton accent. Someone was home. The girl broke away from the painting and turned her attention to what she'd come for.

The safe sat on the floor, no taller than waist height. Unlike the wooden cabinets it was a new addition. It stood out, an ugly afterthought by someone unconvinced by the ample security already on offer.

The girl knelt down, her knees sinking into the soft carpet. The voices were getting louder. She didn't have much time.

She looked at the back of her hand where two sets of numbers had been scrawled in biro. The first set had got her into the room. The second set she began to quickly punch into the safe.

A small, red light came on. The safe gave a short, sharp buzz and remained closed.

The girl looked down at her hand. She was sweating. The numbers had begun to smudge. She took a breath and moving slower this time, she put the numbers in again. One digit at a time. Check the hand, type the number. Check the hand. Type the number. She willed herself to ignore the voices outside, to forget who it was she was stealing from and what he'd do if he caught her.

She pressed the final number and a small, green light flashed on, to the accompaniment of a satisfyingly solid clicking sound. The safe door swung open.

She was greeted with the sight of stacks and stacks of notes and several velvet bags. Despite the voices outside the room, her curiosity got the better of her and she risked a glimpse inside one of the bags. Dozens of uncut diamonds spilled out.

Scattering through her fingers and into the deep pile of the carpet. There was no time to pick them up. She stuffed the bag back in the safe and ignoring the cash and diamonds reached in to take what she had come for. The thing which was more valuable than everything in that entire room combined.

She slipped her prize into the pocket of her padded jacket and, before shutting the safe, pulled out a handkerchief with which she quickly wiped down the keypad and door for prints.

Moving as fast as she dared, she crept out of the room, pulling the door closed behind her, again wiping over every surface she touched.

By the time the heavy, metal door clicked shut she was already halfway out of the window of a downstairs bathroom.

By the time anyone realised what was missing, she had disappeared over that grey, endless horizon and vanished off the face of the earth.

1

The man in the blue shorts swung a leg up and brought it smashing down on the back of the man in the red shorts' head. Red's face registered the shock and pain and for a moment he staggered, threatening to fall.

Smelling blood, Blue pressed his advantage, launching a savage cross into Red's faltering guard.

But Red wasn't out yet. He leaned back and as Blue's looping punch missed him, he reached up and grabbed Blue's extended arm, before pulling him tight to his body and taking them both down to the mat with a well-timed trip.

The fighters' bodies hit the ground with a sickening thud, blood and sweat splattering across the canvas of the ring.

When it had looked like a swift, violent knock-out the crowd had been on their feet, screaming for satisfaction. Now that the fight had progressed to the slow attrition of grappling, their interest waned and they retook their seats as the monolithic roar died down into the broken hubbub of drunken conversations.

At the back of the room one man remained fixated on the fight, never once taking his eyes off the ring. He sat alone at his table, a glass of water untouched in front of him. His mixed-race complexion marking him out in a room full of white faces. A shaved head and deep scar running down the side of his face. Beneath his waxed jacket he was nearly twice the size of the men fighting in the ring. Craig Malton was here on business.

He had travelled all the way out to Hindley, an unremarkable former mining town on the periphery of Greater Manchester, to witness this fight. Having grown up in Moss Side, anywhere this far out of the city felt like countryside to Malton. Out here he was on his own.

But working alone was how he liked it; it meant that the only people who got hurt were the people who he decided needed to get hurt.

Malton glanced around the town hall where the fight was taking place. Parquet floors and ornate details spoke of an era when, thanks to the Industrial Revolution, Hindley had been prospering. A time long since passed. Nowadays the hall was the kind of place that at the weekend would be hosting a local wedding; folding tables of buffet food, a travelling DJ and everyone having the time of their lives. But on this wet Thursday evening people had been lured out with the promise of violence.

Malton noted the hall had several exits: the double doors that led from the entrance, a couple of doors leading to toilets and another couple leading backstage. Too many escape routes for Malton's liking. He'd have to be quick.

He turned back to the man he was here to see. The man who was kneeling over his opponent, raining down blows. The man in the red shorts – Bradley Wyke.

Officially Malton ran Malton Security, a firm that ran doors, protected building sites and installed security systems. Unofficially, and if you could afford it, Malton was the man you came to when you needed something looking into. Something that you'd rather the police didn't know about.

Malton solved crime for criminals. With a mixture of cunning, brute force and a lifetime spent getting to know Manchester's sordid underbelly, there was nowhere he couldn't go. Nothing so well hidden he couldn't drag it kicking and screaming into the light.

He wanted a word with Bradley Wyke and Bradley knew it. He'd not been at his flat this past week and hadn't turned up to the gym he ran either. But this fight had been booked in for months and Malton was sure that however scared Bradley was, there was no way he'd waste the months of gruelling training. Not to mention the thousand-pound purse on offer to the victor.

Malton felt a buzzing in his pocket. He knew straight away who it would be: the man who was paying him to come all the way out to Hindley on a bleak Thursday evening. The most feared man in all of Manchester – Danny Mitchum.

Danny Mitchum sat at the top of a vast pyramid of criminal ingenuity. He didn't just oversee the wholesale importation of drugs from both North Africa and Central Europe, he also commanded a sprawling network of middlemen and street dealers. Despite his operation generating millions of pounds a year and being responsible for the majority of drugs sold in Greater Manchester, Danny was also more than happy to get his hands dirty.

Over the past decade – through a combination of fear, respect and extreme violence – Danny Mitchum had become king of the Manchester underworld.

But Danny had got greedy. Word had got out that he'd been stealing from his suppliers – a group of heavy players from Merseyside who went by the affectionate nickname of the Scouse Mafia. The Scouse Mafia were not the sort of people who took kindly to being ripped off.

Danny didn't wait for the bodies to start piling up. As soon as he found out someone had talked, he'd gone into hiding, tasking Malton with ferreting out who in his organisation had grassed him up.

For the past three months Malton had been wading through Danny's crew. Men like Bradley. Danny Mitchum worked with the absolute dregs. Serial offenders, domestic abusers, sociopaths and violent alcoholics. Any one of them could have been the leak. It was Malton's thankless job to find out which one.

Malton hadn't wanted to take the assignment but he knew well enough that you don't say no to Danny Mitchum. Ever since taking the case he'd been bombarded day and night by Danny's calls, most of which he chose to ignore. Danny didn't text. He couldn't – he was blind. And so instead he left long, foul-mouthed voice notes, which Malton was forced to trawl through into the early hours.

Malton let the phone in his pocket ring out.

Bradley was on his opponent's back, his arms and legs hooked around the man's torso, pinning him to the mat. Blue tried to stagger to his feet, attempting to muscle Bradley off.

Both men were at the peak of physical fitness. Lithe, gym-honed bodies, each covered with tattoos. Blue's thick legs flexed as he attempted the impossible: raising his own weight and that of the man on his back. For a thrilling moment it looked like he would make it. The crowd rose in volume only to crash into disappointed heckling when the weight proved too much and Blue crashed back down to the mat. Bradley kept his grip and for just a moment looked up from the fight and out into the crowd. Directly into Malton's eyes.

Malton saw straight away that Bradley knew who he was and why he was there. Bradley froze in the ring. Torn between finishing off his opponent or turning to run. Fight or flight?

The phone in Malton's pocket started buzzing again.

Bradley made his choice. He loosened his grip on Blue and let the man's tired arms slip down to his sides. Just what Bradley was hoping for. Without hesitation he started hammering blows into his opponent's exposed face. The first punch hit so hard that before Blue knew what was happening Bradley had already unloaded half a dozen more punches.

Scenting blood, the crowd rose to its feet and Malton was forced to stand to keep eyes on Bradley. The referee hovered, unwilling to intervene too soon, but it was clear the fight was over. Blue made no attempt to protect himself. His head swung left and right, his neck loosened with each crushing blow.

Finally, the official stepped in and pulled a frenzied Bradley Wyke off what was left of his opponent. He hauled Bradley to his feet, holding his arm aloft in victory.

Malton was already moving towards the ring, effortlessly pushing past the groups of men intoxicated as much with violence as with alcohol.

Bradley was lost in the moment. Soaking up his victory. The crowd bellowed their approval and he bellowed back. The sight of Malton at the apron shook him to his senses. Bradley took a step back, raised his arms and turned to the mob.

'Let's have it!' he shouted.

The effect was instantaneous. As one the crowd surged forward, screaming obscenities and hurling pints high in the air. Malton was powerless to do a thing as hundreds of bodies flooded the ring.

The last Malton saw of Bradley Wyke was his bloody, sweat-stained torso shaking off well-wishers and slipping out through one of the doors that led backstage.

Malton was outside in the car park just in time to see Bradley's beat-up Mazda tearing away into the evening gloom.

Standing in the damp evening air he began to feel the sweat chilling on his bald head. Freed from the confines of the meeting hall he became aware of the clinging stench of the crowd – beer and BO.

Ignoring the phone that was still ringing in his pocket, Malton got into his racing green Volvo estate and set off back to Manchester. As he drove his resolve began to harden. In his mind he replayed the grind of the past few months, culminating in this latest almighty fuck-up.

By the time he was on the outskirts of the city his mind was made up. He was going to tell the most feared criminal in all of Manchester he was quitting.

As he drove, he imagined how Danny would react to the news. The thought made him smile.

2

Keisha neatly stacked the ten thousand pounds on the table. She'd specifically asked for it in ten-pound notes. Small enough to make the pile look inviting but large enough not to feel like she was offering loose change.

The ten thousand pounds was the trap; everything else was the bait.

Keisha looked around the room. When she'd arrived in this house a couple of months ago it had been semi-derelict. A major benefit of running her husband's business had been that she had complete control of the money coming in. With him being a hugely prolific drug dealer, that meant a lot of money.

One of the ways she had hidden that money was property. When she had bought the detached house in north Manchester eighteen months earlier she imagined it would be used as a bash house – a discreet place to mix pure drugs with cheaper fillers before sending them down the chain.

But her husband had been dead for three months now. His drug business had been carved up and whatever assets he had were under investigation by Greater Manchester Police.

Keisha had fled, taking with her a few thousand in gold and watches along with the keys to half a dozen properties littered around Manchester and hidden from the law behind various shell companies. Properties just like the one she now found herself in.

She didn't mourn her husband. It had been fun while it lasted but she always knew one way or another he'd end up in an early grave. It just so happened that she was more than a little responsible for his death. She wasn't alone in that; she'd roped in an old flame, a man who she hoped might be persuaded to see a future with her. But things hadn't worked out and so now, before Keisha could start a new life, she had one last thing to do.

A score to settle.

The ten thousand pounds was a down payment on that.

The house was in Harpurhey, an overlooked suburb of north Manchester It was far enough out of the city that at one time it was almost pastoral. The elaborate swimming baths and a smattering of large, country house style homes bore testament to what the area once was before Manchester expanded to engulf it. These days it was a mixture of dense terraces and council estate fringed by parkland, dotted with eccentric Victorian houses in various stages of decay.

Despite being in the middle of Harpurhey, the house was isolated, hidden down a potholed, dirt track that ran parallel to the main road north out of Manchester. It was shielded from view by a verge covered in scrubland and trees. If you didn't know it was there you'd never find it. That suited Keisha perfectly.

She had done her best to spruce up the one room that was serving as her bedroom, living room and kitchen. She had put rugs down over the bare boards and hung thick curtains over the windows – not that there was anyone around to look in.

At one end of the room, a six-foot-high mirror leaned against a wall next to the double bed, and at the other sat a table and chairs.

It was late May yet a bone-deep cold hung over Manchester. Several fan heaters were scattered about the room, doing their best to make up for the complete lack of heating in the house.

Despite the warmth they generated, a strong smell of damp still hung about the room, with large, black blooms of mould flowering across the ceiling.

Keisha hoped she'd done enough to make things look inviting for her guest. Even if she hadn't, ten thousand pounds was still ten thousand pounds.

Keisha knew exactly what money could buy you. She'd grown up dirt-poor in Hulme, a suburb of Manchester so unloved it had been levelled not once but twice in living memory. She'd seen the things people would do for money. The humanity they'd give away. She'd watched her mother, a proud Irish woman, try to turn the tide of deprivation. First through residents' groups and trade unions and then through local politics. But as the Nineties came round, she'd seen how quickly all that hope and trust could be wiped away in the face of money. Drug money.

When Keisha found herself alone and at her lowest ebb she'd made the decision to make sure that from then on it would be her with the money. Her buying and selling people. With a fearless charm and a ruthless ambition, she had thrown herself into the Manchester underworld and risen to a place where she thought that no one would ever be able to touch her.

Her marriage to a notorious criminal had given her the wealth and power she'd always craved, but it wasn't enough. No matter how powerful she became she never forgot that three decades earlier the one man she'd ever truly loved had walked out on her. A few months ago the chance finally came to win him back. Certain that she could make up for all the lost years, Keisha had done everything in her power to turn back time. She sacrificed her husband, his entire family and nearly lost her own life in the attempt. It wasn't enough.

After he rejected her yet again, she had made up her mind to destroy him.

Keisha was busy setting up a bottle of wine and two glasses when the sound of someone hesitantly knocking on the door drifted into the room. Keisha rushed over to the mirror and gave herself a last check.

Like most mixed-race women she looked a lot younger than her years. She had flawless brown skin and dark glossy hair that hung down in long, brown curls. She loved her figure and made sure to run several times a week. She never knew when she'd have to run for real.

Rain or shine, indoors or outdoors, Keisha was never without her sunglasses. She wore designer jeans, a baggy grey sweater and a pair of box-fresh New Balance trainers. She didn't do heels. She wasn't into looking helpless. She took a last look in the mirror. Her outfit showed off just enough stealth wealth to impress, but when paired with her beaming smile it made her look eminently approachable. She went to meet her guest.

Nearing the front door she paused for just a second beside the only obviously new addition to the house – two heavy security doors. Each secured with a padlock for which only Keisha held the key. Her eyes were drawn to one of the two doors. She held her breath for a moment. Her body tense as if half expecting the door to burst open.

The sound of knocking brought her back to the here and now. 'I'm coming!' she shouted.

A young woman stood on the doorstep looking unsure. Like Keisha she was dressed for practicality. Unlike Keisha she looked worn down with it. Tatty, loose-fitting jeans, scuffed-up trainers and a black anorak with a carefully repaired but still visible tear down one side. Her hair was braided tight to her head and her skin was several shades darker than Keisha's.

'Diane Okunkwe?' said Keisha flashing a smile that didn't quite reach her eyes. Not that Diane would ever know that, thanks to Keisha's sunglasses.

The woman on the doorstep smiled with relief. Keisha looked past her then and, satisfied that she had come alone, led her inside, closing the door behind her.

'Thank you for coming,' said Keisha as she shepherded Diane through the hallway. 'We're a bit tricky to find out here.'

Diane smiled politely and said nothing.

As they passed through the hallway a loud groan came from behind one of the two locked doors. Keisha saw Diane's hand grasp the strap of her handbag a little tighter. She sensed the woman's steps faltering.

Pretending not to have heard a thing, Keisha ushered Diane into the front room. As the door closed behind them Keisha could see Diane had already forgotten all about that groan.

Her eyes were fixed exactly where they were meant to be fixed – on the pile of money.

Keisha walked over to the table and began to unscrew the bottle of wine that sat next to the stack of cash.

'Sit down, have a drink,' she said.

Diane didn't move. She looked around the room. The rugs and curtains. The giant mirror and the bed. The suitcases and floor heaters. Keisha could tell she was trying to work out just what anyone was doing living like this.

Keisha kept smiling, her focus on Diane, silently urging her towards the table. Diane took a chair and sat down, trying her best not to stare at the pile of money. Keisha knew it was more than she'd ever seen in her life.

Keisha was in the middle of pouring out the wine when another loud groan reverberated through the house.

This time Diane was unable to hide her reaction. They both knew she'd heard it. Keisha kept pouring.

Again it came. Louder this time. A human sound of slow, unbearable pain.

Diane was on her feet, ready to leave.

Seeing her fear, Keisha reached over the table and grabbed Diane's wrist. Diane gasped with shock at the strength of her grip.

The groaning carried on. It sounded more intense, more urgent.

Keisha fixed Diane through her dark glasses. 'You came here for a job, yes?'

Diane was too scared to answer so Keisha carried on regardless.

'A job to earn money to send back to your family in Ghana? Your mother, your father. The operation he needs?'

Keisha watched as this information lit the fuse of Diane's paranoia. Who was this woman? What else did she know about her family?

14

'Ten thousand pounds,' said Keisha, nodding towards the pile of money. Finally Diane let herself look over at the cash. She drank it in.

Sickening screaming now filled the house. Keisha held her nerve.

'It's yours. And all I want are three things,' she said.

'I cannot,' said Diane, trying hard to muster the strength to flee.

Ignoring her protests Keisha continued. 'Firstly, I want your cleaning job. The one you just got. On Monday you are to stay away and I'll go in your place.'

Diane was barely listening. Keisha could see the panic overwhelming her. But still she held her wrist tight.

'Secondly, I want your name. Your identity. I want to turn up as you. Tell them I'm you. Diane Okunkwe.'

Diane looked worried. 'You do not look like me. You are . . . not black.'

Keisha had half expected this. As a mixed-race woman she was more than used to hearing it.

'Where you work, it's white people. Rich white people. You're Ghanaian. I'm a mixed-race Mancunian. Far as rich white people are concerned, we're all black.'

Diane laughed. The two women shared a lifetime of experience without saying a word.

'You said three things?' said Diane. The fear had left her voice.

Keisha knew she had her now. At the sound of yet another moan she let go of Diane's wrist, turned away and shouted, 'Shut up or I'm coming in there!'

Instantly the screaming stopped, melting away to muffled whimpers.

Keisha turned back to Diane. 'Three, I want you to disappear. I don't care where you go, but you go. You take the ten thousand pounds on the table and you vanish. Do we have a deal?'

Diane took another look at the notes and Keisha knew exactly what her answer would be.

Watching Diane leave with the money, Keisha felt a little swell of satisfaction. She always got what she wanted. And right now what she wanted more than anything was to destroy the man who'd wronged her.

Craig Malton.

3

Dean Carter's mouth began watering as the man at Maxie's Desserts placed two plates down in front of him. Each plate had on it a giant waffle drenched in chocolate sauce, M&Ms and chopped nuts. As if that wasn't enough, half a dozen scoops of ice cream ringed each plate, each scoop topped with a Maxie's Desserts branded wafer. Finally, lashings of whipped cream encircled each scoop and covered what little waffle had escaped the chocolate sauce.

Dean nodded approvingly and the man returned behind the counter.

Then he got to work. First, he arranged the plates. One on each side of the table, as if two people were about to sit down to eat. Resisting the urge to steal a swipe of ice cream, Dean took out his phone and spent a good couple of minutes arranging and taking photos of the food.

From behind the counter the man watched approvingly. Everything about Maxie's was set up to be photographed. From the bright pink colour scheme to the extravagantly topped desserts. It wasn't enough for something to taste good anymore. Customers wanted their food to *look* good too. Social media was watching.

That was exactly what Dean was doing. Uploading his posts to social media. But not to his own profile. First, he went to Facebook, then Twitter, then Instagram, TikTok and even YouTube. He uploaded a photo or video with the caption 'treatz wiv bae' to each platform on a profile he'd set up – Dobbzbobbz. He made sure that in every photo the logo of Maxie's Desserts was clearly visible both on the waffles and on the wall in the background.

With all the posts uploaded, Dean got up, went to the counter, paid for his food and promptly walked out of the shop leaving both plates of food untouched.

As he sat in his car across the road from Maxie's he could hear his stomach rumbling. But he couldn't risk spending a second longer back in the café. Not if his plan was about to come off.

Maxie's sat in a narrow row of terraced houses just off a main road. From where he was parked he watched as customers went in and out of the shop. A family with children. A group of young girls. A couple. All of them South Asian. After all he was in Daubhill.

Daubhill, or Dobble as the locals pronounced it in their cheery Boltonian accent, used to be home to thousands of millworkers. As the jobs in the mills dwindled the white workforce was replaced with recently arrived immigrants from India, Pakistan and Bangladesh. When the mills closed they had stayed and made the area their own.

Dean stood out a mile. Bad enough he was white. But he was tall with it. In an attempt to convey a little gravity he wore a suit. It had the exact opposite effect. He looked like a schoolboy, gangly and fresh-faced – apart from the livid, circular scar he'd recently acquired on his left cheek. What's more he didn't speak a word of Urdu or Punjabi. He didn't even have a Bolton accent.

None of this would have been a problem except for the fact that Dean wasn't in Daubhill for fun – although in the three months he'd spent scouring the area he'd become quite fond of the place. He had a job to do. A girl was missing and he'd promised to bring her home. Her name was Olivia. But besides her photo all he had to go on was the name of her boyfriend, a major Bolton gangster known only as Big Wacky. Daubhill was his turf.

Dean had never done anything like this before. Three months ago he would never have dreamed of even trying. But then he'd started working for Malton Security. In that time he'd met some of the heaviest figures in the criminal underworld, he'd totalled cars, narrowly averted a gang war and been shot point-blank in the face. It was the best job he'd ever had.

Dean saw how Malton moved through Manchester relying on native wit and the constant threat of violence inherent in both his reputation and his physical presence. There was nothing Malton couldn't discover. No one he couldn't track down.

Which is why it was a shame that Dean couldn't tell Malton anything about his hunt for Olivia or how he'd been asked to find her by her friend Vikki.

Dean had met Vikki working on another case for Malton. In fact it was down to Vikki's help that Malton had managed to crack it.

So when Vikki had asked Dean to find Olivia he was both glad to be able to return the favour and flattered that she had asked him and not Malton. So much so that when she worried out loud that Malton would be mad at her for taking up Dean's time, Dean had reassured her it would be their little secret.

As much as it made Dean uneasy to keep something from Malton, he told himself this was a great way of proving himself to his boss. Taking on extra work and showing initiative. When he found Olivia there would be no reason not to tell Malton everything. But until then this was strictly a one-man operation.

Walking around Daubhill, Dean had quickly learned two things, one – everyone in Daubhill knew who Big Wacky was and two – no one in Daubhill was prepared to say anything about him to a lanky white guy in a cheap suit.

After several near misses, Dean decided he needed to change tactics.

Malton had spent a lifetime getting to know everyone who made the underbelly of Manchester churn. He'd forged personal connections, loyalties and debts. Dean saw how he went wherever he wanted. There was no door barred to him, no one who wouldn't talk – eventually. Malton had cunning, reputation and a notorious capacity for brutality to help him find out what he needed.

Dean had none of that. But he did have a mobile phone.

These days everyone wanted to be internet famous. Athletes, models, writers, influencers, musicians. Everyone craved their own brand, and criminals were no different. Dean had been staggered to discover how many serious criminals were in the process of cultivating their own online personas. Where once criminals would deliver their threats face to face, now they took to social media. Suddenly anyone with a mobile phone and a morbid curiosity could keep track of the latest gangland feuds.

No one in Daubhill was talking about Big Wacky but online his name was all over the place. Which was why Dean came up with the online handle – Dobbzbobbz. If he couldn't find Big Wacky then he'd let Big Wacky find him.

For over a month now he'd been posting as Dobbzbobbz. Going on local forums, using every hashtag he could think of. Anything that would make it more likely that Big Wacky, who-ever he was, would take notice.

Dobbzbobbz was cocky, fearless and gobby. Most of all Dobbzbobbz hated Big Wacky. Everything Dean posted he made sure to mention Big Wacky's name. He called him a coward, a plastic gangster and a police informant. Anything he could think of to get his attention.

It had worked.

In no time at all, Dean found himself fielding dozens of different accounts threatening him, challenging him to come out from behind his internet handle and make his accusations in the real world.

Dean had absolutely no intention of doing anything as reckless as that. His plan was far more subtle. After nearly a month of whipping up online drama he was aware that Big Wacky knew all about Dobbzbobbz. Big Wacky had made it known that he personally wanted a word with Dobbzbobbz and that anyone who could put them in the same room would be well rewarded.

Dean was about to give Big Wacky his wish. He knew they would be watching his accounts. Driving themselves into fits of rage at his latest attacks. And so having found a suitable venue he'd very deliberately posted the bait – photos of him and his 'bae' sharing a romantic waffle at Maxie's Desserts in the heart of Daubhill. Slap bang in the middle of Big Wacky's territory.

It was the nearing the end of May and despite the early evening sun the streetlights of Daubhill had begun to come on. The sky was dark blue and the smell of takeaways mingled with exhaust fumes.

Dean slid down in his car seat and turned his phone to camera, holding it up high enough to make sure that he had a perfect view of Maxie's Desserts and whoever was about to turn up to interrupt Dobbzbobbz on his romantic waffle date.

Dean felt his scar itching. The wound had barely healed and despite all the creams and pills he'd been given it was a constant, low-level pain.

Suddenly his phone began to silently vibrate. The image of the shop vanished and was replaced with a name – Malton. His boss was calling.

Dean risked a final look at Maxie's before sinking lower still in his seat and taking the call. As he listened to Malton speak his heart sank.

'Yes . . . No . . . Yes . . . Yes . . . I'll be there right away.'

Dean hung up and lay there for a moment, half in his seat and half in the footwell. Malton needed him. Now. He knew he had no choice but still he couldn't quite believe he'd got this far only to fall at the last hurdle.

Struggling up he looked over to Maxie's Desserts. The family were still there. Still eating their ice cream. Dean looked up and down the road. Nothing.

Big Wacky was still out there but for now he'd have to wait.

Dean started up his car, took one last longing look at Maxie's, pulled away from the kerb and drove off towards Manchester, gripping the wheel all the way there to keep from scratching his scar.

A few minutes later a Black Range Rover screeched to a halt outside Maxie's and half a dozen young men piled out and barrelled into the café armed to the teeth with knives, baseball bats and hammers. All of them determined to let Dobbzbobbz know exactly what happened when you bad-mouthed Big Wacky.

4

'In closing, I'd just like to say how honoured I've been to represent the people of Bolton as a councillor and how immensely grateful I'll be to stand for you when I become your new MP.'

Tahir Akhtar finished speaking to the sparse crowd who'd come out on a late May evening to hear the two candidates for the recently vacated parliamentary seat of Farnworth and Great Lever.

He looked around the reading room of the High Street Library, his face beaming from beneath his neat white beard. He wore a baggy suit and his signature glossy red tie that hung down over his gut. Tahir responded to the polite applause by applauding himself, before turning to the three people seated to one side watching and taking notes. A middle-aged white man, a younger white woman and a South Asian man of a similar age to Tahir.

They were the selection board sent by Manchester Labour Party HQ to determine who would be the next candidate for Farnworth and Great Lever. After the unexpected death of the previous incumbent, Tahir had thought it was a mere formality that he would be chosen. He had decades of council experience and was as loyal a Labour Party member as you could hope to find.

Unfortunately for him the young woman sitting beside him had other ideas.

Fauzia Malik was busy looking out over the crowd sitting among the library tables, politely listening. It was a mixture of white and brown faces. Around twenty in all. Most of whom Fauzia recognised.

When she had first joined the Labour Party she'd expected to find a hotbed of dynamic local go-getters. Instead she'd discovered that the old boys' club was alive and well. Even somewhere like Daubhill. For generations now Labour had relied on large block votes from the mixture of Pakistani, Indian and Bangladeshi communities to make places like Farnworth and Great Lever impregnable. A combination of these block votes and the white working class meant that the Tories never even came close. The same faces fought the same seats and won the same elections year after year. Nothing changed.

That didn't put Fauzia off one bit. She loved a challenge. It was why she went to medical school and became an A&E doctor. It was why she moved out of her parents' place in her twenties and successfully stood for election as a local councillor. And it was why when the incumbent MP collapsed of a heart attack she had caused a minor scandal by challenging Tahir Akhtar for the seat.

Whoever won tonight would find themself heading to Westminster. Fauzia was determined that would be her.

She rose to her feet. Her job as a junior doctor at Royal Bolton Hospital meant that she spent most of her time in scrubs and trainers. But with political ambitions always in the back of her mind she'd found an ex-Savile Row tailor up in Hull who specialised in women's tailoring. Tonight she was wearing a bespoke light blue suit. The jacket cut close to her body, the trousers wide legged and high waisted. It looked every bit the two grand it had cost her.

Fauzia was short, with straight dark hair and thin, determined features. But standing tall in her suit she felt like she could take on anyone.

'I'd like to start by thanking my fellow candidate – Councillor Akhtar – for everything he's done for this community.'

Fauzia paused to applaud and a few in the crowd joined in. Tahir kept smiling.

'Which is why it pains me to say that people like him are the problem.'

24

A gentle ripple of surprise went through the crowd. Tahir kept smiling but a subtle look of confusion began to spread over his face.

'Many of you already know me. You know my family whose food processing plant has created jobs in this area. Local jobs for local people. I've worked there myself and I couldn't be more proud of the contribution my parents have made to Daubhill. To this community.'

The brown faces in the crowd nodded along while several of the white faces looked blank.

Fauzia continued. 'Yet there are some in this community who care more about appearances than realities. I love Daubhill. There are schools and mosques and families and businesses and people working every hour of the day to get ahead. And then there are the drugs.'

A gasp went up from the crowd. Tahir had stopped smiling.

'There are gangs. There is violence. And people like Councillor Akhtar think that because it comes from within our community the best thing to do is keep quiet. Save face. Don't let the outside world label it as a problem. But it is a problem and it's one that affects our community. It's our sons selling drugs. Our children taking them. Our families growing up in areas where a violent criminal makes more money in a day than a hardworking family does in a month.'

Tahir was shifting in his seat. He looked furious. All three of the Labour Party vetting panel were frantically writing notes.

Fauzia felt the thrill in the room. Everyone knew something was happening. When she had first decided to run against Tahir she knew she would be up against it. The only thing she had going for her was Tahir's complacency. He'd been as good as told the seat was his. If Fauzia was to change people's minds she'd need to grab their attention.

'Maybe your son's been shot,' said Fauzia, making eye contact with a middle-aged woman sat at the back of the room. 'Or perhaps you've fought your own battle with addiction?' She glanced over to a clean-shaven man in his thirties who was nodding along intently. 'Maybe you wonder why men like Councillor Akhtar make such a fuss when someone tries to bring what's happening to light?' Fauzia looked straight at a woman her own age who was earnestly hanging on her every word.

Fauzia had lived in Daubhill her whole life. She went to school in Bolton and now worked in the hospital. She'd seen it all and she wasn't prepared to stay quiet. Over the past few weeks, in anticipation of this day, she'd made sure to reach out to as many people as she could. The people that the old boys' network ignored. Mothers, recovering addicts, ex-gang members. The collateral of men like Tahir's silence.

Fauzia's whole life was about exceeding people's expectations. Politics would be no different.

She took in the crowd, now firmly on her side.

'I won't be silent anymore. As your MP I will make sure that we are open and we are honest and we stand with one voice and say, no more. No more drugs, no more gangs, no more deaths. We deserve better.'

Fauzia sat down to a round of spontaneous applause. She turned and smiled sweetly to Councillor Akhtar whose face was nearly as red as his tie.

Fauzia felt a buzzing in her pocket. Through sheer force of habit she pulled her phone out, expecting a message from the hospital.

I'M OUTSIDE.

It was her brother Waqar. Annoyed at the interruption, Fauzia was about to put the phone back in her pocket when it buzzed again.

NOW! OUTSIDE LIBRARY! NOW!

A car horn sounded somewhere outside. Fauzia looked out at the audience. They were still applauding. Across the room the panel from the Labour Party were talking among themselves. She kept up her smile but could feel her frustration building.

Not here. Not now.

26

The woman from the panel got to her feet.

'That was quite a set of speeches. I'd like to thank both candidates and now turn to the floor for questions.'

Fauzia's phone buzzed in her hand again. Across the floor of the library hands shot up. She looked down at her phone.

I'M COMING IN.

She slipped it back into her pocket and rose to her feet. Before the moderator could interrupt her she turned to the room.

'I am so sorry. I would have loved to answer any questions but right now I have a family emergency. I'm really sorry,' said Fauzia, the lightness in her voice masking her mounting anger.

The car horn sounded again from outside. And again. Looks of confusion were beginning to break out.

'Thank you for this opportunity to speak,' said Fauzia as she slipped away.

Fauzia rehearsed her furious rant as she headed out of the library entrance and towards her brother's white Audi hatchback. She could see him alone in the driver's seat with his window down. He looked rattled. He would be looking a lot more rattled in a minute when she'd finished with him.

Waqar was older than her by a couple of years. While she had gone to university to study medicine he had stayed behind to run the family business. He hid his resentment at this turn of events behind his lavish lifestyle. A lifestyle that even for the son of wealthy parents had raised more than a few eyebrows.

Her brother was handsome, even Fauzia had to admit that. He was tall and naturally broad with a strong jaw, long nose and large, brown eyes surrounded by almost feminine lashes. He looked out of place on the streets of Daubhill, like a visitor from somewhere far more glamorous who'd simply got lost passing through.

Fauzia was already shouting as she crossed the car park towards him.

'What the hell do you think you're doing? Do you know what tonight is? What it means to me?'

Something was wrong. Waqar didn't look up. As Fauzia got closer she saw he was shaking.

'What have you done now?' she snapped. It had to be something. It always was with him. Ever since he'd failed his entrance exams to Bolton Grammar and been bundled off to the local comprehensive in disgrace, he'd been getting into trouble.

'He's in the boot,' said Waqar, unable to look his sister in the eye.

Fauzia froze, her mind trying to wrap itself around what she'd just heard.

'He came for me, Fauz. Galahad sent him. I panicked. He was going to kill me.'

'Who's Galahad? What do you mean "he's in the boot?"' asked Fauzia. Her brain was still running to catch up but the sense of dread in her stomach knew exactly what he meant.

For the first time Fauzia noticed what looked like blood all over her brother's hands. Her mouth went dry. Her anger replaced by fear.

'What have you done?' she said quietly.

Waqar looked his sister in the eye. He was terrified. 'Just get in the car.'

There was a reason Fauzia knew so much about the gangs in Daubhill. Her brother Waqar was in them up to his neck. Unable to bear her success he'd gone looking for his own cheap status. And now this is where it had got him.

On the night she could become an MP this is what her brother did. Fauzia felt her concern begin to give way to her rage.

'I asked what have you done?' demanded Fauzia, trying hard not to let the fear she was feeling intrude into her tone.

'Please, Fauz? Just get in,' said Waqar, leaning over to open the passenger-side door.

She looked over to the library window. Inside she could see the meeting was still in full swing. No one had seen them. Yet.

'Just get in!' shouted Waqar, revving the engine.

Any moment now someone would be coming out of the library. Maybe the audience. Maybe the Labour Party selection panel. Maybe Tahir. This would be more than enough for him to destroy any chance Fauzia had.

Whatever Waqar had done it was better she knew about it. That way she could control it. Protect herself and protect her family.

With a last look towards the library, Fauzia jumped into the car alongside her brother.

She had barely shut her door before, with a screeching of tyres, Waqar accelerated away.

Brother and sister headed off into the night.

Along with whoever it was in the boot.

5

Malton was on his way to tell Danny Mitchum he was quitting.

It was just starting to go dark and the motorway was nearly deserted as Malton put his foot down and pushed on towards town. The M602 carved its way through Salford in a near straight line, unsentimentally cutting a deep channel through where there once were streets, houses, communities.

Bradley Wyke's escape was playing on his mind. Wyke was a bottom feeder whose amateur MMA career was slowly killing what few brain cells he had to start with.

And yet he'd eluded Malton.

It seemed the thing Malton feared most was finally happening – he was losing his touch. For a man in his position that wasn't just humiliating. It could be deadly.

Malton moved in a world where there was no place for weakness. The people he dealt with could sniff out vulnerability and when they did they pounced like animals.

Wyke would talk. His kind always did. He was probably already out there boasting about how he'd given Craig Malton the slip. Anyone who knew Malton would know that Wyke had simply delayed the inevitable, but for those who were inclined to listen to the drunken chatter of men like Wyke, the seed was being sown. Craig Malton was on his way out.

One-on-one nobody could best Malton. But he couldn't be everywhere at once. He relied on the myth behind the man, the decades of reputation he'd earned with blood, sweat and broken bones. Malton was the figure in the shadows; the knock at your door in the middle of the night. He was the one person you didn't want to get on the wrong side of.

The moment people stopped believing that he was finished.

He had wasted far too much time chasing phantoms for Danny Mitchum. Everyone he talked to was a potential leak. Weak, blustering idiots who wore their criminality with an open pride. Following the lead of the man at the top – Danny Mitchum.

It was clever in a way. Mitchum surrounded himself with people who could barely function in the world, much less plan anything as coherent as a challenge to his power. Danny kept the whole shitshow together with a toxic mixture of loyalty, fear and dependence.

The city began to loom up in the newly minted darkness. The border between Salford and Manchester had been colonised with a dozen new tower blocks. One after another they clustered around the Ship Canal and the River Irwell creating whole new neighbourhoods, albeit neighbourhoods devoid of shops, schools, pubs or anything else that would bind together the people who lived there. Nowhere for humanity to slowly accumulate in the in-between spaces. The spaces where Malton plied his trade.

Manchester was changing. What had started as regeneration had metastasised into an uncontrollable proliferation of the new. Glass and steel and leveraged real estate washing away the decades of gentle, loving decay.

As he crawled through the traffic-calming measures Malton couldn't stop turning over a thought he'd had from the beginning, when Danny had employed him months ago. A suspicion that try as he might, he couldn't silence.

Was Danny Mitchum playing him?

Everyone who knew Malton knew he never took sides. He never made a threat he didn't carry out and he never received a threat without making sure that whoever made it knew the terrible mistake he'd made. But most of all, people knew that when Malton took a job he saw it through to the end. No matter what the cost.

Years ago, when he'd been hired by a distraught low-level street dealer to find the arsonists who'd burned down his house with his young family inside, Malton had traced the crime back to a powerful money launderer with connections to major criminals down in London. Regardless of the repercussions, Malton had grabbed the man off the streets and delivered him to the grieving father. The message went out. Craig Malton's only loyalty was to the job.

Once you hired Malton he finished that job. Whatever the consequences.

So why was finding Danny's grass proving so difficult? These past few months it had become harder and harder for Malton to ignore the voice in his head telling him something more was at play. Was the leak a red herring? Was Danny Mitchum up to something? Something that required Craig Malton to be looking the other way?

It was late. The city centre nearly empty. But with so much of it pedestrianised or turned over to buses and empty bicycle lanes, it took nearly half an hour for Malton to navigate the few hundred metres from the north-east of the city centre to the location where for the past three months he'd had Danny Mitchum tucked up in a safe house.

Crawling past building site after building site, Malton could feel his grip slipping. His city was changing underneath him and unless he got his head together, soon enough it wouldn't be his city anymore. Walking away from Danny Mitchum was a start but things hadn't been right for a while now.

Malton knew exactly what was wrong. That didn't mean he knew what to do about it.

As Malton rounded the corner by the AO Arena and headed up Cheetham Hill Road, he rehearsed in his head how he would break the news to Danny that he was no longer on the job.

He would tell Danny that while he personally was no longer searching for whoever it was that had grassed on him to the Scouse Mafia, that didn't mean he was giving up the hunt. Far from it. He was going to put his best man on the job.

6

Keisha examined what ten thousand pounds had bought her.

Diane's laminated ID card, her cleaner's tabard bearing the logo of the facility where she was due to start work and a copy of the letter she'd received announcing that she had the job. Like the tabard, the letter bore the logo of her employer. It told Diane her shift times and the minimum wage she would be paid for her troubles.

Keisha held the letter in her hands. The paper was stiffly luxurious and the logo printed in a thick, embossed ink read: THE SENTINEL. No wonder they couldn't spare any more than minimum wage if they were spending this kind of money on their stationery.

The photo on the ID could be easily altered and that's all there was to it. Keisha had become Diane Okunkwe. A brand-new start. The chance to be someone else.

Looking round the room at what remained of her old life, Keisha knew it was never that easy. No one ever really changed. Especially not people like her and Craig. Thirty years had passed since they were last together but she knew deep down that who they were was burned into their DNA. They were fighters, they were doers, they were people who had nothing and so could never lose.

When you grow up poor you have to get on with people. You don't have money, or power, or influence. All you have is the people around you in the same boat. You don't have the luxury of splendid isolation.

Keisha could get on with anyone. Fit in anywhere. She had never lost that, even when she started making real money.

33

Truth be told she could never stand her own company for too long. But if you could get on with people then anything was possible. Black, white or mixed race. Rich or poor. North Manchester or South Manchester. Keisha's childhood had taught her how to fit in. Become who she needed to be.

In order to pay Craig Malton back for what he'd done to her she had to become Diane Okunkwe.

The groaning had begun again. Loud and unrestrained. It sounded like someone was dying.

Keisha put down the letter, rose and went to a large, grubby holdall in one corner of the room.

The groans became urgent screams. They began to coalesce into a human voice. 'PLEASE . . . KILL ME . . .'

Keisha opened the bag. It was filled with guns: automatic pistols, a couple of rifles, several handguns. Even a few grenades.

She selected a revolver. Despite its compact size, the gun looked enormous in her hands. A brutal antique. Keisha expertly broke the gun and took six bullets out of the bag, which she slid into the chamber one by one.

'KILL ME . . .'

Keisha closed the gun, zipped up the holdall and went to deal with the noise.

No one would be getting killed today. What she had in mind was far, far worse.

7

Fauzia sat in her brother's car outside an industrial unit, part of a small cluster of similar buildings on the edge of Bolton. She watched as Waqar turned a key that raised the metal shutters to the building. The sound of the shutters rang out through the night but by now it was getting dark and there was no one to hear it.

Just her, Waqar and whoever it was in the boot.

Ever since she'd got into Waqar's car, Fauzia had been doing her best not to think about what was coming next. But as she sat outside her father's factory it finally dawned on her just what her brother was planning. A plan that she was now part of.

With the shutter fully open, Fauzia slowly drove the car forwards and into the building. Waqar followed on foot and the shutter began to close behind them.

Fauzia killed the engine and Waqar waited until the shutter was nearly at the ground before turning on the light.

In an instant the entire room lit up to reveal a vast meat processing plant.

Two rows of six polished metal tables, each with several stations containing gleaming, sterilised blades and shears. At the end of each table was a large, plastic bin on wheels.

Between the rows of tables ran a conveyor belt which passed the length of the building before rising upwards towards the thing that Fauzia now was certain had brought them here tonight.

She had never forgotten the day her proud father had picked her up from school and excitedly driven her to the abattoir to show off his new toy.

He'd led her into the building, very much the same as it was today. Rows of tables manned by dozens of men. Back then most of them didn't even speak any English. Her father's factory was their first step to making a new life for themselves in the UK.

A young Fauzia had watched as the men got on with the job in hand.

Some men processed newly killed meat, removing feathers and beaks. Others worked to sever the organs and viscera from the usable meat. Further down the table yet more men worked to cut meat into the chunks, which would find their way onto kebab skewers and into takeaways all over Bolton.

It was a dirty job and the men worked long hours. But they were thankful to Fauzia's father. He gave them a chance when no one else would. Many of those men went on to marry and have children, their labours rewarded with a better life for the next generation.

Fauzia thought her father was a hero.

But there was one big problem – the waste. Every scrap of fur and feather. Every piece of intestine and internal organ. Fat and bone and gristle. The plant produced a huge amount of waste and back then the entire room stank of it. The salty, sweet smell of decaying meat.

It also cost hundreds of man hours and a small fortune to dispose of it all.

Then he had bought the meat grinder.

It was the size of a small car. Brilliant, silver and clean, it took pride of place at the back of the room. A long, mechanical conveyor belt had been installed between the tables leading inexorably upwards towards its flared metal maw. Fauzia's father had held her up to look inside and she saw the row upon row of razor-sharp blades, curved and overlapped to ensure that nothing escaped their lethally sharp edges.

Every table fed the meat grinder. Every line of production moved towards it.

Fauzia's father had explained that the machine was so dangerous it could not be turned on by one man alone. That way a lone worker couldn't turn it on and then somehow accidentally fall into the blades. The machine could only operate with two people present.

It was Fauzia and her father who had pressed the switches to turn the wondrous machine on that first time. One switch on the conveyor belt itself and one switch on a wall-mounted control panel on the far side of the room.

Above the loud whirr of the blades the workers had applauded for a moment and then returned to their grim task.

From then on there would be no more waste. Everything that could not be processed by hand ended up on the conveyor belt and was fed into the meat grinder.

As the first scraps fell into the machine the shrill, mechanical sound became soft and thick as it tore through the viscera. Then out the end it came. The paste. Thick and pink and greasy. Like a toothpaste made from all the worst things in the world.

The workers collected the paste in large, clear plastic bags. It would soon become burgers and kebabs and sausages. Anything that could be reshaped and remade.

Fauzia remembered how sick she'd felt watching it emerge that first time.

She shook off her memories of the past and looked over to where her brother had hauled the body out of the boot of his car and was dragging it along the concrete floor towards the conveyor belt.

Fauzia's training kicked in. She passed her eyes over the body. A young, white man in an olive tracksuit, soaked red with blood. There were no visible injuries to his head and from the pattern of the bloodstains she guessed he must have some kind of puncture wound to his torso.

Now Fauzia knew why Waqar had brought her here. He wasn't scared or desperate. He knew exactly what he was doing. He needed a second person to turn on the meat grinder.

Waqar was meant to be the doctor. He was the one who was going to go on and do great things. But when he failed his school entrance exams her father simply gave up on him and transferred his affection to Fauzia, who for the first time in her life finally felt noticed.

Fauzia was bright and fiercely ambitious. She loved her father and wanted to make him proud. But at the same time the sudden glare of his attention filled her with a terrible fear that his love might just as quickly be taken away if she disappointed him.

So Fauzia worked harder than she'd ever worked before. She passed every exam, won every prize. Every second of her life was dedicated to the overachievement she felt was the only guarantee of her father's affection.

At the time it never occurred to her that while she was basking in her father's favour, Waqar had been left out in the cold.

It was only much later when she'd see her brother coming home, his head low and his clothes stained from the meat processing plant that it began to dawn on her how hard it had been for him. While she was away at university he was settling disputes between workers, doing paperwork and unclogging the meat grinder. While he was stuck in the family business she was off living the life that had been meant for him.

It was why, when she began to suspect that he was more than a little involved in the local drugs scene, a part of her forgave him. Despite her own feelings towards drugs and criminality she told herself that somehow her brother must be different. He had been driven to it. Led astray. Deep down she wished she could give him her success but that could never happen and so she couldn't bring herself to judge him when he found his life unravelling into criminality.

Now he'd killed a man.

When she had got in the car outside the library she was operating on pure survival instinct, desperate to get Waqar away from the meeting. But now, standing in the meat processing plant watching her brother try to haul the body onto the conveyor belt, everything became crystal clear. She could smell the bare concrete scrubbed clean with bleach. She felt the bone-deep chill radiating inwards from the metal walls. The relentless strip lighting left nowhere to hide.

She couldn't go through with this.

Waqar buckled under the weight and the body rolled off the conveyor belt, hitting the concrete floor with a dull thud. The sound of it brought Fauzia to her senses.

She marched over to where Waqar was trying unsuccessfully to heave the dead man back onto the conveyor belt.

Fauzia took a closer look at the body. His hands were heavy and battered. A fighter's hands. His eyes were closed and on his head, a long-healed scar running front to back. Too jagged to be surgical. Evidence of a violent past. She saw the holes in his tracksuit top. The torn fabric in the centre of the largest patches of blood. Fauzia had seen this sort of thing before in A&E. Stab wounds.

'You can't do this,' she said, more in attempt to convince herself than to persuade her brother.

Her brother looked up at her. 'I'm doing it. You're doing it with me.'

'I won't,' said Fauzia firmly.

Waqar stopped trying to lift the lifeless body onto the conveyor belt and stood up to face his sister.

'You know who this is?'

'It doesn't matter,' she said. 'We need to tell the police.'

Waqar laughed. 'You need to know who this is. This is a guy sent by Galahad. To kill me.'

'You keep saying that name: Galahad. What does it even mean? Who is he?'

'I don't know. That's the whole point. It's an alias. But I do know he's one of the biggest drug importers in the country and he's pissed off with me.'

'What did you do?'

Waqar looked angry. 'What did *I* do? Oh, because it's always my fault? Because I'm not a doctor or an MP? No, I'm just a fuck-up who runs a meat plant. I'm just a joke right?'

'I didn't say any of that. I want to help you. But right now it looks like you've killed someone and want me to help you dispose of the body.' Fauzia could hear her voice rising in volume. She was getting angry.

'So are you going to help me or not?' Waqar shouted back, his voice echoing off the walls, ringing out over the meat processing plant.

The two siblings stood staring at each other. It could have been any argument from the past twenty years, if it wasn't for the dead body on the floor between them.

It was Waqar who broke first.

Fauzia watched as her brother bent down and frantically tried to lift the body. It was a bloody, dead weight and try as he might he simply couldn't do it alone.

As he struggled he began to babble. 'He's going to kill me. He's going to kill Mum and Dad. He's going to kill you.'

'Then go to the police!' cried Fauzia.

Waqar looked up. There were tears in his eyes. 'Oh, sis, if you understood anything you'd know how stupid that sounds.'

Suddenly he wasn't the fuck-up who wrecked everything he touched. Suddenly he was her big brother. He was the one who taught her to ride a bike. The brother she'd once overheard boasting to his friends how clever his little sister was. The one who kept quiet as their parents lavished all their attention on her while he languished.

Waqar turned away from Fauzia and went back to hopelessly wrangling the body. 'If I got to the police then what do I tell Mum and Dad? How do I explain this to them? I can be the disappointment. I'm used to that. But this?'

Fauzia bent down and grabbed an arm.

The body was even heavier than it looked. The man was well over six foot. Both Fauzia and Waqar were tiny by comparison. With each one of them holding an arm they heaved him up off the floor. As Fauzia stumbled under the weight, the man hung between them. As his tracksuit top rode up she glimpsed a cluster of bleeding puncture wounds. The unmistakable signature of a knife attack.

Fauzia was more than used to the sight of blood at the hospital but there was something obscene about seeing it here and now. Oozing endlessly from the lifeless body she and her brother were struggling to haul to its feet.

Finally they stood back, the body on the conveyor belt. Fauzia looked down. Her bespoke suit was covered in blood.

They both knew what came next. Without saying a word Fauzia walked over to the control panel on the far wall. Waqar stayed by the panel on the conveyor belt.

Fauzia took in the scene. Her father's processing plant. Her brother bloodstained and exhausted. The body on the conveyor belt. She closed her eyes and hit the switch.

The conveyor belt started moving and the meat grinder fired into life. The sound took Fauzia back to that day she and her father had turned it on for the first time. She was glad he wasn't here to see her now.

She walked over and stood next to Waqar. Brother and sister watching in silence as the body travelled along the conveyor belt and rose upwards towards the open mouth of the meat grinder.

There was already a clear, plastic bag over the valve where the paste would emerge.

Fauzia couldn't tear her eyes away from the body as it went on its journey towards the spinning blades. She stood numbly and tried to rationalise to herself what she was doing.

She thought back to what her father had said to her the day he'd taken her to see the meat grinder. When he'd seen her disgust at the process he'd pulled her to one side and with a deathly earnestness he'd told her that people will always want meat. They can't imagine living without it. But neither can they imagine the fear and violence needed to turn a living creature into food. People want things but they rarely want to pay the price. And so they turn to men like him. Men like the ones working in his factory. Invisible men locked away from the world in a lightless industrial unit. Men who will do whatever it takes.

His business wasn't meat. His business was doing the things that people were afraid to do but even more afraid to go without.

At the time she had wanted to go home. Get as far away from the place as possible. But now standing watching the body heading towards its inevitable destination, finally his words made sense to her.

However much the thought of helping Waqar cover up his crime scared her, the thought of losing him scared her more.

Fauzia looked over at her brother. He was sweating and shaking. She guessed the adrenaline that had helped him overpower the bigger man and stuff him in the boot of his car was leaving his system. Like a junkie needing a fix his entire body was beginning to rebel.

The body on the conveyor belt was a few feet from the lip of the mincer when it let out a sickening groan.

He was alive! Fauzia had been so overwhelmed by the situation she'd forgotten the most basic rule – check for a pulse.

The man had raised one arm and was letting out a low moan. Still groggy from the blood loss he was trying to escape.

Fauzia pushed past her brother to get to one of the kill switches but Waqar grabbed her arm and held her tight.

'He's alive,' she screamed. Cleaning up Waqar's bloody mess was one thing but having blood on her own hands was something else entirely. Whatever it cost she could not let this happen.

'It was me or him,' said Waqar, holding his sister tightly. Suddenly he seemed a lot less timid.

The man was still moving. One leg dangling from the side of the conveyor belt. It did nothing to slow his progress towards the mincer.

Fauzia dug her nails into her brother's forearm but he didn't release his grip. She looked up at him. He was smiling.

'Who's fucked now?' he shouted across the floor to the man on the conveyor belt. 'Tell Galahad this is what happens when you . . .'

Waqar didn't get to finish his speech. The man reached the lip of the mincer. His screams became lost in the sound coming up from the machine.

Just before he went over the edge he raised his head one last time and held Fauzia's gaze. She saw the raw fear in his eyes, his open mouth spitting out dying words drowned out by the machinery.

Then he was gone. His body toppling over the edge and into the mincer. There was a dull thud as he hit the side of the flared hopper that received the conveyor belt and then a sound that neither sibling would ever forget.

Blades cutting through living bone and flesh. A man's terror literally being ripped out of him.

Then just like that the sound died down to the regular dull grind of meat being processed.

At the other end of the meat grinder the clear, plastic bag began to fill up with pink, wet paste.

Fauzia shook free of her brother and threw up on the floor of the processing plant. Her mind went blank. All she could see was the look on the man's face those few seconds before he died.

The meat grinder had done its job.

There would be no waste.

8

In the half an hour since Dean had been left alone with Danny Mitchum, Danny had threatened to have him killed three times, promised to kneecap him once and called him a 'cunt' so many times that the word had lost all meaning.

Dean had been waiting outside when Malton pulled up at the warehouse where they'd been keeping Danny. He didn't want to go in alone. Even after three months of babysitting him, Dean was still scared of Danny. He felt that was the appropriate response.

Danny wasn't big. Maybe five foot seven at most. And he was scrawny with it. He spoke with a dense, dirty Manchester accent but his voice was high. Almost childlike. It made the constant flow of obscenities all the more jarring.

But nowhere near as jarring as his face. Danny wasn't born blind. Ten years back he was a teenage drug dealer, making too much money, too much noise and too many enemies. Someone had decided to teach Danny a lesson. He'd been jumped by half a dozen men and held down while industrial brick cleaner was poured all over his face. They wanted his death to send a message.

Danny lost both eyes, most of his nose and all the soft tissue around his mouth. What remained of his face was a patchwork of scarring and skin grafts, a dark, bisected hole in the centre of his face, just below the two, flesh-covered sockets.

His lips had been reconstructed out of skin from other parts of his body. They didn't match the colour of the rest of his face and barely covered his snarling mouth.

They'd intended to kill him. Instead they'd created a monster. After it emerged the police had known about the attempt on his life, Danny won a multi-million-pound settlement and with that money began building the biggest organised crime gang in Manchester.

However startling Danny's face was, it was no match for the dark, vile state of his soul.

As a condition of accepting the job to track down the leak in Danny's organisation Malton had insisted Danny go into hiding. Away from eyes of the Scouse Mafia.

It had taken Danny some convincing to disappear from view. His empire hung together around his larger-than-life presence. His reckless visibility. Without him there the whole thing fell apart.

So Malton had made sure that as far as the world was concerned Danny *was* still there. Malton knew all too well the value of reputation. How reputation meant that a single man could cow an entire city.

As Danny went to ground, Malton began to feed the underworld rumour mill with sightings, half-truths and outright lies. Danny had shot a man in Rusholme and was lying low. Danny had set up a torture room in a city centre flat and was personally supervising the dismemberment of one of his rivals. Danny was down in London making peace with the Irish mob.

Danny Mitchum might have disappeared from sight but he most definitely was kept alive in the minds of both those he worked for and those who might get it into their heads to move against him.

Only three people knew the truth of where Danny had ended up – Malton, Dean and Danny's father Stevie. They alone knew where Danny was – in the empty storeroom of a north Manchester hosiery warehouse.

The warehouse was owned by a Jewish family firm that had been in Cheetham Hill for generations but now that times were hard, they were more than happy to accept Malton's offer to rent a room in their building. No questions asked.

Dean had helped Malton strip out the ceiling-high metal shelving and boxes of deadstock. In their place had been installed a bed, a table and a TV as well as a small bathroom, built in one corner of the room.

Malton ensured that while there was always someone on guard outside the room but only he and Dean ever went inside. It was Dean's job to drop in once a day and update Danny with Malton's progress.

Danny's father Stevie never asked about visiting him and Malton never offered. Dean suspected Stevie was enjoying getting the chance to be in charge for once.

Dean hated checking in on Danny. When Danny wasn't on one of his many mobile phones, he would force Dean to keep him company. Talking for hours on end while Dean did his best to stay on his good side.

Right now Danny was as angry as Dean had ever seen him.

'He thinks he can fuck me off? Fuck right off. Fuck. Right. Off. If I get killed, I'm going to come back from the dead and fucking wreck him!' Danny was pacing.

Forty-five minutes ago Malton had broken the news to Dean. He was handing over the hunt for the mole to him. Dean was as flattered as he was terrified. Malton had then gone in to see Danny and tell him personally that he was putting his best man on it.

Dean had sat outside listening to the screaming and swearing until finally Malton had emerged and told him to go in and get started.

Dean was always eager to impress Malton. Whatever was asked of him he threw himself into it. Even when he suspected Malton was simply toying with him, giving him pointless jobs to see just how far his loyalty would stretch.

He'd half hoped that was what was happening when Malton ushered him into Danny's room. That his boss would suddenly have a last-minute change of heart, drag him out and tell him it was all one big joke.

But Dean knew Malton didn't joke.

'You think cos I'm on the run for my life I can't hurt him? I can hurt anyone, Dean. Anyone.'

Danny had a nasty habit of frequently dropping Dean's name. A pointed reminder he was now permanently on Danny's radar.

Danny turned and made a beeline across the room for Dean. Despite losing both his eyes Danny had an almost unnatural sense of his surroundings. Not once had Dean seen him hesitate, falter or trip. If it wasn't for the unpalatable proof etched into Danny's face, Dean would swear Danny was no more blind than he was.

Danny stood so close to Dean he could smell the stale weed on his breath. His bright yellow, two-piece tracksuit done all the way up to beneath his chin.

'No offence but I paid for the full VIP treatment and he's given me the fucking work experience?' Danny grabbed Dean before he had a chance to react.

Danny smiled, his scorched gums and stained teeth a rictus grin of amusement as he sensed Dean's body tense with fear.

'No offence.' Danny let him go and laughed. 'Dunno what you're scared of. I'm the one should be shitting myself. Who's going to protect me now? You? You know what this lot do when they get hold of someone?'

Dean had an idea but he didn't want to say.

'Peel your fucking skin off, set dogs on you, mince you by inches. And all the time they keep you alive. Let you watch. Film it. Keep your family in the loop. What would your dear old mum say if she got a video of you with your arms ripped off?'

Dean had heard the stories about what Danny was capable of. A level of violence that married a deranged imagination with a complete absence of anything approaching a conscience. Danny didn't just kill people. Danny took out eyes with his grubby fingers. He sanded off faces with power tools. Danny did the kind of things that made even hardened criminals sick to their stomachs.

47

Dean knew how much the underworld liked to gossip. Most criminals were worse than a women's knitting circle when they got going. He told himself that Danny's reputation couldn't possibly all be true. Danny was several inches shorter than Dean. Barely nine stone soaking wet. And blind with it. Just how much damage could someone like that really do?

As Danny kept on ranting Dean tried not to think about it. Instead he turned over in his mind just what it was Malton thought he was doing, putting him in charge of the hunt for the grass in Danny's gang.

These last few months he'd hardly seen his boss. While Malton was busy wading through Danny's crew Dean had been left to deal with the day-to-day running of Malton Security by himself. Those few times he had seen Malton he'd seemed distant. As if there was something troubling him. Something bigger than just the Danny Mitchum job.

Malton made it his business to know everything about everyone. So how could he not know about Dean's search for Olivia, Vikki Walker's missing friend?

Dean wondered if Danny knew who Big Wacky was. If Danny ever shut up maybe he'd ask him.

'I got a secret,' said Danny, grinning. 'You wanna see?'

Dean nodded. Anything to get away from the incontinent stream of violent threats. Dean tried not to let Danny get to him but try as he might everything about Danny put Dean on high alert. Danny exuded danger and he knew it.

'Well?' asked Danny. 'You nodding, you thick cunt? I'm blind.'

'Yes,' said Dean quickly. 'I want to see.'

Danny theatrically unzipped his tracksuit top. Dean gasped. There, hanging over Danny's pigeon chest by a thin, gold chain was a hand grenade. The chain threading straight through the grenade's pin.

'Fuck,' exhaled Dean.

Malton had made sure Danny was locked away unarmed. Dean had been there when he'd gone through Danny's stuff

48

and removed a two-foot machete and a Taurus Model 85 handgun. Yet somehow Danny had managed to get his hands on a live grenade.

As far as Dean knew only he and Malton had access to the room. Dean knew he hadn't given Danny a grenade. It was inconceivable Malton would do such a thing.

Danny grabbed the grenade and held it aloft with a smile.

'If those fuckers come for me? They're not taking me alive. One pull.' Danny mimed tugging the grenade.

Dean gasped. Danny laughed, relishing Dean's fear.

Something was badly wrong here. Something that Malton had somehow missed. Suddenly Dean felt very alone.

'Clever, right?' said Danny. 'If we're going to be working together from now on we should get to know each other, right? We should do something to celebrate.'

'Malton says you can't leave this room.'

'Malton says?' said Danny. 'That bastard has put you in charge now. What do you say? I want to leave this room. Are you gonna say no to me, Dean Carter?'

Danny picked up the chain holding the grenade around his neck and started swinging the grenade back and forth across his chest as he waited for Dean's answer.

'Trick question. 'Course you fucking aren't,' said Danny.

He let go of the chain and the grenade dropped back against his chest, nestling amongst the scars, tattoos and gold chains. He did his tracksuit top back up and went over to the set of drawers that had been placed in the room for what few personal belongings he seemed to have.

Danny opened the top drawer. Notes spilled out. The entire drawer was stuffed with cash. Some in bundles, some loose. More money than Dean had ever seen in his life.

Danny stuffed a couple of handfuls into his pockets and turned to Dean.

'Help yourself. Call it a signing-on bonus,' he said.

Dean froze.

'Don't be fucking rude,' said Danny, an edge creeping into his voice. 'Take the fucking money.'

Dean walked over to the drawer and took what he hoped was enough but not too much. All the while Danny watched him through those eyeless sockets.

'Now we got some money. Let's go,' said Danny.

'Go where?' said Dean doing his best to not let his voice betray his escalating dread.

Danny smiled. 'We're in the middle of fucking Manchester. Where else? We're going out!'

9

Malton sat in the waiting room wishing that the sense of relief he'd felt after handing Danny Mitchum over to Dean had lasted just a little bit longer.

Instead, with his thoughts no longer preoccupied with a wild goose chase through Danny's criminal empire, suddenly the one thing he'd been doing his best not to think about had resurfaced in his thoughts.

Three months ago he very nearly had it all. A beautiful woman who loved him and convinced him that maybe even Craig Malton could be happy. Three months ago he had a future and her name was Emily.

A lifetime of being the outcast was finally over. He was no longer the mixed-race kid from a broken home who had to strain every sinew of his being just to feel like he might belong. Three months ago Malton was about to stop having to live as a man apart. He was going to have roots. He was going to have a family.

Then three months ago he lost it all at the hands of a very different woman. A woman who had come from the same streets as Malton. A woman who could go anywhere, be anyone. A woman who wouldn't think twice about violence to get what she wanted. A woman who more than anything wanted Malton.

His ex. Keisha Bistacchi.

Thanks to Keisha, Emily finally saw who Malton really was and she fled. Then Keisha too disappeared and once again Malton was alone.

Since then Malton had been running from his feelings. But now they crashed over him in waves.

Malton screwed his eyes tight shut and heaved in a lungful of office air. A combination of expensive leather furniture, fresh flowers and the faint trace of perfume: Creed's Jardin d'Amalfi. He let the breath back out and opened his eyes, taking in his surroundings and doing his best to keep the darkness inside him at bay.

Every inch of wall space in the waiting room was taken up with framed newspaper articles. Every single one featured the smiling face of the woman whose waiting room it was – criminal lawyer Bea Wallace.

Bea looked nothing like any lawyer Malton had ever known before. She was blonde. Almost too blonde. She always wore her signature blood-red lipstick and thick, black-framed glasses. She was tiny, barely over five foot tall but was never seen out of a pair of vertiginous high heels.

In Malton's experience criminal lawyers looked like down-on-their-luck car salesmen. Crumpled suits, coffee-stained ties and male pattern baldness. Bea looked more like a Fifties pin-up.

Despite appearances, Bea was one of the most ruthless people Malton had ever met. She kept international drug dealers out of the papers and gangland killers out of jail.

Looking round the office Malton recognised more than a few of the faces looking back at him. Here was Bea Wallace dining out at Mana, Manchester's only Michelin-starred restaurant, with a man Malton knew as the accountant responsible for laundering millions of pounds from a string of cannabis farms. And here was Bea attending the wedding of a hired killer, famous in the Manchester underworld for having beaten a man to death in the toilets of Piccadilly train station and who, thanks to Bea, escaped prison with a plea of self-defence.

Malton and Bea's worlds overlapped and intermingled as inside and outside the law they provided their services to the worst Manchester had to offer. Each aware of the other but keeping a professionally astute distance.

But then a few weeks after Emily had walked out and Keisha had fled, Bea reached out to Malton for a job. Nothing too taxing. A client who needed some close protection while he conducted some 'business'. To thank Malton personally she'd taken him out to dinner and he'd somehow ended up back at her place. That was the first time he realised just how persuasive Bea Wallace could be.

She wasn't Keisha and she definitely wasn't Emily but right there and then Bea had been exactly what Malton needed. He had spent so long hiding who he was. Trying to balance his contradictions. He had the body of a brutal thug and the mind of a Machiavellian tactician. To the white world he was black but to the black world he would never truly be black. He had millions in the bank, the ears of the most powerful people in Manchester and could walk through any door in the city, yet every day he felt like an impostor.

But not to Bea. From the first moment she saw him Bea knew everything he was. And she wanted it all. For the last three months Malton had been happy to let Bea have him. Now that he was done with Danny he would have the time to decide whether or not to continue their arrangement.

Malton checked his watch. It was nearly ten. Bea had asked him to meet her at work. She was running late. He could hear her in the next room talking to a client. Bea's no-nonsense, Geordie accent along with the occasional monosyllabic grunt from whoever it was in there with her.

Bea never stopped working. Since he'd known her, Malton had been in awe of how little she slept. Working from her office for ten hours a day before returning to her city centre duplex apartment where she continued to work late into the night – filing court documents, researching her clients' crimes and making the kind of phone calls that carry more weight than any sort of legal argument. In her own way Bea's word meant every bit as much in the Manchester underworld as Malton's.

Malton could still smell the stink from the crowd back in Hindley on his clothes. The stench of beer and sweat stuck to his waxed jacket, impregnated his skin. He wished he'd had time to change before he got here.

'JUST FUCKING DO IT!' a male voice shouted from the next room.

Malton was immediately on his feet.

'I PAY YOU FUCKING MONEY TO DO THIS SHIT. SO FUCKING DO YOUR FUCKING JOB!'

He crossed the waiting room and with one giant, battered fist yanked open the adjoining door. He was greeted with the sight of tiny, blonde Bea sitting calmly on the edge of her desk, legs crossed demurely, while a thick-necked man in garishly distressed designer jeans and T-shirt paced up and down ranting.

Malton immediately recognised Stevie Mitchum – Danny's father, and while Danny was in hiding, the public face of Danny's criminal business.

Bea turned to Malton with a smile. She seemed utterly unfazed by Stevie's outburst.

Realising he was no longer alone with his lawyer, Stevie turned to the open door, screwing his face up in distaste at the sight of Malton poised in the doorway.

'Mr Mitchum was just getting rather passionate about a kilo of cocaine that somehow ended up in the boot of a car registered in his name,' said Bea breezily.

Depending on the company she was keeping and the amount of wine she had drunk, Bea's Geordie accent waxed and waned. When she was in court she spoke in an assertively low RP, with only the occasionally overlong vowel sound giving any hint of her true voice. But when she was talking to her clients she liked to put them at ease and slip back into the unmistakable musicality of her native Newcastle accent.

Stevie didn't move an inch. 'Aren't you supposed to be busy finding out who grassed my son up?' he demanded.

Dealing with Danny Mitchum was a constant minefield of mind games and unpredictability. His father Stevie was tediously simple by comparison. Malton had met hundreds of men like Stevie. Brutal men who had come to realise that the only way they could get a share of the good things in life was to take them. Ideally by force.

What made Stevie stand out was his dumb luck at having Danny for a son. Without Danny, Stevie would be just another meathead waiting for the inevitable moment he picked on the wrong person and came to a nasty end.

Thanks to Danny, Stevie found himself with a mid-life career pivot from local hard man to second- and then first-in-command of the most profitable drugs business in Manchester.

It was clear from what Malton had overheard that without Danny's mercurial touch, Stevie was struggling. While Danny could spin gold from shit, Stevie's talents were very much in the opposite direction.

'I've just come from talking to Danny,' said Malton calmly.

Bea made a show of looking out of the window, her way of letting both men know that she was officially not listening to anything they were about to say.

'I've decided to step things up and put my best man on the case.'

'Your best fucking man? We're paying *you*.'

Malton made a show of looking contrite. 'Unfortunately I've not made as much progress as I'd like, so I thought it would help to have a fresh pair of eyes.'

Stevie floundered in the face of Malton's unflinching politeness. Malton knew Stevie would love the chance to kick off. Malton was utterly confident that if it came to blows he would dispatch Stevie in short order but he always felt that if things did turn physical it was a failing on his part. Malton hadn't lasted as long as he had through brutality alone. Sure, he could dish it out if he had to but whenever possible he preferred de-escalation, negotiation and compromise.

Failing that he always carried a stainless steel hatchet in the gamekeeper's pocket of his waxed jacket.

Bea hopped off her desk and stood between them.

'Boys! Whatever this is about, can I ask that you carry it on outside my office? As your lawyer it's vitally important that I focus on the job in hand,' said Bea, sensing the impasse and butting in.

'What's he even fucking doing here?' spat Stevie.

'From time to time I use Mr Malton for various services,' said Bea coyly.

She shot Malton a flirtatious glance. Stevie was too riled up to notice.

'If you're finding it hard to keep things together I can tell Danny for you?' offered Malton.

Sensing the limits of Stevie's patience Bea began to wind things up. 'Mr Mitchum, I think I've got everything I need to get started. I'll be in touch. And please don't worry, I promise we can make this go away.'

Stevie didn't take his eyes off Malton. Malton knew problems that couldn't be solved with a good beating were beyond Stevie. In a situation like this it was best to simply let him burn himself out.

'I can fucking handle it,' spat Stevie. 'You tell Danny that. I've got this. Don't need him.' He turned to Bea, on a roll. 'I never seen that car in my life. Not my car. Not my drugs. OK?'

He gave Malton a last empty glare and flounced out of Bea's office, leaving Malton alone with her.

They stood in silence for a moment listening as Stevie passed out of the office and disappeared down the corridor.

When they heard the sound of the elevator Bea threw her arms around Malton and kissed him full on the mouth.

It only lasted a few seconds before she pulled away, her face screwed up in disgust.

'Eugh, you smell like a rugby team, where have you been?'

With no one else in the office Bea's accent slipped further into her native Geordie.

Malton smiled. 'Hindley.'

Bea grinned at him as if he were a naughty schoolboy. 'Well let's get you back to my place and get you showered off.'

Malton watched as Bea packed a Gladstone bag with a thick stack of legal papers. He liked Bea. She was easy and fun. She could look after herself and knew what she wanted.

Like Emily she was a nice, white, university-educated girl who had been drawn to the chaos that men like Malton made their own. Unlike Emily, Bea wasn't trying to save Malton from the chaos. She wanted to join in the fray. She thrived going head to head with men like Stevie Mitchum. She was fearless and relished taking on all comers.

In a way she reminded him of Keisha. She was tough and smart and ruthless. But Bea was driven by unquenchable ambition. What drove Keisha was something far more sinister. A slow burning rage that at any moment threatened to erupt and burn the world down around her.

But, unlike Keisha or Emily, Bea felt whole. A complete person whose desire for Malton was based solely on her own agency. There was nothing missing in Bea's head or in her heart. No space for Malton to fill. He found it odd that the knowledge Bea could walk out at any moment didn't scare him. On the contrary. Knowing that she wanted him but that she didn't *need* him, made everything simple. It meant that unlike with Emily or Keisha he would never risk opening himself up. He would never risk falling in love.

Malton looked past Bea, out of the office window and into the night. Keisha was still out there somewhere. Sometimes, alone at night when he couldn't sleep, he let his mind walk the streets of the city. Visiting all the places he thought she might be. But he knew Keisha. She would only be found when she wanted to be found.

He was sure of one thing – she'd be back. And when she returned she'd be bringing hell back with her.

Deep down, part of him was looking forward to it.

10

'Craig Malton put you here,' snarled Keisha.

Across the room a giant of a man lay on a stained mattress, naked and shivering in a pool of his own vomit.

The door to the room had been locked behind Keisha. There was no easy way out for either of them.

By the light of the bare bulb hanging from the ceiling Keisha could see he was easily six-foot-six and despite his current, degraded state his body was packed with sinewy muscles. His greying skin glistened with a sheen of stale sweat.

Every inch of his flesh was covered in tattoos. A photo-realistic tribute to a dead dog across one shoulder, a record of Man City's Cup form down one arm. Across his neck, in ornate, gothic font the single word stood out: *VICIOUS*.

Being alone in a locked room with this man was a risk Keisha didn't take lightly. The revolver she cradled in her lap wasn't just for show.

Keisha sat on an orphaned dining chair, the only other piece of furniture in the room. Chipboard had been hammered over the windows, blocking out the light. Aside from the bulb above their heads the room was in darkness. But nothing lurking in the shadows could hope to project the raw threat that radiated from this defeated giant, sprawled at Keisha's feet.

Once this had been someone's front room. The thick, garish carpet that took pride of place was now soiled and torn. The fireplace had long been ripped out, leaving a gaping, brick hole up to the chimney. A cold draught blew down, filling the room with its icy chill. Between the damp in the walls and the shit and piss soaking the mattress, the room couldn't have smelled worse.

The giant's huge body shuddered. A heavy, tattooed arm rose. A large, knotted hand pressed its palm flat against the carpet.

Keisha watched as the man tried to lift himself up. Even in his compromised state he must have weighed easily nearly twenty stone. A human leviathan.

'That's it. Do you remember who you used to be? How we used to be shit-scared of you? Remember that summer? No one stepped to you. Not Salford, not Moss Side. No one. You were a king. And then he took it all.'

The head lifted for just a moment. A sunken face barely visible behind a long, scruffy beard. Veins on his neck pulsed beneath the VICIOUS tattoo. For just a second a dim light shone in his weary eyes. His lips moved over dry gums. It was too much. He fell back into his own filth.

Keisha knew that however clever she was, however ruthless and quick, she was still a woman in a man's world. The furious, unavoidable truth was that as a woman almost every man she met could overpower her. Easily.

It enraged Keisha. The depth of her fury and ambition outweighed any man she'd ever met. Even Craig. Yet the lowest, weakest punk could fancy his chances against her. She had cunning and she had weapons, but even they weren't always enough.

That was why she had found this man. Why she had locked him away in preparation for the moment when she would unleash him on the world.

When she first sought him out he was a junkie. A ruined shell of his former self. For months now Keisha had been feeding him the heroin that controlled his every waking thought. It had been enough to make him her compliant, unquestioning slave.

But now she needed something more than a slave. She needed a warrior.

'See this?' Keisha held up the revolver. 'If you had this you could shoot me. You could get out of here. You could do whatever you want.'

Keisha held up the gun for him to get a good look and then gently placed it on the floor in front of her.

A low growl erupted from deep within the giant ribcage. It had been nearly a week since Keisha last injected him with heroin. Without the safety net of methadone, she was detoxing him in the most brutal way imaginable.

All that time locked in this room.

Three months ago Keisha had brought Manchester to the brink of gang warfare, in a bid to wrench Craig Malton from his comfy, middle-class life and bring him back to her. Despite everything her plan had failed. But Keisha couldn't move on. Not yet.

She loved him too much to walk away. But that didn't mean she could forgive him. Whenever the thought of moving on crossed her mind all she had to do was close her eyes and think back to a day almost thirty years ago. A day that meant she could never go back.

Keisha staggered through the night. All around her were people. Faces looming up from the blackness and disappearing back into the dark. She could smell burning.

The night air was cold on her skin. She could barely walk. Every step was agony and yet, try as she might, she couldn't find the strength to cry out for help.

If only she could make the few feet back to the open door of her flat. The flat where a few months earlier Craig had walked out on her.

It felt like walking through thick mud, every step a tiny victory. As she reached the door she turned around and saw it.

The entire world was on fire.

Because of what happened that day Keisha wouldn't stop until Craig Malton was destroyed.

Keisha watched as the enormous body hauled itself off the mattress and began to crawl towards the gun. She remembered who he had been before he became just another helpless addict. She remembered the fear his name inspired. The damage he'd done.

'I know you will come back. And when you do I know what you want. You want to hurt the man who put you here. The man who put a needle in your arm. Who made you like this.'

The colossus dragged himself towards the gun. A big hand inching across the floor and hauling his huge bulk forward along the carpet. Each finger stained blue with long-faded tattoos.

'That's it!' said Keisha. 'One inch at a time.'

Keisha needed this man to remember who he once was. A human wrecking machine. A violent lunatic. She needed him to be her chosen representative. A living avatar of her own rage. Keisha couldn't physically match men head to head. But with this man on her side she wouldn't need to.

She leaned forward and addressed the shuddering body on the mattress. 'That's your brain, unable to produce the dopamine you need just to feel human. All that heroin, your brain got lazy. 'And without it . . . ?'

The man groaned and thrashed.

'But there is another way to produce dopamine. Another way to kick-start your head back to the land of the living. Violence.'

He pulled his body off the filthy mattress and onto the carpet. He didn't have the strength to raise his head, dragging it along the floor with him. The gun was a few feet away now.

'You remember how that felt don't you? When it all kicks off? The fear and adrenaline? The rush? That feeling when you're hitting them or they're hitting you. It doesn't matter, does it? It's all one great big explosion in your brain. I'm done giving you drugs. Now I'm going to give you something better.'

It wasn't pure chance that Keisha had chosen this man to be the weapon she'd use to take aim at Craig. He and Malton had met before. Nearly five years ago. Back when Keisha was still alone and drifting through Manchester's underbelly. Before she had found a husband. Before she had decided it was time to win Craig back. Before all of that.

His name had been Leon Walker. And when the whole of Manchester was quaking in fear at his unquenchable brutality, only one man had dared to step to him. That man was Craig Malton. On the sixth floor of a deserted multi-storey, they had nearly killed each other. But when it was over Malton had walked away and Leon Walker lay six floors down, splayed on the pavement; his back was broken.

If anyone wanted to hurt Craig it was Leon Walker.

A huge hand reached out, fingers brushing the metal handle of the gun.

'That's it, Leon. Take it. Take it back. Take it all back,' said Keisha.

She smiled like a proud parent.

'Pick it up, Leon. Pick it up.'

Greasy, delirious fingers slithered over the gun, desperately trying for purchase. Leon's hand slid into a grip.

'Now imagine I'm Malton,' said Keisha.

Something filled Leon Walker's body. A glimmer of the power that was once there. The head rose, the eyes blazed and suddenly a bottomless rage, every bit the equal of Keisha's, swelled in him.

Leon Walker's scabby, broken mouth opened and a bellow of pure, primal fury filled the room.

Keisha was on her feet now. 'You feel it don't you? That old memory of what it's like to have the power over life or death.'

His arm raised the gun and pointed it up at Keisha.

'Malton did this to you. Make him pay,' said Keisha.

A finger tightened on the trigger.

Click. Click. Click.

Leon Walker managed three times to fire an empty chamber before his strength left him and with an anguished cry he dropped the gun back on the carpet.

Keisha bent down close to him and held out six bullets in her palm.

'But you can't do this without me. Do you understand?' Leon Walker muttered wetly.

'I asked you a question,' she said, her voice losing the gentle, encouraging warmth. She thrust her fingers into his long greasy hair and yanked his head up so he was looking her straight in the eye. 'Do you understand me?'

'Yes,' said Leon Walker almost inaudibly, sweat and drool running down his chin.

Keisha dropped his head back into the soiled carpet, stood, picked up the empty revolver and left Leon to his own private hell.

Leon Walker wasn't ready yet, but when he was Craig Malton wouldn't know what hit him.

11

Dean felt the eyes of every single person in the pub watching them. As if Danny's face didn't attract enough attention, he also didn't have an indoor voice. If anything it seemed like he was deliberately talking even louder than usual.

This was really bad. For three months Malton had managed to vanish Danny off the face of the earth. Dean had been on the job less than an hour and here they were, out in the open. Danny making up for lost time.

As Danny held forth about the last time he was in the Derby Arms, Dean's mind raced as he tried to think of a way to get Danny back to the safe house with as little fuss as possible.

He knew Danny wouldn't make it easy.

'So I think, this is fucking it. Now or never. I follow the prick into the toilets. Filthy fucking toilets. Get hepatitis from the door handle toilets. See him go in the cubicle. Just me and him. You following, Dean? Smash. Kick in the door. Bang. Door hits him in the face, he goes down, twats his head on the toilet and so the cunt's already pissing blood before I've even put hands on him. He looks up at me and you know what he said?'

Dean sneaked a look around the Derby Arms. It was nothing like Danny had described it. Danny had talked about a cavernous brewery pub with stark linoleum floors, wipe-clean walls and the kind of invasive strip lighting usually found in bus stations and hospitals. According to Danny the clientele was a mixture of derelicts, prostitutes and people wanting to meet somewhere no one with a shred of decency would be seen dead.

The Derby Arms had evidently changed since Danny was last here. It wasn't just refurbished with cheap and cheerful pub fittings and dusty house plants. It had been taken over by people in their twenties living across Cheetham Hill Road in the new Green Quarter flats. Hipsters had colonised the Derby Arms.

The world Danny Mitchum described was a relic. A distant bit of folklore.

Dean wondered about faking a call from Malton. Inventing a threat on Danny's life. Spiriting him back to the safe house. Anything to minimise the damage that had already been done to Danny's cover.

'Fucker closed his eyes, started singing Amazing fucking Grace? You believe that? Couldn't fucking make it up. Never seen anything like it. Course, I still smacked him about. Only right.'

Dean laughed nervously at the punchline.

Danny grinned with satisfaction, picked up his pint of Guinness and downed half in one go. Stout dripped from the corners of his reconstructed mouth but he didn't seem to care.

The dozen or so twenty-somethings who'd been discreetly hanging on Danny's every word returned to their own private conversations.

Danny terrified Dean. The thought of lying to his face seemed almost suicidal. Despite being blind Danny saw everything. Dean didn't trust that Danny couldn't see right into his soul.

Lying wasn't an option. Dean kept thinking. Keeping one eye on Danny and the other on the rest of the pub.

It was clear to Dean that how Danny saw Manchester and how it really was were two very different things.

It had started as they walked through the backstreets of Cheetham Hill. Dean began to realise that Danny Mitchum's memories of Manchester were unchanged from back when he lost his eyes just over a decade earlier.

Walking down winding north Manchester streets he'd swing round, finger extended as he pointed to his own,

personal landmarks. A safe house where he'd tortured someone to death or a shop he'd torched to settle a drug debt.
More often than not, while Danny pointed, relating his tales
of violence and intimidation, Dean found himself following
Danny's finger, only for it to be pointing to newly erected
luxury flats or freshly cleared plots of empty land awaiting
a developer.

Since Danny's accident Manchester had changed out of all
recognition. Dean felt it too. The walk to the Derby Arms had
included dozens of new buildings he didn't recognise. He was
used to it. Every time he went out in Manchester it was like
the city had grown overnight. Skylines altered and streets took
on new shapes.

Dean could feel Manchester racing ahead into the future. It
made him want to run and keep up.

But Danny Mitchum saw none of that. He saw the old
Manchester. A tightly knit world of decay and decline. A play-
ground of violence where he had made his name.

So when they'd arrived at the pub only to find it had fallen
to the irresistible wave of gentrification, Dean was unsure how
to break the news to Danny.

It didn't help that Danny was still wearing that grenade
around his neck. Dean could see the bulge it made under
Danny's tracksuit top.

Scanning the fresh-faced punters that filled the bar Dean
recognised New Manchester. The Manchester that lived in the
city centre and ate out every day of the week. Renting flats,
working temp jobs. Riding the wave of change that was sweep-
ing the city. The last people who would have any idea of who
Danny Mitchum was.

But Dean wasn't prepared to bank on that. It would only
take one person for the word to get out. Then some of the
worst people in the world would be making a beeline straight
for the Derby Arms.

Danny finished his pint and barked, 'My round, what you
having?'

Dean cursed his inaction. Now they would be there for another pint. More precious minutes out in the open. But he knew better than to refuse the offer of a drink from Danny Mitchum.

'I'll get it,' said Dean getting up.

It was enough of a shock to see Danny stride into the Derby Arms and without the benefit of eyesight somehow pick his way around punters, a pool table and several bar stools to seat himself in the far corner of the bar.

Every time it looked like he was about to collide with something, Dean's heart missed a beat. Danny was like a bundle of dynamite. It would only take the slightest nudge to set him off.

'Fuck off. Sit down. It's my round,' Danny snarled. 'My money not good enough for you?'

Dean gently sat down under the withering, eyeless gaze.

'Pint of Carling please,' he said.

'That's a top pint that, Dean,' said Danny and headed off to the bar.

They couldn't stay here any longer. Dean had to make a move.

Malton Security ran dozens of venues across the city. If he could get Danny to one of those then he'd have backup. He could make sure the place was secure. Call Malton. He'd hate to admit defeat but if the Scouse Mafia really were after Danny's head, the longer they were out in the open the more danger they were both in.

Dean decided that the Diamond Lounge fitted the bill. It was a strip club and midweek would be relatively empty. If strippers couldn't lure Danny away then what could?

Just as Dean rose to go and tell Danny the change of plan a student carrying three pints turned away from the bar and walked straight into Danny, tipping all three pints down Danny's tracksuit.

The whole bar went silent. They'd heard his tales. They'd seen his face. What was left of it. They might not know the name Danny Mitchum but it was clear that wherever this disfigured stranger had come from it wasn't the world of new-build flats, boutique club nights and Instagram accounts that now filled the Derby Arms.

Danny exhaled.

The student opened his mouth to apologise.

Before a sound had come out, Danny's hand had shot up, grabbed the boy by the back of the head and slammed him down face-first as hard as he could into the bar.

The student's face smashed off the bar, showering blood and teeth over the stunned barmaid.

The three pint-glasses dropped from his hands and before he'd even hit the floor the screaming started.

Dean was halfway across the room but Danny was already up on his toes. He was only just warming up.

He turned on the student lying whimpering at his feet, spat a ball of phlegm from his lipless mouth onto his prone body and began to stamp down on him as hard as he could. Between each stamp he spat out a single word.

'Do . . .' Stamp. 'You . . .' Stamp. 'Know . . .' Stamp. 'Who . . .' Stamp. 'I . . .' Stamp. 'Am?'

Chaos erupted. People were fleeing. A couple of mobile phones were out filming. Dean could see the barmaid on the landline, her hands barely able to hold the receiver still, she was so scared.

This was as bad as it could be. As Dean got near the bar he faltered. He felt his gut clench in the only rational, sensible reaction to confronting a man like Danny Mitchum. Dean was afraid.

Danny stopped momentarily to catch his breath. He raised his face, taking in the bar and the terrified customers, who were mesmerised as Danny addressed the entire room.

'I see you cunts. I see all of you. This is my city. Not yours. Mine. I was here first. I'm Danny Fucking Mitchum and don't you forget it.'

This was too much. However scared Dean was he had to act. He stepped over the prone student and sidled up behind

Danny. Trying to sound as casual as possible Dean whispered, 'Think we should be going, Danny.'

Danny gave the student one last stamp and turned to Dean with a grin.

'And I never even got you a pint.' He laughed and sauntered out of the Derby Arms.

Dean briskly walked after him. Careful not to break into a run. With Danny out of the pub, drinkers rushed to the fallen student. A couple watched Dean leave, wondering whether they dared stop him. With one look from Dean their courage deserted them. On his way out he looked up, straight at the CCTV he knew would be there.

This couldn't have gone any worse.

Dean raced to catch up as Danny walked across four lanes of speeding traffic and back towards the safe house.

In the distance he could already hear the police sirens.

12

'All this was about a phone?' said Fauzia, barely able to keep the incredulity out of her voice.

Waqar was sitting on the large, white sofa in her flat, wearing her dressing gown and drying his hair with one of her towels. Fauzia had already tossed her suit jacket into a bin liner. She could smell the blood on her. She'd clean up once Waqar had gone. But her brother still lived with their parents and couldn't very well go home covered in a dead man's blood.

'It's more complicated than that,' said Waqar, carelessly tossing the wet towel onto the hardwood floor. 'It's encrypted. Runs an app called DLchat, a totally private network. It cost ten grand just to buy the phone. Another ten grand to get on DLchat. It's end-to-end secure. The servers, everything. No one can crack it. Not FBI, not MI5. Not the police.'

After taking nearly an hour to hose down and sterilise the meat grinder and then making sure the bags of warm, pink paste that were once a human being had been disposed of in amongst all the other hundreds of bags of waste generated daily by the takeaways of Daubhill, Fauzia and Waqar had driven to Fauzia's flat in a converted mill on the edge of Bolton town centre. All the way there Fauzia had been trying, without success, to work out just what was going on.

'The man you killed stole your phone?'

'No.' Waqar was beginning to sound frustrated. He was never the most articulate child. As soon as the glow of parental affection transferred to Fauzia he had clammed up for good.

'It works like this,' he said and leaned over Fauzia's glass-topped coffee table. 'This is Bolton,' he said picking up an apple from the fruit bowl. 'And this is Huddersfield.' He picked up an orange. 'And this is Oldham.' A banana. 'And this is Bradford.' Another apple.

'You've lost me,' said Fauzia.

'That's us. Asians, big South Asian communities. And each one has their own drugs operation. Their own bosses, their own suppliers, their own territory.'

Fauzia knew all this already. It was the exact situation that men like Tahir had allowed to perpetuate. What she wanted to know was where her brother fitted in to all of this.

'So you're in trouble with whoever it is that runs Bolton? What's his name?'

Waqar leaned back on the sofa, spreading his arms across the back and grinning proudly.

'Waqar Malik. I run Bolton.'

Fauzia shook her head with disbelief. 'You?'

'You're not the only one in this family who can do things, Fauz,' said Waqar, sounding hurt. 'Nothing gets sold in Bolton without my say-so.'

'Even if that's true . . .'

'Oh it's true.'

'Even if it is true, who was the man you . . .' She couldn't bring herself to say it out loud.

'Killed? You mean the man *we* killed. He was from my supplier. Galahad.'

Galahad. That name again. 'Who is Galahad?' said Fauzia.

'I don't know. That's the whole point of the encrypted phone. I call him Galahad. That's what comes up on my phone. I message Galahad and he gets back to me. About shipments and prices, dates and stuff. We never meet. I'm a professional.'

Fauzia's head was spinning. She had assumed her brother had been leaned on for cash. Or that, eager to prove his street smarts, he'd been dealing to his mates. But here he was telling her that he was no victim. He was the one calling the shots. He was the one running Bolton!

For a moment Fauzia caught her reflection in the dark glass of the window. Instantly her mind filled with the man's face. His eyes bulging with fear. His final, unheard words. She shook the image away and turned back to her brother.

'If you really are the biggest dealer in Bolton. If . . .' The words sounded ridiculous coming out of her mouth. 'Then why keep your phone in Mum and Dad's safe?'

'Friday innit? Everyone's down the mosque. The one time everyone knows where I'll be. I can't afford to lose that phone. So I stick it in the safe while I'm out.'

Waqar shook his head a little as if this was simply common sense.'

'Someone knew you'd be out,' said Fauzia, flipping Waqar's logic back on him.

Waqar went to reply but as he opened his mouth the steel trap of Fauzia's reasoning closed around him. He scowled and looked down.

'So tell Galahad what happened,' said Fauzia, eager for this not to descend into one of their regular arguments.

Waqar smiled condescendingly. 'Can't. No phone. No way of contacting him. The guy in the boot, he'd been sent to find out why I'd gone all quiet.'

'And you killed him?' said Fauzia incredulously.

For a moment Waqar looked like he did when their father was tearing strips off him. A small, scared little boy desperately trying and failing to fight his corner.

'He wouldn't take no for answer. I told him I didn't have the phone on me. He didn't believe me. Said if I didn't show it him he'd come round Mum and Dad's looking for it. Galahad knows I've lost it. Trust me Fauz, if he thinks I've lost a phone that could be traced back to him? I'm fucked.'

All the bravado was gone now. Waqar hunched over, nervously wringing his hands, unable to look Fauzia in the eye. He was back to being her big brother.

Fauzia took a breath. This changed everything. Back at the factory she told herself she was saving her brother from dark forces beyond his control. More and more it sounded like the exact opposite. Her brother had gone looking for trouble. And he'd found it in the worst possible way.

'So where was the phone when you last saw it?' she said, doing her best to treat this situation no differently than all the other times she'd helped Waqar clean up his mess.

'I left it in the safe in Mum and Dad's strongroom. Someone took it. Bradford or Huddersfield or Oldham. One of that lot,' said Waqar shaking his head angrily. 'They didn't dare make a play for me themselves. They knew if I pissed off Galahad he'd do the job for them.'

Fauzia's mind reeled. Her parents' safe was located inside a locked room that itself was easily as secure as a safe. A safe within a safe. Hidden again inside her parents' house. It would be virtually impossible to break in.

But if by some unimaginable feat of ingenuity someone had managed it that meant they didn't just know where her parents lived. They'd already been in their house.

She put the thought out of her mind and pushed on. If she was going to solve this she needed to know everything about Waqar's world. So for the next half an hour she listened as he outlined how he'd risen to become the king of Bolton.

The more Fauzia heard the less she could believe it. By the time he'd finished Waqar's chest was puffed out, his mouth a cocky sneer. Her big brother looking every bit the triumphant kingpin.

After everything she'd been through that night Fauzia couldn't resist bringing him back down to earth.

'And what happens if you can't find the phone?' she asked.

The smile slowly left Waqar's face. He looked down at his feet.

'Galahad will kill me,' he said. 'And he'll kill Mum and he'll kill Dad.' Suddenly something occurred to Waqar and he looked up at his big sister. 'And he'll definitely kill you.'

Fauzia's blood went cold. She looked out of the window into the black Bolton night. Once more she saw the face of someone realising they were about to die.

This time it was her own.

13

Malton wasn't making love. He wasn't having sex. He was fucking. Like a man possessed. He was fucking Bea and it felt great.

She knelt on the bed in the master bedroom of her apartment. Malton had never seen a Caesar bed before he met Bea. It was twelve feet wide and eight feet long, every part of it bespoke. It was bigger than most people's living rooms.

Bea had led him into the flat and headed straight for the bedroom while he hurried into the bathroom to shower off the Hindley stink. Later on she'd be working late into the early hours while Malton slunk off – to where, she never asked. But before that she wanted to work out the day's tensions.

Bea had a very specific type of client. Rough, violent men. Men who'd grown up respecting nothing except brutality. The kind of men who never imagined that a woman like Bea existed. A woman who could take their unreconstructed thuggery and not just use it to tame them like dogs but get off on it while she did so.

Malton had no illusions as to what Bea saw in him. He didn't know for sure what he saw in Bea but as long as she was happy for them to keep each other at arm's length he didn't care.

Their whole relationship was a negotiated stand-off punctuated with sex. After what had happened with Emily that suited Malton just fine.

Bea's clothes, discarded on the floor of the flat, formed a trail all the way to the bedroom where she now hovered, naked on the edge of the bed, the vast expanse of the mattress playing out in front of the two of them.

Bea felt good against Malton's powerful body. Her skin was flushed and pink. Beneath her work clothes she had several tattoos floating over her body. Mementoes from a wild adolescence of rebellion and bad decisions.

It had never occurred to Malton to ask about any of them and it had never occurred to Bea to tell him.

Bea reached a hand behind Malton's back, pulling him deeper into her. Digging her nails into the taut brown flesh.

Malton responded urgently, grinding her backside against him.

He looked down at the tattoo of a bee that sat at the base of Bea's spine, its delicate wings spreading out over her hips. The worker bee. The symbol of Manchester's industry and unity.

Like so many Mancunians both born and adopted, Bea had got it in an act of defiance and solidarity after the murder of twenty-two innocents by a godless maniac.

He tried to lose himself in the pleasure of the moment. But tonight something felt different. He couldn't focus. The physical pleasure wasn't enough to keep his thoughts at bay.

Suddenly his brain stopped spinning and he saw clearly what was distracting him – Emily.

No sooner had she left a note and walked out on him than he'd started working for Danny. He'd taken the job because saying no wasn't an option. But more than that, he wanted it. He needed something that would consume him. Stop the pain he felt at losing Emily. Now he was off the job that pain came flooding back.

As he knelt on the bed, pressed up against Bea, it was clear that he had to go looking for Emily. Properly this time. There was no amount of sex and violence in all of Manchester that could stop him thinking about her forever. About what they'd had. About what they were going to have. It had taken a lifetime for Malton to finally allow himself to dream of a family. Of taking the risk and making himself vulnerable like that. But no sooner had he made that choice than Emily left and it was snatched away.

He needed to know for sure that the future he'd dreamed about, even for those few days, truly was over.

Bea leaned forward, pushing her face into the soft, cotton bedding, her blonde hair spreading out over the covers. Her backside rose up and Malton grabbed on to her thighs to keep himself inside her.

He had no doubt that Bea's thoughts were just as cluttered as his own. He knew she used sex to clear her mind. Get ready for an evening's work. She was using him just as much as he was using her. There was no need to make things any more than they were.

Whether or not he'd break things off with Bea he couldn't say, but he knew that he wouldn't be sleeping in this obscenely large bed tonight. He'd be returning to his vast, empty house in Didsbury. The house he avoided as much as possible thanks to all the memories of Emily it still held.

Malton was about to climax when his phone went off on the bedside table, all the way on the other side of the bed.

'Leave it,' said Bea, pre-empting Malton's instincts.

But it was too late. As the phone rang and rang, Malton felt himself dragged out of the moment. He ground to a halt.

Bea shook him off and spun round on the bed, her legs spread wide as she looked at him with coy disappointment.

'I know,' she said. 'Work.'

Without taking her eyes off Malton, her hand slid between her legs as she began to play with herself.

'If you're not up to the job someone's got to finish it,' she said with a smile.

Malton turned his back and tried to focus. He could still see Bea's reflection in the ceiling-length windows as she squirmed on the bed. He did his best to ignore it.

His caller ID said – Dean. It had been a big ask leaving Dean alone with Danny. It had only been a couple of hours. Malton had hoped the boy would have lasted longer. He answered.

'What?' said Malton, making sure to keep the dread Dean's timing was stirring inside him at bay.

'They're here to kill Danny!' screamed the voice on the other end of the line before being drowned out by the sound of gunshots.

14

Someone was hammering on the security door to Danny Mitchum's bolthole. The room within the textile warehouse where for the past three months Malton had been keeping Danny hidden. The room that Dean had hustled Danny back to after the incident at the Derby Arms.

The room that they were both now trapped in.

Whether it was people uploading clips to social media, leaks within Greater Manchester Police or good old-fashioned word of mouth, after what happened at the pub word had most definitely got out. Someone had found where Danny was hiding.

'Is that all you got?' screamed Danny at the locked door. Still buzzing from the violence back at the pub, he was on the balls of his feet, his body tense and ready for a fight. Dean sincerely hoped it wouldn't come to that. Again.

It had started with the sound of someone breaking into the main warehouse. The owners had all gone home. Dean and Danny were alone in the building. Then he'd heard the shouts. Demanding that they come out. Of course Danny had shouted back at which point they opened fire on the door.

Malton had tasked Dean with not only investigating Danny's organisation but keeping Danny safe while he did so. That had only been a few hours ago. Since then Dean had let Danny walk out of his safe house, watched as he beat a man half to death in front of a packed pub, CCTV and half a dozen camera phones, and now he was trapped and helpless as what sounded like a heavily armed death squad did their best to break into the room and kill them both.

This was not how Dean had planned things. With no other option he'd done the one thing he didn't want to do. He'd called Malton.

Malton was on his way but whether or not they'd still be alive by the time he got there was down to Dean.

The gunfire died down. The door was still intact. Then the hammering started up again. It sounded like they had some kind of battering ram. A heavy, hollow crashing, shaking the door in its frame.

'I'm going out there,' said Danny. 'Open the fucking door.'

'I can't let you.'

Danny turned on him. 'You going to stop me are you, Dean?' he sneered.

Dean took a step back. He'd finally seen the casual, unhinged violence erupt from within Danny Mitchum. It hadn't been a fight; it had been a slaughter. There was no warning and no escalation. Danny had gone from zero to attempted murder in the blink of an eye. And on top of all that, he still had a live grenade around his neck. His precaution against torture was beginning to seem less and less unhinged by the second.

Dean was trapped between the armed killers outside trying to get in and the unarmed killer inside trying to get out. Still, he held his ground and, mustering as much authority as he could summon, said, 'I'm getting us out of here.'

Danny laughed. 'The fuck you are. One way in, one way out. Craig Malton's not a man who likes variables.'

'He's also not a man who puts all his eggs in one basket,' said Dean crossing the room.

It was true there was only one exit. For now. But Dean had seen something he shouldn't have.

Dean had been watching Danny for the past three months. In that time he'd made sure he knew the building inside and out. While Danny was locked away Dean had walked the surrounding area, considered escape routes and if trouble came, which direction it would be coming from.

In that time he'd noticed something peculiar. On the outside of the building there was a fire door. But try as he might he had been unable to find the corresponding door on the inside of the building. It simply wasn't there.

Dean had taken to pacing it out. Mapping the building to himself. Discreetly but comprehensively he created a plan of the entire building, which was when he realised where the inside door for the fire exit was. It was within Danny Mitchum's room.

The corner of Danny's room had been converted into an en suite. Tiled and plumbed in. A proper room within a room. It wasn't quite the luxury Danny was used to but it was enough to make being locked up for three months bearable. Behind those tiles lay what until very recently was the fire exit door.

There *was* a way out.

The hammering stopped for a moment. A few seconds later there was a loud, deep bang. Dean recognised it as a shotgun round. Someone was unloading shot after shot into the door. The shrill ring of metal on metal filled the room as nearly imperceptible little bulges began to appear on their side of the door. It wouldn't hold forever.

Whoever had come to kill Danny Mitchum wasn't messing around.

There was no time to waste.

Dean rushed into the bathroom.

'I'd be shitting myself too if I were you.' Danny laughed as Dean scurried past him.

Dean looked around the small en suite. A shower, toilet and sink. The floor was covered in thick, vinyl onto which a geometric pattern had been printed, while the walls had been tiled to the ceiling.

Danny appeared at the doorway. 'Get back here and open the door,' he snarled.

'We're leaving,' said Dean as he grabbed the heavy, ceramic lid off the toilet cistern. It made a loud clunk as it hit the floor.

'Down the fucking toilet?' said Danny.

Dean didn't have time for this. Ignoring Danny he turned to roughly where he imagined the fire door to be, hidden behind the glossy, black tiles, and he started to smash the cistern lid into the tiled wall.

Danny jumped back startled. Dean didn't stop. Shards of tile showered the room. Dean had to squint to avoid being blinded by the debris flying off with every hit.

'He built this over a fucking door didn't he?' said Danny Mitchum, a smile of comprehension crossing his ragged lips.

'Help me,' said Dean. The tiles were almost gone now. Behind them was chipboard. That would be harder to shift. But behind that there had to be the fire exit and their best shot at getting out of this alive.

'I don't have time for this. Give me the keys to the main door,' said Danny.

Dean turned to argue and saw that Danny was holding a gun.

Dean's guts flipped over. First a grenade and now a gun? But with a supreme force of will he betrayed nothing to Danny.

Danny frowned, disappointed at the lack of reaction.

'You know what this is, right? You think your sweet family of bra merchants can't be bought like anyone else? Quick phone call, someone meets them late one night with a bag full of cash and next thing you know someone's accidentally left a gun under the ceiling tiles. So open that fucking door so I can kill whoever the fuck thinks they can walk in and shoot me dead.'

Danny raised the gun and pointed it straight at Dean.

Dean flashed back to the last time someone had pointed a gun at him. Malton's ex, Keisha Bistacchi. He moved his jaw a little, feeling the still-fresh scarring where the bullet had entered his mouth and left via his cheek, taking half a dozen teeth with it. He could feel the scar throbbing.

He was in no rush to get shot again.

'You don't need the gun. You're under my protection,' said Dean hoping he sounded like Malton would in this situation.

'You're fired,' said Danny Mitchum. 'Now give me the fucking keys to that door.'

Dean stared into the carnage that was Danny Mitchum's face. The patchwork of skin and reconstructed flesh. Danny was impossible to read.

Dean had failed to keep Danny hidden. He wasn't going to compound his fuck-up by getting Danny killed. He turned and started hammering at the chipboard beneath the tiles. His eyes screwed shut, his heart racing as he smashed away. Waiting the whole time for the sound of Danny's gun going off.

Suddenly the chipboard gave way and Dean felt the heavy ceramic weight of the cistern bounce off something hard and unyielding. He risked opening his eyes. It was the fire door!

BANG. BANG. BANG.

Dean dropped the cistern lid. But he felt nothing. No impact, no searing pain.

Danny was no longer in the en suite. Then he realised what Danny was doing. He was shooting his way out. Unloading his weapon into the lock of the steel door separating the two of them from the men with guns hell-bent on murdering them.

The sound of gunfire from both sides of the door rang out. Both Danny's gun and – on the other side – the shotgun.

Dean raced out of the en suite in time to see Danny heave open the severely damaged door, utter a gut-wrenching scream and rush into the building beyond. From the brief glimpse Dean got, the warehouse was on fire.

Instantly there was more gunfire. Some from Danny's handgun, some from what sounded to Dean like a shotgun and then more automatic weapon fire.

He heard Danny scream in pain.

Dean didn't even hesitate. Unarmed and without a plan he rushed after Danny. He was halfway across the safe room when the explosion came.

A cloud of shrapnel and flesh blew into the room, knocking Dean off his feet.

Then he blacked out.

15

It had taken Malton nearly three minutes to get from Bea's flat on the sixty-fourth floor down to the underground car park where his Volvo waited.

It had been another six minutes from her apartment block at Deansgate to get out to Cheetham Hill. Manchester city centre was slowly squeezing out cars with more and more streets blocked off. Traffic cameras and pedestrianisation. The council's hope: that if they made driving in the centre of Manchester so slow that it became faster to walk, then motorists would be forced to abandon their cars.

Malton did no such thing.

He had pulled across the tram tracks behind the Midland Hotel and – going the wrong way down a one-way street – had made his way onto Deansgate where he hurtled down a bus lane before breaking into the traffic crawling through the inner ring road.

He'd lost a precious two minutes before he was able to cut across two lanes and wind his way around the roads that were optimistically referred to as the Green Quarter.

Finally Malton pulled up outside the warehouse where he'd stashed Danny Mitchum.

The entire building was ablaze.

Then he heard the explosion. The sound came from deep within the building. A second or so later Malton saw part of the roof begin to collapse inwards.

He didn't pause. Barrelling out of his car, he rushed through the double doors that bore signs of having already been smashed open.

He found himself in an inferno.

The warehouse was a single-storey building. It was laid out very much the same as it had been for the last hundred years. Heavy, metal shelving went all the way up to the ceiling at a height of around twenty feet. The shelving created corridors and alleys, breaking up the otherwise vast space of the warehouse floor.

Every inch of shelving was covered in brown boxes packed full of underwear. Some awaiting delivery, some deadstock, some junk that no one could bring themselves to throw away.

It was all burning.

The heat was unbearable. Nylon and cotton in a conflagration. The boxes were packed so tight that no sooner had one gone up than all of its neighbours burst into flames. The whole place was nothing more than fuel.

Malton rushed through the maze of shelves, keeping himself alert. Whoever had broken the doors down and set the place on fire was still inside. Whatever the explosion he'd just heard was, it meant that he was dealing with some heavily armed people.

Malton reached into his jacket and pulled out the small, polished steel hatchet he carried with him at all times. It wouldn't have been his weapon of choice against an armed death squad but it would have to do.

He rounded a corner and found exactly where the explosion had taken place.

One of the huge shelves had toppled over, causing the neighbouring shelf to topple in a domino effect. Boxes had fallen off shelves onto the floor where they caught fire. The flames rose up into the night sky through a ragged hole torn in the ceiling by the force of the blast.

There was more too. Blood, flesh. Among the telltale scorch marks of explosive, Malton recognised human remains. He had to get into the safe room. Find out if Dean and Danny were still alive.

But his way was barred.

The explosion had upended a large, wooden cutting table, sending it flying across the warehouse floor. The table was solid enough to remain intact but had been flipped and now leaned at an angle against the fallen shelves, blocking the door to the safe room.

Malton felt the fire at his back. The air was thick with smoke. There wasn't much time.

A box blown open by the explosion caught his eye. Undershirts were scattered across the floor. Bright white against the darkness. Malton snatched one up and, tying it around his face, used it to form a makeshift mask. It wouldn't hold up long but it was better than nothing.

He put his hatchet away and walked up to the table. It was vast. Easily ten feet long and made back when things were built to last. Heavy, dark wood, polished to a high gloss through decades of use.

Malton planted his feet and squatted before the table. His hands sought out a grip on the wood, his fingers straining to hold it as tightly as possible.

He took a breath and tasted smoke through his mask. It was now or never.

Malton tensed every muscle in his body and, pushing all his strength through his legs, he began to lift the table. Malton could squat 220 kilograms easily, but this felt almost impossible.

His fingers clasped at the smooth wood, straining to keep a grip as his legs pushed upwards, engaging his glutes.

The table began to move.

Malton leaned in, putting all his strength into it. His teeth gritted. He felt sweat running down the back of his shaved head.

Inch by inch his legs straightened and the table rose.

Malton paused for a moment at the height of the lift. He knew that in seconds his strength would desert him. With one last Herculean effort he twisted his body and wrenched the table off the shelves on which it was resting.

He leapt back as the table crashed to the ground in front of him.

Malton didn't have time to feel any sense of triumph. He was already vaulting over the table and into the safe room. Behind him he heard the heat-warped metal shelving crash onto the cutting table, blocking the way out completely.

16

Dean came to at the sound of smashing wood. He lay quite still for a moment as he flexed his extremities one at a time, checking they were all still there.

He could feel the heat coming from the open door. Outside the safe room was an impassable inferno. He began to choke as the smoke filled his lungs.

Still he heard the sound of smashing wood.

Deciding that enough of him was still there to at least investigate, Dean pulled himself to his feet in time to see Malton emerge from the en suite, clutching his hatchet.

'Where's Mitchum?' asked Malton.

Dean remembered Danny's screams. The explosion that could only have been the grenade around his neck.

'He's dead,' he sputtered back.

Malton didn't miss a beat. 'You found the hidden exit?'

Dean felt a little surge of pride. For everything he'd got wrong tonight at least he'd uncovered Malton's escape route. That was the smashing sound. Malton always had a plan B.

'If Danny's dead,' said Malton, 'then we're done here.'

Dean didn't know whether he meant done as in they'd finished the Danny Mitchum job or done as in he'd failed, he'd let Danny Mitchum die and now his time at Malton Security was at an end.

Either way he took one last look at the flames consuming the warehouse before following Malton out of the fire exit and away into the night.

17

In the soft morning light The Sentinel looked like the best luxury hotel you'd ever seen. Nestled in beautiful woodland on the edge of Ashton-in-Makerfield, west of Manchester, it was spread over three buildings, each one emerging from the trees as a blend of glass, steel and exposed wood.

The grounds had been carved out of the surrounding forest as sympathetically as possible. Curated gardens blended in with guided woodland walks and there was even a paddock with horses for the use of the guests.

Looking at The Sentinel the only things that gave away its true purpose were the twelve-foot, rigid metal fence that ran around its entire perimeter and the constantly manned gatehouse, which anyone hoping to visit The Sentinel had to pass through.

It had been a nightmare to get here. Keisha would have driven, but Diane Okunkwe didn't have a car. That meant Keisha couldn't risk being seen in one. And so she had taken a train and two buses. Nearly two hours door to door before Keisha would even begin to earn minimum wage.

No wonder Diane had taken the ten thousand pounds.

The final stretch had to be on foot. A long, country road broke from the main road and meandered deeper and deeper into the forest before suddenly the trees parted and the gatehouse appeared, the high metal fence spreading out from either side of it and disappearing into the woods. A barrier blocked the road, stopping traffic and visitors from proceeding.

Keisha took a deep breath, lowered her eyes and approached the gate house. It was an old building, a relic from the country estate that used to occupy the grounds of The Sentinel. Now its ornate stonework and sturdy buttresses were all that remained.

She was dressed like Diane. As well as the logoed tabard she'd bought from her, she'd been round the Harpurhey charity shops and was now dressed in the signature style of someone working seven days a week and still worrying about being able to feed her family.

Cheap Primark jeans and a sweater top underneath a bulky but insubstantial anorak. She wore unbranded trainers on her feet and had gone without either perfume or sunglasses.

After a lifetime of wearing sunglasses the daylight stung her eyes as she waved through the window of the gatehouse to the security guard inside.

The guard looked up from his phone. Keisha guessed he was local. He was young, probably in his twenties but already piling on the pounds. Every part of him swollen and red, from the sausage fingers that pawed his phone to the piggy face that stared up at her.

Keisha thought about how Craig would never have given a security job to a guy in that state.

She smiled nervously. The security guard struggled to his feet, walked to the window of the gatehouse and slid a panel aside. He had to stoop to be level with Keisha.

Keisha did her best to look small and meek as the security guard looked her up and down.

'You with the cleaning crew?' he asked. He was talking loudly and slowly as if he thought Keisha might be confused.

Keisha nodded and passed him Diane Okunkwe's badge, on which Keisha had replaced Diane's photo with her own.

The guard didn't even look at it.

'In future buzz yourself in. I'm working,' he said gruffly, then shut the window and went back to playing with his phone.

The barrier rose and Keisha continued on her way.

It took another five minutes to reach the main buildings of The Sentinel. From the sports cars and high-end SUVs in the carpark Keisha guessed that most of the guests hadn't walked.

The three buildings were in a U-shape around a garden, all connected to each other with glass corridors. The building nearest to her had large, glass double doors through which she could see a reception desk where a pretty, young woman was on the phone.

Keisha checked her watch. Leon Walker should be awake by now. The night before had been a breakthrough. He would never fully recover from the damage done to his system thanks to his drug use. But Keisha didn't need him to fully recover. She needed him well enough to do what needed doing. Already his natural strength was slowly flowing back into his huge frame. His body would look after itself. Keisha needed to make sure that his mind was hers.

He would be safe in the first of Keisha's two locked rooms. There was no need for him to be going anywhere. Not just yet.

Keisha walked up to the main entrance and held Diane's ID against a scanner to one side of the doors.

There was a brief pause and then the double doors slid open. A blast of warm air flowed out and around Keisha. It was a sunny May morning but inside The Sentinel the heating was going full blast.

She paused for just a second on the threshold. The reception was a large, double-height lobby with wide, airy corridors leading into the building. Almost all the ground-floor walls were glass and it gave an impression of enormous light and space.

She caught a glimpse of a few bodies wandering about further down the corridors. The guests.

In a way she was sad that Craig would never know just how much effort she was going to in order to utterly ruin him. Once upon a time she had been driven by a love that felt so intense it made everything else pale and dull by comparison. That love was still there somewhere deep inside Keisha's heart. If she didn't love Craig she would simply have killed him. But because, somewhere deep down, she loved him, Keisha was willing to go the distance to do something far worse.

Keisha put her head down, walked through the doors and they closed behind her. She marched at a pace, heading past the reception and into the building.

She'd just passed the desk when she heard, 'Excuse me?'

Keisha froze.

'Excuse me? Can I help you?'

Keisha turned and walked back to the reception where the pretty girl at the desk was smiling. But only with her mouth.

'Are you with the cleaning crew?' she asked.

Keisha nodded and the girl began typing something on her computer. Keisha's heart skipped a beat. She'd altered the photo on the ID but what if The Sentinel had Diane's photo on file?

'Name please,' said the girl. Now that she knew Keisha was a cleaner all trace of warmth had gone out of her voice.

Keisha had braided her hair down into cornrows. It wasn't exactly the same as Diane's hair but she hoped it would be near enough. Hair was the least of her worries. Diane was a black, Ghanaian woman with a thick Ghanaian accent. Keisha was a light-skinned Manc with an accent that placed her squarely in the Hulme/Moss Side postcode.

'Diane Okunkwe.'

'This is your first day?' said the girl, not looking up from the computer.

'Yes.'

The girl stopped typing and for a moment looked at her screen. She then turned and looked up at Keisha and then back at the screen. Her eyes narrowed, her face deep in thought.

She pressed a few more keys.

Keisha felt the heat of the room pressing in on her. Her clothes clung to her with the sweat of the long walk up to The Sentinel. But she held her ground.

'Down the first corridor, last door on the left. Please don't speak to the guests and if possible avoid looking directly at them,' said the girl without looking up.

Keisha and Diane were from totally different worlds. They looked as dissimilar as it was possible to look. But to a white person, especially one with a million other things to do that day, there was only one thing they looked like: a black cleaner.

Keisha was about to turn and go when the girl looked up.

'Wait!' she said, a touch of impatience in her voice. 'In future, don't come in the front way. Round the back.'

The girl went back to her computer.

Keisha nodded meekly and headed into the depths of The Sentinel Luxury Rehab Facility.

18

The morning air stank of smoke as Malton stood behind the police line watching the fire service withdraw from what was once a warehouse and was now a smouldering crime scene.

Danny was dead. That was a problem.

Malton's reputation rested on the knowledge that he always stayed true to his word. News would eventually get out that he hadn't been able to keep Danny safe. The only way to repair the damage would be to find his killers.

Luckily, while the list of people with a grudge against Danny Mitchum was endless, the list of people with the muscle, smarts and guts to carry it out was far shorter.

Among the firemen soaking down the last of the charred embers and the uniformed officers diverting traffic, a woman in a baggy jumper and a bright purple, hiking anorak stood shaking her head.

Malton patiently waited until she'd seen all that she needed to before she turned and wandered over to the police line where he stood waiting for her.

Malton had known DS Benton since he was a kid. Benton was the first police officer to ever arrest him. But despite getting off on the wrong foot they'd both kept an eye on each other over the years. Her, as Malton built up Malton Security and him, as Benton rose through the ranks of the Greater Manchester Police.

Malton didn't have time for most police. He knew enough about the inner workings of the law to know that it was a rigged game and that GMP had a history of playing fast and loose with the rules. But he also knew that Benton spent her whole career going against all of that. When she bent rules she did it to get the right people behind bars. And when she was asked to look the other way by those higher up, it only made her dig in harder.

'You know what,' said Benton as she approached, 'I think Danny Mitchum might just be dead.'

She was joking but her face didn't show it. She bent under the police tape and carried on walking away from the scene of devastation. Malton fell into step alongside her.

Benton reached into her coat pocket and pulled out a Greggs paper bag containing a muffin. She ate as she walked and talked, crumbs and blueberries scattering as she went.

'I'd heard you were protecting Danny Mitchum,' she said. 'Who from?'

A few months ago, a tip-off from Malton to Benton had prevented a bloodbath at Danny Mitchum's fortress-like home in Hale. Ever since then Benton had been feted as the detective who could unwind the labyrinthine threads of Manchester's underworld.

'I'm working on it,' said Malton.

It was taking all his focus not to think about Emily. He hoped for her sake she was a long way away from all of this.

Benton had finished the muffin and had moved on to scraping the paper wrapper with her teeth.

'Thing is, ever since I saved Danny's life he's kind of been my thing. Keep an eye on Mitchum. Work up the ladder. Roll them all up. You know, basic war on drugs stuff,' said Benton.

She'd reached her car. A black, police-issue Vauxhall Corsa.

'So what's your professional opinion?' asked Malton.

'Sure, he survived having brick cleaner poured on his face. And for a nasty little shit with no eyes he seemed pretty light on his feet. But call me a miserable realist' - she turned back to look at the blackened ruins of the building - 'he's not walking away from that.'

They both silently looked at what was left of the warehouse. He hoped the family who owned it had been keeping up their buildings insurance. Either way he'd be paying them a little extra for the inconvenience.

'We both know what happens now,' said Malton.

'Danny's the biggest dealer in town. He's gone. Someone's going to step up,' said Benton.

'Everyone's going to step up. It'll be carnage,' said Malton.

'You don't want that,' said Benton. 'The police don't want that. And I know for a fact all the "respectable businessmen" who've managed to claw their way off the streets and move in next door to some lad from Man City's first team don't want that. So that leaves the big question . . .'

'Who wanted him dead?' said Malton, finishing Benton's sentence.

Benton stuffed her muffin wrapper into one pocket and pulled out a can of Diet Coke from another. She cracked it open, leaned against her car and drank.

'Fuck me, I thought it was hard when Greater Manchester Police were determined to bury my career. Now they actually want me out there doing the job, I'm exhausted,' she said.

Benton was a solid woman. The sort of female police officer who men are happy to call on for backup. She was never one of the boys but she was happy to take licks alongside them and that had earned her a sort of grudging respect. A respect she had worn paper-thin over the years with her refusal to play the game.

Right now she looked well on the way to a nervous breakdown.

'You know I'll help if I can,' said Malton.

Benton laughed.

'Now you come to mention it, I do have one suspect,' she said.

Benton was suddenly deathly serious. Malton knew what was coming but kept his mouth shut and listened.

'If you were to ask me, who has a grudge against Craig Malton, is crazy enough to try and kill Danny Mitchum and clever enough to actually do it? Well that's a very short list. That's a list of one: Keisha Bistacchi.'

Malton stiffened. He'd been doing his best not to think about that possibility until he absolutely had to.

'When did you last see your ex?' asked Benton. 'I mean the criminally insane one. Not the posh one who does cakes.'

Malton loved how even in the darkest moments Benton would try and find something to laugh at. He knew full well that if Benton wasn't laughing, the horror of what she dealt with day to day would overwhelm her.

'Last I saw of Keisha, I left her chained up in my office with Dean watching her,' said Malton.

'Oh yeah,' said Benton, feigning recognition. 'The time she shot him in the face and legged it into the night. I can't tell you how to run your love life, but I can tell you that if I were you, I'd be wondering exactly what Keisha was up to right now.'

'You think this is Keisha?' said Malton, gesturing at the blackened warehouse.

'There's a lot of people out there waiting for the day that Craig Malton finally slips up. The day they can think about making a move on him without shitting themselves at the very thought of it. If I wanted to make you look just a little bit vulnerable, offing Danny Mitchum feels like a pretty solid play.'

Benton grinned. 'But that's just me thinking aloud. If you do find anything don't forget your good pal DS Benton.'

Benton drained the Diet Coke and put the empty can back in her pocket before turning and walking back to the blackened ruins where Danny Mitchum was last seen alive.

Malton suddenly felt impossibly tired. He hadn't slept but his mind was too occupied for anything as easy as sleep. The longer he stayed awake, the more distance he could put between himself and all the ghosts of his past who were forever on his heels.

Something about Danny's murder had dredged up one ghost he knew he'd never outrun. A man called James.

Along with everything else in his life, Malton's sexuality was split down the middle. He'd never imagined falling in love with a man but when he met James all that changed. Then thanks to what Malton was and the world he came from, James was taken from him, tortured for days and finally put down like a dog.

Malton had never forgotten James. Never stopped looking for the people who killed him and vowed never again to let his guard down. Loving Malton got James killed. After last night he needed to make sure that history wasn't repeating itself.

The possibility that Keisha was behind this both terrified and thrilled him. If it was her, that meant she was back in his life. But then that also meant that this was just the start.

There was only one thing he knew for certain. Whoever had killed Danny was still out there. If they could get to Danny they could get to anyone.

Not just Malton but anyone connected to him.

Someone like Emily.

Keisha was a suspect but there was someone far more obvious. Someone far closer to Danny Mitchum. Someone with not just the means but the motive.

Someone who was right under Malton's nose.

19

Fauzia could feel something small, hard and sharp beneath her feet. She bent down and ran her hand along the thick carpet that covered the floor of the strongroom in her parents' house.

Every few millimeters her fingers brushed up against something nestled in the carpet. Diamonds. She picked them up, one at a time and put them on top of the safe. Seven in all. Each worth around fifty thousand pounds.

She gave the safe door a quick tug. It was locked.

Fauzia looked around again, but as much as she searched, it appeared everything else was still there.

The watches and jewellery in the display cabinets. The Lowry painting that she knew for a fact was worth just shy of a million on its own. Even the diamonds. Nearly half a million worth of stones, which could have easily been stuffed in a pocket, had simply been ignored.

It didn't make sense.

After sending Waqar home Fauzia had stripped out of her bloodstained clothes and showered, shampooing her hair twice before she was satisfied she could no longer smell the blood. Having cleaned her nails and combed her hair for any stray traces of blood, she put Waqar's clothes in the bin liner along with her ruined suit before going to bed where she lay wide awake until dawn, unable to put the night's events out of her mind.

Her brother had killed a man. And she'd helped him do it. Now she was helping him cover it up.

In one stupid moment everything that she worked for was in danger. Not just her job and the election but her father's love. That was what scared her the most. Ever since she passed the eleven-plus her father had looked to her to see the culmination of everything he'd worked so hard to achieve. Thanks to Fauzia's relentless drive he'd never once been disappointed.

The fear of letting him down had led her to excel in everything she turned her hand to. Lying awake in bed she resolved that covering up a murder would be no different.

Nothing that happened last night had been her fault. Waqar had taken her by surprise. She only did what any loyal sister would do. Waqar's business was his own. What mattered now was how she handled the fallout.

Giving up on falling asleep she had risen just as it was getting light, made herself a pot of coffee and sat down to think.

Fauzia's flat was in a large, converted mill and spread over two floors. She had three bedrooms, a large open-plan living area and a brand-new kitchen, which she had yet to use. It was expensive for Bolton but for a junior doctor the rent was easily affordable. It was far enough from her parents in Daubhill to flex her independence but not so far away that she felt she'd turned her back on the place she'd known all her life.

While it was expected that they would both live with their parents until they married, Fauzia had been allowed to move out without question. Yet another proof that when it came to her and Waqar there was one rule for the golden girl and another for her big brother.

She sat at the breakfast bar in the kitchen. The cooker and hob were brushed steel and untouched. The large Smeg fridge contained a pint of milk and little else.

Whenever Fauzia had the time for a sit-down meal she'd head up the road to Daubhill and her mum's cooking.

She checked her phone. She counted fifteen missed calls. Most were supporters she'd brought along to hear her speak the night before. One immediately stood out: Labour Party HQ. They'd called about half an hour after the debate. Whatever they thought of last night, they wanted to let her know about it.

She'd barely given the meeting a second thought. There she was, on the verge of securing a nomination that would in turn lead to her becoming an MP, and all she could think about was the sound the meat grinder made when the man fell into it.

She'd finished her coffee, slung the bin liner of blood-stained clothes in the boot of her car, a slate-grey BMW 2 Series Coupe, and drove over to her parents' to examine the strongroom.

The front garden of her parents' house had been paved over and turned into a driveway. When Fauzia arrived there was only a single car still parked on it. Both her father and her brother's cars were gone.

Her father – Iffat – owned dozens of properties all over Bolton and spent his days in a flurry of activity managing them. He regularly rose early and set off to complete the never-ending list of jobs that being a landlord required of him.

But Waqar had only left Fauzia's flat a few hours ago. He'd told her he was coming home. Wherever he'd ended up, at least if he wasn't home it meant Fauzia could examine the strong-room in peace.

Letting herself in the front door, Fauzia heard her mother Samia cooking in the kitchen. Knowing that if she bumped into her she'd be trapped for at least an hour being updated on the lives of her aunties, uncles, cousins and neighbours, Fauzia crept past the kitchen where she could hear her mother listening to the early morning Quranic recitation on Asian Sound, and headed to the strongroom.

Maybe Waqar had no idea who Galahad was but that didn't mean Fauzia couldn't try to find out.

Standing in front of the formidable metal door she briskly tapped the numbers she knew by heart into the keypad. With a discreet click, the locking mechanism disengaged and Fauzia let herself in.

Once in the room she made straight for the safe. She kneeled and punched in the code and the light went green, and then the door opened. She couldn't believe what she saw inside.

Everything was still there. The piles of currency, the black velvet bags, each one containing a dozen diamonds. Nothing was missing.

She took out the nearest black velvet bag and tipped the contents onto her palm. Four diamonds, just like the ones she'd found on the floor, fell out. One was missing.

Fauzia combed the floor once more but found nothing.

Someone had got into the room. Someone had opened the safe. They had seen the cash and even opened a bag to discover the diamonds. And after all that the only things they had taken were a single diamond and the encrypted phone Waqar claimed he was storing there.

'How was your speech?'

Fauzia turned to see her father – Iffat – standing in the doorway to the strongroom, an eager look on his face.

He must have returned from fixing something at one of the rentals. Her dad had worked all his life. He was still working now. He was short and slim. Dressed in the plain, black trousers and shirt he always wore. He had earned millions over his life but still spent like he did back when he was starting out, when he and his wife were living in one room of a boarding house in Daubhill. They had the money now to move out of Daubhill and up the road to the mansions of Chorley New Road but Daubhill was where his heart lay.

Fauzia stood up and leaned back on the safe, discreetly shutting the door with her legs. 'It went well. I had to go before the end though. Needed at the hospital.'

Iffat looked sympathetic. He knew a thing or two about putting work first.

'You have to beat that idiot Tahir. I know it's him holding up my wedding hall.'

Now that Waqar had been entrusted with the meat processing plant, Iffat's next grand scheme was the construction of a giant, one-stop-shop wedding hall smack bang in the middle of Daubhill. He'd bought up a giant parcel of land that was sandwiched between terraced houses and abandoned mills and was in the process of constructing a huge venue. A banqueting hall, wedding boutique and beauty parlour all in the one place. A venue where families wanting to throw an extravagant wedding for hundreds if not thousands of guests, could spend vast sums on the big day without ever having to venture out of Daubhill.

It had been a building site for over a year now. After Iffat's retrospective planning permission had been blocked, the project had ground to a halt. Now he spent his time shuttling between the council and his solicitor, attempting to break the deadlock and resume work.

'I'll do my best,' said Fauzia honestly.

Iffat smiled indulgently. 'You will beat him and get my planning permission. I know you will. You are my proudest achievement.'

Fauzia puffed a little at her father's praise. With a lifetime to get used to it, she still thrilled a little when her father talked about her like that. The thought of that feeling ever going away terrified her.

'What are you doing in here?' asked Iffat curiously.

'I just wanted to look at my wedding jewellery,' said Fauzia, the lie instantly springing to her lips.

She indicated to a couple of the cabinets where on display was a collection of ornate gold jewellery.

Iffat gazed happily at his daughter.

'Don't you be getting married just yet. You've got work to do!'

It was one of the oddities of life at the Maliks'. While Fauzia's friends lived with brothers who could do no wrong and parents who wondered out loud daily when their daughters were going to get married, Fauzia found herself an honorary boy.

After Iffat turned his back on Waqar it was like he had decided that he didn't have a useless son and a brilliant daughter, he had two sons. One of whom just so happened to be a girl.

Fauzia often wondered what her life would have been like if Waqar had passed his entrance exam.

'Your brother didn't come home last night. Again. I give him an easy job, running the factory. And what does he do? There's nothing that boy can't mess up.'

Fauzia felt awful hearing her father talk about Waqar like this. She thought about what her father would say if she told him how wrong he was. His son had found his niche. He was the biggest drug dealer in Bolton.

But he was right about one thing: Waqar had messed up. Badly. Now that Fauzia was folded into the chaos she needed answers before things could escalate any further.

'At least I have you.' Iffat beamed. 'My daughter the MP! Your mother is cooking. I want you to come and tell us everything that happened last night.'

Everything that happened last night flashed through Fauzia's mind. In that moment whatever doubts she might have had vanished. She had come too far and worked too hard to let one night ruin everything.

'I'll be there in a second,' she said.

Iffat smiled at her and left.

Fauzia waited until he was gone before leaning forward against the safe and doing her best not to throw up. She sucked in the dry, solvent air of the strongroom and retched in the absolute silence afforded by its reinforced walls.

When she regained her composure she stood up and took a final look around.

If someone had broken in and taken the phone like Waqar said there was only one way they could have done it.

They had the key codes.

20

The Sentinel rehab facility was committed to providing a warm and caring environment in which, with the very best therapy, medication and counselling, its guests could confront, process and overcome their addictions.

Keisha had looked at their website before she came and so she knew that the room she was currently cleaning belonged to a guest who had paid at least forty thousand pounds a month for the privilege.

There was a large double bed, which Keisha had changed, a relaxation area with sofas and a fireplace, which Keisha had hoovered, and a large, en-suite bathroom, which had taken Keisha the best part of half an hour to put back to something resembling what it must have looked like before its current occupant had last used it.

Having set the room back the way it was, she had changed all the scented candles in their ceramic holders before lighting them and filling the room with the healing smell of sandalwood.

The aroma from the candles was a world away from the stench of Leon Walker's room and the soiled mattress on which he found himself performing his own, far less glamorous detox.

Keisha looked around and smiled. Everything was going according to plan.

Just as she expected, the moment she put on the cleaner's tabard and began pushing her trolley stacked with dusters and cleaning products around the facility she was as good as invisible.

All round her the pampered addicts of The Sentinel went about the very expensive business of getting better.

Outside in the gardens there was a yoga session in progress as several unusually plump, rosy-cheeked addicts downward-dogged their way to wellness.

It was coming up to lunch and the smell of organic, vegan, home-cooked food was filling the building.

It had only been one morning but Keisha felt like she'd successfully enmeshed herself exactly where she needed to be.

Alone in the now clean room old habits took hold.

Checking the coast was clear she slid open the drawer beside the bed.

It was filled with dog-eared brochures and check-in paperwork, an eye mask and ear plugs and underneath all the clutter – a passport.

Lynne Harris, a beautiful brunette in her early fifties looked up at Keisha from the pages of her passport. She had managed to sneak a very sultry pout past the passport office. As well as the passport there was work correspondence for Lynne. All the parts of her life that even rehab couldn't put on hold.

Keisha had just replaced what she'd found and shut the drawer when from behind her she heard a voice demanding, 'What are you doing in here?'

Spinning round she found herself face to face with the real-life pout of Lynne Harris. She was even more radiant in the flesh. Her long brown hair glossy and immaculate.

Keisha had read that there was a salon in The Sentinel. It looked like Lynne was making full use of the facilities.

'Bad enough you did such a piss-poor job yesterday and left this place an absolute tip, but today I come back and find you trying to steal from me!' cried Lynne walking past Keisha, pulling open her drawer and eyeing the contents suspiciously.

'It's my first day,' said Keisha honestly.

Lynne was quiet. Keisha could tell she was looking her up and down. Trying to work her out. From the scruffy trainers to the make-up-free face, everything about Keisha told the world she was nothing. She was no one behind her tabard. A faceless presence who arrived, cleaned and left. She was not worth a woman like Lynne Harris getting upset about.

'What's your name?' asked Lynne.

'Diane,' said Keisha, not looking up.

'Well, Diane, I'm pretty sure this isn't your first day and lucky for you I'm late for my massage. But if I find you snooping around again one word from me and you'll be out of here and back to wherever you came from. Do you understand?'

Keisha understood perfectly. She came from Hulme and everything she'd ever done her whole life was to make sure that no one could ever talk to her like Lynne was talking to her now.

But all she said was: 'Yes, ma'am.'

Lynne gave a last glower, grabbed a towel and left.

Keisha continued to clean the room for a few more minutes until she was sure Lynne had gone before she went back to the drawer, pulled out several letters and Lynne's passport and took photographs of all the relevant parts before replacing them exactly as she'd found them.

If Lynne Harris was locked up in The Sentinel, then in the outside world there was a vacancy. After the way Lynne had spoken to her, Keisha resolved to have some fun filling it.

Keisha packed away her trolley and left the room.

As she headed down the corridor and on to the next job she paused for a moment by another patient's room.

Looking through the small window in the door she saw a room very different to Lynne Harris's. This room looked more like a hospital, albeit a very expensive, very exclusive hospital.

A bed was surrounded with monitors and drips all attached to the woman who lay in it, heavily sedated as she went through her medically supported detox.

Her eyes were closed and the curtains drawn but Keisha recognised her immediately.

Her name was Emily, the woman who'd walked out on Craig Malton and the reason Keisha had smuggled herself into The Sentinel.

21

Dean knew he was in trouble. He just didn't know yet quite how much trouble.

As he drove the metallic yellow Crossland, which he'd bought with his first paycheque, from the flat he shared with his mum in Burnage across town to Malton Security, he practised in his head how best to recount the events of the previous night to Malton.

Danny Mitchum was dead. Murdered. And only hours before his murder Dean had been personally entrusted with his security. Whichever way Dean turned it over in his head, things didn't look good.

Ordinarily Dean enjoyed the drive to work. He loved his car. It wasn't quite Malton's Volvo with its vintage styling but the Crossland was technically an SUV, even if it did look more like he should be dropping the kids off to football training than driving cross-country. What's more, being a sour, yellow colour it had come in at nearly a grand cheaper than an identical model in the more popular blue or red. The dealer had almost seemed relieved to find someone actually willing to drive it out of the showroom.

On a normal day he'd arrive early, check the local news and most importantly help himself to the free breakfast that Malton Security put on for its staff coming off nights or just getting started for the day.

But today, driving to work, he felt like a condemned man.

Dean arrived before Malton and sat in the cramped canteen surrounded by doormen and security guards, listening to their conversations as they feasted on greasy bacon and eggs washed down with strong, dark tea loaded with sugar.

Malton Security employed over sixty staff. A handful of women for when a client needed female door staff and the rest of them the kind of bull-necked, barrel-chested men whose very presence was a deterrent. Usually Dean enjoyed sharing breakfast with them. Hearing their war stories from the night before and doing his best to learn every last scrap of gossip coming from the streets.

Working with Malton he'd learned that knowledge was always more powerful than muscle. Unlike Malton, knowledge was all he had.

But as he sat listening to the stories of drunken brawls, illicit encounters and long, uninterrupted spells of boredom, Dean felt a terrible sadness creeping over him.

He'd miss this.

In his first few weeks Dean had been first ignored and then teased. It hadn't helped that early on he'd made an enemy of Alfie, the office manager. Alfie was a morbidly obese bully whose role at Malton Security was a constant source of mystery to Dean. The most office managing Alfie ever did was refilling the coffee pot and occasionally pushing a hoover around. The rest of the time he sat playing on his phone or eating.

Alfie was put in charge of Dean and extracted every last ounce of misery his tiny shred of power afforded.

But as soon as Malton shone his light on Dean all that was over. Dean went from the firm's whipping boy to a kind of company mascot. He might not have been able to work a door but Malton saw something in him and from that day on Dean was untouchable.

Even Alfie grudgingly laid off him.

Now that Danny Mitchum was dead all that was for nothing.

Malton appeared just as breakfast was winding up.

The last few stragglers swallowed down their food, nodded an acknowledgement to their boss and headed out to work or back home to sleep through the day ready for the night shifts.

Without saying a word, Malton scooped what was left of breakfast together into a large, white barm cake and poured out the last of the stewed tea into a couple of mugs for him and Dean before heading to his office.

Dean took the open office door as his silent cue to follow. Which he did, his heart heavy and his mind racing.

He perched on a battered sofa, sipping his tea in silence while Malton ate at his large, leather-topped desk.

Dean was fairly sure Malton was still wearing the same clothes he'd been in the night before. Heavy jeans, thick knitwear and the waxed jacket he was never without. The strong smell of smoke that filled the office confirmed his suspicions. Malton hadn't been home.

Besides the desk and the sofa the only other piece of furniture in Malton's office was the weights bench on the far side of the room. Hundreds of kilograms of plates were neatly stacked up. Having seen Malton lift, Dean could confirm they weren't just for show.

Across the wall of the office, half a dozen Ordnance Survey maps of Greater Manchester had been joined together giving a vast picture of the great conurbation. Hundreds of unmarked pins dotted the maps. Dean knew that each one represented a job Malton had done for someone.

Since he'd been working at Malton Security, Dean recognised a couple of the pins as jobs he'd been involved with. The rest were an unspoken mystery.

Malton didn't keep records. It was all in his head. Every one of those pins held its own dark secrets. Secrets that Dean longed to know but knew better than to ask about.

He watched Malton finish off his breakfast and then for a moment they sat in silence, Malton not offering to start the conversation and Dean unsure just how much trouble he was in.

Finally Malton spoke. 'Tell me everything you saw last night.'

Dean did his best, racking his brains. He told Malton about the trip out. How Danny had managed to smuggle both a grenade and a gun into the locked room. The former his insurance against torture, the latter used to shoot his way out of the locked room.

Dean described Danny's behaviour. How it was as if he wanted people to see him. His sickening assault and the numerous witnesses.

As he recounted the events of the night before, Malton peppered Dean with questions. *Did he show you the grenade? How was it attached to his neck? How do you know it was live?*

Knowing better than to try and lie to Malton, Dean gave as honest an account as he could. But as he did so he realised that despite living through the events of last night he had very little in the way of actual information.

Ending his story with Malton's appearance in the hidden room, Dean fell silent. He desperately wanted to look down in shame but forced himself to hold Malton's gaze. Letting him know that whatever was coming next, he would meet it head on.

'In summary,' said Malton, 'you heard gunfire. You didn't see anyone. Danny Mitchum had a gun and he used it to break out of the room. You gave chase, heard an explosion, the force of which threw you back into the safe room and then you blacked out?'

When put like that, Dean felt like an abject failure. With nothing left to lose he took a sip of his tea and went on the attack. 'I was thinking about who it might have been,' he said.

Malton held his gaze, silently bidding him to continue with this line of thought.

'He spoke about the Scouse Mafia? Cartels? I don't know much about that sort of thing but it seems to me if that was the case why haven't they gone after his operation? If they couldn't find him they could have put the screws on his people, forced him out into the open. From everything we've seen his setup is a shambles. Without him running things they're sitting ducks.'

'And no one made a move,' said Malton.

Encouraged, Dean went on. 'We know Danny was in hiding. And from everything I've heard these past three months, thanks to all the rumours you put out, nobody for one moment suspected the truth. If anything people were more scared of the Danny they couldn't see.'

Malton gave a little smile. Dean's heart leapt and he continued before his boss had a chance to stop him.

'So how did they find him? No one would have the first clue where he was,' said Dean, thinking out loud.

Dean wasn't under any illusions. He was far from home free. Danny's death didn't just affect him. Danny had been under Malton's protection. That meant whoever killed him hadn't just destabilised Danny's crew, they had put a target on Malton too.

It had already occurred to him the night before. What if the target wasn't Danny at all? What if the whole point of killing him had been to bring down Malton?

Every pin in the map on Malton's wall was a job. Every job was another brick in the legend of Craig Malton. He was just one man but his reach was immense. That wasn't due to muscle or knowledge alone. It was due to the fact that everyone knew that when you hired Malton the job got done. He found your missing drugs. He tracked down the rat who grassed you up. He brought your daughter home and broke her pimp's legs for good measure.

Malton had spent his entire adult life among some of the most violent people in Manchester. That he was in neither Strangeways nor Southern Cemetery was testament not to his physical strength but the strength of his reputation.

Danny's death threatened to sweep away all of that. Tear every pin out of the map and leave Malton dangerously exposed.

Dean could only think of one person who hated Malton that much. The person responsible for the livid, throbbing scar on Dean's cheek. Malton's ex – Keisha Bistacchi.

But as much as he wanted to say her name out loud he held back. He knew just how tangled and intense Malton's relationship with Keisha was. He didn't want to even speak her name out loud before he was sure of his suspicions.

Malton broke the silence. 'You're sure *no one* knew where he was?'

Instantly Dean knew exactly who Malton meant. The only other obvious suspect. Relieved to have a lead that wasn't Keisha, Dean dived in.

'There was only one person apart from us and Danny who knew what was really going on. The only person who knew he was in hiding. The person who had to be told, because he'd left him behind to run things day to day,' said Dean, leaning forward eagerly.

'The man who last time I saw him was making a pig's ear of doing it,' reflected Malton.

Malton swallowed his cup of tea and set the mug down on a pile of invoices.

'His dad – Stevie,' said Dean.

22

After leaving her parents' house, Fauzia met Waqar at his office above one of his kebab shops. Since taking over the meat processing plant, he'd bought a dozen such shops all over Bolton. A whole chain – Solitaire Kebab. He had borrowed the money from Iffat who was relieved to see his son finally taking some initiative and expanding the business. It made complete sense. The factory supplied the meat, the kebab shops sold the meat.

Fauzia hadn't told Waqar at the time but she was proud of him. He had finally started knuckling down and making the best of where he'd ended up. Whatever pride she'd previously felt had been replaced with dread anticipation at what new revelations were still to come about her brother and his illegal activities.

Labour HQ hadn't rung back yet. Fauzia couldn't decide if that was a good thing or not. Was informing her of her failure to beat Tahir simply a low priority now they had their new candidate? Or was the machinery already in motion? Had she been anointed the heir apparent to Farnworth and Great Lever?

Either way it would have to wait. There would always be another hustings, another empty seat, another election. None of that would matter if she couldn't put last night's business behind her for good.

She was back on shift at the hospital shortly, where she planned to toss the bin liner of bloody clothes she was keeping in the boot of her car into a clinical waste bag and send it off to the hospital incinerator. That still left Waqar's missing encrypted phone to track down.

It was this that brought her to Waqar's office. After finding out he hadn't returned home the night before she guessed this must be where he would be. She found him in the room above the kebab shop, sitting in a tatty armchair between two tottering stacks of pizza boxes. The room looked more like a clubhouse than an office. Several chairs, a table with the remains of a spliff spread out over it and a large TV balanced on an old fridge. Tucked away in the corner were a small chipped desk and a laptop. Fauzia got the impression that whatever it was Waqar did here, it wasn't working.

'I already told you,' he said angrily, 'I didn't give anyone the passcodes. Not to the safe or the strongroom.'

Waqar was sulking. His balled fists stuffed between his legs, his head bowed. This was the Waqar Fauzia knew. Not the drug dealer. Not the killer.

'Then it doesn't make sense. No one even knows the strongroom is there. And even if they did, they couldn't get in without blowing the door off. And if they blew the door off they'd have to do the same with the safe.'

Waqar looked at his feet and shrugged like a naughty school-boy. A lifetime of dealing with her older brother's moods told Fauzia that he was holding something back.

'They didn't take anything else. It's all still there. Well we're down a diamond,' she said looking at Waqar accusingly.

'I didn't take nothing,' he argued. 'Are you thick, sis? I told you – they knew what they were after.'

'How would they even know it was there? Are you sure you didn't show anyone the room? A friend? A girlfriend? Anyone?'

Waqar went silent again.

Fauzia changed tack. 'There's only one explanation I can see. If, as you say, you didn't give anyone the code, then whoever took the phone already knew it. So that's me, Dad and you.'

Waqar looked up, his face indignant. 'What you saying?'

'I know it wasn't Dad. You've seen his phone. An old Nokia. He wouldn't even know what a smartphone was, never mind try and steal one.'

They both knew what was coming next.

'That leaves you and me,' said Fauzia.

'So you think it was me?'

'I know you turned up with a body. I know you tricked me into helping you dispose of it. I know the explanation you gave. And I know that explanation is sounding more and more like bullshit. But more than any of that, until last night *I* had no idea the phone even existed. So either you've somehow lost this phone or there never even was a phone in the first place.'

'You think I'm lying?' said Waqar angrily.

'I think it doesn't make sense that someone could have taken it. Unless you have a name in mind?'

Waqar's eyes darted away. He looked like he was mulling something over in his mind. He opened his mouth to speak at the exact moment of the explosion.

The windows above the kebab shop blew inwards with the force of the blast, showering Fauzia with shards of razor-sharp glass.

At the same time as she instinctively crouched into a ball, Waqar sprung to his feet. No sooner had the glass blown in than he was running across the small room, knocking over boxes to get to the window.

He had a gun in his hand.

Fauzia glanced up but she didn't see her brother. She saw a ruthless gangster, armed and ready to kill.

On the pavement outside flames were consuming Waqar's Audi. Whatever the explosion was it had come from within the car. A broken window and an explosive device tossed inside. The exterior of the car was still mostly intact but the windows were all gone and now thick flames billowed out of the empty holes, sending black smoke into the sky.

Fauzia was there beside him in time to see the scruffy blue VW Golf, DIY tinting peeling off the windows, its rear bumper held together with masking tape. She saw the man whose face was covered with a mask and hood getting into the back of the car and she saw him drive away, nearly running over a couple of onlookers who'd been drawn by the sound of the blast.

She also saw the phones. The modern response to public tragedy – pull out a phone and start filming. If Labour HQ *had* been impressed by last night's speech, this was the last thing she needed.

She grabbed Waqar, pulling him away from the window.

Waqar turned to his sister. He looked suddenly alive. Like he'd been expecting this and now it had happened things could truly begin.

'Still think I invented a stolen phone?' he said.

Fauzia looked from the burning car to her brother, the gun in his hand. She could feel the heat rising up from the flames.

Suddenly everything became sickeningly real. This wasn't just another of her brother's screw-ups.

If the phone was real and Waqar *hadn't* taken it, that meant whoever did was still out there and this was just the beginning.

Fauzia had already unwittingly helped her brother to kill a man and cover up his crime. If she was going to get out of this alive she would have to go even further.

23

Stevie Mitchum threw the quad bike into a doughnut and clung on for dear life as the machine tore a perfect circle out of the lawn at the back of Danny Mitchum's giant, modernist mansion.

From the look of the vast back garden this had been going on for some time. A couple more quad bikes and half a dozen scramblers lay scattered around what was left of the lawn.

Dressed in shorts, a T-shirt and flip-flops, Stevie was clearly enjoying his time as man of the house.

What a house it was. Where there had previously been a large, Victorian country villa now stood a fortress-sized cube of a building. Covered in white render and glass, its modernity jarred with the leafy, suburban surroundings of Hale. The entire house was ringed by a high wall, discreetly topped with razor-sharp spikes.

The only way in was through a giant sliding gate to the front of the house. To Malton's surprise, when he and Dean arrived, the gate was open. They simply wandered in.

Malton and Dean stood patiently on the veranda watching as half a dozen of Stevie's hangers-on cheered and whooped while ear-splitting music came from the open windows of a ground-floor room.

Malton had to wonder what Stevie's neighbours made of this. This part of Hale was rich enough for each house to boast not just dozens of rooms and outbuildings but also vast grounds. Even so, Stevie's antics couldn't have escaped the attention of the company directors and premiership footballers who had the misfortune of living nearby.

As they watched, a young woman emerged from inside the house, brushed past them and stood on the lawn waving to Stevie.

She was hard to miss. Lithe and tanned in shorts and a sloppy tracksuit top. She was barefoot with long back seams tattooed up the backs of both legs, ending in an ornate bow just below her buttocks.

It wasn't just her legs. From what Malton could see there were tattoos all over both hands as well as running up her neck and behind her ear.

She waved a dainty hand, manicured with long, Tippex-white nails, at the doughnutting quad bike.

Stevie pulled out of the spin and hurtled towards the house at a speed that made Dean take a step back and the woman dive for cover behind a large, gas-fired grill built into the veranda.

Malton stood stock-still as Stevie drove towards them. At the last minute the quad bike pulled itself around ninety degrees and came to a halt, scattering turf up the side of the house and narrowly missing Malton.

As Stevie killed the engine, the woman emerged from behind the grill and ran to him.

Stevie stepped off the bike and ignoring Malton grabbed her and lifted her up. She wrapped her tattooed legs around Stevie's thick waist and they kissed messily.

With his companion still hanging off him Stevie turned around to face Malton and finally made a show of noticing he was there.

'Let yourself in, did you?' he said.

Malton studied Stevie's face. Searching for the tell. Did he really not know his son was dead? It had been nearly twelve hours since the fire. Was Stevie really this out of touch?

It was time to find out.

Stevie shook off the woman and stepped up onto the veranda.

'Can't hide behind your lawyer girlfriend now,' said Stevie, picking up where they had left off the night before.

'I'm not here about that,' said Malton. Maybe Stevie really didn't know. If that was the case then Malton was about to tell him the worst news any parent can get.

'I'm here about Danny,' he said.

'What about him?' barked Stevie. He sounded brash but Malton detected something else there. He couldn't tell if it was fear or guilt or something else entirely.

'He's dead.'

Stevie's tiny eyes screwed up in confusion. 'No he's not. You're watching him. We're paying you fifty grand a week. He's not dead.'

If Stevie was acting then he deserved an Oscar.

'Someone raided the safe house where we were keeping him. Turns out Danny had a grenade with him. It went off and killed him.'

'Bollocks it did,' said Stevie disbelievingly, before he turned and walked into the house.

The woman looked at Malton for a second, confusion on her face. Then she hurried inside after Stevie. Malton and Dean followed them both. The gaggle of men who'd been watching Stevie tear up the lawn lurked at the edge of the veranda. If Danny was dead then who was calling the shots?

Malton found Stevie sat on a giant sofa facing an equally huge TV screen, embedded into one white wall of the enormous lounge. The TV was on, blasting out while Stevie belligerently flicked through the channels.

The woman was curled up next to him like an affection-ate cat. Stevie's meaty hand had already disappeared into her tracksuit top where it was roughly fondling her breasts.

In the kitchen next door the men from the lawn had started drifting in. Malton could see them doing their best not to look like they were eavesdropping.

'This is Miyah Mai,' said Stevie not looking up.

'Hi,' she said.

Looking at her for the first time Malton guessed she was closer to Danny's age. A slim, toned twenty-something whose

118

tattoos, tan and nails spoke of someone who'd never existed outside the male gaze.

Stevie settled on a music channel. Loud dance music filled the room.

'So who did it? Those Scouse pricks?' demanded Stevie, shouting above the television, his eyes firmly focused on the screen.

Malton thought he detected a waver in Stevie's voice.

'I don't know yet, but seeing as the only people who even knew Danny was in hiding are in this room right now, I thought I should probably start here.'

Malton had to raise his voice to be heard. In the kitchen Stevie's men edged closer to try and catch the conversation.

There was a long pause until finally Stevie turned off the television, stood up and turned to face Malton. He looked crushed. 'You think you're fucking clever don't you?' said Stevie.

Everyone's clever compared to you, thought Malton but kept it to himself.

'Thing is everyone's seen you now, caught with your dick in your hand,' Stevie said, his voice breaking with emotion.

Malton lowered his voice. 'Right now I need to find out who killed Danny. Only three people even knew he was in hiding. Me, Dean here, and you.'

Malton motioned to Dean whose face gave nothing away.

The men in the kitchen were stock-still. Hanging on every word.

'Fuck you saying?' bristled Stevie.

Malton couldn't be sure but it looked like Stevie was trying to remember how to cry. Every argument Malton had ever made to himself about why he shouldn't bring children into the world played out on Stevie's face. Emily might have changed his mind but watching Stevie's reaction to the news of his son's death Malton suddenly felt an intense sense of relief to know he would never be vulnerable in the way Stevie Mitchum suddenly found himself.

But there was no time to pander to Stevie's emotions. Malton needed to be sure of the facts.

'I'm fairly certain I didn't kill him, and Dean here promises me he didn't either. So that just leaves you,' said Malton.

Stevie's face screwed up. With one giant hand he tore off his T-shirt and squared up to Malton, his giant, bare chest an immovable wall of muscle.

'I'm not scared of you, Malton. I know dickheads like you. Let's go. Right here. You and me.'

Malton didn't react. 'So you're saying it wasn't you?'

'Course it fucking wasn't. Why would I kill my own boy?' Stevie's voice was cracking.

A single tear squeezed out of Stevie's left eye. He turned away. A huge fist rising up to wipe it.

'Jealousy? To take over his organisation? To just steal his stuff and fuck off? Rage? Shame? I don't know,' said Malton out loud not expecting an answer.

Stevie stood his ground. Malton could tell it was taking all his resolve not to fly at him. A small, cruel smile came over Stevie's face.

'What about your psycho ex? Keisha Bistacchi?' he said, looking Malton straight in the eye.

As much as Malton already suspected Keisha could be behind Danny's killing, that didn't make it any easier to hear her name in Stevie's mouth.

Stevie sensed he'd hit a nerve and continued. More at home on the attack than in his grief.

'She tried to kill Danny before. And I heard it was Keisha shot your boy in the face.' Stevie turned to Dean. 'Fucking look at him.'

'Workplace accident,' Dean deadpanned. Malton couldn't be prouder.

'I'm not ruling anyone out,' said Malton, purposefully staring down Stevie.

'I told you, I didn't do it.'

Malton held Stevie's gaze. Daring him to look away. Just as Stevie's eyes began to water Malton shrugged and looked away. He had his answer.

Whatever else Stevie Mitchum was, he wasn't the sort of man who'd murder his own son.

'I know you didn't do it. Not after what I've seen today.'

Stevie's eyebrows knitted. Malton saw Dean suppress a look of surprise.

'What you've seen today?' said Stevie.

Malton nodded. 'First of all, I think you loved your son. But second of all, he's dead and I find you here doing doughnuts in your back garden.'

'I didn't fucking know,' spat Stevie.

'Exactly,' said Malton. 'Because if you did know he was dead then you'd know that the minute news got out, every single lunatic, psychopath, hardman, plastic gangster and street dealer would know that your whole operation is up for grabs. I've spent the last three months going through Danny's business and the one thing I've learned? Without Danny it's nothing. He's the brains. He's the reason no one dares take a shot. But now he's gone. And if you knew that then right now you'd be getting ready for war.'

In the kitchen a few of the hangers-on started to shuffle nervously. Being part of the Mitchum crew was suddenly starting to look like a much less exciting prospect.

'I'm not fucking scared,' said Stevie. He sounded scared.

Malton almost felt sorry for him.

'Danny's death happened on my watch. It's up to me to sort it. And I will.'

'Good,' said Stevie, unsure what else he could say. 'You better. Start with those Scouse fucks who were threatening him.'

'That's a good idea,' said Malton. 'Danny said it was the Scouse Mafia after him.'

'And you did fuck all,' croaked Stevie.

Malton was letting Stevie save face. Depending on how this all turned out he might be needing him further down the line.

'So what you going to do about it now?' said Stevie. He puffed his swollen chest out and did his best to look like he was the one in control.

Malton had been thinking through this exact question all morning. Finally he'd come to the inevitable conclusion that there really was only one place to start.

One man who could tell him for sure whether or not the Scouse Mafia had killed Danny Mitchum.

Unfortunately for Malton that man was spending the rest of his life in the category-A wing of a supermax prison.

24

Dean was dropped back at HQ by Malton with instructions to check in with everyone on staff. Find out if there had been anything unusual to report the night Danny died.

For months now Malton had been giving Dean an increasing amount of responsibility at Malton Security. It was clear he'd never be up to door work but that didn't matter. Malton already had several dozen meatheads on the payroll. Hired muscle that would flex and extend on command. Dean had something none of them had – Dean thought like Malton.

Since starting at Malton Security, Dean had studied his boss. What made him tick. The details that piqued his attention and the red herrings he ignored.

Dean would never be Malton's physical equal but he hoped that one day, just like his boss, he'd be able to think his way through the darkest reaches of Manchester's shadows.

Dean set himself up in Malton's office and spent a couple of hours going through everyone on staff one by one. There were fights, break-ins and police reports. Just a usual night shift for Malton Security. Nothing out of the ordinary.

With nothing to show for an afternoon's work Dean decided to take matters into his own hands. Rising from Malton's desk he headed out to see first-hand the aftermath of the night before.

It was getting on and Manchester was beginning to cool under the late May sun. A chill ran through the railway arches and Victorian infrastructure that made up Cheetham Hill. It had once been home to a large Jewish community but thanks to their success they had mostly long since moved out to

Prestwich and Cheadle, leaving Cheetham Hill to the next generation of migrants.

The family who owned the warehouse were one of the few Jewish businesses still trading. Operating a few hundred metres from one of the oldest synagogues in Manchester, a beautiful building now restored as a museum, documenting the community's rich history.

Dean walked past the lock-ups and industrial units. In amongst the newer buildings he glimpsed the occasional terraced house – an incongruous vestige of the slums that used to cover the area.

He reached the remains of the warehouse to find that the police line had shrunk to a few feet from the building and a squad car was parked up outside, its driver nowhere to be seen.

Dean hung back on the other side of the street. There were never many people about in this part of Cheetham Hill, even fewer this time of day. Streetwalkers and drug addicts made up most of the pedestrian traffic.

Wherever the police officer to whom the car belonged was, they didn't look like they were coming back.

Dean took one last look and skipped out into the light, across the road, past the empty police car, under the police cordon and back into the gloom of the ruined building.

Wet ash and torn fabric squelched under foot as Dean picked his way through the black, tangled wreckage. Shelving units had buckled in the heat, toppling in on themselves and creating a macabre thicket of twisted, scorched metal.

Using his mobile phone as a torch he picked out the bright yellow plastic markers laid down by the forensics teams. Places where he assumed they must have found bullet casings.

Finally he found what he was looking for. The spot where Danny Mitchum died.

A black circle marked out the radius of the explosion from the grenade around his neck. Debris was scattered in a perfect blast pattern. The force of the explosion had bent the heavy, metal shelves around it. Dozens of police markers were spread all over, mapping out all the tiny pieces that once made up Danny Mitchum.

Dean's hand went to his mouth. A small sob caught in his throat. Danny had bullied, threatened and terrorised Dean the whole time he'd known him. But now he was dead Dean found himself overwhelmed by a feeling he didn't expect. He'd miss Danny.

Dean took a breath and stepped back. He was glad his boss wasn't there to see him. As much as he could think like Malton the one thing he still couldn't do was feel like Malton. Or rather not feel anything at all. Under all the broken bones and bullet wounds and threats and promises were living, breathing people. Dean felt for them all.

He said a little prayer to no one in particular and feeling a bit better turned and made his way out of the warehouse.

On the walk back to Malton Security he turned over all the unanswered questions in his head. *Could* the Scouse Mafia have pulled this off? And if they did who told them where Danny was hiding? Did Danny pull the pin on the grenade? In all the time Dean had been minding Danny he'd come to appreciate that beneath the manic façade was a mind every bit as cool and calculating as Malton's. If Danny was confident enough to rush whoever was attacking, why would he pull the pin seconds later?

And then of course there was Keisha. Dean had seen how Malton had tensed when Stevie Mitchum mentioned her name. If even Stevie could make the connection then surely Malton was looking into it?

But what if he wasn't? What if Keisha was his blind spot? What if their shared history meant that despite everything pointing directly towards Keisha, Malton couldn't or wouldn't make a move? Should Dean be the one to follow up the lead?

The more he thought on it the more seemed off about the whole thing.

Dean was so deep in thought that he didn't even notice the woman who was standing outside Malton Security, nervously looking around as if uncertain she was in the right place.

He was about to go inside when she called out and he finally noticed her.

'My name's Fauzia Malik,' she said. 'I need to speak to Craig Malton.'

25

Keisha watched as Leon Walker shovelled the instant noodles into his mouth. Stock dripped down his chin and soaked into his beard as he gave up on his fork and drank the remaining noodles and soup straight from the bowl.

No sooner had he finished than he turned to the pile of instant noodles beside him and tore open another packet.

Keisha watched as he filled up the kettle she'd given him with bottled water and set it boiling while he decanted the various sachets of freeze-dried vegetables and greasy sauce into the bowl.

'Feeling better?'

Leon glared up at her. There was a purpose in his eyes she'd not seen before.

He was still far from the being the man who for a brief summer terrorised the Manchester underworld, but the broken junkie she'd taken in off the streets was finally taking his leave.

He stared up into Keisha's dark glasses. She held his gaze until he faltered, noting with satisfaction his eyes lingering for a moment on her cleavage before falling back to the filthy mattress on which he was sitting.

Keisha was going out tonight and she was dressed to impress. She was squeezed into a daring, black leather midi dress with a heavy, metal buckled belt across the middle that cinched in her waist, showing off her hips and bust. With deep reluctance she swapped her trainers for a pair of knee-length scarlet leather boots with just a touch of a heel.

She looked a world away from Diane Okunkwe who'd spent the day cleaning up after wealthy drug addicts at The Sentinel.

It was tough, boring work but now she'd confirmed Emily was at The Sentinel things could finally start moving.

As soon as Leon was ready it would be time to get the party started.

Keisha finished her outfit off with a Bottega Veneta handbag. Heavy black leather sewn into a quilted pattern and a thick, gold chain. The bag had cost a couple of thousand pounds from Selfridges in town. The gun she was hiding in the bag cost a few hundred pounds and to Keisha's knowledge had been used to shoot a man dead in Nottingham before being trafficked up north.

Whatever else Leon Walker was he was still a very, very dangerous man. Even in his weakened state it was wise to be careful.

He watched impatiently as the kettle started to boil.

'You want to know what Craig Malton's doing right now?' she said.

Malton's name snapped Leon to attention.

'Maybe he's eating dinner in his great big house in Didsbury? Or perhaps he's fucking his new girlfriend, a lawyer who lives in a big penthouse in the city centre? Or maybe he's just walking around without a permanent limp and three fused vertebrae?'

The kettle clicked off. The water was boiled. Leon Walker didn't move.

'That's what all this is about, locking you in here. Cutting you off. Tough love.'

Leon snorted.

Keisha smiled. 'No, you're right. I don't really give a shit about you. But I know that you give a shit about Craig Malton. About making sure he suffers for what he did to you. A broken back? Six months in traction? And then all the time in the world for everyone you'd ever terrorised to get their own back. What was that like, Leon? Suddenly no one's scared of you anymore? Suddenly it's your turn to be afraid.'

From the savage look in his eyes Keisha knew she was pressing Leon's buttons.

'Since you last went head to head he's only got stronger. If you couldn't beat him before, what are you going to do now?'

She let that thought hang.

'That's why I'm going to help you. I'm going to give you your chance not just to hurt him but to destroy him.'

Leon Walker opened his mouth to talk but only a low groaning sound came out. Somewhere between a yawn and a stutter. Then finally he began to remember his voice. 'Shoot . . . the . . . bastard,' he stammered, shaking the whole time.

Keisha felt a moment of doubt. Was this man up to what she needed him for? Had Malton's beating and the years of addiction stripped away too much?

She smiled like a patient mother. 'You can shoot him. Bang. He's dead. Over. Done. Is that enough for what he did to you? The years of humiliation, suffering, making you less than nothing? Don't you want something worse?'

Keisha didn't wait for an answer. She got to her feet. 'Your kettle's boiled,' she said as she turned and let herself out of the room, leaving Leon Walker alone with his thoughts.

She quickly shut the heavy, metal door, locking it behind her, and checked her watch.

Lynne Harris, the patient whose details she'd stolen earlier, had been invited to a fancy reception in town for prominent Mancunian women. Keisha would be attending as Lynne but couldn't help feel that if you were celebrating the most powerful women in Manchester and you hadn't invited Keisha Bistacchi then you didn't know the first thing about what really made Manchester tick.

Keisha had been on the backfoot ever since her husband had been killed. She was sick of hiding. It was time to flex her muscles. Prove to herself that there was nowhere she couldn't go. Nothing she couldn't do.

She had half an hour before her taxi arrived, so having double-checked Leon was locked up tight she turned to the second locked door.

There was only a single lock on this door and it slid open easily.

What she saw as she opened it sent her hurtling back thirty years.

Keisha staggered to the bed, alone in the freezing cold flat. There was blood on her hands, blood on the sheets. Her blood. It was still warm. Wet and slick. Raising her head off the mattress she could see the flames outside. Burning shadows danced on the bare walls. Keisha closed her eyes and waited for the end.

The sound of a taxi's horn hauled her back to the present. Having reminded herself exactly why she was doing all this she locked the door behind her and headed out into the night.

26

In the immediate aftermath of the car bomb, Waqar had insisted his sister make herself scarce. After making him promise to hide his gun and call the police, Fauzia had left for her shift at the hospital.

For the next twelve hours the guilt had been building until by the time her shift ended she couldn't quite believe what she'd done. She was in line to become an MP and she'd fled a crime scene. She'd left her brother alone to face the police. Even if he was the victim, could he be trusted not to implicate himself? Or worse – her?

At least the firebombing had got rid of any DNA evidence left in Waqar's car.

By the end of her shift, Fauzia had decided that abandoning Waqar to his fate wasn't an option. As always it would be up to her to fix things. And this time she would need help.

As a local councillor Fauzia found herself privy to the constant stream of gossip, rumour and legally suppressed information that flows through local government. Pay-offs, NDAs, plea bargains and executive decisions. It had been eye-opening to say the least.

She'd become aware of the names of prominent criminals, corrupt politicians and cynical businessmen. People who spent their time just about getting away with it. A who's who of Manchester's sleaziest bottom feeders.

Craig Malton's name had been different. When people talked about Craig Malton there was almost a reverence. He was talked about like a folk hero. A white knight walking alone through the underworld.

Out of curiosity Fauzia had looked him up and to her surprise discovered he was the CEO of a security company. A security company that held dozens of council contracts.

Fauzia's political instinct immediately sensed something was off. Malton Security was a run-of-the-mill security firm. Large but nothing special. Yet Craig Malton's fingerprints seemed to be all over the city.

Unable to find out more through conventional channels, she'd done some digging of her own.

What she found out was scarcely believable. Somewhere, under all the official contracts for doors and private security, Malton Security – or to be more exact Craig Malton – was running some kind of unofficial, underworld enforcement agency. Solving crimes for the criminal fraternity.

It was too farfetched. Too unbelievable. At the time she thought whoever Craig Malton really was could wait for another day. Fauzia had bigger fish to fry. She had set her sights on the recently vacated seat for Farnworth and Great Lever.

As she worked her shift, going through every possible course of action in her head, she kept coming back to Craig Malton. The man who people talked about in whispers. The man who they said could find anyone, solve any problem, settle any score.

Fauzia knew Waqar had manipulated her into being an accomplice to murder. Initially she had suspected he'd concocted the missing phone story to excuse entangling her in the mess he'd made. But there was no way he would have arranged the firebombing of his beloved Audi. And he seemed genuinely fearful of Galahad, the criminal higher up the chain who he claimed was responsible.

She had thought she knew her brother. That despite everything he had done, he was still the same Waqar she grew up idolising. But seeing him at the window, brandishing a gun, suddenly Fauzia realised she had been dragged into a world in which all her achievements and ambition counted for nothing.

This wasn't something she could go to the police about. Not without terminating her political career for good. That meant that however desperate it might seem, it was time to test the legend of Craig Malton.

But now, as she sat in the tatty office talking, not to Craig Malton, but to an impossibly young-looking, lanky, white lad with a livid, round scar on one cheek, everything about this course of action seemed foolish.

'I still don't really understand what it is that you want,' said the boy who'd introduced himself as Dean.

His clothes looked like he'd been sleeping in them and he smelt faintly of smoke. His fingers kept going to the scar on his cheek. From what Fauzia could see it looked inflamed, maybe even infected.

'I need to talk to Craig Malton,' she said.

'I told you,' said Dean, 'he's gone for the evening. But I promise you, whatever you'd say to him you can say to me.'

Fauzia looked at the weights bench, the missing ceiling tiles and the flat, stained pile of the carpet. On one wall was a collection of maps covered in pins. She had no idea what it all meant.

Could she say it out loud? And what if she was wrong? What if this was just a regular security firm? She thought back to the burning car. The gun in Waqar's hand. She realised she had nowhere else to turn.

'I've been told that Mr Malton can do certain things. Things that sometimes need doing,' she hedged.

Dean got up, walked across the room and shut the door. 'I think I know what you want. And I think you know what you want but unless you ask, I can't help,' he said.

Fauzia wondered if the room was bugged. She chose her next words very carefully.

'It's my brother. He had an encrypted phone that he used to contact a man called Galahad.'

'An encrypted phone?' said the boy, curiously fishing.

Fauzia didn't rise to it. She was only going to tell this underling what she deemed absolutely necessary to bring his boss Malton on board.

'The phone was stolen. If my brother doesn't get it back, this Galahad will kill him and me and our entire family.'

She took a breath. Saying it out loud made it all painfully real.

The boy sat listening. His fingers rubbing back and forth across his scar.

'What happened to your face?' asked Fauzia.

The boy's fingers pulled back as if he'd been caught with hand in the till. 'I got shot,' he said almost proudly.

'I think your wound might be infected. If I were you I'd get some antibiotics as soon as you can.'

The boy looked worried for a moment. Without thinking, his fingers reached back up to his face before he caught himself.

'What's your brother's name?' he asked.

'I want Craig Malton,' said Fauzia firmly. She'd told this underling enough.

The boy nodded sympathetically. 'I work directly with Mr Malton. Right now he has a big job on but I'll be seeing him tomorrow and I'll tell him personally you want to retain his services. What's your name?'

'Fauzia.' She wasn't going to give him any more than that and the boy didn't ask.

'And your brother? I only need his name. That'll be enough for Malton.'

Fauzia sucked her lips to her teeth and turned over in her head the pros and cons of giving away enough information to identify herself beyond reasonable doubt. There were more than enough Fauzias in the world. Not as many with a brother called Waqar.

There was no way around it. If this truly was what she was set on doing she would have to take the risk.

'Waqar,' she said curtly.

Sensing things had arrived at an impasse, the boy reached into the leather-topped desk and produced a business card. It said Malton Security and had a mobile phone number

134

beneath. He crossed out the mobile number and wrote his own in biro.

'If you need anything, you call me on that number,' he said. 'I'm Dean.'

Fauzia looked down at the altered business card. This wasn't going how she expected. Still, she'd not told him anything that could hurt her. If Craig Malton really was just a myth then all of this was for nothing anyway.

Suddenly the boy called Dean spoke. 'People don't come to us unless they're desperate. That's OK. Desperate is what Malton does best. I promise you there is no door in this city that can keep him out. Once he's working for you he can't be bought, threatened or lied to. Every criminal in this city knows who Craig Malton is and he'll do everything he can to retrieve that phone.'

'Everything within the law,' said Fauzia, still mindful of the possibility of a hidden recording.

'Everything,' said Dean.

For a moment there was an uneasy silence. It felt to Fauzia like neither of them were not quite used to what was happening here. Both of them doing their best to play their part. It didn't fill her with confidence. But compared to tackling her brother's mess alone this was the best she had.

'I should go.' Fauzia got up. Dean rose with her, hurrying past to open the door.

It was as she was on her way out that one last detail occurred to her. A detail that had scarcely registered among all the other revelations Waqar had told her about his secret life as a major criminal player.

Fauzia was still wary about giving away too much information, especially to Malton's underling. But having got this far she wanted to make sure that there was at least a chance for the risk to pay off.

'My brother. His name's Waqar. But on the streets . . .' She paused feeling foolish saying it out loud. 'On the streets he's known as Big Wacky.'

135

27

The naked flesh of Bea's back was pressed against the floor-to-ceiling window. She wrapped her legs around Malton's waist and hung on to his broad shoulders for dear life.

If anyone was watching from outside they would have seen the room bright against the dark night sky, the bee tattooed at the base of Bea's spine imprinted against the glass and the intense look on Malton's face as he drove into her.

They would never have guessed that at that very moment Malton was weighing up in his mind a very short list of suspects for Danny Mitchum's murder. Danny's father Stevie, Keisha or the combined might of the Scouse Mafia.

But they were sixty-four floors up at one of the highest points in the city and so no one saw Bea grab Malton to her as he closed his eyes and came.

For a moment everything in his head dissolved into brilliant white. For just a second Malton felt a sense of total clarity.

By the time he opened his eyes it was all clear and he knew exactly what he had to do.

He was about to step into the shower in Bea's guest bathroom when she appeared at the door. They had only had sex ten minutes ago but she was already fully dressed as if off out for the night. A black, strapless dress, with a bright green blazer thrown over it. Lawyerly but not too lawyerly.

'Going somewhere?' asked Malton, suddenly feeling underdressed.

'And you're coming with me,' said Bea. 'I need a plus-one.'

Malton hadn't come to Bea for sex, he'd come for a favour. He needed to get into a maximum-security prison and Bea was just the woman to help him do it.

But before he could work out how best to ask she was tearing off his clothes and silencing him with her open mouth. And now here she was asking her own favour.

'I haven't got a stitch to wear,' he said honestly.

Bea smiled back. 'You're a forty-four-inch chest aren't you? Don't answer that. I know you are. I checked. There's a midnight blue, mohair evening suit hanging up in the spare room. Shoes, socks. The lot. My treat.'

After the day he'd had Malton didn't have it in him to argue.

Part of him was even glad. Everyone in Malton's life was either a threat or a liability. He either had to protect them or to protect himself from them. Not Bea. Bea existed quite happily without Malton. She saw the city just as he did – a collection of brutal, sordid compromises, misdeeds and buried bodies. Bea made no bones about what she wanted or what she'd do to get it.

Malton wondered how different things would have been if he'd met Bea years earlier. Her icy intelligence and utter fearlessness combined with a relentless sex drive was starting to make its mark on him.

'Come on then. Hurry up and get showered. I can't take you out smelling of sex now, can I?' she said as she fiddled with her earlobes, inserting a pair of gold, drop earrings.

Malton quietly enjoyed being toyed with.

'Before you pop in the shower, there's something else I want to ask you.'

This was the wrong way round. Malton had come here tonight to get a favour from Bea. She had not only got him to agree to a night out but now there was more?

'Ask away,' said Malton stepping into the shower and turning on the water.

It was a capsule shower. A large, tiled area sealed off by a sliding glass door.

Malton left the door open but let the water hammer down from the rainforest showerhead, forcing Bea to raise her voice as she talked. The louder she got the more Geordie she became.

'I'm always working. You're always working. We're people who live for our jobs. Thing is, I think I might quite like you. You're not like most of the men I tend to go for. Not as stupid as you look.'

Malton didn't stop scrubbing himself. His rough fingers scouring every remaining trace of smoke and tiredness from his thickset body. He realised he hadn't showered since the fire. Events had assumed their own momentum and he'd let himself be carried along. An evening out with Bea would be the perfect chance to pause, if only for a moment.

'I've got a proposition,' she said.

Malton rinsed the soap from his shaved head. It smelt faintly of perfume. A reminder of the sensory delights that Bea brought into his life.

He turned the shower off and stood for a moment dripping wet until Bea picked up his cue and tossed him a fluffy, white towel.

'We both fix problems for a certain class of people. Me legally, you . . . in your own way. It makes perfect sense.'

Malton knew what was coming before she said it.

'We should go into business together.'

28

Keisha's feet were killing her as she looked around at the great and the good of Manchester's power women.

The downstairs of the Manchester Assurance building had finally been given the makeover it deserved after a couple of decades of languishing as the scruffy bar of an even scruffier hotel.

The days of dark wood, hotel carpets and damp were long gone and now the room was every bit as opulent as originally intended when it was built over a hundred years ago.

It was the perfect setting to hold Northern Power Women, an event celebrating the region's female movers and shakers.

A giant open space of glass, ceramic and plants created an almost tropical environment for the high-achieving guests to enjoy while enthusiastic youngsters bearing silver platters of nibbles and champagne wandered among them.

Coming here wasn't part of the plan but after the way Lynne Harris spoke to Keisha the plan had changed.

Armed with Lynne's information, Keisha had done a little digging and discovered a highly successful businesswoman who'd exploited the fashion for non-surgical cosmetic procedures to create an empire of trainee aestheticians paying tens of thousands of pounds each for the privilege of being taught how to inject fillers into the faces of the women of Manchester.

Keisha would never dream of getting work done. She was proud not just of how good she looked for her age but also of how her body was her proof of who she was and what she'd endured to get here. Every inch of it was perfect and she'd take serious issue with anyone who said otherwise.

She'd walked into the event and picked up Lynne Harris's goody bag without comment, the young PR running the desk handing her a lanyard with a welcoming smile.

With Leon Walker on the mend and Emily firmly in her sights, tonight was a little reward. A chance for Keisha to let her hair down. Literally. She'd unpicked the braids that she needed to pass as Diane Okunkwe and her voluminous, dark brown hair spilled off her head in rich, shining curls.

But it wasn't just about fun. This was a chance for Keisha to flex the skills that she'd used to survive these past thirty years. Her ability to fit in wherever she went. From East Manchester cocaine importers to South Manchester academics. Keisha had spent years learning how to become whoever she needed to be to get ahead.

Keisha had no doubt that there wasn't a woman in this room who'd achieved what she had or would even dare try.

She spoke to a human rights lawyer from the chambers down Brasenose Lane. Then pivoted to a deeply boring ten minutes listening to a senior management consultant at KPMG who worked out of the gigantic, white offices overlooking the town hall. After making her excuses she enjoyed sharing bitchy comments with an artist who stood out not just by dint of her youth but as being the only woman not in a dress. Instead wearing long, baggy black trousers and a kimono style jacket paired with severe, black-rimmed glasses and a bowl cut.

Important people, all filled with their own importance and too self-regarding to ask too many questions of the woman who said her name was 'Lynne'. She knew that there must be people in that room who would know Lynne Harris. She rode that edge of danger. Feeling her senses sharpen, her instincts working overtime. Feeling out each person before she gave away just enough of herself to keep the conversation moving.

Experience had taught Keisha that the best way to lie was to lie big. Lie loudly. Lie with a smile on your face while you look them in the eye and dare them to contradict you. In a way she was no different to anyone else in that room. Keisha knew you never got past the velvet rope without telling a few porkies. You never got in the VIP enclosure without stepping on a few toes. You never made your first million without fucking over a few people.

Every single woman in that room had clambered over the competition to be there tonight.

Keisha felt herself swimming through the currents that made Manchester the city it was. A city just small enough to delude yourself that you could conquer it and just big enough to make that a tantalising impossibility.

She didn't want to conquer Manchester, but when her plan came to fruition she would at least be leaving a scar.

Keisha was listening to a senior member of the council laughingly dismissing local protests over a library closure when she saw them.

She was blonde, petite and striding into the room in a dazzling green blazer over a black cocktail dress, black nylon legs in tottering heels.

He was in a dark blue mohair evening suit.

Keisha instinctively gripped her Bottega bag, feeling the gun she was still carrying sitting heavy inside.

For a moment she thought about making a quick exit, wondering if she could get out before she was noticed.

By then it was too late. He'd already seen her.

Her ex: Craig Malton.

29

The comforting smell of onion frying in turmeric and cumin filled the silence of the dining room.

Fauzia could tell her mother was anxious from the amount of food covering the table. Samia's inner turmoil very precisely matched the amount of time she spent cooking. Unlike Fauzia's expensive, immaculate kitchen, her mother's was saturated with decades of cooking. Every inch was covered with spices and pans and knives and plates. Everything she needed to feed her family.

Upon hearing the news of the firebombing, her mother had retreated to the kitchen and for the next few hours threw herself into preparing enough food to feed half the street.

While Fauzia was working her shift, Iffat and Waqar had been talking to the police. They even had to miss going to the mosque.

When she arrived home the police were wrapping up. Iffat was angrily batting away suggestions from the detectives about 'vendettas' and 'gang rivalries'. His son was no gangster. He was an honest businessman.

Waqar was silent. Playing the good son.

Fauzia had barely flinched when she told them that she couldn't help. She hadn't been there. She was at her flat getting ready to go on her shift.

Waqar was watching her as she lied. Once again he had forced her to participate in his sordid world. But now Fauzia wasn't just a helpless dupe. She had Malton. She had already decided she wouldn't tell Waqar. Waqar had his secrets; this would be hers. If Malton reported directly to her then she could control the situation. Keep a lid on things. Do what she always did and fix Waqar's mess.

Besides, if Tahir got wind of any of this he'd gladly use it to destroy her.

Before the police left, Fauzia had taken the officers to one side and made it very clear just how sensitive this whole issue was. How it might look to the community. The police digging into the family of a prominent Asian councillor. A female Asian councillor. A female Asian councillor who was in line to become the area's next MP. While offering all the help she could, she left them in no doubt that one wrong step and the whole thing could turn very nasty, very quickly.

Even as she said the words she knew exactly who she sounded like: Tahir Akhtar. A councillor who had spent his entire career hiding behind vague threats about the dire consequences of bringing 'the community' into disrepute.

Labour HQ still hadn't called her back.

Usually family mealtimes were a raucous mixture of parental admonishments and sibling rivalry. But with all the questions about the firebombing of Waqar's Audi lying heavy on everyone's mind, they ate in silence.

Across the table from her Waqar was shovelling food into his mouth. Seemingly unaffected by the chaos he'd created.

As far as Iffat and Samia knew, her brother was a helpless victim. An innocent man caught up in something that was nothing to do with him.

Fauzia knew that was a lie. Her parents still saw the disappointing son who ran the meat processing plant and a string of kebab shops. She knew different. She now knew that alongside all of that Waqar was living a parallel life as a ruthless drug dealer who called himself Big Wacky.

She could barely reconcile everything she'd heard about Big Wacky with everything she knew about her brother Waqar. They were like two different people.

But if the police ever got a whiff of who Waqar really was then it was a very short walk to them looking into the body she had helped him dispose of.

She had been so distracted during her shift that she had forgotten to get rid of the bloody clothes. They were still in a bin liner in the boot of her car. This wasn't Fauzia's world and she was running just to keep up. She would have to deal with them on her next shift.

Now everything would depend on whether or not Craig Malton lived up to his reputation.

At this moment in time all she had were the reassurances of his worryingly young-looking underling and the business card he'd given her.

She tried to ignore the dark sense of dread she felt building in her chest. To blot out the image of the dying man's face, screaming forever as he tipped into the merciless maw of the mincer.

Samia was clearing the plates when Waqar spoke up. 'I'm going to find out who did this,' he said.

Samia looked horrified.

'You will do no such thing,' said Iffat.

'That's the police's job,' said Fauzia, much preferring to trust in Greater Manchester Police's atrocious clean-up rate than to have Waqar running around escalating things.

'We know the police won't do a thing. They don't care about us lot,' said Waqar.

'I'm a councillor about to become an MP; believe me, we can trust the police,' said Fauzia, hoping she sounded more convincing than she felt.

'Dad, when your first butcher's shop got burned down, who helped you? Was it the police? And, Mum, when your car got nicked, who got it back? The police? It was us, the community. We look after our own,' said Waqar.

Fauzia didn't like where this was going. She had always thought Tahir and his kind were relics. An old boys' network, out of touch with the modern world. The more she was drawn into Waqar's mess, the more she was realising how little she knew.

'Someone firebombed your car. I don't know why they would do that. You run a kebab shop. Why would anyone want to target you?' said Fauzia with just enough innocent incredulity in her voice to rile her brother.

Waqar glared across the table at his sister.

'A chain of kebab shops *and* a meat processing plant,' he said with belligerent pride. Leaving out his drug dealing he turned and took Samia's hand. 'Mum, all I want is for us all to be happy. To be safe and to enjoy the things we've earned. Those white detectives, you think they're going to go home to their little houses and their little wives and spend a single moment worrying about the brown family with the nice cars and the big house and the daughter who's an MP?'

Samia looked unsure.

'Oh come on,' said Fauzia.

'I'm doing this for all of us. I'm so proud of you, sis. I don't want some scumbag to spoil it for you,' said Waqar.

Fauzia had to hand it to her brother, he was a convincing liar.

'So let the police do their job,' she implored.

'I will,' said Waqar. 'But they can't stop me asking around. Whoever did this, someone out there knows.' He turned to Iffat and Samia. 'You two gave jobs to hundreds of people in this community. Their parents and cousins and brothers and sisters. People haven't forgotten that.'

He turned back to Fauzia. 'Just let me ask. I promise I'll be careful,' he said.

'You're a good boy,' said Samia, clutching Waqar's hand.

Fauzia knew from Iffat's silence that despite what she said being true, Waqar's words meant more. The community had made him what he was today. As proud as he was to have a daughter about to break into parliament, he could never forget that. He'd been alive to see police turn the other way as the NF beat up his friends. He'd been there when the BNP had tried to burn Oldham to the ground. And he'd lived through a decade when suddenly anyone with brown skin was a terrorist.

His head said trust the police. His heart said trust the community.

Fauzia put on her best, most political smile. 'Just you be careful,' she said to Waqar through clenched teeth.

Malton had better find that phone, and fast.

30

'Actually we're thinking of going into business together,' said Bea.

Malton watched Keisha's practised smile as she nodded enthusiastically.

'Working with your other half?' said Keisha. 'Could be messy,' she teased.

Malton could tell she was staring at him under her sunglasses.

'Lot of men don't like strong women,' continued Keisha. 'We scare them.'

Bea laughed just the right amount.

Malton thought how what was going on in front of him was no different to him and Stevie Mitchum. Two alphas slowly feeling each other out. Working out the pecking order in the most bloodless manner possible.

'I'm bored of talking about me,' said Bea. 'What about you?' Bea looked down at Keisha's lanyard. 'Lynne?'

For just a second Malton saw the confidence and poise drain from Keisha. He recognised the exact moment it happened. The moment she realised that for all her confidence and bluster she had just fucked up. She'd given Malton a name.

Keisha smiled widely. Hiding her slip behind dazzling, white teeth. 'Non-surgical cosmetic procedures,' she said.

'Fillers and things?' said Bea.

'Exactly,' said Keisha.

'You look fabulous with it,' said Bea, her smile never waning.

Unseen, beneath the dark blue mohair of his evening jacket, Malton flexed the muscles in his back. Letting the stress of the encounter flow from his powerful shoulders down his traps and spread into his glutes.

It had been nearly three months since he'd last seen Keisha. As a parting gift she'd shot Dean in the face. In Malton's office.

He'd known on some level that she must still be out there. His last encounter with Keisha had seen her husband and in-laws wiped out. Malton wondered how she'd possibly top that.

Killing Danny Mitchum would fit the bill. If she knew Malton was protecting Danny then his death would be the perfect way to land a body blow against him. To show the world that Craig Malton wasn't quite as invincible as he liked to make out.

He had only come along tonight as quid pro quo for the favour he needed from Bea and now here he was, face to face with the woman who very well could have murdered Danny.

'What do you do, Craig? Bea here's a top lawyer, where do you fit in?' said Keisha playfully.

'I work security,' said Malton.

'Oooh, you're a bouncer? I should have guessed from all that muscle. He beats them up and you put them away? Something like that?'

Bea and Keisha laughed performatively. Malton didn't make a sound.

'Dorothy!' Bea's attention shifted as she waved to a woman on the other side of the room. She turned to Keisha. 'Lovely to meet you, Lynne. If you ever need a lawyer . . .!'

'I like to stay out of trouble,' purred Keisha.

'Back in a minute,' said Bea, squeezing Malton's arm. He watched as she tottered across the room and started air kissing a tall woman with dazzling, grey, shoulder-length hair.

Malton was alone with Keisha.

'You're looking good, Craig,' she said. 'I like your girlfriend. She's fun. What happened to Emily?'

Malton knew he wouldn't have much time before Bea returned.

148

He took a step closer. The smell of Keisha's perfume was overwhelming. It tugged him back to years before, when he'd first met her. But there was no time for nostalgia.

He had one shot at this. Keisha was near impossible to read but if she was to give anything away he needed to take her by surprise.

Malton lowered his voice and looked Keisha directly in the eye. 'Did you kill Danny Mitchum?'

Keisha was silent. She didn't speak. She didn't react. Her eyes unreadable beneath her sunglasses. Malton watched her face, scouring her features for the slightest tell.

Keisha burst out laughing. 'Craig, come on. What would I want to do that for?'

'To get to me.'

She pulled a face. 'Were you working for Danny Mitchum?'

Malton didn't react but he could see Keisha already figuring it out in her head.

'Oh my God. You *were* working for him. And someone killed him? On your watch?'

She put a hand to her mouth to stifle more laughter. Keisha took a breath and composed herself. She became deathly serious.

'Look at you,' she said. 'In your fancy suit, surrounded by all these nice, posh people. You and me, we're not like them. They'll never let you join the club, Craig. You know that don't you? You know where you really belong.'

'I wonder what Lynne Harris is doing tonight,' said Malton calmly.

Before Keisha could answer, Bea returned. She was bearing two glasses of champagne.

'I saw you two were still chatting away and thought you could do with a drink.' She offered the glass to Keisha.

Keisha smiled back. 'Aren't you sweet! Meeting you two has made my night but it's well past my bedtime. Got to get home for the little one!' She turned to Malton. 'If I ever need protecting, I know where to come,' she flirted as if Bea wasn't standing there beside him.

Malton watched Keisha sashay between partygoers and out of the room. The slightly faltering steps in her heels. The amazing silhouette her cinched black dress gave her. He saw other men in the room unable not to snatch glances at her. She exuded something intangible.

Those who didn't know might put it down to attitude, sex appeal or just straight-up confidence. Malton knew better. Keisha was lethal.

The only thing Malton had to go on was her claim that she didn't kill Danny Mitchum. He'd seen her mask slip for a moment when he clocked the name on her lanyard. He still knew her tells. From her unvarnished delight at learning Danny had been killed on his watch it was clear she hadn't even known he was dead.

He made a note to look into who exactly Lynne Harris really was. Keisha may not have killed Danny but she was back in Manchester. There was only one thing that could have brought her back and it made his blood run cold.

She was back for him.

She would have to wait. With Stevie Mitchum and Keisha crossed off his list of suspects there was only one name left in the frame for Danny's murder.

The only way he could get to that suspect was through Bea.

So for the rest of the evening he smiled, let her show him off and dutifully fetched drinks. Knowing that at the end of the evening he still had to ask his favour.

He had to ask her to get him an appointment to see one of her clients in the maximum-security prison he called home.

The head of the Scouse Mafia.

31

Dean took the stairs up to Vikki Walker's flat two at a time. She lived in one of the tower blocks standing in what was left of Salford's town centre.

Salford council had ripped the heart out of their own city, replacing it with a low-rise shopping precinct and an impassable one-way system. There, in the middle of it all rose a single high rise – SALFORD SHOPPING CITY – stuck down the side of it in giant, plastic letters.

Vikki lived halfway up the tower block. Dean didn't even bother to check on the lifts. After his last visit, being trapped in a broken lift for a couple of hours with nothing but his phone and the smell of piss for company, he was happy to take the stairs.

He was propelled upwards by the news that he'd finally discovered Big Wacky. Or at least Big Wacky's sister had discovered *him*. The woman who'd come looking for Malton to track down a missing, encrypted phone belonging to her brother had revealed that same brother was none other than Big Wacky himself, the key to finding Vikki's missing friend Olivia.

Dean knew that he couldn't keep Fauzia from Malton forever but with the hunt for Danny Mitchum's killer still ongoing, he felt like he had a day or so to conveniently 'forget' to mention a new client to Malton.

As long as Fauzia went through him he could keep things ticking along until he'd had a chance to get to Big Wacky.

He paused on the eighth floor for breath. Out of the window he could see the giant Tesco that was now next to Salford

Shopping City. A doomed attempt to correct the civic vandalism already done.

Once he'd tracked down Olivia then he could tell Malton everything. When it was a done deal. Until then he didn't want Malton thinking he was taking jobs on the side.

Dean could feel the sweat starting to soak into the shirt and jacket he wore for work. He knew Malton didn't expect him to dress like the boys who did the doors and he didn't want to simply dress like a mini-me to Malton with his jumpers and heavy denims. Desperate to not make the wrong decision Dean had bottled it and bought himself the least conspicuous suit he could find. He looked like an eager estate agent.

Reaching Vikki's door on the fourteenth floor he found it already unlocked for him – having rung the bell at the ground-floor entrance. Dean let himself in.

He was instantly struck by the smell. Vikki had been cooking. The aroma of something homely filled the small flat. Vikki emerged from the kitchen into the front room that made up the main body of the flat. She was wearing dark tights under a baggy T-shirt that hung down like a dress and on her hands were a pair of floral oven gloves. She looked very different to how she had when Dean first met her.

Back then she'd been abandoned by her father and left in a semi-derelict flat to fend for herself with only her dog Fury for company. The flat was a foul-smelling hovel and she was a wreck.

Now the flat felt warm and inviting and Vikki was glowing. Her wary scowl had been replaced with a warm, open smile.

Fury came jogging over and nuzzled Dean's leg. He was the softest Staffie he'd ever met.

'When you said you were coming I ran over to Tesco, got some food. Sausage and mash? I'm doing onion gravy.'

Vikki was flourishing. Her pale, underfed skin had cleared up and now shone. Vikki was tall, not as tall as Dean, but big like her father. And strong too. Her whole body radiated health.

After she'd helped Dean and Malton with a case, Malton had made sure to take care of her. The flat had been done up and she had a regular stipend put in a bank account to ensure she could feed herself and heat the flat.

Dean would never ask Malton outright what had gone on between him and Walker. Instead he'd put together bits and pieces he'd overheard at work along with what he'd found out from keeping his ears open while travelling all over Manchester for Malton.

The story was a simple one. Leon Walker had been a force of nature. He and Malton had clashed. Leon Walker hadn't come out on top.

Dean wondered just how much of Malton's concern for Vikki came from his guilt over crippling her father. After all that Malton had done for her, she could have easily asked him for his help in tracking down Olivia.

The fact she had instead asked Dean had put a flutter of hope in his heart, which the sight of her emerging from the kitchen midway through preparing a home-cooked meal did very little to calm.

Dean caught his breath. He wiped his sweaty palms on the back of his suit trousers. As the blood pumped through his body he could feel the scar on his cheek throbbing. Maybe Fauzia was right: he should be on antibiotics.

'You took the stairs?' Vikki said. 'I know there was that one time in the lift but still?'

'I like the stairs,' said Dean, bent double catching his breath.

'So is that a yes to sausage and mash?'

Dean pulled himself upright and did his best to look composed. In the months since he'd met Vikki she'd gone from a troubled, lost girl to a vital, focused young woman. She'd just turned seventeen. Only a year younger than Dean.

'I won't say no,' said Dean with a smile.

Fury the dog rolled over on the newly laid carpet and wiggled his legs in the air hopefully. Dean was powerless to resist, bending down and rubbing the Staffie's exposed belly.

He had hoped to burst in and immediately give her his good news. But the promise of hot food and Vikki's company won him over.

Dean saw a lot of himself in Vikki. She'd been given a chance by Malton and grabbed it with both hands. She'd gone back to college in preparation for applying for a fashion degree. She'd also joined a women's rugby team and taken to the sport like a natural. The Walker propensity for violence finally finding a legitimate outlet.

Watching her set the table, he knew that when he'd agreed to find her friend Olivia he was motivated not just by the desire to prove himself to Malton. There was something about Vikki's drive. The radical way she'd reshaped her life.

He wondered if he was falling for her.

Dean hoped that wherever Leon Walker was right now he was a long, long way away. Out of his daughter's life for good. From what he'd learned asking around it was clear Leon Walker had been a miserable excuse for a father.

Vikki put a plate of food down in front of Dean and, without waiting for his response, sat down herself and began to eat.

Delicious-smelling steam rose off the pile of mash, drenched in thick, rich gravy.

'You said you had some news?' she said through a mouthful of food.

Dean marvelled at how she utterly lacked anything approaching table manners. But this wasn't the starving feral girl he'd first met. This was a young woman, rough around the edges but confident. Happy even.

Dean paused to give the moment a little drama. 'I've found Big Wacky,' he announced.

Vikki froze. She swallowed the food in her mouth and put her cutlery down. A smile slowly forced itself across her face.

'You know where Olivia is?' she said.

Dean had hoped for a little more enthusiasm.

'Not yet, but I've found Big Wacky. Or rather his sister found me. She came into the office. Can you believe it?'

Vikki looked like she was thinking. 'What did she come in for?' she asked warily.

Dean's mouth was watering at the smell of the food. His body was screaming for him to eat, having endured the climb to the flat. But he was focused on Vikki. Something about her reaction to his news didn't quite feel right.

'Big Wacky, her brother, had his phone stolen. She wants it back,' he said flatly.

'A stolen phone?' said Vikki.

'Not a regular phone. An encrypted phone. Big Wacky's a drug dealer. All his contacts are on it. His connection to *his* dealer.'

Dean stopped himself. What was he doing telling her all this? Was he trying to get her to react like he'd hoped? To throw her arms around him and thank her knight in shining armour? However disappointed he might be in her muted response to his news, there was no need to show all his cards just yet.

As if sensing Dean's confusion Vikki broke into a smile. She reached across the table and clasped Dean's arm.

'That's brilliant. I know you'll find her,' she said, before going back to her food. Almost as an afterthought, through another mouthful of food she added, 'Did you tell Malton yet?'

Vikki paused, a forkful of mash suspended mid-air, waiting for Dean's answer.

'No,' said Dean and gave a weak smile back.

'That's good. He's done so much for me already. I don't want to keep asking him for favours,' said Vikki.

As she raised the paused fork to her mouth, the contents slid off and into her lap.

Vikki shot up as did Dean. He rushed over to the kitchen and started searching for something to mop Vikki down.

'It's OK!' said Vikki shaking her head and laughing to herself. 'I'm such a messy eater.'

Dean had located a greasy-looking tea towel and was running it under the tap when Vikki simply stripped off the T-shirt dress she was wearing, leaving her standing in just her bra and tights.

Flustered, Dean's eyes strained to stay focused on Vikki's face.

Their eyes met, both of them realising at the same moment in time the awkwardness of the situation.

'I'm sorry!' blurted out Dean, turning away.

Vikki was too busy laughing to feel embarrassed. 'Don't be daft. I'm just so used to you being round. I forget you're here sometimes. I'll go and get changed. You just carry on eating.'

Dean cautiously turned around. The sound of Vikki's laughter was far more of a turn-on than any amount of exposed flesh. The easy joy that felt so different to how she was when they had first met.

Dean couldn't help himself. He too started sniggering as he took his seat back at the table.

'Don't look!' teased Vikki as she turned to go, making a comic display of attempting to cover her rear as she disappeared into the bedroom.

Dean was about to go back to eating when he saw the phone on the table. Vikki's mobile. It lay there, glowing, unlocked.

All thoughts of Vikki in her underwear vanished from his mind. Instead he was back to dwelling on Vikki's muted reaction just now to the news that he'd found Big Wacky. Was it his imagination or was there something going on? If Dean didn't know better he'd say she was scared.

Dean reached over and grabbed up the phone.

He could hear Vikki pulling out drawers in the next room. He didn't have long.

His heart raced as he clicked around at random. Instagram, TikTok, a WhatsApp group for her college friends, lots of photos of Fury. The phone of a normal, teenage girl.

Still Dean couldn't shake the feeling that something was wrong.

He clicked the phone app and looked at Vikki's call log. A collection of the usual cold call numbers. Untraceable call centres and ambulance chasers. Nothing of note for the first few screens.

'Don't let it go cold,' shouted Vikki from the next room.

Dean had run out of time. As he went to close the phone app he brushed the contacts list and suddenly the screen changed to a list of every number in Vikki's phone.

There was no one under A and so B was right there at the top. Or to be more precise a single name under B.

Big Wacky.

Dean's heart leapt. With stumbling fingers he closed the app and put the phone back where he thought it had been sitting on the table just as Vikki emerged wearing a baggy, turquoise tracksuit top and a short, black skirt.

'You not eating?' she asked.

Dean began to eat, all the while wondering just how much trouble he was in.

32

Cans of energy drink. Snickers bars and a bag of bananas. Keisha angrily slammed Leon Walker's food for the day onto a chipped, melamine tray and headed to the locked room where she was keeping him.

Last night had been a disaster and it was all her fault. She'd got sloppy. The night out as Lynne Harris was meant to re-assure her that she still had the guts and cunning to stay ahead of the pack. A dry run for when she emerged from her bolthole and picked up where she left off. Instead she'd run into Craig. He'd seen her and her name badge.

She knew he'd be looking up Lynne Harris, trying to fig-ure out what she was up to. This meant she was out of time. The plan would have to start moving and start moving straight away.

Whether Leon Walker was ready or not was now irrelevant.

Keisha picked up the tray and headed out of her room into the hallway where she set it down on the dusty floorboards and started unlocking the door.

She would have to move on Emily now too. She had planned to take things slowly. Make sure she'd covered every possible angle. Keisha hated being rushed. She hated having to rely on brute force. For her, violence was an absolute last resort. A last resort she was happy to visit but nonetheless one that created more problems than it solved.

But she knew she wasn't the only one on a ticking clock. Someone had killed Danny Mitchum and Craig was caught up in it all. With that kind of distraction Keisha felt certain that he would never see her coming until it was far, far too late.

On top of that there was the woman she now knew as Bea Wallace. The brochure in her goody bag contained a profile of every woman there. Bea Wallace – a celebrated criminal lawyer. Looking over the list of her clients and cases, Keisha recognised several very heavy underworld figures. It was clear to anyone in the know that Bea specialised in keeping the criminal elite out of prison.

The final nail in Craig's coffin would be Emily but it wouldn't hurt to drag Bea into things along the way.

Keisha was so distracted that having picked up the tray and opened the unlocked door with her foot she was totally unprepared when the giant frame of Leon Walker barrelled through the open door, knocking her to the ground and scattering the contents of the tray across the bare floorboards.

Keisha rallied almost instantly and turned to see the shoeless, near-naked Leon hurtle out of the front door.

She was dressed ready for work at The Sentinel but still had the presence of mind to make sure she wasn't walking in on Leon Walker unarmed.

She pulled the revolver out of the bumbag around her waist, got to her feet and took off after him, making it outside only a few seconds behind him.

Bursting out of the front door she found him crumpled on the ground. The front yard of the house was vast. A huge, dirty patch of rough ground hemmed in on all sides by a large, brick wall.

Beyond the wall was the sound of the main road running through Harpurhey, the road itself hidden behind a canopy of trees.

If you didn't know any better you could imagine you were just about anywhere.

Leon writhed and coiled on the ground, his hands clamped over his face. He'd spent the last few months in a dark room with only a light bulb for company. In the full glare of daylight his already fragile constitution had crumbled.

Keisha looked round the yard. There were a couple of scrapped cars. Piles of mattresses. Some broken up asbestos roof tiles and various mounds of rubble among which were any number of things that could be used as a weapon.

The wall around the house ended in a large, six-bar gate over which sheet metal had been welded. It was tall but Leon could easily get over it.

Keisha raised her gun. 'Get back inside,' she said, her voice cold and dead.

Leon turned, his eyes screwed tight shut against the light. His head swung side to side trying to see where Keisha's voice was coming from.

'Get back inside.'

He unfolded himself from the ground and rose to his full six-foot-six height.

He was naked except for pyjama bottoms and in the sunlight Keisha could properly see his body, riddled with tattoos and neglect. He had been massive once, a ten-man job. The mass had gone but the residual strength remained. Keisha had felt it when he'd barged past her out of the house. She saw it now all over him. Maybe he was more ready than she thought.

Leon was not more than a dozen feet away from her. If he charged she would only get off one shot before he was on her.

But he didn't charge. He stood his ground, staring at Keisha through squinting eyes.

'Where are you going to go, Leon?' she asked.

He didn't move.

'The world thinks you're dead. The world doesn't care. It carried on without you. There's nothing out there for you anymore.'

He took a step towards Keisha. A low growling sound was coming from him.

'You leave now, naked, alone. To do what? Become a junkie again? Like how I found you? Shivering in your own shit in some derelict mill. You and all the other ones who didn't make it? Is that what you want?'

Keisha saw Leon's fist bunching and unbunching. He was thinking.

'Or maybe you go back to your daughter? Little Vicious. I hear she goes by Vikki these days. Has a whole new life, even though you left her with fuck all. Now her flat's been done up. She's got money coming in. Going to college and everything.'

She saw the look of confusion on his face.

'You're wondering how? Thinking – I left her with nothing but despair and drug debt. How is she doing so well while I'm stood here about to be shot down like a dog? I'll tell you – Craig Malton.'

The name had an immediate effect.

'He paid to do up her flat. Paid for her to get back to college. He didn't just take your life. He took your family too. He's playing at being daddy. You think that's cos he gives a shit about her? He just wants the world to know he took everything from you. So what are you going to do about it?'

Keisha lowered her gun.

'Rush me? Kill me? Sure. Then head out there and see how long you last. See how easy you find it to get even with Craig Malton. We both know you won't get through the night.'

Keisha felt her heart pounding. This was what she lived for. The reckless gambit. The high-stakes throw of the dice. She was fifty-fifty whether she could get the gun back up in time if he charged. Her kind of odds.

'Or you stay here with me. I feed you. Heal you. And then I give you the tools to get the one thing you want most: revenge.'

Keisha let the word 'revenge' hang in the air. It felt so satisfying in her mouth. Revenge, the one thing no one can truly resist. The primal desire to right a wrong.

Leon Walker started to move. Small, faltering steps. His filthy, bare feet treading through the debris and garbage littering the front yard. He was coming straight for Keisha.

But she held firm. Her gun by her side. Leon was closing the gap. He was only six feet away now. If she drew, it would be point-blank. If she even got a shot off.

She'd made her call.

Keisha kept the gun by her side and held her breath as Leon stumbled past her and back into the house.

She waited a few seconds before, alone in the yard, she let out a deep sigh of relief. Wallowing in the euphoria of her bluff paying off.

She found him back in his room. On the mattress cross-legged. He said one word to her: 'Revenge.'

She gave him his food for the day and before she left, set down a washing-up bowl, a disposable razor and a can of shaving cream.

Then she locked him in and headed off to The Sentinel.

Leon Walker was half the plan, but without Emily Keisha had nothing.

33

Malton knocked on the sage green door of the four-storey, semi-detached house and waited for an answer. The house was one of a dozen that ringed a small park and was lost amongst a cluster of mature trees that created the impression of being somewhere deep in rural England.

In reality the street was a stone's throw from the centre of Cheadle village, a leafy south Manchester suburb, and home to a large number of Manchester's Jewish community.

This was where Emily's father lived.

Upon retiring he'd moved from the family's giant house in Hale Barns to a still-considerable property in Cheadle. Here he was walking distance from everything he needed to enjoy living out the rest of his life in the comfort that having several million in the bank gave a person.

Malton knocked again. He didn't have time for this. Bumping into Keisha last night changed everything. Maybe she wasn't behind Danny's murder but that just meant that whatever she was up to was one more thing he now had to deal with.

Her timing couldn't have been worse.

Malton heard the sound of a lock being loosened and then the large door was opened by Mayer Haim, Emily's father. Mayer was a striking man who'd been blessed with a ferocious metabolism. He drank and ate without restraint yet remained rake-thin with a full head of the same thick, black hair that Emily had.

Mayer didn't smile to see Malton but nor did he look surprised. Malton respected Mayer too much to waste time.

'I need to know where Emily is,' he said.

Mayer frowned and took a breath. 'I should never have called you.'

But he had. All those years ago it was Mayer who'd hired Malton to rescue his daughter from the boyfriend who was pimping her out to keep them both supplied with drugs.

'I'm sorry for what happened,' said Malton.

'Do you actually know what happened?' asked Mayer suspiciously.

Malton knew Emily had gone but that was all.

'I want to help,' he said.

Mayer looked sad. Malton sensed the effort it was costing him to hold back his true feeling. Mayer held Malton's gaze. 'Emily doesn't need your help. She's safe. That's all you need to know.'

Malton took a breath. He didn't want to scare Mayer but he had to tell him.

'I think someone might be after Emily. Someone who wants to hurt her. To get to me.'

Once Malton knew for sure who had made the move on Danny then he could do something about it. But until then he couldn't take any chances.

Mayer shook his head angrily. When he looked up the stoicism was gone. All that was left was raw emotion.

'I thought you could keep her safe. I told myself it was all OK. It wasn't. It never will be. But all I can do for Emily now is keep you away. I hope you understand.'

'The person who is after me will do anything to hurt me – and that includes the people I've been close to.'

'I'm not thinking about you. I'm thinking about my daughter. Trust me when I say she's somewhere safe. I'm sorry, Craig, but that's all I can tell you. If you want to try and get it out of me. Go ahead.'

Mayer held up his arms in surrender. They both knew Malton would never lay a finger on him.

Driving back into Manchester Malton tried to put Emily out of his mind. He'd done as much as he could. He realised now what he felt for her was no longer love. It was guilt.

He had so wanted to be part of her world. The world of pub lunches and leafy suburbs and tasteful wealth. To live a life that felt easy. To finally belong somewhere.

For that very brief time before Emily left he had embraced the idea that maybe he could grow old like Mayer Haim. Happy and secure. Surrounded by family and good memories.

Now he knew better.

Malton didn't do guilt. It was a new feeling for him and he didn't like it. He'd been the one to bring Emily into his world. It was he who believed he could protect her. He thought he could be the man Emily believed he was. Kind and brave and hopeful.

But deep down he was the man Keisha knew he was. An outsider who if he stopped for just a moment would be consumed by the chaos that was always following a few steps behind him.

After parking his green Volvo Estate on one of the roads surrounding Strangeways Prison, Malton made his way to the visitors' entrance.

Bea had done her bit and now he had an appointment with her most notorious client – Callum Hester.

Most of the criminal world knew him as the Boss of the Scouse Mafia.

To Malton he was as close as he would get to family. Callum was his former lover James's older brother.

34

Dean did his best not to wince as he watched the film of a technician in a coral-coloured lab coat use a syringe to inject filler into the face of a smiling patient.

He gripped the underside of his chair and nodded along as the next scene showed yet more needles going into lips and foreheads while the narration explained how Femme Visage was started by struggling single mum Lynne Harris who through a combination of hard work, pluck and charisma had turned the brand into a multi-million-pound beauty empire.

The promotional film ended with a lingering shot of Lynne surrounded by a dozen of her employees, all wearing the distinctive coral Femme Visage uniform.

They all looked deliriously happy.

Dean fought the urge to scratch the scar on his cheek. That morning, on Fauzia's advice he'd been up early and visited a private GP in the city centre. One of Malton's many contacts. It had cost him a hundred pounds for a consult but he'd left with a prescription for antibiotics and a warning about the dire consequences of not keeping his wound clean. The young woman in the coral uniform closed the laptop and smiled across the desk at Dean.

Dean had been in work early. Staring at the map on Malton's wall and thinking about last night.

Vikki had Big Wacky's number. Could it be that she'd simply forgotten he was in her phone? She'd given him Big Wacky's name to help track down Olivia. Why not his number too?

Dean thought how eager Vikki had been for him not to tell Malton about what he was up to. At the time he had been secretly flattered she trusted him to do it alone. Now he felt sick.

He was wondering just what he should tell Malton when his boss had turned up and given him the name Lynne Harris.

Glad of the distraction, by lunchtime he had found out about her company, her husband, looked at her house on Google Street View and booked himself an appointment at his nearest Femme Visage under the pretext of wanting to buy some vouchers for his mum's birthday.

Dean's mum worked ten hours a day as a carer visiting people all over Manchester. Changing beds, making meals, cleaning bathrooms and more often than not being the sole point of human contact for her clients in an otherwise long and empty day.

She hardly had time for sleep, never mind ten two-hour sessions injecting fillers into her face.

But as a cover story it was good enough.

'Your mum's very lucky to have such a thoughtful son,' trilled the young woman behind the desk.

'It all looks very . . .' Dean searched for the word. 'It looks very professional.'

The woman beamed. 'All Femme Visage staff have to complete a full training course and earn their Certificate in Advanced Aesthetics.'

'And Lynne Harris runs those courses?'

The woman nodded fondly. 'Mrs Harris supervises the courses personally. She's my inspiration.'

'She seems amazing,' lied Dean.

'Oh she is,' gushed the woman. 'Do you know she started Femme Visage in her front room? Selling fillers to the mums of children in her daughter's nursery group?'

Dean nodded and smiled. He had no idea why Malton needed to know about Lynne Harris and after the visit from Fauzia Malik the night before he desperately needed to get ahead of whatever it was that was going on between Vikki and Big Wacky.

Up until he'd found Big Wacky's number in the phone he thought he'd been falling for Vikki. Now he had a horrible suspicion she had simply been the bait.

Whatever Lynne Harris was about, it was wasting valuable time. Sooner rather than later he would have to tell Malton about Fauzia's visit. When that happened it would become much harder to track down Olivia without Malton discovering that he was moonlighting for Leon Walker's daughter.

'I think my mum would love to meet her. Is it possible to get a personal appointment? I think she'd really be thrilled.'

Something like a look of concern crossed the woman's face.

Dean quickly followed up. 'My mum's birthday is next weekend. If there's any chance she would be about at all? At any of the locations?'

The woman did her best to smile through her obvious nerves. 'Mrs Harris is currently on a four-month sabbatical.'

Up until now nothing about this meeting had seemed the least bit interesting or important. But the look on the woman's face as she said the phrase 'four-month sabbatical' set alarms bells ringing.

'Is she OK?' said Dean, trying to sound worried.

'She is taking time away from the company to work on her inner goals of actualisation, visualisation and self-realisation.'

The woman beamed as if she'd just negotiated an especially difficult tongue-twister.

'Where has she gone?'

'I'm afraid that's confidential.' She smiled. 'So what can I put your mother down for? Lips? Eyes? Forehead? How about the whole facial rejuvenation package? I'd love to sign her up for something.'

The woman's voice had an edge of desperation to it. Under all the fillers in her face Dean detected more than a few worry lines.

Dean left with two hundred pounds' worth of vouchers and a sense that there was something he wasn't being told.

He knew the first question Malton would ask was where had Lynne Harris gone for four months?

But Dean had far more pressing questions of his own. Starting with why Vikki Walker had Big Wacky's number in her phone.

35

'Everyone's on the rob. Everyone.'

Malton sat across from Callum Hester in the small, windowless room set aside for visits from his legal team. The guards were outside but couldn't hear a thing.

Callum tilted his head and smiled fondly back at Malton. For nearly a decade Callum had dominated the importation and supply of drugs from South America to North Africa and then from North Africa across the water to mainland Europe and beyond. He'd forged links with German and Dutch gangs on the continent, corrupted police officers in half a dozen countries and gone as far as to travel all the way to the homes of the cartels in South America.

Callum Hester was as fearless as he was ruthless. He wasn't scared of anyone or anything and so it never occurred to him not to do the things that no one else would dare. That had been his downfall. While his peers fled to Dubai, Callum refused to leave Liverpool. The city he considered his own.

'You know this, Craig. I know you know this. Don't mean you suddenly start killing people,' said Callum, a twinkle in his eyes.

Callum was in his fifties and prison life clearly agreed with him. With nothing but time he had been working out non-stop. Already a large man before he went inside, Callum had shredded down and now bulged with the solid muscle of a man thirty years his junior.

Despite his size and his reputation, Callum had the native charm of the city of his birth. Whether he was complimenting or threatening, he did it with a lightness and a charisma that had wrong-footed both allies and enemies alike.

While Malton would never think of Callum as a friend, Callum was as near as he'd ever come to meeting his equal.

Back when he'd been starting out, the constant turf wars between Liverpool and Manchester had brought Malton into Callum's orbit. Both men recognising each other as the apex predator that they were. Malton knew Callum could burn down half the city with just a word and Callum was quick to realise that having a man like Malton in Manchester was much better for business than a protracted gang war.

Callum's reach was near limitless. There was nothing and no one who was safe if Callum Hester turned against them. Inside prison the only way the authorities could curb that power was to isolate him. From other prisoners, from guards and staff, and especially from visitors.

The only two people Callum Hester had seen in the last five years were the guard who unlocked his cell in the morning and locked him up at night and the lawyer who was working on his appeal – Bea Wallace.

Bea had made sure Malton got in as one of Callum's legal team. He didn't know what strings she pulled but he knew that he owed her big time. Next time she suggested going into business together it was going to be a lot harder to say no.

'Danny Mitchum was stealing from you?' asked Malton.

Callum burst out laughing, shaking his head as if hearing a particularly good joke.

'Danny Mitchum was one of my biggest customers. He bought wholesale. I mean the entire shipment wholesale. You know? The amount of money that lad was putting our way, so what if he nicked a little round the edges? You don't think every little toerag who works Danny's operation isn't dipping into his pocket? It's how it is. You of all people know that, Craig. Keeps you in business.'

Nothing Callum said came as news to Malton. It was true. The drugs world wasn't known for the probity and reliability of the people who worked in it. Everyone stole from everyone. Scores were settled, sometimes with money, sometimes with words, sometimes somewhere remote where no one could hear the screams.

Callum had come alive in the half hour Malton had been in the room. Malton knew he was the first person aside from Bea that Callum had spoken to face to face in years. Between smuggled phones and Bea he still ran his empire, but the minute Malton had walked in the room it was clear the one thing that Callum didn't have. As much as Malton needed Callum's information, it was a sign of his respect for Callum that he gave him what he so obviously craved – human contact.

The prison service knew what it was doing keeping Callum Hester in isolation. It wasn't just about stopping his business. It was about breaking him. Punishing him. He would only live so long but until he died they could make it hurt.

'So how's Manchester treating you, Craig?' said Callum changing the subject.

'Aside from Danny Mitchum getting blown to pieces?'

Callum frowned. Disappointed to be dragged back on topic.

He sat back and stared down at Malton. His nostrils flared as he took a breath, choosing his next words carefully.

'Listen, Craig, you know I'd rather kill my own than grass. So when I tell you what I'm about to tell you, it's cos it's you. We got history. Don't matter that our James isn't here no more. Far as I'm concerned, you and me, we're family.'

For a moment the twinkle in Callum's eyes dimmed. He took a breath and dragged a heavy hand across his face, as if wiping away tears.

'I never stopped looking for the bastards that did that to our lad.'

Malton wondered when Callum would bring up his younger brother.

Back when James was murdered Malton and Callum had turned Liverpool upside down looking for his killers. James was nothing to do with the underworld. Whether it was his lover Malton or his brother Callum who got him killed didn't matter. They shared an unspoken bond of responsibility to avenge the man they both loved.

But despite Callum's muscle and Malton's cunning they came back empty-handed and James's death went unanswered.

James had taught Malton the true price of family.

'I never stopped looking either,' said Malton.

Callum pushed his chair away and leaned back. He shuddered, as if shaking off the dust of their terrible past. When he leaned forward once more he was back to being Callum Hester – a god among criminals.

'Three months ago Danny Mitchum stopped buying,' said Callum.

Malton sat up.

Callum looked uncomfortable but he continued. 'He bought regularly. Ships came in, he'd buy the lot. Huge amounts. One of our best customers. Like I said, so what if he nicked a little here or there? I always thought of it like casinos, how they give you the drinks and the food? Long as you keep playing the game. House always wins.'

Malton's mind started to assemble a timeline of what he was being told. For the entire time he'd been guarding Danny, his organisation had been cut off from their main supplier.

'Thing is, the year before he overbought. Pinched other people's shipments. Paid nearly double for them. I couldn't say no to that. Fuck knows what's going on with that one. Ask me, he's a bit . . .'

Callum spun his finger around his ear in the universal hand gesture of 'cracked in the head'.

Whatever else he was, Danny was clever. He'd stockpiled enough product that when he stopped buying there would be nothing to tip Malton off he was up to something.

'So if you stopped dealing with him, who was his new supplier?'

Callum shrugged. 'Much as it pains me to say it, in here, I know fuck all. I get bits and bobs from Bea but if it carries on like this, if I ever do get out I'm going to be starting from scratch.' Callum burst into a wide grin. 'You should join me. Be like old times.'

Malton spent his entire life running from 'old times'. 'When's the appeal?' he asked.

'End of the year. Few more months yet.' For a moment Callum looked sad. He glanced round the small room. A larger-than-life character reduced to an animal in a cage. 'I know I did some terrible things. But I never did anything like what they did to James. I never, Craig. You know me. I'm one of the good guys.'

Malton wondered if the people who'd crossed Callum Hester would describe him like that. The policemen targeted in their homes. The junkies tortured over drug debts. The dozens of men who were beaten and worse in Callum's fruitless hunt for his brother's killers.

Callum sensed Malton's silence and eager to get him back onside said, 'Whoever it was he started going to, you know two things. One: they were bigger than me, and two: they were big enough to move on Danny Mitchum. Someone that big? That's a short, short list.'

Malton knew he was right. Currently it was a list of none.

'I'll miss Danny. He was a laugh. I remember last time I heard from him. Still in here of course. He'd leave voicemails and Bea would bring me a phone in to hear them. Mad little kid.'

Malton had to hand it to Bea, she knew what her clients wanted and she delivered.

'You talk about being on the rob. Goes both ways,' said Callum. 'Last I heard he was bitching about his own people nicking from him.' He laughed. 'Like I said, everyone's at it.'

Malton felt the tiniest glimmer of something useful. He reached out to grab it. 'Did he say who was nicking from him?'

Callum sucked his bottom lip as he thought back to the call. Then as the information returned to him a broad smile broke over his giant face. 'Some guy who worked for him. Into a bit of the old boxing I think.'

'MMA?'

'Yeah, that's the lad. You know him?'

36

Keisha had spent all morning pushing her cart around The Sentinel, cleaning rooms and scrubbing floors.

No one paid her the least bit of attention. Diane Okunkwe was not part of The Sentinel. She wasn't there to help the people who could afford the obscene fees to get over the addiction to whatever it was they used to make the pain of their privileged lives a little more bearable.

Diane Okunkwe was there to clean the carpets, scrub the toilets and plump the pillows, merging into the background as she did so.

Even the staff ignored Keisha. They looked away or even right through her.

Just as she'd hoped.

She'd steered clear of Lynne Harris. There was no contact with the outside world allowed at The Sentinel but even so, after bumping into Craig the night before she was going to be extra careful. Her plan was in motion now. There could be no room for errors.

It was just after lunchtime when she finally found herself alone outside the door to Emily's room.

Through the window she could see Emily exactly as before – lying asleep in a hospital bed. Completely alone.

As a cleaner, Keisha had every reason to be in the room but even so as she opened the door she couldn't help but take a look around to make sure that no one saw her as she slipped inside.

The lights were low and the curtains drawn. A soft table lamp shone over Emily's sleeping face. Her skin was alabaster white and her hair dark brown, almost black. She was beautiful, no two ways about it.

She reminded Keisha of Snow White. After she'd eaten the apple.

Like all the other addicts at The Sentinel, money had shielded her from the ravages of her illness. The same money that now was curing her in the most luxurious conditions imaginable.

Emily was on a medically supported detox. She had been given drugs to ease her off the heroin in her system.

Keisha knew it was heroin because it was Keisha who had given it to her. A parting gift after the last time she and Craig crossed paths.

Emily stirred. Her eyes screwed tight and soft lips opened and closed as she muttered something indecipherable. She was dreaming.

Keisha froze to the spot and watched until she settled down.

She couldn't do anything with Emily in this state. She needed her on her feet. Moving and biddable.

Keisha searched the room for medical charts. Unlike an NHS hospital there was nothing on view. She supposed the brittle pride of The Sentinel's clientele meant that everything was kept as discreet as possible. Letting everyone convince themselves that they were somehow different from the junkies clogging up streets and hostels all over Manchester.

Once more Emily began to mutter softly. Her dark eyebrows furrowed and her shoulders shifted.

She turned in the bed, sloughing off the covers.

It was then Keisha saw it.

There on Emily's arm was the telltale bump of a subdermal implant. Immediately Keisha knew exactly what drugs Emily was on.

Buprenorphine. A painkiller given to opioid addicts to ease the pain of withdrawal. Unlike other painkillers, it had a ceiling dose, meaning that users couldn't take it in ever-increasing amounts. It was junkie-proof.

The subdermal implant meant a dosage nearly one hundred times stronger than morphine. It was a powerful tool but it also meant drowsiness and memory loss for those taking it. Hence Emily's troubled dreams.

But none of that mattered to Keisha. What mattered most was why she was on it.

There were two drugs used to treat morphine withdrawal in heroin addicts. The most common drug was methadone. It had its drawbacks but it was tried and tested. She'd seen other patients at The Sentinel taking it.

Buprenorphine was much rarer. It lasted longer in the system and was less suited to a dynamic withdrawal.

So much so that there was only one category of recovering addicts for whom buprenorphine was routinely prescribed.

Methadone had one huge side effect. It has been shown to lead to neonatal abstinence syndrome. Babies were born addicted to the methadone taken by their mothers. Whereas buprenorphine didn't cross over to the unborn child.

Keisha looked down at the tiny bump in Emily's arm. This changed everything.

Gently she pulled back the covers and looked down at the almost imperceptible swelling in Emily's tummy.

She was pregnant.

37

Fauzia watched the young man wince as the nurse wrapped his horrifically burned arms in a protective layer of cling film before slipping his burned hands into clear plastic bags and taping these round his wrists.

He couldn't have been more than twenty years old but, lying shivering on the hospital bed, he looked like a child.

Fauzia was nearly at the end of a non-stop shift when he'd come in. A rough sleeper who'd been smoking spice in his tent when he'd passed out and set the tent on fire.

Luckily for him, he was one of the increasing number of rough sleepers who'd started moving their tents onto the pavements of Bolton town centre. A council street sweeper had spotted the flames and dragged him clear. Saved his life.

As tired as Fauzia felt, the young man looked worse. His skin was pitted and scabbed. It hung on him, grey and lifeless. He had a scruffy beard and his hair was greasy and lank over his scalp.

An indescribable smell came off his naked flesh. Stronger than the airless smell of disinfectant that filled the hospital. It was deep and wicked and spoke of a human being utterly adrift.

Fauzia did her best not to notice it as she finished her work on him.

Both arms and hands were badly burned. For the next six to eight months he'd need constant care and attention.

From the look of him Fauzia imagined he'd not had either of those things for a long time.

As she thanked the nurses and went off shift, she couldn't help but wonder if the spice that had burned his tent down and nearly cost him his life had come from her brother Waqar – Big Wacky.

After the visit from the police the day before Fauzia had spent the night at her parents' before heading straight to the hospital. She had scrubs in her locker at work and after changing into them let herself be sucked into the whirlwind of chaos that was the Saturday shift at Royal Bolton A&E.

Drunks, fights, heart attacks and road accidents. From the moment she stepped in the door she hadn't stopped. She'd found it a welcome relief.

But now that she was coming off shift, suddenly everything started to come back to her. Waqar's burning car. Her visit to Malton Security. The lies she told the police and Waqar convincing their parents that he had it all under control.

Exhausted, she risked closing her eyes and letting the promise of sleep lightly brush up against her.

In that split second she saw the face of the man as he tumbled into the meat grinder.

Fauzia's eyes shot back open. Her heart was racing.

She had imagined that somehow she'd be able to get a handle on things. Calm them down and restore some kind of order. She saw now that there was never any order. Her brother's world was endless chaos and now she had been dragged into it.

Not wanting to return to her empty flat or her parents' questions, she sat in the staff room decompressing on her phone.

As a councillor she had access to various online resources and she used them now, searching the minutes of the licensing committee for every mention of Malton Security.

Half a dozen incidents involving firearms. Employees charged and cleared of GBH on three separate occasions. Absolved of any wrongdoing following the drugs death of a seventeen-year-old clubber. And most tellingly – rolling contracts to provide security on an ongoing basis for several council buildings.

It was nothing she didn't already know.

Fauzia had hoped that bringing Craig Malton on board would put her mind at ease. Quell her instinct to try and fix the problem herself. Instead it had simply given her one more thing to worry about.

She told herself there was nothing she could do now except let things take their course. She had done all she could.

Whatever Waqar was planning, it was better she didn't know.

The best thing she could do now was head home, shower off the smell of her shift and sleep.

Before she could do any of that her phone lit up with a call.

Fauzia's heart jumped. The steady, doctor's hands that had seen her through her shift deserted her as she fumbled to answer.

'Hello?'

On the other end of the line a posh, woman's voice said, 'Hello, Fauzia! This is Sophie calling from Labour Party HQ. I wonder if you'd be free to pop over and see us this evening?'

38

Malton looked down at the black, irregular-shaped lump of carbon on the table in front of him.

'That's Danny Mitchum,' said Benton. 'Or at least we think it is.'

Malton had never visited the labs used by Greater Manchester Police before. He'd had no reason to, much less any way of getting inside. Now that Benton was back in GMP's good books, she seemed a lot less concerned about keeping her connection to Malton private. The way she saw it she'd been squashed for doing her job to the letter of the law, so if they were going to come for her again she may as well get the benefit of pushing the envelope a little.

That meant Malton got his visitor's lanyard and was ushered through what looked a lot like an old university building and into where GMP processed the bodies of crime victims.

'DNA?' asked Malton.

Benton laughed. 'He's fucking charcoal. He's a briquette. If that even is him. Seems he was hiding out in a secret room at the back of the warehouse.'

Benton let that hang for a moment. 'Don't worry, Craig, you're nothing if not cautious.'

'What about the gunmen?' asked Malton.

Benton rolled her eyes. 'Lots of bullet holes, lots of bullet casings and that's your lot.'

That would mean Danny didn't even take any of them down with him. He hadn't gone out in a blaze of glory. He'd been put down like a dog.

'How do you know this is him?' said Malton looking down at Danny Mitchum's earthly remains.

'Best guess. Science is a bit like detective work. You got to tell everyone you know what you're doing. Throw in some jargon and a title and maybe you might start believing you actually do have a clue. But at the end of the day, beyond a certain point, no one knows anything.'

Malton knew a few things. He knew that he was out of suspects. Keisha and Stevie's reactions to the news of Danny's death was enough to nudge them into the clear for now. And while it was true Danny had been stealing from the Scouse Mafia, Callum himself had shrugged it off as the cost of business and said how much he'd miss Danny.

He also knew he needed to find out why Danny had overbought from Callum Hester then stopped buying altogether. Had he found a new supplier or was he winding his operation down and tricking Malton into protecting him while he set up his retirement? Either way the plan had gone wrong in the worst way possible. Most of all he knew he was running out of time.

Malton had felt bad about not telling Benton he had been hiding Danny. Benton had risked her job dozens of times to help him out. It wasn't like Malton hadn't returned the favour, with tip-offs and inside information. Then there was the time he'd learned a violent rapist with a grudge was stalking Benton's house. Benton still didn't even know about that one. Malton liked to have a few of his own secrets. Especially when they involved a rapist getting handed over to some especially brutal men with a strong sense of irony and a very private, very secure BDSM dungeon.

After meeting Callum Hester his first phone call had been to Benton. Hester was the sort of man the police never got anywhere near. Sure they arrested him on a trumped-up assault charge but they had no more idea what he was planning now than they did when he was at large.

Even Benton had been impressed with his debrief. So much so that to show just how thankful she was, she'd invited him here to view what was left of Danny Mitchum.

'Funny thing is,' said Benton, 'there's been nothing. Biggest player in the city dies, you'd think all the shitbags would be climbing over their own mothers to take up the slack.'

'But?' said Malton.

'Nothing. Not the Scousers, not Salford, not any of the Asian crews.'

'Maybe they don't know,' said Malton.

Benton gave him a look. 'Or maybe while you had him locked up you were working double time to make it look like he was still hiding around every corner waiting to pounce.'

Malton knew Benton wasn't asking; she had already figured it out. Danny's operation only worked if Danny was there. Scaring the shit out of everyone from the top down. Take away Danny and there was no loyalty.

Malton was quietly pleased that his efforts to cover Danny's absence were still proving so effective.

'Of course,' said Benton, 'you'll only get so far bullshitting the dregs that make up Danny's operation. Eventually even drug-addled street dealers will start to wonder when they last saw their boss turn up to a collection in person.'

She was bang on the money. The belief that Danny was still alive and out there somewhere would only last so long. As soon as word got out he was dead, finding his killer would become academic. The whole of Manchester would erupt.

'I'm going to take another look at Danny's crew,' said Malton.

'The meth users and the domestic abusers? That'll be fun,' said Benton.

Malton wasn't looking forward to retracing his steps but unless he found out who had turned the most feared man in Manchester into a lump of carbon then he could well be next. Until then everything else was on hold. Thanks to Callum Hester he at least had somewhere to start – the MMA fighter who got away: Bradley Wyke.

184

That just left one thread hanging.

Malton looked down at the tray filled with Danny's remains and casually as possible said, 'Keisha's back.'

Benton turned, her eyes wide. 'You kept that one quiet, didn't you? When?'

'Bumped into her last night. Calling herself Lynne Harris.'

Benton suddenly sounded deadly serious. 'Just be careful, Craig? Remember what happened last time.'

Malton could hardly forget it. Keisha had cost him Emily and nearly killed Dean. He couldn't imagine what she was planning to do for an encore.

They stood in silence, pondering all that was left of Danny Mitchum.

Finally Malton said, 'I should be going.' He turned to Benton with a loaded look. 'Unless you've got any better leads?'

From the pained expression on her face Malton could tell there *was* something. Some piece of information she hadn't planned on telling him. He wondered if his news about Keisha had changed her mind.

'I tell you this thing, you need to promise me the minute you get anything, I mean *anything*, you tell me first?' said Benton warily.

'You know I'm good for it,' said Malton.

Benton didn't look at all convinced but carried on nonetheless. 'Rumour is there's a bigger player out there. One who supplies the Asians, maybe Salford too. Someone bigger than even the Scousers. Scary thing is we have zero intel. He's been operating through an encrypted phone network, which means we have no way of monitoring him. It's like we can see the waves he's making but we can't see him. He's everywhere. Fingers in everything. And all we have to go on is a name.'

Benton looked down at the fist-sized lump of black matter that was once Danny Mitchum and shook her head, chuckling at the absurdity of it all.

She turned back to Malton. 'Calls himself Galahad.'

39

Fauzia hated visiting the headquarters of Manchester Labour Party. Despite being in power in Manchester for decades, or maybe because of it, the Labour Party had made their base of operations a converted office building in Hulme.

The Wesley Centre was owned by the Methodist church. In keeping with the rest of rebuilt Hulme it was a low-rise, brick building in the style that had seemed thrusting and modern for around six months in the mid-Nineties.

To Fauzia's eye it was worse than anonymous. She thought of the beautiful mosques back in Bolton. Each one built by subscription from the community and each one bigger than the last. The rivalry between Indian and Pakistani Muslims leading to an arms race of extravagant architecture. Defiant, glorious statements of belonging. Elegant domes springing upwards above rows of terraces. The mills and factories were gone but the mosques were still there.

Fauzia wasn't overtly religious but she appreciated her community's unapologetic display of pride.

The Wesley Centre inspired no such awe.

Hulme was also a nightmare for parking. Its proximity to the city centre along with the density of housing meant that almost every other street was residents' parking. Fauzia had driven around for nearly a quarter of an hour before finding somewhere she wouldn't feel anxious leaving her BMW.

She had barely had chance to sleep over the past forty-eight hours but the adrenaline from the phone call was just about keeping her moving as she walked through the backstreets of Hulme to the Wesley Centre.

Hulme had been demolished and rebuilt twice in the last fifty years. The iteration that finally stuck was one of unambitiously modest, brick houses and endless cul-de-sacs. There was a high street of sorts as well as a covered market and a giant ASDA where once there'd been a particularly rough high school.

Fauzia was a Bolton girl but she knew the urban history of Manchester. As someone active in the Labour Party she'd seen how politics had shaped the face of the city. The desire to turn a stolid, northern industrial hub into a thrusting city of the future. All glass and steel and money – wherever it might come from.

Manchester was rebranding itself, turning towards the world as an international city at the same time as its suburbs were beset with poverty, hunger and crime.

Fauzia truly believed in Manchester. Not the Manchester of the brochures and the Chinese investment fund money but the Manchester that she grew up with. The city not that different from Bolton where her father had made his fortune. A city built on people, not slogans.

It was why she'd got into politics. To protect what mattered to her.

She was buzzed into the Wesley Centre. The overwarm air of a modern office washed over her. Ringing phones, raised voices and workers' chatter from the half dozen organisations who shared the Wesley Centre filled her ears. Labour didn't even have the building to themselves.

The moment she set foot in the Labour Party office she could feel something in the air. Staff at desks turned to look at her. People smiled as they passed. But everyone kept their distance.

Fauzia's mind began to spin. Was this it? Had she got the nomination?

Before she had a chance to go any deeper down that rabbit hole the door to an office on the far side of the room opened and Tahir Akhtar emerged followed by a professional-looking white woman.

The woman shook Tahir's hand and he gave her a tight smile before walking through the office towards Fauzia.

He stopped as he drew level with her. 'I don't need the Labour Party to take this seat,' he whispered to her, the fierce smile still on his face.

Then he turned to face the room, grabbed her wrist and without warning jerked it upwards. 'Let's hear it for the new MP for Farnworth and Great Lever!'

The office erupted into applause.

Fauzia did her best to look humble, strong, grateful and excited all at the same time. It was all she could do not to burst out laughing in surprise at what was happening to her.

Before the applause had even died down, Tahir had seen himself out.

Someone handed Fauzia a bouquet of flowers and the next half hour was spent having the same, happy conversation over and over as everyone involved rushed to congratulate her.

Fauzia felt wide awake. She'd done it. A girl from Daubhill was going to be an MP. Of course there was the election but that was a formality. Farnworth and Great Lever was a safe Labour seat.

It was only when she was walking back to her car that she turned her mind to Tahir's words. *He didn't need the Labour Party.*

Suddenly the euphoria was gone. Tahir was going to run as an independent. He was going to split the vote. Maybe she'd still win but now she wasn't being handed the keys to Westminster. Now she would be dragged into a vicious local battle for control of Farnworth and Great Lever.

A battle that she knew would quickly turn dirty.

Tahir would use whatever he could. That meant Waqar. His money, his business and what he was doing the night he and Fauzia killed a man.

Fauzia was so terrified that for a moment she thought she'd forgotten where she parked.

Glancing up and down the street she checked again. This was the spot. Outside the Zion Centre, near the Rolls-Royce memorial.

It was gone. Her car had been stolen.

Then it hit her. The one thing she absolutely couldn't forget to do. The one thing that in all the chaos had slipped her mind entirely.

The bin liner was still in the boot.

The bin liner full of her and Waqar's bloodstained clothes.

40

The last time Malton saw Bradley Wyke he had been fleeing into the night.

Bradley clearly had something to hide, but that didn't mean he killed Danny Mitchum. Men like Bradley were always up to something. If it was true that he was stealing from Danny then that would be reason enough to flee.

Stealing from Danny Mitchum was a bad move but would Bradley double down? Would he think the best way out of his dilemma was to kill Danny? Malton doubted someone like Bradley Wyke would even dream of such a move. Much less be able to pull it off.

The same couldn't be said about Galahad. Assuming he was as real as Benton seemed to think he was. A super-supplier. Someone above the entire supply chain. Someone like that wouldn't think twice about moving on Danny Mitchum.

Finally Malton had a lead worth chasing. But first he had to satisfy himself by paying a visit to the one that got away.

Malton and Dean were parked down the road from Bradley's gym. Malton had been here several times, looking for Bradley. It was less a gym and more a blank space beneath a railway arch just beyond what was left of the red light district underneath Piccadilly station.

The double doors to the gym were wide open, revealing a space scrubbed clean and fitted out with minimal gym equipment. The Manchester sunshine shone through the cold. They sat in the car and watched Bradley working with his client – a fiercely energetic young woman. Bradley was barking a few inches from her ear while she went through a series of push-ups, burpees and kettlebell swings.

Malton and Dean both ate their stuffed bacon barms in silence. The irony of their greasy, calorific breakfast was not lost on them as they watched Bradley bully the calories out of his client.

'I got what you asked for about Lynne Harris,' said Dean, finishing his bacon barm.

Malton looked at him encouragingly and Dean continued.

'CEO of a beauty company. Worth a few million at least. Big house in Chorlton. I dropped in to book some treatments and was told she was on leave. For the next four months.'

Malton raised an eyebrow. Ordinarily he could imagine a millionaire CEO treating herself to nearly half a year of holiday. But coming alongside bumping into Keisha using her name to gatecrash an event it was worth further investigation.

'I know,' said Dean. 'I'm looking into where she's disappeared to.'

Malton smiled. This is exactly how he hoped Dean would turn out. An extension of his own thought process. A trusted second who could take over when Malton ran out of hours in the day. After Dean's debrief about the events of the night Danny was killed, Malton had said no more about it. He preferred to keep Dean guessing. Have him feel the need to overcompensate for what in fairness had been an impossible situation.

Wherever Lynne Harris was, Dean would track her down.

Right now he had to talk to Bradley Wyke. To cross him off the list of suspects in Danny Mitchum's death and in doing so see what insights could be squeezed out of him as to the ongoing state of Danny's operation.

Even if Bradley didn't kill Danny, he had been working for him. It was possible he knew something about Galahad and didn't even realise it.

Bradley's client was finishing up. She was towelling herself down and beaming with the post-workout endorphin rush.

Malton waited until she'd got into a Land Rover and headed off towards the ring road before he got out of his car, Dean close behind.

Bradley was standing in the entrance to his gym on his phone.

Malton covered the distance quickly enough that he was only a few feet away when Bradley looked up.

He still wore the signs of his fight a few nights before. His face puffy and red, one eye a livid purple colour.

Bradley instantly recognised Malton. He also knew he was cornered. His phone went straight into the pocket of his track-suit bottoms and he assumed a fighting stance.

Malton stopped dead. Behind him Dean tried to look like realistic backup.

Malton held up his hands in surrender. 'I just want to talk,' he said.

Bradley took all of three seconds to consider this before launching a flying kick towards Malton, who stepped aside, grabbed Bradley as he passed and tossed him onto the hard tarmac of the road.

Bradley hit the ground, rolled and scrambled to his feet.

He got straight back into a fighting pose.

Aware that Dean was hovering, looking unsure what to add to the situation, Malton raised a hand for him to stand down.

'I don't want to fight you,' said Malton as Bradley lunged at him, swinging punches left and right.

Malton raised his guard but only in defence. The punches he couldn't dodge he blocked with his thick forearms. 'I've not got all day,' said Malton, a slight impatience creeping into his voice.

Bradley was a trained MMA fighter. He spent hours every week practising his craft. But Bradley was easily four or five stone lighter than Malton. A lightweight at best. For a man the size of Bradley, no matter how well he trained, going up against a man the size of Malton, there was only ever one outcome.

Bradley stopped advancing. He stayed in a boxer's stance, up on his toes, moving, essaying, readying his next attack.

A few yards behind him a pink Mini was pulling up.

Looking past Bradley, Malton saw Stevie Mitchum's girlfriend Miyah Mai climb out of the Mini, dressed in a tracksuit the same shade of pink as her car. She was on her phone.

Oblivious to what was going on behind him Bradley took Malton's distraction as his cue to launch another attack. He swung for Malton's head with a high kick. Malton elegantly ducked and smashed an upper cut into Bradley's guts.

Bradley staggered back, barely able to keep on his feet.

At that same moment Miyah Mai looked up from her phone and saw a winded Bradley bent double next to Dean and Malton.

She turned and started to run.

'Get on it,' ordered Malton.

Dean turned and took off after Miyah Mai. She was small but she was fast. She'd already reached the end of the row of railway arches and had jinked right, heading down the long road that would eventually bring her into Gorton via a series of unloved office buildings.

Dean disappeared after her.

Malton turned back to Bradley. The smaller man was gasping for air, reeling from the punch.

'Can I ask you my questions now?'

41

Dean tore round the corner and under the railway bridge after Miyah Mai.

Despite his long legs he wasn't a natural runner. It took an immense amount of focus for him to ensure all four limbs were doing what he wanted them to do and doing it all at the same time.

As he heaved in air, his mouth wide open, he felt the skin around the wound on his cheek pull taut.

Up ahead of him Miyah Mai was receding into the distance. She moved like a gymnast, her whole body a tightly wound machine.

She ran away from town, past cheap office space and a lone burger van touting for business amongst the MOT garages beneath the railway arches.

Dean sprinted past the burger van and watched as Miyah Mai dived down a back alley. Obviously she hadn't spent as much of her youth as Dean had wandering the streets, soaking up the city and its secrets.

She'd just run down a dead end.

Dean slowed just a little, safe in the knowledge she was going nowhere. He composed himself. Compared to him she was tiny. But that didn't mean he wanted it to get physical. Especially not with a woman.

The last time that happened he'd ended up getting shot in the face.

As Dean caught his breath he felt glad of the distraction from the gnawing realisation that time was running out for him to tell Malton not just about Fauzia's visit to HQ but about his search for Olivia and Big Wacky.

Dean slowed to a trot and worked out in his head what he'd say to Miyah Mai. How he'd take the heat out of the situation and talk her into coming with him back to Malton where this whole thing could be worked out.

All of this became moot when rounding the corner he saw a flash of movement as Miyah Mai sprung from behind a communal bin and with both hands swung a traffic cone as hard she could at Dean's knees.

Tangled up and in excruciating pain, Dean hit the ground as Miyah Mai vaulted over him and started running back the way she came, a blur of pink.

Dean knew where she was going – to her car.

Heaving with exhaustion and agony he hauled himself back upright and, limping along, took off after her.

He saw her hurtle past the burger van and back round the corner of the railway bridge. She could run.

The prospect of losing her trumped the burning sensation in his lungs. He pelted along, his legs barely keeping him upright.

He rounded the corner in time to see Miyah Mai diving into her car.

Malton's car was there but Dean couldn't see him or Bradley anywhere.

Miyah Mai was still nearly a hundred metres away. Dean hammered towards the car, telling himself that the fastest a man had ever run a hundred metres was just under ten seconds. If he could just get near that time then he might have a chance.

But then the car engine started.

Defeated, Dean stopped in the street. There was one way in and one way out. His final desperate plan was to block the car with his exhausted, broken body.

Up ahead, Malton emerged from the gym under the arches. At least now if he got run over, Malton would see that he'd tried.

The engine kept revving. And revving. Then with a hideous screech of metal on metal the pink Mini started to drag itself round to face Dean.

That was when Dean saw the wheel clamp. While he was chasing Miyah May, Malton must have put it on her car. He always carried one in the boot of his Volvo. Now every tiny movement of the car dragged the metal of the clamp up and into the guts of the wheel arch.

The noise became more and more shrill as the engine began to overheat. Every metre the car moved, more pieces were sheared from the chassis until eventually with a defeated 'phut' the engine gave up and died.

Dean walked up to the car. Miyah Mai was still clutching the steering wheel with both hands, staring straight ahead, locked in flight.

Dean tapped on the window. The sound shook her out of her trance. She looked up at Dean – breathless, limping and covered in the filth of the back alley where he'd fallen.

She smiled apologetically.

'Sorry,' she said.

42

Keisha was sure she hadn't been found out. There was no way they could have worked out she wasn't Diane Okunkwe. As instructed, Diane had texted her to let her know that she had taken the money and returned to Ghana. As far as The Sentinel was concerned, there was no other Diane Okunkwe than the woman in the tabard and cheap jeans standing in the waiting room of the facility director, ready for him to call her into his office.

Since discovering that Emily was pregnant Keisha had spent the next twenty-four hours passing through shock to dismay until finally arriving at excitement.

A baby would change everything.

Her original plan had been to take Craig apart. Dismantle the legend and break the man. Targeting anyone and anything close to him. Loved ones, clients, anyone who relied on Craig Malton to protect them was fair game. Then once word was out that Craig was no longer quite as untouchable as he once was, she'd let the Manchester underworld finish the job.

Whoever had killed Danny Mitchum had given her a head start but now that Emily was pregnant the plan would have to change.

Keisha would still break Craig. Leave him less than she found him all those years ago. But now, before she did that she would give him one last chance to have everything he ever wanted.

The door to the facility director's office swung open and Lynne Harris walked out. As she passed Keisha she gave her a tight, smug smile.

Keisha looked back at her blankly. Her head was too full of grand plans to give a moment's thought to someone like Lynne Harris.

'I'm ready for you,' said the facility director, holding the door open for Keisha.

First Emily's baby, now this. The Sentinel was certainly keeping her busy.

Half an hour later, having been fired from The Sentinel on trumped-up charges of stealing from a guest's room, Keisha was on her way home. She had paid for a taxi to drive her back to Harpurhey. The whole way back she wore her sunglasses and an enormous smile.

She and Craig were finally going to get to be a family.

43

Fauzia was exhausted. After getting a taxi home from Hulme she'd spent the rest of the evening agonising over whether or not to report the theft of her car to the police.

If it got out that she didn't report it, there would be questions. But if she did report it stolen and the police found it and what was in the boot then the questions would be even worse.

She kept telling herself it must just be bad luck. She'd parked an expensive car in Hulme. Someone took a chance and stole it. Deep down she didn't believe it for a second. It was far too much of a coincidence. But she knew if she fully embraced the terrifying possibilities of what really happened to her car, the fear would overwhelm her.

She couldn't believe that she'd forgotten the one thing that was completely within her control. It would have been a matter of minutes to dump the bag with the bloody clothes in the incinerator at Royal Bolton. Instead whoever had taken her car now had evidence of her part in a murder.

She had no choice. She would pass it on to Malton Security. The biggest risk was already behind her. She had made the initial approach. She had nothing to lose handing this over to Malton. For all she knew the people who stole her car were the same ones who were after Waqar.

For the rest of the night, Fauzia had been unable to sleep. She lay in bed in her flat, her brain spooling through all the different scenarios.

Just a few hours earlier she'd been as good as told she was on her way to becoming an MP.

That seemed like a very long time ago now. Everything was coming apart and people like Tahir would be waiting to see her fall.

Every time it felt like she was about to tip over into the sleep she so desperately needed, she would hear the screams and the sound of the meat grinder in motion.

She ended up sitting on the sofa, drinking coffee and staring out of her window at the looming shape of Winter Hill, far in the distance.

Just as she felt herself finally drifting off for a couple of hours of desperately needed sleep, her phone rang.

In truth her phone rang near constantly. As a junior doctor working a brutal shift pattern she was fair game for those at the hospital to dump jobs on to. There was always a long list of items waiting for her when she started her shift.

But this number was different. It was private. Fauzia stared down at the phone as it rang, her sleep-deprived brain trying to catch up. Was it Labour HQ? Or Malton? Or maybe Waqar calling from a new phone.

She had gone for nearly twenty-four hours without sleep. Kept upright with fear and adrenaline. She wasn't on shift until midday. A few precious hours when she should be trying to snatch some rest. But this was far more important.

Her heart in her mouth, she answered. She listened numbly to a voice on the other end, low and precise as he told her he wanted to meet. Gave her instructions on exactly when and where.

The voice went quiet. Fauzia could hear her own breathing, shallow and panicked. But she needed to know. Whether she believed her brother or not, even after all this time, she needed to hear it for herself.

'Who are you?' she said, her voice trembling with fear.

There was a long pause. And then one word before the line went dead.

'Galahad.'

Fauzia needed to act now.

Her next call was to a local twenty-four-hour car rental. Thirty minutes later they'd delivered her a grey BMW nearly identical to the car she had lost the evening before.

She signed for her car and was on the move.

Galahad wanted to meet at her father's semi-completed wedding hall. Said if she didn't come to him then he'd come to her. She didn't want him to come to her.

As she drove through Daubhill, Fauzia wondered if he had stolen her car. Had he been following her? Was he following her right now? The call had taken her by surprise. Exhausted and scared she had simply got in her car and driven. But as she neared the wedding venue her rational brain began to kick in.

She was driving to a deserted building to meet a violent criminal who wanted to kill her brother and possibly her. If she wasn't so bone-tired maybe she would have pulled over, thought it over for just a few minutes. But her mind was in freefall, her body slipping into the autopilot so familiar to any doctor who's worked twelve on, twelve off.

As the terraced streets flew by Fauzia felt her eyelids drooping. After a sleepless night finally her body was beginning to cotton on. She still had an entire shift ahead of her. If she lived that long.

With no time for sleep she stopped briefly at a pharmacy run by an old school friend and wrote herself a prescription for ten 200mg tablets of modafinil. A drug used to treat narcolepsy.

Fauzia had heard other doctors boast about doing this. She'd seen it happening. An in-group secret. A rite of passage even. Fauzia had never once considered it. But now, with everything else she'd already done, a little prescription fraud felt like nothing.

Back in her car she took one 200mg tablet with water and headed off.

Five minutes later she was turning down the side street that led to the wedding hall.

Surrounded by terraced houses and small, industrial work-shops, the wedding hall rose several storeys to loom over its sur-roundings. The roof of the building was a giant glass dome. Or it would be just as soon as the contractor delivered the glass. Cur-rently it was an ugly, rusting metal frame, letting rain cascade down into the building.

The site was surrounded by temporary metal fencing but as Fauzia drew close she saw that someone had ripped one of the fence panels aside.

By the gap in the fence stood a man dressed in a black tracksuit and trainers, a hood and mask covering his face.

Fauzia stopped and stared as the man pointed for her to drive on through the gap and on towards the wedding hall.

She suddenly felt very calm. For the past few days she'd been doing her best not to think about Galahad. She knew so little about him that all she had to go on was fear and suspicion. Galahad was everyone and everywhere. He could break into her parents' strongroom. He could strike at random. He could send men to kill her. He was a dark god against whom Fauzia had no recourse but to tremble.

But now she was going to meet him. Face to face.

Fauzia had been in the dark, waiting for the blow to come. At least now she would be able to face it with her eyes open.

The ground floor of the wedding hall was going to have glass doors all round it, for the rare occasions when the Bolton weather would permit guests to venture outside. But the same contractor who had yet to finish roof also had failed to deliver the glass for the ground floor.

Without the glass doors around the lower floor, it was tem-porarily boarded up.

As Fauzia drove slowly past the masked man she saw that one of the panels had been torn away and a second masked man, also dressed in black, was pointing for her to drive her car on into the building.

Fauzia could feel her heart racing. The modafinil was doing its job. She was wide awake. Her mouth was dry and her head beginning to throb.

The way she felt right now, if they were going to kill her in her own father's wedding venue it would almost be a mercy killing.

Fauzia drove on past the second man in black and into the wedding hall. Construction on the wedding hall's interior had yet to commence. The structure itself was nearly finished but without electricity or fittings the space more closely resembled a concrete, multi-storey car park. The rain from the unfinished roof dripped down the walls and lay in freezing puddles all over the floor.

Inside she was greeted by a third man dressed all in black and the battered blue VW Golf she recognised from the fire-bombing of Waqar's Audi.

Something was lying on the bare concrete floor a few metres in front of the man.

Fauzia stopped her car engine and got out.

A fierce chill was baked into the bare, grey walls. Everything smelt damp.

What light there was came from the unfinished roof. It was enough for Fauzia to recognise what lay on the floor in front of her.

It was her bloody jacket.

'That's for you,' said the man in black by the VW Golf. 'Go on. Take it.'

His accent wasn't local. Fauzia wasn't even sure it was northern. More a flat, neutral English. Like someone who wasn't speaking it as their first language.

But in the half light, with his face covered, she could barely make him out at all.

Fauzia bent down and picked up the jacket that until yesterday had been in a bin liner in the boot of her car.

The blood had dried but the expensive flannel still felt thick and luxurious to the touch.

There on the inside was the tailor's label with their logo and, hand-written alongside it, Fauzia's own name and the date she'd had it made. There was a similar label on the trousers.

As good as a signed confession.

Fauzia swallowed hard and tried to sound brave. 'Are you Galahad?'

The man laughed and shook his head. 'We work for Galahad.'

'What does he want?' she asked. Her head was throbbing with the modafinil. She felt sick. There was no time to be scared now.

'You know what he wants. He wants the phone.'

'It was stolen,' said Fauzia honestly.

The man went silent for a moment. 'By who?'

Fauzia detected just the faintest hint of upward inflection in his voice. A question with a touch of desperation. Peering through the gloom she saw the eyes staring out at her. Just a man. A man who sounded like maybe he was just as scared of Galahad as she was.

Suddenly her fear had a very human face.

Politics and medicine had taught her that as an Asian woman she had to make a first impression. She had to blow away any doubt that she deserved to be in the room. She had to go all in.

'I'm trying to find out. But I can't do that if you keep this up. First Waqar's car and now this?' she said, the confidence in her voice echoing off the concrete.

The man was quiet. He was thinking.

'If we don't get that phone, you know what'll happen.'

Fauzia was an A&E doctor. She'd seen more horror than most. And since watching a man fall into a meat grinder, she felt like there was nothing left that this man could throw at her. No sly innuendo or vague suggestions.

She took a step towards the masked man.

'Where's my car?' she demanded.

The man shook his head. Fauzia knew it was long gone.

'What if I go to the police?'

The eyes beneath the mask flashed anger. 'We can ruin you. We can kill you.'

There was an incredulous anger to his voice. That he was being talked to like this. By a woman like Fauzia. It was a tone she was depressingly used to. A tone that she brushed off without a second thought.

'Then you won't get your phone,' said Fauzia defiantly.

If they wanted to kill her then they would. She couldn't stop them. But if she could just keep the ball in the air until Malton did his thing then maybe she stood a chance.

'We can help you,' said the man, his tone suddenly veering towards conciliatory.

'I don't need your help,' Fauzia replied firmly.

'You're going to be an MP. We can make sure that happens without any drama. Tahir Akhtar's not going to go quietly.'

Fauzia didn't expect that. Who were these people? How did they know so much about her?

'I said I don't need your help.'

The man shrugged. Fauzia realised the other two men in black had walked into the hall while they were talking.

They passed by her without saying a word and got into the VW Golf.

The third man was about to get in when he stopped for a moment. 'Whatever you decide, we need that phone.' He got in the car and pulled the door shut.

They gunned the engine and slowly pulled away towards where Fauzia had driven in.

As the Golf passed her it stopped and a window wound down.

'And just so you know, if your brother tries anything, we're going to burn this place to the ground. With your family in it.'

The window went up and the car screeched away, the sound of tyres echoing through the concrete shell of the wedding venue.

Back in her car, Fauzia pulled out the card that Dean had given her a few nights ago. Ignoring the number he'd written in biro she turned on the interior light and held the card up so she could see the crossed-out number beneath.

Dean had said to call in an emergency. This felt like the kind of emergency that required the organ grinder. Not the monkey.

As the phone rang through to voicemail she heard a deep, Moss Side accent say, 'Leave a message.'

44

With his ankle handcuffed to a thirty-two-kilogram kettlebell, Bradley Wyke was going nowhere.

Miyah Mai sat beside him on the only chair in Bradley's gym.

Malton had closed the doors behind him leaving the four of them – Bradley, Miyah Mai, Dean and himself – alone in the converted archway.

The walls had all been stripped back to the bare brick of the viaduct above them. From the way the light hit them, Malton guessed some sort of resin had been painted over the ceiling to seal the bricks. The concrete floor was painted a bright white, and from the lingering smell of fresh paint Malton could tell this whole set-up was still quite new.

Every few minutes the whole space shook with the sound of another train passing overhead.

There were a couple of convection heaters in one corner of the room but none of them were currently plugged in. Despite Manchester crawling into summer time, deprived of direct sunlight the vaulted room was horrendously cold.

Both Miyah Mai and Bradley were visibly shivering. Miyah Mai wrapped her arms around herself for warmth while Bradley tried to tough it out, standing erect as if ready to keep on fighting, regardless of the weight chained to his ankle.

'Where did you get the money from for this place?' asked Malton.

Bradley said nothing.

Malton sighed and began to pace. Despite turning up in a heavy jeep coat with a shearling collar, he too was freezing.

'Does beating up blokes in a church hall pay well?' Malton asked.

'We'll give Stevie back his money,' said Miyah Mai. 'Please don't tell him about us.'

'Shut up,' said Bradley, shouting with such force that his breath emerged as a thick, angry cloud of condensation.

Malton made sure not to betray any surprise at what he'd just heard.

'Danny Mitchum's dead,' said Malton.

'Don't fucking care,' said Bradley defiantly.

Malton reached up and rubbed his shaved head. Partly it was for the theatre of it all, partly he was thinking. Putting together several different stories into one coherent narrative.

He'd very deliberately made sure Stevie's crew were in earshot when he told Stevie about Danny's death. With so few leads to go on, he didn't have a choice. Whoever had killed Danny Mitchum would have to make their move eventually. If word was out Danny was dead, then it wouldn't only be Malton on a ticking clock. Depriving Danny's killer of their head start against the rest of the underworld was the least Malton could do.

'Danny Mitchum was stealing from the Scouse Mafia,' said Malton.

Bradley smiled. 'Everyone fucking knew that. He bragged about it,' he said.

This was news. When Danny had hired Malton he told him he needed to find the leak. If Danny was simply broadcasting his crimes to people as low down the chain as Bradley, then the leak could have been absolutely anyone. In fact the leak was probably Danny himself. Perversely it was their loyalty to Danny that had stopped them talking to Malton about their boss's lack of discretion.

First he was stockpiling drugs from Callum Hester and then employing Malton to help him vanish off the face of the earth. It was clear now that the leak was just a cover story. Danny was up to something. Something that had got him killed.

He was dead and still wasting Malton's time.

'Danny said that if you could nick something, you should. And if you got found out, you got what you deserved,' said Bradley.

'Did he get what he deserved?' asked Malton.

Behind him Dean had started to march on the spot, hugging himself tight against the cold.

'Stevie showed me Danny's safe,' interjected Miyah Mai.

'Shut up!' shouted Bradley. He moved to grab Miyah Mai but forgetting the kettlebell ended up tripping and falling on his arse.

'Let her speak,' said Malton and turned to Miyah Mai.

'After Danny went under the radar, Bradley had an idea. Stevie, his dad, he's not like Danny.'

'He's a fucking idiot,' said Bradley.

Malton couldn't disagree.

'Danny's house is full of stuff. Valuable stuff,' continued Miyah Mai.

Malton had been to Danny's house several times. It was a dumping ground of expensive trash. Designer bags, high-end watches, televisions, bikes, cars. It was like for all the money he made, none of it really meant a thing. Money wasn't the point for Danny. It had always been about the power.

'He doesn't use it. Can't fucking see it can he?' said Bradley. 'Like he said, if you can steal it, you should steal it.'

'So you've been stealing from Stevie?'

'The dickhead gave her the combination to the fucking safe! What sort of div does that?' said Bradley.

'It's true,' said Miyah Mai. She was warming into the confession now. 'I didn't even ask. He was showing off. It was full of gold and guns and explosives. No one kept track of anything. But we didn't kill Danny.'

'Why would we? It was going great.'

'Your girlfriend sleeping with Stevie Mitchum so you could rob him?'

'My wife,' said Bradley defensively. He gave a protective look to Miyah Mai who looked back adoringly.

Malton had all he needed. 'That's great. I'm glad for you. Because whoever killed Danny Mitchum, now they're top dog. They're the one with a target on their back. More so, because everyone's scared of Danny Mitchum. Well, they were. But this new guy? They'll want to take him out before he has a chance to get comfy. I'm glad that's not you two.'

Bradley shot a look to Miyah Mai. She looked terrified.

'We didn't kill him,' she said, her voice pleading for Malton to believe her. 'And we'll stop stealing from Stevie.'

'Don't do that,' said Malton. 'I need you to carry on stealing. Like none of this happened. I don't want him suspecting that you've started reporting back to me what's going on at the mansion.'

'We're not grasses,' spat Bradley.

Miyah Mai's eyes widened. 'Do you think Stevie killed his own son?'

Malton gave her a conspiratorial smile but didn't answer her question. 'Can you do that for me?' he asked her, purposefully ignoring Bradley.

'No,' said Bradley firmly. 'We're done with Stevie Mitchum.' He turned to Miyah Mai and repeated for her benefit, 'We're done.'

Malton looked from Bradley to Miyah Mai, trying to decide who was the weakest link.

'OK,' blurted Miyah Mai.

'Fuck's sake! I said no,' shouted Bradley.

'We don't have a choice, babe,' she pleaded.

'Smart wife you got there, Bradley,' said Malton. 'You could learn a thing or two.'

'You want to know about Stevie? I'll tell you about Stevie,' spat Bradley defiantly. 'Stevie is fucked.'

'Fucked?' said Malton with exaggerated surprise.

'People know something's up. When Danny disappeared there was talk but at least with Stevie running things it's fun.

With Danny you never know when he's going to explode. Stevie's . . . easy?'

Malton feigned surprise well enough for Bradley to start looking very pleased with himself. So pleased that when Malton asked, 'So how is he fucked?' he carried straight on talking.

'Everyone's saying Danny's dead. Without Danny no one's going to follow Stevie. He's got maybe a couple of guys left in the mansion. There's no gear coming in either. Hasn't been for a few weeks now. Got so bad Stevie went out himself to make a buy. Fucking idiot got caught doing it too.'

Malton remembered the overheard conversation between Stevie and Bea in her office. Bradley seemed to be enjoying being the centre of attention so Malton let him continue.

'Nothing to sell. No business to keep ticking over. And then there's him.'

'Him who?'

Bradley went quiet as if realising he'd said too much. It spoke volumes about the state of what was left of Danny Mitchum's business that he felt free to say as much as he had.

Miyah Mai piped up: 'Stevie says there's someone out there. Someone bigger than Danny ever was. Someone who wants to take the business. I bet they're the one who killed Danny!'

Bradley glared at Miyah Mai.

She shrugged off his disapproval. 'Stevie's an idiot but he's sweet. I'd hate something to happen to him.'

Malton could feel something big coming into focus. The disorder of the last few days began to align itself in his mind. 'Did he say who?' Malton asked. He already knew what she was going to say.

Miyah Mai looked defiantly over to her husband and then back to Malton. 'They got a stupid name. Like it's made up.' Miyah Mai rolled her eyes as she struggled to recall it. 'Glad hand . . . Gala something . . . Gallagher . . .'

'Galahad?' interjected Dean before he could stop himself.

A smile broke over Miyah Mai's face. 'Yeah! That's the one. The man who was gunning for Danny, Stevie said his name was Galahad.'

Malton didn't have to look at Dean to know the expression he'd have on his face.

The look of someone who'd just been caught out.

45

Dean had fucked up and he knew it. He had been so eager to impress Malton, so keen to show off, that the word 'Galahad' was out of his mouth before he realised that there was no way he could know about Galahad without admitting to Malton that he had yet to tell him about the visit two nights ago by Fauzia.

And if he told Malton about Fauzia's visit, then he would have to tell him about Vikki and what he'd seen on her phone.

Dean had been hoping to get ahead of Big Wacky, make his own enquiries and set up his own leads without having to tread on Malton's toes. But events had overtaken him. His eagerness to impress Malton had betrayed him. He was out of time.

Now all he had left was damage limitation. To choose whether to simply tell him that Fauzia's visit had slipped his mind or to give the full story. Tell him about Vikki and Olivia and his moonlighting in attempting to track her down. To reveal his suspicion that Vikki and Big Wacky were somehow connected. That he'd been duped.

Dean sat in the passenger seat and watched through the windscreen as outside his boss dialled a number on his phone. Dean could only guess who he was talking to, but once the call was finished he waited for Malton to get back in the car before he let rip.

'I should have told you sooner, there was a walk-up. Someone looking to hire you.'

Malton didn't say a word. He started the engine of the Volvo estate and headed off towards the ring road.

Without any other option, Dean continued. 'She didn't tell me much but I managed to look her up. Her name's Fauzia Malik, and she's a prospective MP. From Bolton. Her brother Waqar is into drugs, had the encrypted phone he runs his operation on stolen. Someone's been leaning on him to get it back. Someone who goes by the name of Galahad.'

They passed down the stretch of ring road the council had earmarked as a European-style boulevard. What they ended up with was a six-lane road flanked by looming blocks of flats, with private gyms and noodle bars occupying the ground floors.

Nothing Dean had said was a lie. He hadn't mentioned the name Big Wacky or his search for Olivia but he'd told Malton everything else.

Still Malton kept driving in silence. He drove past the giant, glass Co-Op offices shaped like the bow of a cruise ship and down past yet more railway arches as he headed towards Regent Road and the motorway beyond.

Dean had seen Malton do this to other people. Simply shut down and force them to fill in the silence. Make them talk when they should have kept their mouths shut. He was determined not to be sucked in, but he found Malton's stonewall so oppressive that he simply had to keep talking.

'I should have told you sooner but I was out looking for Lynne Harris and then this today. I got tunnel vision. The whole Danny Mitchum thing.'

Malton made his way up Regent Road. Past the Salford Lads' club made famous by The Smiths and past a collection of edge-of-town stores, one of which had been burned down twenty years previously in a show of gangland strength.

Manchester's unstoppable expansion was even reaching this far out. Over the Salford boundary and filling in the derelict brownfield sites with block upon block of flats. Cut-price city centre living over a mile out of the city centre and a stone's throw from Langworthy Road and what was left of the real Salford.

They were crossing over onto the motorway when once more Dean found the complete lack of response unbearable.

'So what now?' he asked. He wasn't sure if he meant what now with Fauzia, what now with Danny, or what now with his time at Malton Security. Either way he needed answers.

As Malton sped up onto the motorway he turned to Dean, his face not giving away a thing. 'You said Fauzia Malik's from Bolton? Let's go visit her.'

Dean sat back into the soft leather of Malton's car upholstery and kept his eyes on the road.

He had no idea if he'd just got away with it or he was being led to the scene of his execution.

46

It was a risk taking Leon Walker out into the big wide world, but Keisha no longer had the luxury of time. If he couldn't do his part in the plan, then he was useless to her.

Currently he was exceeding expectations.

Keisha was parked up in a black Mercedes across the road from Lynne Harris's house, waiting for Leon to finish up. No longer working at The Sentinel she was back in her own clothes. Faded, skin-tight jeans and a matching trucker jacket over a heavy, white T-shirt. Black Airforce Nikes to match her black sunglasses.

Lynne's house was a large, detached Victorian property in Chorlton. The kind of house that could easily sell for over a million. Like the other houses on her road, it was set back at the end of a short driveway with a large front garden, which had a modern wood and steel fence encircling it. It was out of keeping with the house but it provided a great deal of privacy.

Perfect for Keisha.

Lynne had got her fired but this wasn't about that. Craig knew Lynne's name. He'd be looking into her. Slowly putting it together. Hitting Lynne's house with Leon Walker was Keisha's way of letting him know that she was still thinking about him. Still one step ahead. She would strike first before Craig could figure out what she was doing.

A statement of intent written with Leon Walker's battered fists.

Had there been more time, Keisha would have researched who might be in the house. As it was, she knew that Lynne's husband would be home. Anyone else Leon found there it would be up to him to deal with.

Now that heroin wasn't firing the dopamine receptors in Leon's ruined brain it was time to reacquaint him with his first addiction – extreme violence. Shaking off years of drug abuse and reviving the muscle memory of senseless brutality that had made his name shine so bright and so briefly.

From the way Leon had reacted to the man who opened the front door, Keisha was confident the old Leon was in there somewhere. No sooner was the door open than that six-foot-six frame swung into action, smashing a fist into the face of a man Keisha assumed must be Malcolm Harris, Lynne's husband.

From where she was parked, Keisha saw the man fly backwards into his house followed by Leon. She was impressed Leon had the presence of mind to close the door behind him.

Keisha had bought a couple of burner phones. With the first phone she had called the second phone, put it on speaker and given it to Leon to take in with him. Giving her a crude but effective way to eavesdrop on the carnage.

That was seven minutes ago. Keisha had given Leon very precise instructions. He was to be inside for no more than ten minutes. There were still three minutes left on the clock.

Keisha looked around the road. Large houses. Full-grown trees. Multiple cars. No litter or graffiti. No people on the streets. She thought how the people on this street had paid so much money to live in their gilded bubbles. Sparing themselves the worst of humanity but also denying themselves the chance of ever experiencing its flipside.

Growing up Keisha had seen both. She'd seen how low people could fall but she'd also seen the pure, glowing kindness that thrived in the darkest places. It meant a man like Leon Walker held no terror for her. Keisha knew his kind all too well and she knew how to handle them.

But to the people who lived on Lynne's road, hiding from the world in their million-pound properties, secure behind locked doors and fences and alarms, Leon Walker would be all their worst fears made flesh.

'Please, no! Please, don't!' came a man's voice over the phone. Keisha guessed it must be Lynne's husband. He sounded half crazed with fear. There followed a series of loud crashing sounds and then in the silence that followed the sound of a man wetly weeping.

While the crash of breaking glass came over the phone, Keisha thought over her new plan.

When she'd known Craig all those years ago he swore he would never have children. He was fastidious about it. Obsessed even. He said that children made you weak. They were a vulnerability he couldn't afford.

The day Keisha was to tell him he was going to be a father, Craig had walked out on her. He never knew he was a dad and she never got the chance to know if he would have changed his mind and stayed.

Now Emily was pregnant, she had a second chance to find out.

A woman's voice came over the phone. She was talking in a foreign language. Spanish maybe? Perhaps Portuguese. Keisha didn't understand what she was saying but she recognised the defiance in her voice and the sound of Leon Walker's fist crunching into her face.

Leon's heavy breathing came thick and fast over the phone. Whatever he was doing he was doing it with a ferocious intensity. That was good. For her plan to work Keisha still needed him with a taste for carnage.

She checked her watch. Less than a minute left.

Right now if she reached out to Craig there was a chance he would turn her down. He still had the life he'd built himself. His business, his reputation, Bea Wallace. Keisha would need to make sure he was a broken man when she finally told him they could be a family again. Stripped of everything he clung to in order to give his life meaning.

It would be just like when they had first met. Back when Craig was so young and scared and it was Keisha who had taken him under her wing, fallen in love with him and shown him just who he could be.

But first she had to break him.

Keisha's watch beeped. Ten minutes was up. A few seconds later Leon Walker strode out of the house. The ruined junkie was gone. The monstrous giant who'd terrorised Manchester for those few, brief months was back.

Keisha had raised Leon Walker from the dead and turned him into her personal agent of violence. Now she would use him to remake Craig into the man she'd known he could be ever since she first set eyes on him over thirty years ago.

Keisha was going to deliver the most violent love letter imaginable. By the time she was done, Craig would never be the same again.

47

Fauzia watched Malton as he methodically walked the strong-room. He ignored the watches and the jewellery. Didn't even pause at the Lowry. The craftsmanship that caught his eye was the room itself.

Malton looked impressed.

Not half as impressed as Fauzia.

She was about to start her shift when he had called her back, having listened to her voicemail, and asked to come over to her parents' house as a matter of urgency. Fauzia had phoned in sick and headed over.

It was the first time she'd seen her parents since winning the nomination. With everything else that was happening the most exciting news of her life had simply slipped her mind.

It meant that after seeing her mother and father crying tears of joy at her success she was able to spin the news that a man would shortly be visiting the house to check on her family's security. All standard procedure for the next of kin of an MP in waiting.

She watched as Iffat's chest had risen with pride. His daughter was important enough to need security. Samia had peppered her with questions – first all the upheaval with Waqar and now their daughter needing security. Iffat did Fauzia's work for her, calming her mother down and making sure she knew that such measures were simply a sign of how well their daughter was doing.

Any remaining worries she had vanished upon Malton's arrival. He was everything his reputation had made him out to be and so much more.

For starters he was enormous. Not tall but wide. A fearsome scar ran down his face and his hands were like sledgehammers. But he dressed well and took his shoes off without even being asked.

More than that he had a stillness. A sense of quiet purpose that instantly dragged the room down to his speed. Without saying a word he made the world around him slow down to his own internal chronometer.

The boy Dean from the office was with him but he stayed silent while Fauzia led them both straight through, carefully avoiding her parents in the kitchen.

Fauzia noticed the wound on his face was still livid and she wondered if he'd taken her advice.

Once they were safely in the strongroom the real work started.

Malton paced the room, tapping on the walls, listening for the sounds he heard back. Fauzia was almost certain he was counting his paces, measuring the size of the room. Was he comparing it to the footprint of the house? Checking for hidden sections? She couldn't imagine but it was clear she was watching someone very special at work.

'I need the passcode for the safe,' said Malton as he knelt down in front of it.

'9367856,' said Fauzia without a moment's hesitation. He had been in the house less than ten minutes but she trusted him completely.

Unlike the boy. Ever since he'd arrived he hadn't been able to stand still. Everything about him said he'd rather be somewhere else. Fauzia half wondered if he'd had a dressing-down from his boss for not passing on her details sooner. Either way he was irrelevant now she had Malton on the case.

As Malton knelt to inspect the safe, Dean finally spoke. 'Can I use the toilet?' he asked.

Malton seemed oblivious as he continued to check over the safe.

'First floor, second door on the left,' said Fauzia, far more intrigued by Malton's process than the boy's bathroom request.

Malton didn't even look up as the boy slipped out. Alone together, Fauzia stood alongside Malton and bent down, looking over his shoulder as he worked.

Malton opened the safe a couple of times. Again he ignored the diamonds and cash inside. Instead he ran his fingers along the lock, examining the mechanism for signs of tampering.

Finally he rose to his feet and turned to Fauzia. From the look on his face she could tell he had something to say.

'You think it was your brother, don't you?' he said.

Fauzia didn't react. She took a step back and gently shut the door to the safe room behind her.

'Now we can talk,' she said.

On the phone she'd told Malton just what she'd told Dean. Now they were face to face in the privacy of the strongroom she could tell him the whole story.

Malton didn't move. The spotlights on the ceiling threw shadows over his tough, worn face. The scar running down one side was thrown into stark relief. He waited to hear what Fauzia had to say that required this level of privacy.

'My brother's in over his head. He's been dealing drugs and it's gone wrong. He's in danger. We all are.'

Malton nodded along, taking in every word. 'How much do you know about Big Wacky?' he asked.

Fauzia was briefly thrown to hear someone other than her brother use his nickname out loud.

'Big Wacky? That's just my brother's nickname. He thinks it's all a game. Playing at gangsters is what got him in this mess.'

Malton gave the faintest of smiles. He glanced away for a second as if rehearsing what he was about to say.

'Your brother doesn't deal drugs,' he said. 'Your brother sits at the very top of a giant organisation that deals drugs. The head of the drug trade in Bolton. More than that, your brother has done something almost no one ever does. He's got clean.'

It was one thing to here this from her brother but to hear a man like Malton singing his praises? She realised that despite everything there had been a voice in her head doubting what Waqar had told her. Putting it down to his usual bullshit and bravado. That voice now fell silent.

'But my brother isn't really a gangster. He's in over his head,' she said. 'He's not part of this world. He still lives at home with Mum and Dad.'

Malton smiled a little. 'Biggest dealer in Oldham? Lives with his parents. Main man in Huddersfield? Still living with his parents. So are his wife and kid. Bradford? Well he's out on his own. But he's not long for this world. Not if Oldham's got anything to do with it.'

Fauzia was speechless. This man knew her brother better than she did.

'Whoever your brother is to you, to the Manchester Underworld he's a near legend. Big Wacky, the drugs boss who cracked the hardest part of the whole thing – laundering the cash. Any idiot can buy drugs and stand about on street corners selling them. Any idiot with a mouth on him can persuade other people to do the dirty work for him. But to know what to do with the money when it starts coming in? That's the hard part.'

Suddenly Fauzia thought of the string of kebab shops Waqar had bought. Shops that dealt mostly in cash. The kind of place where you could funnel limitless amounts of drugs money.

For just a moment she felt a burning glow of pride. Her parents had been wrong about Waqar. He *was* special. He *was* smart. They didn't let him prove it the normal way and so Big Wacky was born.

But then she remembered what Big Wacky brought with him. The meeting in her father's wedding hall, the burning car, the body in the mincer.

It was only the solid, reassuring presence of Malton standing before her that stopped Fauzia from breaking down at the thought of it all. He stood as still as he had when he'd first arrived. Unshockable, immovable, immense.

'Can you find the phone?' she asked. Her voice sounded thin. All the hours without sleep were finally catching up to her.

'Yes,' said Malton definitively.

'And what about the people who bombed his car? And stole mine? Galahad?'

Malton thought for a moment and nodded. 'That too,' he said. 'Is there anything else I need to know? Anything you haven't told Dean?'

Malton looked at her and for just a moment Fauzia was convinced he knew everything about that terrible night at the meat processing plant. But there was no way. Of the three witnesses, one was Waqar, one was her and one was dead in the most horrific way imaginable.

In the deadened silence of the strongroom Fauzia began to feel the tiredness pressing down on her. An impossible gravity slowing every second to a crawl, stretching out every moment.

Suddenly the weight of what she was carrying became too much.

She took a breath and said out loud what had been haunting her for the past few days. The events of that terrible night.

Malton listened in silence. Whatever he felt about what he was hearing, his face betrayed nothing.

The air in the room tasted of solvent. Fauzia felt her heart start to pound so fast it was as if she could hear it. A frantic drumbeat signalling her body finally giving way to the inevitable stress and fatigue.

The strongroom suddenly felt like nothing so much as a prison cell. She had to get out; she couldn't breathe.

Fauzia spun round and punched in the code for the door.

As it swung open the room was filled with the sound of shouting coming from upstairs.

Malton didn't say a word. He pushed past her, out of the strongroom, down the hallway and up the stairs towards the sound of raised voices.

48

Dean looked up into the eyes of the man pointing a gun in his face. The man who he now knew to be Big Wacky.

'Who the fuck are you?'

He was taller than he'd imagined. And better-looking too. Like a model. But Dean didn't pay too much attention to Big Wacky's firm jaw or his big, brown eyes. He was more focused on his gun.

In the car it seemed Malton had accepted Dean's excuse. Finding Danny Mitchum's killer was the number-one priority and Fauzia's missing mobile had simply slipped his mind. He'd kept his powder dry all the way to Bolton, telling Malton everything he could about what Fauzia had said to him.

He hadn't said a word about Olivia.

But the moment he set foot in the Maliks' house he knew that it was now or never. This could be the last chance he had to find something connecting Big Wacky to Olivia or Vikki. Something that would either help him track Oliva down or discover just what sort of game Vikki was playing.

Now Malton was working the Fauzia angle, it had become much harder for Dean to do anything without arousing suspicion. He'd either have to come clean or abandon his hunt for Olivia.

Neither of those two options appealed to him and so when he got the chance he'd slipped away from the strongroom and made his move.

When he'd seen the bedroom he knew he had to take the risk.

It looked more like the room of a sullen teenager than a major drug dealer. Black walls, a framed *Scarface* poster and built-in cupboards with floor-to-ceiling mirrors. Two dozen boxes of trainers neatly piled up beneath the window.

Dean had barely set foot inside when he'd been hit from behind with something hard and heavy and knocked onto the bed.

'Did Galahad send you?' shouted Big Wacky, now waving the gun wildly.

Before Dean could think, Malton burst in the room quickly followed by Fauzia.

Big Wacky swung round and pointed the gun at them. Upon recognising his sister he lowered it a little and took a step backwards, his back to the window.

He glared at Fauzia, shifting from foot to foot like a cornered animal. 'Who the fuck are this lot, Fauz? In my room?'

'I was looking for the toilet,' said Dean weakly. He stayed lying on the bed, unsure whether or not he should get up.

'I hired them. To find your phone,' said Fauzia, desperation in her voice.

Waqar stopped moving. He looked from Malton to Dean and back before letting out a high-pitched laugh.

'These two clowns? I told you who I am, sis. I told you what I can do.'

'You're Big Wacky,' said Malton. 'I know all about you.'

Waqar frowned. He still had the gun in his hand. Dean rolled off the bed and got to his feet, joining Fauzia and Malton on the other side of the room.

'Then you know what I'm capable of.' Waqar grinned.

'I know your sister is worried. I know your car got torched and hers was stolen. With the bloodstained clothes in the back from the murder the two of you committed at your parents' factory.'

Dean saw the look of incredulity spread over Big Wacky's face.

'What the fuck have you been saying?' he said, pointing the gun accusingly at Fauzia.

'I'm scared. You need help.'

'I don't need no one. You still think I'm your fuck-up brother. I'm not him. I'm Big Wacky. I make shit happen. Yeah?'

'I know,' said Malton. 'I don't think your sister quite understood who you were. I filled her in. I'm only here to help you get your phone back. This Galahad, I think he might be involved in other business of mine. I want to meet him just as much as you do.'

'I'm not scared of Galahad,' said Waqar. He almost sounded like he believed it. 'If you know who I am, then why the fuck do you think I need help?'

Malton shrugged. 'Maybe you don't. But your sister's paying us so you may as well let us do our job.'

'Job? Who the fuck are you?'

Malton made no move to extend a hand. He simply looked Waqar in the eye and said, 'Craig Malton. Malton Security.'

Dean saw Waqar go pale. The gun hung limp at his side and he staggered back a little, looking from Dean to Malton with a new-found horror.

He started to shake his head. Broken laughter tumbled from his mouth. The cockiness was gone. He seemed in shock.

'They're here to help,' said Fauzia.

Waqar snapped back to attention. He stuffed the gun into his trousers and covered it up with his top. Dean kept his eyes on it.

Waqar glanced from Fauzia to Dean to Malton, as if working out where the most immediate threat lay.

He turned to his sister. 'You fucked up,' he said before barging past Malton and Dean, down the stairs and out of the house.

49

Leon Walker stared at the YouTube video playing on the phone propped up on the table in front of him. In his giant hands he held an MP5 submachine gun.

The bag filled with guns lay on the floor beside him.

The video was instructions on stripping an MP5. Keisha had let him out of his room and installed him in her own room along with the phone, a gun-cleaning kit and a pile of rags.

Now that her plan was in action, Leon Walker would need to do more in his down time than simply shit himself to sleep with heroin withdrawal. To demonstrate her growing trust in him Keisha had given him the job of cleaning up the bag of guns. Of course, she had made sure that all the ammunition was safely secured in the second locked room, but even so it was a huge leap from the Leon Walker who twenty-four hours earlier had tried to make his escape.

Keisha did her best to push away all thoughts of the moment she would finally win Craig back and become a family. That was the prize, but before the prize came the fight.

She sat across the table from Leon. As a reward for a job well done, Keisha had bought them a bucket of KFC on the way home. Unfortunately for Leon, his detox diet of noodles and methadone hadn't prepared his stomach for anything as solid as fried chicken. Having devoured his first piece he'd immediately thrown it up all over the floor.

After Keisha had made him clean it up, she set him to work on the guns while she finished the KFC herself. It wasn't a patch on the chicken she used to get back in Moss Side. KFC mistook salt and sugar for actual spices. The skin was crispy but dry and the chicken beneath indifferent. It was nothing like the soft, moist flesh doused in strong, spicy jerk seasoning and grilled to a crisp that she had grown up on.

But this wasn't Moss Side. This was Harpurhey. This wasn't home. This was a base of operations. And Leon Walker wasn't a friend. He was a weapon who would very soon be ready to be aimed and fired.

Just a day earlier she had been planning to wipe Craig Malton off the face of the earth. Now she would be using that same unstoppable force to win him back once and for all. Her love and hate two sides of the same coin.

The guns had spent several weeks buried. In that time the damp Manchester soil had begun to work its way into the bag. Since digging them up a few months ago, Keisha had left them untouched. She'd had other priorities.

But now that she needed her arsenal she had set Leon to work cleaning and servicing each gun individually.

As it was Leon who would be using them, it seemed only right that he should be the one to make sure they were up to the job.

Keisha watched him work, his lips moving silently. His focus split between the video on her phone and the gun in his hands, the same hands that a few hours earlier had broken Lynne Harris's husband's arm and given her housekeeper a concussion.

Keisha never felt guilty about collateral damage. Growing up she'd seen whole communities written off as acceptable losses by a government too wrapped up in its own ideology to even begin to care. The people at the very top got there by shutting off their hearts to the bodies they stepped over to reach the summit.

Some of her peers went into politics. Determined to right the wrongs they saw all around them. Keisha learned a very different lesson. If you want to succeed, then someone else has to fail. If you want to rise to the top, then you need to throw everyone else down. The only way to get what you want is to take it from someone. And if they won't give it to you, then it's up to you to give them hell.

By the time this was over there would be many more bodies caught in the crossfire. But it would all be worth it to start over with Craig and a child of their own. The child which she would take from Emily.

Leaving Leon to clean the guns, Keisha wiped the chicken grease off her fingers and went to remind herself what all this was about.

The door to Leon's room was open now. There was no need to lock it except at night. The second door was still locked.

It was that second door that she opened and slipped inside, closing it behind her.

Blackness.

For just a moment she was back in Hulme.

The noise outside the flat was deafening. A mob screaming into the night. There must have been hundreds, maybe even thousands. Massed together against the freezing cold. They were only a few feet away, but alone in her flat Keisha couldn't even cry out for help.

Instead she lay on her bed and counted out each breath. The pain was unbearable but she knew now no one was coming to help. If she was to survive the night, it would be down to her and her alone.

Keisha pulled a cord switch and lit up an ornate lampshade hanging from the ceiling. She was back in the house in Harpurhey.

The room was small. Little more than a box room but the walls had been painted a bright, optimistic blue. The floor had been carpeted recently. It was as if it belonged in a different house altogether.

The bag filled with ammunition had been dumped in a corner. It looked dirty and out of place with the one other thing in the room: the crib.

It was a large, waist-high, white crib. A delicate, lace canopy providing cover from the light above. It had cost several thousand pounds. Delivered from a specialist shop in London.

Keisha slowly approached the crib, a fond smile spreading across her face.

Her mouth felt dry as she leaned over and looked into the crib. Her eyes grew wet but she wouldn't cry.

One hand went into the crib and rested on what lay inside it.

A small, white coffin. Broken and decaying from decades underground but still sealed tightly shut.

On top of it a rusted, brass plaque that read – *Anthony Malton. Born Asleep.*

50

Malton closed the door of his office. Now it was just him and Dean.

They had driven back in silence. Malton had hoped that the weight of his disappointment would be enough to break Dean but for the whole journey he had stayed silent. Malton could tell when someone was wrestling with their conscience and so he kept quiet and let Dean's guilt do the job for him.

Dean wasn't stupid. He wasn't lost on his way to the toilet. He was in that bedroom for a reason. What was he looking for and what would he have done if he hadn't been surprised by Waqar?

What else was Dean hiding? It was time to find out.

Malton turned to face the young man. He was pacing the room, but never with his back to Malton. He looked almost ready to bare his soul and so Malton simply took a seat at his desk and waited.

Finally Dean stopped, stood still, took a deep breath and began. 'Vikki Walker asked me to find her friend. A girl called Olivia. She's missing. All I had to go on was the name of the boyfriend: Big Wacky. For the last three months I've been try-ing to find her. Vikki said not to tell you. Said she didn't want to bother you.'

From the way Dean looked at him, gauging his reaction to this information, Malton could tell there was more to come. This was a revelation to be sure, but it was the build-up to the main event. He kept quiet and let Dean continue.

'I was at Vikki's flat the other night. I've been . . .' He tailed off, lost for the right words. 'We're friends.'

Malton hoped that Dean didn't see the tiny smile that crossed his mouth.

'She was out of the room for a few moments and I looked at her phone. I don't know why. I just did.'

'What did you find?' asked Malton gently.

'She had Big Wacky's number in her phone.'

Malton hadn't seen that coming. But he kept his surprise to himself and kept things moving. 'How did you go about finding Big Wacky? If all you had was a name?'

Dean lit up as he began to explain exactly how he'd gone about tracking down Olivia.

Malton listened with mounting amazement as Dean outlined his hunt for Big Wacky. Dobbzbobbz, his online antagonism, and its culmination in a honey trap designed to lure an enraged Big Wacky out from his Daubhill bolthole and into Dean's crosshairs.

Malton was still furious that Dean had kept all this from him, but he couldn't help but be impressed with how he had gone about his manhunt.

Dean may have been strung along, but whatever was going on between Vikki and Big Wacky it had been Dean's relentless curiosity that had uncovered it.

For the past few months Malton had been looking out for Vikki Walker. She'd helped him out and he was happy to return the favour. He'd had her flat done up, paid her bills and ensured she was back in college.

Malton saw it less as charity and more as insurance. After what he'd done to her father – Leon Walker – the last thing Malton needed was a traumatised kid growing up into a vengeful adult and coming to look for payback.

Dealing with Leon Walker had been the closest Malton had ever come to death. Before then he'd been shot and tortured but his fight with Walker had very nearly been the end of him. It was sheer luck that he'd come out on top. He had no desire to repeat the experience with Walker's offspring.

In all that time if she had wanted someone found, she only had to ask. But instead she had gone to Dean. Whatever it was she was doing she didn't want him involved.

'If you ever lie to me again you're done,' said Malton. There was no emotion in his voice. He wasn't threatening Dean, simply telling him the facts as they lay.

Unless he could trust Dean completely he had no use for him.

'What now?' asked Dean. He sounded like a scolded child. His voice low, his eyes downcast.

Malton was spoiled for choice. Questions were stacking up and answers were thin on the ground. Waqar Malik had fled in terror at the name Malton Security. That was curious. Malton would need to find out why that was. And then there was Galahad, whoever or whatever that was. It wasn't just Stevie Mitchum who was spooked. Big Wacky was too. If Galahad was big enough to go after Danny Mitchum and Big Wacky at the same time, then who else was in his sights?

Dean interrupted his thoughts. 'I promise I'll never keep anything from you again,' he said. A touch of hope in his voice.

Dean looked wretched. Malton felt bad for the boy. He was the last person to judge someone for letting their feelings cloud their judgement.

But maybe this was just the break he was looking for.

Malton leaned forward. 'Vikki Walker told you her friend had gone missing, yes?'

'She said she'd been hanging out with Big Wacky and suddenly disappeared,' said Dean.

'White girl, Asian guy, what did you think?' prompted Malton.

Malton saw several thoughts pile up in Dean's mind, tripping over themselves as he put it all together.

'Be honest. Did you think – grooming gangs? Asian men? Vulnerable white girls?' said Malton.

From the look on his face it was clear that was exactly what Dean had thought.

'When someone tells you a lie, it's not just about what they're saying to you. It's about what they think you'll hear. The best sort of lie is the lie that confirms what the person hearing it already believes,' said Malton.

Dean smiled as he finally began to see exactly how he'd been played.

Malton continued, 'Right now Vikki Walker thinks you see her as a vulnerable girl who needs protecting. You're her white knight. You're going to use that to find out why she really asked you to find her friend, why she didn't want me to know about it and more importantly how she knows Big Wacky.'

Dean knew a second chance when he saw it.

'And then you find Olivia.'

Dean looked confused. 'But Vikki lied to me.'

'Doesn't matter,' said Malton. 'You made a promise. Whether it's Olivia or Danny Mitchum, you keep that promise. If you don't follow through now, then why would you follow through the next time or the next? Every time you break your word it makes your word mean less. Doing what we do, reputation is the only thing that keeps you alive. Not muscle or stab vests or guns. Your reputation.'

Malton was deadly serious. No job was ever straightforward. People lied, facts shifted, bodies piled up. But Malton always kept his word. It was why he was still here to tell the tale.

Dean's face said that he understood completely. He had betrayed Malton's trust. He wasn't going to betray Malton's creed.

'No more second chances,' said Malton.

'I won't need them,' said Dean firmly.

Somehow Big Wacky, Danny Mitchum and Galahad were all connected. At the back of his mind, Malton quietly wondered if the key to it all had been under his nose all the time.

A girl called Vikki Walker and her missing friend Olivia.

51

'I can do things you can't do. Go places you can't go. And you know it,' said Bea as she dissected the intricately plated dish in front of her.

Malton had finished his monkfish almost as soon as it had arrived. Three large mouthfuls and it was gone.

It was Sunday night and all around them diners picked away at elaborate plates of food, surrounded by what once was an old-school Salford boozer.

The Black Friar had been the last building standing, sandwiched beside the inner ring road and the River Irwell. While all around it fell to the developers' wrecking ball, the Black Friar had a stay of execution and was done up to serve the recently installed residents in the brand-new tower blocks that now loomed over it.

Malton remembered it back when it was tied to the Boddingtons Brewery. Another bit of Manchester's past long since lost to memory.

He wished he'd taken a little more time with his food. It had tasted exquisite. What there was of it.

'We'll be the only ones to know, you and me,' Bea carried on.

Ever since she'd brought it up a couple of days earlier, Bea had been relentless about them going into business together. Malton had seen her go to work on Crown Prosecution solicitors and storied QCs. He'd seen how this tiny, blonde powerhouse bent people to her will. As much as he could feel her all-out assault having an effect, still he hung back.

'What I do, you don't want in on that,' he said. He was now on the tail of Danny Mitchum's killer: Galahad. No one needed that kind of heat.

Bea swallowed a forkful of gnocchi and leaned in secretively.

'I used to dance,' she said. 'Ballet. I was even thinking of doing it professionally. I was that good. Every hour I had, all I did was practise. Because if I'm going to do something, I'm going to be the best at it. Or else why bother?'

Bea held her hands up as if demanding a response to her rhetorical question. Sensing she wasn't finished talking, Malton let her continue.

'But then . . .' She smiled and theatrically pushed out her considerable chest. 'Puberty. I didn't grow up, but I did grow out. They'd still let me do it, mind. But I knew I couldn't be the best. That meant no more ballet. So I chose law.'

'Ballet's loss,' said Malton noncommittally.

A couple of hours earlier after sending Dean home, Malton had got a call from Bea saying she had a rare evening off and wanted to treat him. Malton had suggested the Black Friar.

No sooner had they set foot in the restaurant than Malton was greeted and taken to their best table before being sent over a complimentary bottle of wine.

He used to love it when he was out with Emily and people treated him like that. Watching her astonished reaction. But Bea didn't blink an eyelid. She was used to getting what she wanted.

But it wasn't Emily or Bea who he found himself thinking about as he watched Bea eat. Despite everything that was happening he found his thoughts pulled to Keisha. She was back.

She and Malton needed each other. Not like how Emily had relied on him to keep her safe from the violence and horror of his world. And not like how he and Bea traded favours.

When Keisha was around suddenly they both came alive.

Bea continued, oblivious to Malton's thoughts. 'And now I'm the best at what I do. And that means I want to work with the best. That's you. You're more than just a pretty face.'

Malton smiled. It was easy with Bea. He couldn't imagine her ever needing protecting from anything. Still, he didn't want to risk changing what they had. Working together would do just that.

'You're worried about us, aren't you?' said Bea, smiling at her own intuition. 'Don't be. Nothing I find out about you is going to change that.'

'You don't know what you're going to find,' said Malton, starting to enjoy himself.

'Like that you're bisexual?' said Bea, casually popping a gnocchi into her mouth.

When he'd first got involved with Bea he'd made sure to find out everything he could about her. He always imagined that she had done the same. He couldn't tell if she was expecting a reaction – either to her digging or to her knowing about his sexuality.

Malton expended an enormous amount of energy controlling the competing impulses and desires that churned away inside him on a daily basis. But never once did he question his sexuality. He felt he owed it to the memory of James to never be ashamed of who he loved.

Before he could rise to Bea's bait, he felt his phone ringing in his pocket.

Half expecting Dean, Malton pulled the phone out of his pocket. The number he saw made his heart race.

He stood up from the table. Bea carried on eating unfazed.

'Give me a minute,' said Malton as he left the restaurant.

Standing on the pavement outside Malton answered the phone.

It was Mayer Haim. Emily's father.

52

The pedestrian had been on a zebra crossing when they were hit by a car travelling at over fifty miles an hour. The ambulance was on the scene within minutes and now what was left of the pedestrian was on the way to Royal Bolton Hospital.

A&E was a flurry of activity as the staff prepared for the worst. The next fifteen minutes would determine whether the person hurtling towards them in an ambulance would live, or whether they would die.

Fauzia moved as if on autopilot. She watched the nurses set up the bed in the trauma unit while other doctors put calls through to various specialists throughout the hospital. Summoning them down to deal with the inbound carnage.

The bright ward lights seemed to pulse in time with her headache and the air smelt of disinfectant and blood. Every tiny noise echoed off the hard, scrubbed surfaces. Each sound driving itself deep into her brain.

She hadn't heard from her brother since he found Malton's assistant in his bedroom and pulled a gun on him.

Since then nothing. He hadn't returned home or reached out to Fauzia. Nor had she heard from the masked men who claimed to be working for Galahad. But now Craig Malton was on the case.

Since meeting Malton, Fauzia felt as if a great weight had been lifted off her. He was everything people said he was and more. He was charging her a grand a day but compared to the alternative he was cheap at twice the price. She'd had her first full night's sleep in days and woken up refreshed and ready to go on shift.

She almost felt normal.

Shouts rang out through the ward that an operating theatre was being prepped and an anaesthetist dragged in at short notice to be on standby.

There were half a dozen calls from Labour Party HQ waiting to be returned but they could wait. Right now Fauzia was high on the anticipation of a road traffic collision arriving. This was what she had trained for. The exciting, high-stakes, life-and-death medicine that made all the long hours and tedious repetition worth it.

A senior nurse loudly informed everyone that the RTC was being unloaded. The electricity in the room dispelled the fog of the past few days. The world snapped into focus. Voices became louder, lights bright and everything was clear. She heard her own voice shouting orders. Functioning as part of a well-oiled team.

Fauzia braced herself. This was where she was meant to be. Whatever else was happening with her brother, with Malton and Galahad, right here, right now she was in control.

With a beautifully ordered chaos the trolley appeared surrounded by nurses and paramedics.

As Fauzia stepped forward ready to go to work she froze.

There on the trolley – battered, bloodied and barely alive – was her former rival for Farnworth and Great Lever – Tahir Akhtar.

53

'So let me get this straight,' said Benton as she dusted the safe for prints, 'whoever killed Danny Mitchum is the same person who's after his dad and also the same person who's trying to put the squeeze on Big Wacky?'

'Galahad,' said Malton.

'I'll give him one thing – he's ambitious,' said Benton without looking up.

The strongroom looked a state. Every surface was covered in black fingerprint dust. The smell of it overwhelmed the scent of solvent that hung about the room. In the past few days the strongroom had seen more traffic than it had in all the years since it was built.

Fauzia had called ahead before going on shift to convince her parents that this was all still part of her beefed-up security. Malton was happy to leave it to her to explain why the immaculate strongroom was now black with dust. He had more important things on his mind.

Malton had called in a favour from Benton. She'd arrived dressed in black and looking just about as professional as Malton could have hoped for. She brought with her a box full of tricks.

It hadn't been easy to convince her to do him the favour. Since getting her detective career back on track Benton had been far more cautious about the kind of help she gave to Malton. She knew there were more than enough people in GMP waiting for her to slip up so they could bury her for good. But she and Malton had too much shared history to simply cut him loose.

Besides, they both knew that without the other's help they would be lost. In the end, that was the promise that had secured Benton's help. Malton gave his word that as soon as he knew who Galahad was, she would be the first to know.

Whoever he was, he was looming over the wreckage of Danny's crew as well as terrorising Big Wacky. Then there was Olivia – Dean's missing girl – and Vikki her friend who'd sent Dean looking for her. Both of them with some kind of connection to Big Wacky. The coincidences were starting to pile up in a way that made Malton distinctly uneasy.

Right now the only thing he felt confident about was what had happened with Big Wacky's missing phone.

Waqar was getting to the kind of size where it no longer suited him to be buying from the man above him in the chain. He had the cash and clout to jump up several levels and start dealing with the really big boys.

When that happens, someone's going to lose out. And that's when the violence starts. Malton's hunch was that the whole phone story was concocted as a cover for the fallout from Waqar attempting to sidestep Galahad.

Even if there ever had been a phone, with no way in or out of the room without the codes to both the strongroom and the safe, it was implausible anyone could have broken in. Malton wanted to check the strongroom for fingerprints to make sure he hadn't missed anything before he confronted Waqar with the truth – that he had staged the theft to cover up the extent of his criminal operation to his sister.

Having heard from Fauzia about the night at the meat processing plant, it all made sense. With no one left that he could trust Waqar turned to his sister. But knowing she would be loath to help a hardened criminal he had made up the phone story. Painting himself as the victim. Going as far as to stage a break-in to give weight to his lies.

Malton knew if he was going to convince Fauzia that her brother had used her like that he'd need cast-iron proof.

The investigation with Benton was a welcome distraction from thinking about the call he'd had last night from Emily's father – Mayer. After doorstepping him a few days ago Mayer had made it very clear that he didn't want Malton anywhere near his daughter. After everything that had happened, Malton couldn't blame him.

But when he'd called last night something had changed. Malton could hear it in his voice.

It was a quick call. Mayer was calling on behalf of Emily. She wanted to talk.

That was it. Not when, not why. Just enough to start Malton's mind wandering over the possibilities.

Which was why, right now, Malton appreciated having something to focus all that nervous energy on.

He watched Benton diligently lift every print she could find from the room. To watch her you'd never guess she was really a senior detective who did a two-day crime scene course ten years ago as part of her training to become a junior officer.

This was as much about closing off the phone investigation as it was about gently testing just how far he could take Benton. Now she was back as a detective she could be far more valuable to him than she was in uniform. He needed to make sure she was still open to that sort of cooperation.

From what he'd seen this morning she was more than happy to keep their relationship going. As long as he had the goods to offer in return.

Benton had not just brought powder and brushes, she'd brought a brand-new toy. An electronic fingerprint scanner. Every print she lifted, she gently laid the tape down onto what looked like a card payment terminal. The machine scanned the print, connected with the central database and if it found a match returned the information seconds later.

'This has been sat in a cupboard for months,' said Benton, gesturing to the machine. 'Typical GMP – no money for officers or investigations but let's blow fifty grand on some kit that no one's been trained to use.'

'But you have?' said Malton.

'I read the instruction manual last night,' said Benton with a grin.

Under the cover of Fauzia's security story Malton had fingerprinted Iffat and Samia in order to eliminate any of their prints they found. Fauzia had given her fingerprints and Waqar had been arrested years ago for a late-night fight and so his prints were already in the central database.

Malton's own hands were also stained with ink. Even when Benton assured him that she would be discreetly deleting all records of the morning's searches he had still insisted Benton check his prints by eye. He wasn't on any police database and that was how he wanted it to stay.

Benton started dusting round the Lowry, taking great care to avoid the painting itself.

'Who do you think Galahad is?' she asked, in between gentle sweeps of her brush. 'Cos between me and you, GMP don't have a fucking clue.'

Malton wished he had more than he did. Since talking to Bradley he had got no closer to identifying who or what Galahad was.

Despite Bradley's objections Miyah Mai had been true to her word and started sending Malton regular updates from Hale. Stevie Mitchum was on a war footing, holed up in his son's mansion under lock and key. His crew had seen the writing on the wall and were leaving in droves, with rumours of 'Galahad' beginning to spread through the wider organisation.

With Danny dead the whole shitshow was rapidly disintegrating around Stevie Mitchum's ears, just as Malton had predicted. It meant his window for finding Danny's killer was closing fast.

Benton finished lifting prints from the frame she'd been dusting and began to systematically run each lifted print through the electronic scanner.

Each time there was a tantalising pause before the machine gave a sad little beep to indicate a print that Benton had already eliminated.

'Soon as I find anything, you'll be the first to know,' said Malton.

Benton kept working through her stack of prints. She didn't look impressed.

'So that means you know fuck all then?' she said bluntly. 'When you asked me to do this for you, you told me you had information to share.'

'The information being that I'm working on it,' said Malton, hoping his tone conveyed just how little he wanted to keep up this line of questioning. They both knew that Benton would be getting a couple of grand for the morning's work. Rejoining the ranks of plain-clothes detectives hadn't done anything to blunt Benton's sense of her own value.

'First you get me, a seasoned detective, out here to play at crime scene technicians and then you give me fuck all. It's like you don't want to know what came across my desk this morning.'

Benton let her scrap of information hang there, waiting for Malton to bite while she kept feeding prints into the machine. Each time being greeted with the same frustrating noise. No match.

Malton dug a hand into his pocket and produced a roll of notes as thick as his wrist.

Benton saw what he was doing and laughed. 'You think because I'm here doing some spec work for a semi-legal, supposedly reformed criminal who runs an off-the-books police service for totally illegal actual criminals, you can buy me off?' she said with a grin.

Malton started counting out money. He felt Benton's eyes watching, counting with him.

Benton's face went through the motions of giving the minimum acceptable amount of resistance to taking a bribe before she threw up her arms and said, 'OK. I'll take your money but it's very important for me that you know I would have told you anyway.'

'Told me what?' said Malton as he finished counting out a round thousand in twenty-pound notes. Benton had made three grand and it wasn't even lunchtime.

Benton took the bundle of notes from Malton, getting black fingerprint dust all over them as she folded them into her pocket.

'You mentioned your ex popped up calling herself Lynne Harris?'

Malton's heart leapt. The call from Emily's father the night before had left him acutely aware that he'd let Keisha fall off his radar in the face of everything going on with Galahad.

Mayer Haim could tell him to stay away from Emily until he was blue in the face; that didn't mean Keisha would do the same.

'Dean already looked into it – she owns a cosmetic firm. She's off on leave or something,' said Malton.

'Good lad that one. Keen. I hope you're being nice to him,' said Benton.

Malton decided not to tell Benton how Dean had been running his own operation on the side or how it had worryingly crossed over into his own job for Fauzia Malik.

The idea of gossiping about someone else's mistakes held no interest to Malton. It was tantamount to grassing. Everyone deserved a second chance and right now Dean and his hunt for Olivia could well be the missing piece of the puzzle that would pull this whole sorry mess into some kind of focus.

'What do you know about Lynne Harris? How is she connected to Keisha?' Malton said, steering the conversation back on track.

'Lynne Harris,' Benton began. 'Her husband Malcolm turned up at Manchester Royal Infirmary yesterday with a broken arm. Same time as Daphne De Souza, his housekeeper, showed up with a fractured skull. Malcolm said he'd

246

fallen off a ladder, hit Daphne on the way down. I talked to a couple of nurses. They said it looked like someone had beaten the shit out of him. Someone violent. Very violent.'

Malton knew exactly what she was thinking. He was thinking the same thing too. Last time he'd tangled with Keisha she had Leon Walker in tow. But back then he was a helpless junkie.

Benton looked worried. 'If Keisha's got Leon Walker back on his feet and smacking around whoever she asks him to . . .'

Malton's hand went to the scar on his face. He didn't need reminding what Leon Walker was capable of. '*If* it was Leon Walker,' he said. He knew how Keisha's mind worked. How for her everything had meaning. Everything was part of one long head fuck. Bringing Leon Walker back from the dead would be exactly the sort of thing she'd pull.

She was sending him a message. Letting him know she was close.

Malton looked around the strongroom. It was plastered in black dust. Dusting for prints was always the last job at a crime scene. Purely because of the mess it created.

Leon Walker was fighting fit and still working for Keisha. His daughter had asked Dean to go after Big Wacky in search of her missing friend.

It was all connected. Each random event, each unexpected coincidence. Malton felt his mind swell with the momentum of it all. He was no longer facing a battle on multiple fronts. Whatever was happening it was looking more and more like one single foe.

Galahad.

But until he knew who or what that foe was, no one was safe.

Suddenly an unfamiliar noise broke his train of thought. He turned to see Benton holding up the electronic fingerprint device, a huge grin slapped across her face.

'I'm worth every penny,' she said. 'You got a hit.'

54

Vikki was talking but Dean was only catching every other word. Something about her college course. Fashion design? Something with textiles. As she talked she gestured with her arms, threw her hair back over her shoulder and played with the dozens of beads around her neck.

Dean's heart beat like a butterfly's wings. The dread he'd felt at coming clean to Malton paled in comparison to the task before him.

Vikki had used him. Now he needed to find out why. Why had she insisted he keep Olivia from Malton and how were she and Vikki really connected to Big Wacky?

Dean had asked Vikki to meet him at one of the hot-desk bars that had popped up just outside the city centre. The ground floors of the warehouses that had stood empty and unloved for decades had, one after another, been transformed. Stripped wooden floors, bare brick walls. Brutal, metal downlights and rough-and-ready bars made from chipboard and scaffolding. A mixture of elegance and industry.

Across the table from him Vikki looked like a regular.

She arrived wearing a near full-length, floral dress with long sleeves. Oxblood Doc Marten boots peeked out from under the hem. She wore several necklaces and bangles and carried a tote bag slung over one shoulder.

Watching her talk and laugh and drink her coffee it finally dawned on Dean why he was finding this so hard.

He really had fallen for her.

Vikki had visited him almost every day after he'd been shot. Since Malton had done up her flat, Dean had been round there so much that his mum had started to suspect he had a girlfriend. Hardly a day had passed in the last few months they hadn't seen each other.

It didn't matter now because now what he said next would be the end of everything.

'I need to talk about Olivia,' he said.

Vikki put her hands in her lap, her whole body tightening at the mention of the name. The gaiety was gone.

'Have you found her?' she asked.

Dean ignored the question and ploughed on. 'When you asked me to find her you told me her name and that she'd been seeing a guy called Big Wacky, up in Bolton.'

'That's all I knew,' said Vikki.

Dean couldn't look her in the eye and so he stared down at the empty coffee cup on the table in front of him.

'I think you didn't tell me everything,' he said.

Now it was Vikki who looked away. It was the smallest tell but it spurred Dean on.

He took a deep breath and ripped the plaster off. 'Last night at your flat, when you were out of the room. I looked at your phone.'

'Who do you think you are?' Vikki shot back. The coyness was gone. In its place anger flared.

Dean continued, 'I know. And I'm sorry. But I saw something. Big Wacky's number in your phone. And believe me, I wish I hadn't seen it. But I did and now I've got to find out what's really going on here.'

'You went snooping and you didn't like what you found?' said Vikki tartly.

Dean felt the energy draining from him. Malton would put the accusation out there and then let the silence do the work for him. Instead Dean felt an overwhelming need to talk.

'I'm so sorry. But I did see. And I know you must have a good reason. I think maybe something happened between you and Olivia and Big Wacky. I don't know what, but I think you didn't want to tell me. And I know you didn't want me to tell

Malton about it. But things have got serious. Someone's trying to kill Big Wacky.'

Vikki looked shocked. 'You think that's me?'

'I think when you asked me to find Olivia you didn't tell me the whole story. And now I need to know why.'

Dean sat back. It was done. He'd said it. Vomited out his accusations. The hard part was over.

Vikki was very still. 'What's happened?' she asked.

'I met Big Wacky, in his house. In his bedroom actually. He pulled a gun on me.'

Vikki's eyes flashed with fear. 'Where is he now?' she blurted out.

'He ran off, he seemed . . .' Dean tailed off. How had he seemed? At the time he thought he was just annoyed to find someone in his room but thinking back to what he said to his sister – 'you fucked up', it felt like something more. Like Big Wacky was scared of something.

Vikki clasped her hands in her lap, wringing them together guiltily.

Dean finally looked her in the eye. If he was going to do this then he may as well put all his cards on the table. It was now or never.

'The thing is,' he said slowly, 'I like you. I don't want anything to happen to you. And I think something might be happening. Something with Big Wacky. Something bigger than you and Olivia. The only way I can help you is if I know everything. I want to help you. And I want you to know, whatever happens, I'm going to keep my promise. I'll find Olivia.'

He suddenly felt very calm. This was like when he'd first met Danny Mitchum or when Keisha had pointed the gun at his face. It was as if he'd stepped outside himself and was now an incredulous observer watching as unbelievable events unfolded. Whatever was going to happen next, it was out of his hands.

'You're right,' said Vikki sadly. 'I didn't tell you everything. Because . . . I like you too. And I didn't want you to know who I really am and leave.'

Dean thought about the state she'd been in when he first found her. Abandoned by her junkie father in a filthy flat with no food or money. He couldn't imagine what more she could have to hide.

'I promise that whatever it is, I'll fix it,' said Dean.

Malton was right, when you made a promise you had to keep it. If you didn't have your word then you had nothing.

Vikki downed her coffee and then told him everything.

'They call it supported accommodation. After my dad walked out and never came back that's where I ended up. They know they won't have to deal with you for much longer so they ship you out to these shared houses for the last couple of years before you turn eighteen.'

Vikki shuddered at the memory.

'They've got staff but they don't do anything. You cook for yourself, clean for yourself. Suddenly you turn sixteen and it's like you haven't spent the last ten years getting fucked up by the system. Suddenly you're meant to be just fine on your own.'

As Vikki spoke Dean could see the hurt and anger that was still there, just beneath the surface.

'There were ten of us in the house where I met Olivia. It was crazy. People kicking off. Windows breaking. Drugs. The word got round what the house was and then we had dealers turning up, wandering the corridors. Staff didn't do a thing. There were fights there were guns. And drugs. So many drugs.'

Vikki stopped and looked down at the table.

'I'd lived with my dad. Seen what he went through. But I'd never been so scared in my life.'

Dean instinctively reached across the table and took her hand. Her skin was warm and delicate. She let his hand rest on hers and continued.

'Then I met Olivia. She was different. Like she hadn't given up. She wouldn't let them in. She wouldn't let the place drag her down. She'd just come from a proper foster home. An older couple, but there was some mix-up with paperwork and suddenly she hit sixteen and the council took her off them. Dropped her with all of us.'

Dean squeezed Vikki's hand, as much to keep himself together as to comfort her.

'Did Big Wacky come to the home?'

Vikki gasped. Dean saw her struggle with the memory. 'You've got to understand, we had nothing. No one gave a shit about us. Olivia – she was so strong. She fought it all. But you can't fight your whole life. You just can't.'

Vikki looked down at the table. Dean felt tears in his eyes but he held them back. He tried to remember how Malton sounded when he was at his most intense.

'Go on,' he said, shocked at the lack of warmth in his voice.

Vikki continued. 'One day this guy turns up. He wasn't like the others. He was together. He was nice. He seemed nice. Good-looking too. Really, really fit. And he had money. Lots of money and a car, this big white Audi.'

Vikki looked up. She seemed worried. Unsure how her story was landing.

'Big Wacky?' asked Dean.

Vikki nodded. 'There were two other guys who used to hang around. Real dickheads. But when Big Wacky turned up, they were terrified of him. He sent them packing. Told Olivia how brave she was standing up to them. It was like he was on our side. Olivia, she went in his car.'

Vikki looked up and Dean saw her harden as she caught the surprise in his reaction.

'It's not what you think. Big Wacky was good to her. He was kind.'

Dean failed to conceal a look of disbelief.

'It's so hard. People think you're in care, it's your fault. You're weak. You're nothing. But it's so tough. If they had to do it for just a day. If someone offers you a way out. You take it. Doesn't matter what it is. What Olivia had with Big Wacky? I just wanted some of that.'

Vikki's shoulders shook and tears began to roll down her face. Dean clenched his jaw. It made no difference. He found tears welling in his own eyes.

'He was kind. Sweet. We just drove around. He bought me stuff. Wanted me to see his shops and his factory. I was ready to do whatever he wanted to make him like me. But it was more like he wanted *me* to like *him*. In the end when we . . . '

Vikki caught Dean's eye and looked away.

'I kind of felt sorry for him,' said Vikki.

She looked up at Dean and he felt a jolt of shame that she would see him crying. He thought how much he wanted to be like Malton. To be the immovable, emotionless force moving through the darkness, dragging the truth into the light.

It finally occurred to him – he could never be like Malton.

As Vikki smiled back at him he realised – maybe that wasn't a bad thing.

Vikki wiped her eyes on her sleeve. 'If I could take it back I would. You got to believe that. And it was only one time. Olivia wasn't there and Big Wacky showed up. He asked if I wanted to come for a ride.'

Vikki started to cry again.

'You got to understand. He was a good guy. He was normal. And in a place like that you'd do anything to feel normal. But then Olivia found out . . . She was my only friend and I did that to her.'

'It wasn't you,' said Dean. 'It was the place's fault.'

'We had a huge row. Olivia ran away from the supported accommodation. She said she never wanted to see me again. That she was going to make Big Wacky pay for cheating on her.'

Dean had met Vikki, fearing the worst. Tales of addiction and abuse. There was no denying that Olivia and Vikki had been through hell, but to think that all this started with two friends falling out over a guy. Despite himself, Dean felt an immense sense of relief.

'I still don't understand. Why didn't you want me to tell Malton?' asked Dean.

Vikki looked embarrassed. 'After Olivia went I couldn't stay. I ran away. Back to my dad's flat. I thought if Malton knew he would stop helping me out. Make me go back there. Besides, I had you.'

For the first time since she'd started talking Vikki looked happy, her tears flowing into the creases in her smile.

'Did the staff from the home go looking for either of you?'

Vikki laughed. Dean felt foolish until she squeezed his hand and flashed him a smile.

'I just want her back. To tell her I'm sorry, to tell her I miss her,' said Vikki softly.

Suddenly it all made sense. The missing phone. Olivia wanted revenge – what if she knew about the encrypted phone and somehow managed to steal it from Big Wacky? A final fuck you. If that was true it meant that wherever she was now she couldn't be in more danger.

Dean felt himself straightening up. Becoming bigger. Just like Malton.

No. Not like Malton. Malton had strength. He had the strange remove that let him weather the storm. That wasn't Dean. Dean could go wherever Malton went. He could do whatever Malton could do. But from now on he would do it his way.

With feeling.

'I'll find her,' he said. 'I need to call my boss. Let him know what you've told me. I'll be back in a minute. Get us some more drinks.'

In one motion Dean rose from the table, pulled out his phone and put down a tenner for the coffee before swiftly exiting the café to make his call.

When Malton answered, Dean blurted out everything he'd learned, keen to bring him up to speed. So it was something of a shock when Malton thanked Dean for his digging before informing him that he had just pulled up outside of Olivia's new home.

55

Cherrington Road was a quiet suburban street in Urmston, west Manchester. The sort of place where dentists rub shoulders with bank managers and head teachers. Neat lawns, friendly smiles and the gentle reassurance of an easy life.

Malton sat outside the modest, semi-detached house that Benton's fingerprint-recognition device had given as the address of Olivia Dunn – the girl Dean was looking for. The girl whose fingerprint had been found inside a locked strongroom at the Maliks' house in Daubhill.

A single arrest for shoplifting had meant that Olivia was on the system. From piecing together what was on file about her, Benton had deduced that at one time the couple living in this house had fostered Olivia Dunn. Then when she turned sixteen, for some reason she left and was moved into supported accommodation.

Malton knew exactly what that meant. He shuddered to imagine taking a child from this unassuming normality and dropping her into the hellish finishing school of the foster system known as supported accommodation.

But Olivia's story had a happy ending. She had returned to Cherrington Road. Sue and Trevor Moss were in the process of adopting her before she turned eighteen.

Growing up, Malton had met a lot of foster families. It was always a welcome break from his alcoholic father and the constant infighting of Moss Side. Of course he was too young and too stupid to realise the chance he was being given at the time. Every placement ended the same way – in violence and disappointment and a return into the system and inevitably back to his father who in rare moments of sobriety would promise to do better.

Then he had met Keisha and she had changed everything.

Benton's sleuthing had got him this far but now he was on his own. Under-the-table crime scene investigation was one thing but Benton drew the line at hoodwinking members of the public.

Luckily getting people to do exactly what he wanted was Malton's speciality. So when he rang the bell and a scrawny, middle-aged man with a neat little goatee beard answered, it wasn't too long before Malton found himself invited in and sat on a sofa in front of Olivia's parents-to-be, Sue and Trevor.

Malton had been sure the theft of the phone had been a lie. An implausible story concocted by Waqar Malik to hoodwink his sister. But there *had* been someone else in that strongroom. The girl Dean was looking for. The girl who had been seeing Big Wacky. The girl who just might now be holding the key to Galahad's identity, Danny Mitchum's killers and the campaign of violence against Waqar Malik: Olivia.

It was a homely front room. Not fashionable or modern but tidy and warm. Dozens of photographs of children hung in frames on the walls. A huge extended family of foster children. Some as kids, others in gowns at graduations. Half a dozen children at Christmas, each one's face aglow with delight at discovering something approaching normality.

Malton looked at the smiling faces and tried to find any sort of common ground between those children and what he remembered of his own childhood.

'My daughter Vikki used to live with Olivia,' said Malton softly, hanging his head and doing everything he could to shrink the air of menace that his size and appearance imposed. He felt the whiteness of the space acutely. Their eyes on his skin, on his scar, on everything he represented.

'Did Olivia ever talk about Vikki?' he asked. He would be the one asking the questions. Driving the conversation. As long as he kept a firm grip on the reins he could do this.

'How did you get this address?' asked Trevor politely, leaning forward on the sofa. He had a short, grey beard and white hair. It made him look older than he was.

His body language was all compliance. Open and honest. Ready to help in any way possible. A million miles away from the people Malton usually dealt with. Even so Malton wasn't about to tell him how he'd found his way to Cherrington Road.

Ignoring the question he continued, 'Me and Vikki's mum separated. She stayed with her mum. I didn't know what was happening to her. Then I found out Vikki had left home. Gone into supported accommodation. Do you know what that means?'

He saw Sue and Trevor nodding along.

'Those places are just criminal,' said Sue, a touch of anger in her voice. 'You wouldn't put an animal in some of those homes.'

'When I was told she was in a home I thought . . . I don't know what I thought. Not what I found. Drugs and gangs. I tried to get her back but it was like no one cared,' said Malton, finessing his story.

'No one does care,' said Trevor with indignant authority. 'When the council messed up the paperwork and took Olivia to that place, we were so worried.'

Now he had them on side. He had let them see him as just like them. A loving parent outraged by the care system. An ally.

'When did you last speak to your daughter?' asked Sue, pouring Malton a cup of tea from a brightly coloured ceramic teapot. She was a thin woman with a short bob haircut dressed in shapeless jeans and a faded T-shirt from an old folk festival.

Again Malton swerved the question. 'They told me she ran away from the home a few weeks ago. But they've only just told me now. I came here because I didn't know what else to do.'

Malton watched his practised performance work its magic on these two kind, open-hearted people. It was like he always suspected. Children made you weak. There would always be people ready to prey on that weakness.

Malton's childhood had bred all the weakness out of him. His line of work had taught him the extreme cost of letting your guard down. As much as he envied the easy happiness of people like Sue and Trevor, it was something he knew he couldn't afford to indulge in.

'That's why we want to adopt Olivia. We'd fostered her for years but then when she turned sixteen there was some kind of mix-up and while we sorted it out she had to go and stay at that place. We visited her there . . .' Trevor drifted off, his voice cracking with emotion at the thought of it.

'I don't know how we let it happen to her. But we're not letting her go this time,' said Sue, loading her voice with forced cheer to counter her husband's wavering tone.

Malton considered how it was always the people who were most blameless who carried the most guilt. He'd done terrible things and hurt people who he claimed to have loved. Yet he felt no urge to justify himself to anyone.

'Is Olivia home?' asked Malton. 'I just want to see if she's heard from Vikki. I don't know what else I can do.'

'She's in her room revising,' said Sue.

Suddenly Malton felt them looking at him. Seeing the stocky, black man sat on their sofa. His face scarred, his eyes dead. He would need to speak to Olivia alone but despite all their tea and sympathy he would be the last person they would want left unattended with their daughter.

'I'll go and get her,' said Trevor, rising from the sofa and heading upstairs.

Alone with Sue, Malton sipped his tea, making no move to fill the sudden silence.

A few moments later Trevor returned, bringing with him a young girl. Her hair was held back with an Alice band and her face free of make-up. She had the same happy, carefree look as her prospective parents. An easy, middle-class comfort.

But Malton saw what her foster parents did not – the girl clocking him in an instant. Whatever prejudice Trevor and Sue had, their nice, white liberal politics made sure that they would never be anything other than unfailingly polite to a man who looked like Malton.

Not Olivia. Olivia immediately saw exactly what Malton was. A lone wolf. Just like her.

What Malton said next would decide whether or not he'd retrieve the missing phone, discover the identity of Galahad and find Danny Mitchum's killers.

56

Keisha pulled up outside the large, red-brick house on a tree-lined street in Didsbury, south Manchester's most desirable suburb. The whole street reeked of money. Spacious Victorian houses, all sloping roofs and large, green gardens filled with mature trees and acres of lawns. Over time, owners had piled even more money into them so that now houses boasted extensions made from glass and steel, Oriental-inspired landscaping and deliberately modern loft extensions erupting from the once-neat roof lines.

This was where Craig had tried to make his home.

It was also where Keisha had first tried to bring him back into her life a few months ago. Her campaign to win him back had been announced to the world by Leon Walker unloading a shotgun into his front door.

Back then Leon was a very different man. A heroin addict at his very lowest ebb. A wreck of a human being. Keisha too had been very different. She thought that she knew Craig. That she could win him back to her with a combination of cleverness and brutality – appeal to the man she knew all those years ago.

She knew now that Craig would not be so easily swayed. The ugly shotgun blast that Leon had inflicted on his front door was long gone. A brand-new door stood there as if nothing had happened. As if Keisha's message to Craig hadn't been loud enough.

This time it would be different.

She knew exactly what she wanted Leon to do. He was going to target everything that meant anything to Craig. His home, his business, his lover. Keisha would use Leon to destroy them all. But more importantly than any of that, she would use Leon to shatter the aura of invincibility that Craig had spent so long building up.

She would kill the myth of Craig Malton.

And when he was totally broken that would be when Keisha would give him a second chance. She would tell him they could finally have their family. Have their happy ending. She was too old now but Emily wasn't. Emily was a junkie. A pampered rich girl with no business raising his child. They would take her with them and when the child was born they'd take it and raise it as their own.

Emily was disposable.

Keisha had lost her baby. Why shouldn't she get to finally become a mother? With Craig there beside her. It would be as if the last thirty years were just a bad dream.

That would be her offer. What happened next would be up to Craig.

Leon sat in the back of Keisha's black Mercedes. On his lap was the pump-action shotgun.

It had taken weeks of long, hard detox and finally the enormous risk of giving Leon Walker access to an arsenal of loaded weapons but the look of hungry anticipation on Leon's face was enough to let Keisha know her plan had worked.

Leon was about to embrace his original addiction – violence.

He was dressed in black combat trousers and boots with a dark donkey jacket over the top. Unseen beneath the donkey jacket he was wearing a stab vest. He was ready.

Keisha had given him his instructions. This was the beginning of the end for him and he knew it.

'Set your watch,' said Keisha, glancing in the rearview mirror at Leon.

Leon raised a thick wrist and with his giant fingers pressed two tiny buttons. The watch gave a beep.

'You have five minutes, in and out. The house is empty. This is a wrecking mission. Send a message.'

Leon nodded.

The attack on Lynne Harris's home had been a prelude. This was a full blown statement of intent. Starting with where he lived, Keisha would let him know that nothing was off limits. No one was safe.

She watched as Leon got out of the car and strode towards the house.

Keisha had planned everything down to the last second.

What she couldn't have planned was what happened when Leon reached the house.

As he was raising his shotgun to blow the hinges off the front door he stopped, paused and bent down to get a closer look. Like he was examining the lock for something.

He then lowered the shotgun and pressed a giant hand against the door.

It swung open.

Keisha watched as Leon crept inside.

A few moments later she heard the first scream.

57

'You know you can tell us anything,' said Trevor, standing half in half out of the front room.

Sue hovered beside him. Neither of them looked sure of what they were about to do.

'Don't you trust me?' said Olivia, an edge to her voice.

Malton watched Olivia's parents squirm as she exploited the exact same innocence he had just moments earlier.

He saw her read them expertly and change tack. She looked away, her mouth pursed.

In a quiet voice she said, 'Please? I don't want you to hear about the home.'

The response was almost instantaneous. Halfway to tears Sue threw her arms around Olivia.

'You know there's nothing you can say that will make us love you any less,' said Trevor as Sue hugged Olivia hard.

'I promise I'll be quick. I just need to hear what she knows about Vikki,' said Malton.

Trevor looked torn. Malton knew that any naivety a person might have was soon dispelled by the foster care system. For every solid foster family that went on to change lives there were dozens who realised just what an emotional burden it was. People like Sue and Trevor might seem soft but you could never put your heart out like they did without having an inner strength that few shared.

Trevor looked straight at Malton, weighing him up while his wife hugged their soon-to-be adopted daughter.

He looked to Olivia but it was obvious he was addressing Malton when he said, 'We'll be in the kitchen.'

As they left Trevor gave Malton one final look. Searching for any kind of tell that he was making the wrong decision.

Malton hunched his shoulders and did his best to look as harmless as it was possible for an eighteen-stone ex-bouncer to look.

No sooner was Malton alone with Olivia than she reached her hand into the back pocket of her jeans and produced a phone. 'This is what you want isn't it?' she said, holding it up.

It looked just like a regular phone. Black, matt metal and a large, blank touchscreen. But this was the phone that held the key to everything.

'Can I have it?' asked Malton calmly.

Olivia held the phone tight. 'How do I know you don't work for Big Wacky? I give you this phone and then he sends you back round here to hurt me. Or my parents. Or Vikki.'

Malton thought for a moment. 'Why did you take it?' he asked.

Olivia shrugged. 'I don't know. There wasn't a plan. He cheated on me. I was mad at him. Mad at Vikki. Mad at everyone. And he'd shown me the strongroom. The safe too. I wrote down the codes. By the time I'd taken it I wasn't mad anymore. But then Trev and Sue got back in touch.'

'You give it to me, I promise that's the end of it.'

Olivia looked doubtful. 'Why should I trust you?' she asked.

'If you wanted to get back at him, stealing that phone has caused him more than enough bother.'

Olivia smiled. But only for a moment. 'Is Vikki OK?'

'Vikki's fine. She lives in a flat that I pay for. She's going to college. She's thriving.'

'You pay for her flat?' said Oliva, a tone of suspicion creeping into her voice.

'I knew her father. Wanted to give her a better start than the one he gave her. That's all.'

'So you help people out of the goodness of your heart?' she taunted.

'I help people when it helps me,' said Malton plainly. 'I've been paid to find that phone. Now I've found it – that's a start.

Next I need to make sure that all the trouble that's been caused by it going missing goes away. That includes making sure that once I have it, no one ever comes looking for you.'

He could see her wanting to believe him. Straining against a lifetime of suspicion to take this one leap of faith.

'You really know Vikki?'

'Vicious?' said Malton.

He saw the smile creep across Olivia's face.

'I remember pissing myself when she first told me. She never tells anyone her real name. At least not people she doesn't trust.'

Olivia looked Malton over one last time, shook her head and held out the phone.

Malton took it from her, never once taking his eyes off her until he had it in his own hand.

'Can you tell Vikki I forgive her?' Olivia said hopefully.

'Of course,' Malton replied.

'I'd do it myself but when I heard that Trevor and Sue wanted to adopt me I made the choice – I had to leave all of that behind. I can't risk them changing their minds. I'm not going back.'

Malton knew all too well the struggle to become someone new, someone better. Whether it was his house in Didsbury or the expensive clothes he wore. At the back of his mind was always the gnawing realisation that he was doing his best to fit in somewhere he didn't belong.

'I'll tell her,' said Malton, examining the phone. He looked up. 'Do you have the PIN code?' he asked.

'One, One, One, Two.' Olivia smiled. 'Wacky's not the sharpest tool in the box.'

Malton pressed a small, inlaid button on the phone and the screen came to life. He tapped in the PIN code.

The phone started to vibrate. It didn't stop as hundreds of backed-up messages finally reached their destination.

'I turned it off as soon as I heard about the adoption,' said Olivia. 'I was hiding it under my mattress.'

Malton looked down at the phone. All the messages were texts. All of them sent from similarly encrypted phones under pseudonyms. All except one name – Galahad.

Every message from Galahad was a voice message. Not a single text.

'What will you tell Trevor and Sue?' asked Olivia cautiously, for the first time betraying a hint of nerves.

'I'll tell them you were very helpful, but couldn't tell me where Vikki was. Wish them well with the adoption,' said Malton.

He meant it.

'Where is Vikki?' asked Olivia, a note of concern in her voice.

'Safe,' said Malton.

'Can you tell her about the adoption? Why I couldn't risk seeing her?'

'If you want, when this is over and done you can tell her yourself.'

Olivia considered the offer. 'Maybe. I'd like that. Until then. Can you give her this?' Olivia reached into another pocket and slipped something to Malton. Taking care to slide her own hand into his. The practised gesture of someone well used to the passing of illicit items.

Malton immediately knew what it was. 'I'll make sure she gets it,' he said.

Ten minutes later Malton was parked up a few streets away and scrolling through the phone.

While the phone itself was an ingenious mixture of passwords, hidden operating systems and key-shortcuts that, at a moment's notice, could wipe the entire phone clean, the reason it was so special was the app that it contained.

The DLchat app was no different to any other messaging app save for one important distinction. Everyone on it was a hardened criminal paying thousands of pounds a year to access what they assumed was a secure network. Malton had already heard rumblings about someone having cracked the servers, rumours that the police were already on DLchat harvesting information.

If that was true then a lot of people were going to be getting a very unexpected early morning visit from Benton and her mates in the very near future.

But for now all he was concerned with was Galahad.

He selected the latest message from Galahad, sent that morning, and pressed play.

A voice filled the car and when the message was over, he played it again, and then a third time. Finally, when he was sure he'd heard what he thought he'd just heard, he turned the phone off and tucked it away in an inside pocket of his waxed jacket.

He now knew who had killed Danny Mitchum.

No sooner had he put the encrypted phone away than his own phone went off. Without thinking he took it out to see who or what wanted his attention now.

It was an alert from the alarm system in his house. Ordinarily Malton hated cameras. He preferred to rely on what he could find out for himself. But after the last time Keisha had paid a visit to his house in Didsbury he'd taken the precaution of fitting the entire place with security cameras on a wireless network. If anything were to trip those security cameras then his phone would receive an alert and he would be able to remotely access the feed to see the inside of his house wherever in the world he found himself.

Malton pressed a button on his phone and the screen filled with images from the cameras covering his house.

He saw carnage.

58

MALTON HOUSE. HALLWAY CAMERA

The front door is open. A man lies face down in the hallway.
Beneath him a large red stain spreads into the carpet.

MALTON HOUSE. KITCHEN CAMERA

A shotgun lies on the island unit.

A man flies into frame, barrels over the island unit and crashes
into the cooker.

The man tries to get to his feet. He cannot. He is large. A white
man with shaggy hair.

Leon Walker appears in frame.

Leon Walker picks up the man with one hand, with the other he
turns on the hob. The convection plate glows red.

Leon Walker drags the man to his feet and presses his face into
the halogen hob.

The man struggles but Leon Walker is too strong.

After a few seconds, Leon Walker rips the man's face up from
the halogen hob, smashes his head onto the corner of the oven and
leaves him on the kitchen floor.

The man doesn't move.

Leon Walker collects the shotgun from the island unit and leaves
frame.

MALTON HOUSE. FRONT ROOM

Leon Walker appears, sweeps the empty room and goes.

MALTON HOUSE. BEDROOM

Waqar Malik hides behind the door of the master bedroom, in
his hand a gun. He is shaking.

MALTON HOUSE. LANDING

Leon Walker jogs up the stairs. He's moving faster now. The shotgun is still in his hands as he heads to the bathroom.

MALTON HOUSE. BEDROOM

Waqar Malik slips out from behind the bedroom door and raises the gun.

MALTON HOUSE. BATHROOM

Leon Walker stands for a moment looking at his reflection in the mirror. He pauses and holds up the shotgun. He is admiring himself.

MALTON HOUSE. LANDING

Leon Walker emerges from the bathroom with the shotgun lowered. From out of frame Waqar Malik fires.

The shot misses Leon Walker who discards his shotgun and rushes towards Waqar Malik, who comes into frame with a gun raised.

Waqar Malik goes for a second shot. Leon Walker reaches for the gun and wrenches it from Waqar's hand.

The gun falls over the banister and out of frame.

Leon Walker turns on Waqar.

MALTON HOUSE. HALLWAY

Waqar Malik plummets into frame from above. He hits the banister on the way down before sliding down the remaining steps.

Lying next to Waqar are the shotgun and the handgun as well as a second, inert body.

Ignoring the weapons and the body, Waqar stumbles to his feet and flees out of the front door.

A second later Leon Walker appears, picks up the shotgun and casually walks out of the front door.

59

Tahir would live. He'd lost a lot of blood. Both his legs were broken and he had internal bleeding. His face was black with bruises from where he'd landed hard on the road.

But he was alive.

Fauzia and her team had saved him.

The worst over, Fauzia stood a few feet back watching the nurses tending to him. Against all the odds he had regained consciousness. Now he lay bandaged and battered, sucking ice chips and grunting weakly in answer to the nurses' questions.

Fauzia couldn't take her eyes off him. She needed to speak to him. She needed to know that this was just a terrible coincidence. Tahir getting run over had nothing to do with the bloody events of the past few days.

Her head had started to ache again and now her stomach clenched with protest at the fact she'd gone nearly all day without a break to eat.

As she sat down and waited for the moment the nurses would leave and she could speak to Tahir alone, she tried to remember how she'd ended up here.

All Fauzia ever wanted to do was the right thing. As a councillor, as a doctor, as an MP and as a daughter and a sister. She wanted to help.

She'd thought she was helping Waqar. That she could somehow play this game and walk away. Do just enough to save her brother and then go back to living her normal, law-abiding life. She saw now how deluded that was.

Once you started playing it never ended. There was never any rest. You had to keep running as fast as you could.

Ever since she'd walked out of the library and got into Waqar's car it was like she had gone from the light to the dark. In that darkness up was down, black was white. Waqar was Big Wacky and Fauzia Malik employed men like Craig Malton to do whatever it took to keep one step ahead of ruthless murderers.

She remembered the words of the masked man at her father's wedding hall. They knew all about her campaign to become MP for Farnworth and Great Lever. They knew about Tahir. What was it he'd said? 'We can help you.'

Looking down at Tahir's broken body, the meaning of those four little words held the key to everything.

If Tahir's accident *was* down to her, that meant she was no longer the one fleeing the darkness. She had become it.

Ever since that night at the meat processing plant, Fauzia had told herself that she was as much a victim in all this as the man they had killed. She was simply a bystander to the horror. But if that was no longer the case, then who was Fauzia Malik?

She hadn't heard back from Malton. Whether or not he found the phone didn't matter now. All that mattered was knowing that Tahir's accident was simply that. A random misfortune.

She worked in A&E. She knew full well that day in, day out, normal people had life-changing accidents. Death lurked far closer than most people ever realised.

'Can you keep an eye on him?' The nurse's words shook Fauzia out of her morbid reverie.

She looked up to see the nurse cleaning up the mess left after the initial admission. He was looking at her, waiting for an answer.

'Of course,' said Fauzia, getting back to her feet. The nurse gave her a smile and hurried off, laden with assorted bits of medical waste.

Finally Fauzia was alone with Tahir.

271

She knew she didn't have long. After checking the coast was clear, Fauzia drew the curtain around Tahir's bed and crouched down beside him.

His face was a mess. Skin loose, bruised and going a sickly shade of purple. His eyes were shut but she could tell from how he shifted and moved that he was still just about conscious.

'Tahir? Can you hear me, Tahir?' whispered Fauzia into his ear.

Tahir's face screwed up. His eyes stayed closed.

'It's me, Fauzia Malik. I was the doctor on call when you came in. You're safe now. It's all OK.'

With great difficult Tahir swallowed. Fauzia picked up a glycerine swab and gently moistened Tahir's mouth.

Fauzia continued. 'I just need to know. It was an accident right? Just an accident?'

Tahir tensed. His eyes shot open and he looked straight at Fauzia. He tried to lift himself up off the bed but his injuries defeated him.

Fauzia looked around. It had been too long. Someone would be coming back any minute.

'Tell me it was an accident,' she said trying to keep the desperation from her voice.

Wide-eyed and terrified, Tahir shook his head.

'What does that mean? It was an accident. You got run over. They found you in the road. It happens.'

Tahir continued to shake his head. His tongue shot out and licked his swollen lips. He took a breath and Fauzia saw just how painful it was to do so.

He looked up with bloodshot eyes and hissed out a single word: 'Galahad.'

Before Fauzia could reply the curtain was pulled back. The nurse had returned.

Fauzia snapped back into being a junior doctor. 'Make sure he's on top of his pain meds. I'm going to chase up about getting his scan sorted.'

She didn't wait for a reply. She was already moving.

Along corridors, past wards. Through the endless bowels of Royal Bolton. Her body fleeing, her mind knowing she was trapped.

She turned and pushed through double doors into an outdoor courtyard. At one time it had been a place for patients to sit out. Now it had become a dumping ground.

Fauzia looked up at the Bolton sky and breathed in the air.

Galahad. He had said Galahad.

As her mind began to slow down and absorb just what that meant her phone started ringing.

It was her brother.

She took a deep breath and pressed 'answer'.

She heard Waqar's voice. Breathless and urgent.

'I'm dying, Fauz. You got to help me. I'm dying!'

60

Driving to meet Stevie at Danny's house in Hale, Malton couldn't shake the feeling that time was running out.

But now that Waqar had launched an assault on his home, the time for reflection was over. Losing the phone had put Waqar and his family in Galahad's sights and yet his first move had been against Malton himself – the man who was trying to help him.

What was it he didn't want Malton finding out? That he hadn't simply lost the phone but that it had been stolen by a teenage girl? If that got out then Big Wacky would be finished. Whatever reputation he'd built up would vanish overnight. Better to endure Galahad's displeasure than the humiliation. In Big Wacky's world an internecine gang feud was a far more respectable hill to die on.

If Waqar Malik knew it was Olivia who had taken his phone, he definitely had good reason to try and kill Malton to stop that information from ever coming to light.

He'd called Dean and told him to secure his house in Didsbury. He would deal with the bodies there later. After the damage he'd seen Leon Walker inflict on Waqar, Malton doubted he would be too hard to find. At a hospital or a morgue. And besides, Malton didn't need him anymore – he had recovered the phone and with it discovered the identity of Danny's killer.

The first person who needed to know was Danny's father: Stevie Mitchum. Which was where Malton was heading right now.

The fastest way to reach Hale was to skirt the edge of the city along a semi-rural rat run. Through the scruffy greenery of Trafford and on to the escalating opulence of Altrincham. By the time Malton set off, he was well into rush hour and the way was clogged solid with commuters heading out of the city.

As he crawled past Dunham Massey, his mind scrambled to impose an order on events.

Keisha was playing for keeps. She'd armed Leon Walker and set him off on a path of destruction. His thoughts drifted to the phone call from Emily's dad. What was it she wanted to talk about after all this time apart? Did she want him back? Malton wasn't sure that the man who Emily fell in love with still existed. That man had thought he wanted a family. That man had thought if he tried hard enough he'd finally get the nice, white, middle-class respectability he so craved.

In a way he was thankful Keisha struck when she did. If she'd been just a few months later then he and Emily would have been trying for a baby. The thought of Keisha using a child as leverage against him chilled Malton to the bone.

But his concerns about Emily paled when compared to the visceral thrill he felt knowing that Keisha was entering the end game. First Lynne Harris's home, then Malton's own house. She was moving closer and closer. Malton had no idea where she would strike next but now that the first shots had been fired it wouldn't be long before she would be coming for him.

When she did he would be ready.

Malton felt as if he was finally getting on top of things. The feeling lasted right up until he arrived at Danny Mitchum's place.

The large gates that offered entry through the high wall that surrounded Danny Mitchum's fortress-like house were wide open.

Beyond the unscalable, white, rendered walls, the front garden had been paved over. Ordinarily there were at least half a dozen cars parked up here. Today there were just two. Danny's

Man-City-Blue Range Rover and parked up next to it Miyah Mai's pink Mini, the makeshift repair to the front wheel arch a reminder of the last time she and Malton crossed paths.

Something was desperately wrong. It was like Miyah Mai had said: the rats were deserting a sinking ship.

Malton pulled up and got out of his car. He already had the sick feeling in his stomach that he was too late.

As he walked through the already open front door, he reached into his jacket pocket and took out the polished steel hatchet he always carried with him.

Danny's house was in even more of a state than usual. The pearl white carpet was a mess of muddy footprints. Without Danny around any pretence of keeping it clean had gone out of the window.

Also gone were various bits of furniture. There were bare spaces on the walls where people had helped themselves to the priceless art and memorabilia with which a blind Danny Mitchum had surrounded himself. Pointless signifiers of a level of criminal wealth he had neither the time nor the temperament to spend.

It was a vast house. Dozens of rooms, none with any obvious purpose. Some were completely empty of furniture. Others seemed to have evidence of people using them as makeshift bedrooms. Sleeping bags and mattresses. Empty cans and the remains of takeaways.

But not a soul.

As Malton climbed the broad, semi-circular staircase that dominated the vast entrance hall he noticed the first drops of blood on the carpet.

Then a few red pools of it on the stairs, which carried on to the landing and towards the front of the house.

Malton quickened his pace. He was low now, crouched like an animal ready to pounce on its prey. He gripped the hatchet firmly in one hand, the other hand out in front of him waiting to deal with whatever came his way.

His work was about intelligence. Piecing together scraps of information. Cajoling, threatening and forcing the issue. If trouble came he didn't run but if he was in a situation where he was fighting hand to hand for his life, then something had gone very badly wrong.

Up ahead he heard a sound. Something moved. Someone was there.

Malton froze. He turned slowly to where the noise had come from. He was on the landing now. It stretched around the enormous hallway creating a kind of mezzanine. Malton crept around the landing, heading towards the front of the house.

The landing ended in a door to the master bedroom. The trail of blood led straight into the bedroom.

Before the bedroom there was one other door. It was closed.

The noise came again. It was coming from behind the closed door.

Malton crept along the landing, never once taking his eyes off the door. He was now eye-level with the giant chandelier that dominated the hallway, and out of the corner of his eye he noticed that someone had thrown a bra up into it.

As he neared the door he slowed down. He made sure he was standing so that when the door opened whoever was inside would have to get through him to escape. He reached out for the handle with his free hand and squatted down, making himself as low as possible. If whoever was in there had a gun then there was a good chance they'd aim high. If they aimed low then that would be that.

Malton gripped the hatchet, turned the handle and pulled the door open.

Miyah Mai screamed, turning her body away from Malton, her hands covering her face.

The door was to a storage cupboard. It was filled with pallets of bottles of water. And there in amongst them cowered Miyah Mai.

'He killed him; he killed Stevie,' she shrieked.

Malton didn't have time to ask more. He was already heading towards the bedroom. Following the blood trail to what he now suspected was its terminal destination.

The master bedroom was enormous. Huge windows looked out over the front garden, with a double-height ceiling and a bed lost in the middle of the great expanse of thick, luxurious carpet.

Stevie lay on the bed, his limbs splayed out, staring at the huge mirror attached to the ceiling. A handgun lay on the sheets beside him.

His gut was stained red. Rising and falling slowly. Each time giving out a wet, wheezing hiss.

Stevie turned his head and frowned as he saw Malton, the effort required simply to move those few inches making him grimace in pain.

Malton stood at the foot of the bed. There was nothing to be done for Stevie Mitchum. He'd been shot in the stomach. There wasn't long left now.

'It had to be fucking you,' said Stevie, struggling with every word.

It had been Malton who had tipped Keisha off that he was working for the Mitchums. Back when he'd bumped into her at the Northern Power Women event. This was all down to him.

'Leon Walker?' asked Malton already knowing the answer.

'You always were a know-it-all. Didn't help you stop him, did it?'

Stevie began to cough. Huge gouts of blood erupted from his mouth and ran down the sides of his thick neck.

'Fuck me,' he said, a quiet sadness filling his eyes.

'Where is everyone?' asked Malton.

'Fucking cowards,' spat Stevie, his anger suddenly giving him a burst of energy.

Malton almost felt sorry for him. Without Danny there was no way that Stevie could hold the whole, insane mess together. Danny had been the key. Without him it was always going to end this way.

Malton had found out who killed Danny and uncovered Galahad's true identity. But it had come too late for Stevie.

Malton hadn't seen this coming. This was heavy even by Keisha's standards. If Stevie Mitchum was fair game then no one was safe.

Stevie let out a long, wheezing groan. It wouldn't be long now.

'Stevie!'

Miyah Mai had plucked up the courage to emerge from her hiding place and follow Malton into the bedroom.

She ran across the floor and, ignoring the blood that saturated the bed, knelt down beside Stevie.

Stevie raised a giant, gnarled hand, wincing at the effort. Miyah Mai grasped his thick fist with both her hands and hugged it to her.

A weak smile spread over Stevie's face.

There were tears in Miyah Mai's eyes. 'I'm sorry,' she wept.

Stevie's enormous hand gently squeezed against her own slender fingers.

Malton let them share a moment. He couldn't save Stevie's life but he could at least finish the job he'd been hired to do.

'I found out who killed your son,' said Malton.

Stevie didn't move. He stared up at the ceiling. His own reflection looking back at him. His eyes grew wet.

Malton watched as this monstrous man, pumped full of steroids and aggression, gutshot in the mansion his son's drug money paid for, suddenly became maudlin at the thought of his dead son.

'Tell me,' he rasped.

Malton knelt on the bed next to Stevie and told him what he'd learned.

As Stevie listened a smile broke out over his face. A smile that turned into a laugh. Blood sprayed everywhere as his ruined body pumped his lungs one last time.

'The fucking cunt,' he said gleefully. He turned to Miyah Mai and, as he opened his mouth to tell her that he loved her, he died. The words still in his throat, a smile on his lips.

Malton left them there. Someone else could deal with the clean-up. He had a much bigger mess to deal with.

First his house, then his biggest client. Malton wasn't prepared to wait to see what Leon Walker hit next before he jumped to the inevitable conclusion – Keisha was targeting anyone and anything under his protection.

Right now that meant there was only one place in the city he needed to be.

61

Malton hadn't said much in his call to Dean. Only to drive to his house in Didsbury and secure the building.

Dean didn't have time to fill Malton in on Vikki or ask about Olivia. From the brevity of the call Dean got a sinking feeling that something big had happened. Events had moved on and Dean was back to playing catch-up.

He didn't have time to start imagining what those events were. He was walking up the driveway to Malton's house when through the half-open front door he thought he saw a body.

Without hesitation Dean slipped inside and shut the door behind him.

A man was lying face down on the hallway floor in a pool of blood. A handgun lay next to him.

Bending down to get a closer look Dean recognised him.

He was one of Big Wacky's men. Having spent nearly three months in Daubhill tracking Big Wacky, not to mention all those hours on social media taunting him from afar, Dean had got to know all of the crew who surrounded Big Wacky by sight if not in person. The man's name was Jay.

Next to Jay lay the gun that a few days earlier Big Wacky had pointed in his face.

Dean knew better than to touch anything. Stepping over Jay he moved on towards the kitchen where he found a second body, its face seared off. Burnt lumps of flesh were stuck to the hob. Dean felt his stomach turn.

He didn't need a face to identify this second body. It was Chrissie, the only white face in Big Wacky's crew.

Both Jay and Chrissie were dead. They looked like they'd been beaten to death.

A quick tour of the rest of the house confirmed that whatever had happened here it had been brutal in the extreme. But there was no sign of Waqar.

Dean crept back outside and gently pulled the door closed making sure to wipe down everything he touched.

Back at the Malik house Big Wacky had seemed shocked to learn who Malton was but nothing Dean could recall suggested his next move would be this bloody.

Events really had moved on but Dean was more than ready for it.

Putting some distance between him and Malton's house he drove as far as Moss Side before pulling over to a discreet, terraced road behind the Heineken brewery and pulling out his phone.

After three months of searching for Olivia online as Dobbzbobbz, Dean knew all about Big Wacky.

He began to scroll through all the Dobbzbobbz social media accounts.

Dean had gone silent the past few days, but the social media chatter hadn't. Dozens of accounts were calling him out for not being at the ice cream parlour. Still more were challenging him to step out from behind the phone and meet Big Wacky face to face.

Dean had no way of identifying any of them. Each of them was anonymous. He would have to be clever.

First he looked at the accounts posting threats against Dobbzbobbz. There were several. One after the other he took the username and searched for any other accounts on different platforms or forums who were using the same name.

Man543, Shizzzza_4, RRK-_*#, BWnnn0.

Just as he was beginning to lose heart he got a hit.

Ganghill45.

The same username was registered to a forum about breeding miniature bulldogs.

Dean's fingers shot across the touchscreen of his phone as he typed in the address for the miniature bulldogs forum – Bullies. Post after post showed the kind of men who wouldn't look out of place working for Malton Security as they showed off newly minted litters of bulldog puppies or touted auctions of sperm from their top studs. The sums being exchanged were in the tens of thousands.

Ganghill45 had commented on several posts. Admiring litters and idly talking about getting into breeding himself.

At the bottom of each post his profile had a link to a forum about drill music. The dark, beat-driven rap hybrid.

Dean was already clicking on the link where he was presented with yet more message boards discussing new tracks, beefs between artists and promoting events.

He clicked on Ganghill45's post history. A list of posts came up. Several of them original posts from Ganghill45.

Dean clicked on the most recent and was greeted with an embedded video – Dogzz.

Clicking on the video Dean's car filled with the sound of a drum machine backing track over a speeded-up female vocal. But he wasn't listening to the music, he was watching the video. There was who he assumed was Ganghill45, a skinny white kid wearing an enormous chain studded with what looked like diamonds but what Dean knew were almost certainly low-value crystals. In each hand he had a newly born miniature bulldog. The tiny, velveteen animals poured into his palms.

As he rapped, in the background there were half a dozen other men, nodding along.

There at the back was Waqar Malik.

Now Dean was getting somewhere. He paused the video and stared hard at the room they were in. It didn't look like someone's house. It looked more like a scruffy mancave. Several chairs, a television and a low table covered in drugs paraphernalia. There was even a mattress in one corner and a desk by the window. There were also huge stacks of something all around the room. At first Dean assumed it was some kind of building material. Tiles maybe?

He scrolled forward a little and the camera lurched forward into Ganghill45's face. Dean paused it again and took another look at the stacks in the background.

They weren't tiles. They were pizza boxes. Each on bearing the logo of Solitaire Kebab.

Why would they be above a kebab shop? He had hardly asked himself the question when the answer came to him. A search on Companies House's website and his suspicion was confirmed. The director of Solitaire Kebab was none other than one Waqar Malik.

Dean's heart raced. He was getting closer. What would take Malton hours of shoe leather and leverage to find out he was digging out of the internet in a matter of minutes. An entire generation of criminals living their lives online.

If Waqar and his mates hung out and shot videos above a kebab shop would it be too much of a stretch to imagine that he'd use it as a safe location to lie low after a run-in with Leon Walker?

It was a leap but it was all Dean had.

There were eight Solitaire Kebab shops all over Bolton. He needed more.

Dean kept watching. The camera stayed tight on Ganghill45 and the dogs. In the background Waqar bounced along to the beat.

But then as the video ended the camera moved. The cameraman swept to one side and out to the window, ending the clip staring out over Bolton.

To be more precise, staring out over a park.

It didn't take Dean long to search through eight Solitaire Kebab shops and find the only one that faced onto a park. It was in Daubhill. Big Wacky's territory.

Half an hour later, sitting outside the kebab shop Dean was enjoying the smell of the air freshener that hung off the rearview mirror of his yellow Crossland while he waited for the fire engine he'd called from a burner phone, to turn up.

The police were too risky and he knew that calling an ambulance was no guarantee of it arriving any time soon. But when he found a *Manchester Evening News* article about a firebomb attack outside the very same kebab shop where he was now parked up, everything fell into place. The fire brigade would come sirens blazing and sound just enough like police to do the trick.

Dean's yellow Crossland was immaculate inside. He made sure to clean it out every night and to hoover it thoroughly every weekend before going to his local hand car wash and paying a little extra to have it fully valeted.

With the Crossland, all of Manchester had opened up to him. Before, when it was just his bike, his world was hemmed in by the M60. Now he could range over the entirety of the conurbation. From the city sprawl and surrounding suburbs to the outer reaches of the region.

His mum had been so proud of him when he first drove it home.

Dean heard the unmistakable sound of sirens in the distance. The noise bouncing off tightly packed, terrace houses. A few seconds later he saw the flashing lights of the fire engine. All eyes were on the bright red engine as it bumped onto the pavement and firemen swarmed into the park that Dean had claimed was the scene of a conflagration.

But Dean wasn't watching the park. His eyes were fixed on the upstairs window of the kebab shop where he was immensely gratified to see a face appear at the window above the kebab shop.

It was the bloody, scared face of Waqar Malik.

62

'You need to stay still,' ordered Keisha.

Beneath her Leon Walker grimaced in pain and did his best to comply.

Leon lay on the mattress in his room back at Keisha's hide-out in Harpurhey. The mattress was soaked with blood. The dense, salty odour of it mixed with the smell of stale urine and general decay. The room felt like a place things went to die.

Keisha sat astride his giant body. She knew her weight wouldn't hold him down for long, but it was better than nothing. Leon was badly injured. If she didn't act now then he might not make it to the end.

Keisha had come this far and she wasn't ready to quit now.

She had cleaned up the minor cuts and grazes Leon had received fighting off Waqar's men but what was giving her greater cause for concern was the ugly bullet wound in Leon's left thigh that he'd received at Danny Mitchum's place.

The mansion had been nearly deserted. The sight of a heav-ily armed Leon Walker striding through the grounds had been enough to send the final hangers-on running for the hills.

Alone and cornered Stevie had made his final stand. It hadn't lasted long. He got a single shot off before Leon mowed him down in a hail of bullets, leaving him to bleed out on his bed. It was only when he was getting into Keisha's car that he realised he'd been shot.

By the time Keisha had got him home he was bleeding badly. The back seat of the Mercedes looked like an abattoir. Leon had staggered inside, propped up on Keisha's tiny frame, before dropping down onto the mattress where he stayed.

Keisha needed Leon back on his feet. The dizzying high of violence had been replaced with the agonising pain of his wounds. She couldn't risk letting him have pain medication. Leon was an addict and the smallest amount of drugs in his system could be enough to trigger a relapse. She needed him focused on the task in hand – breaking Craig down to his lowest ebb. Ready for Keisha to save him.

Everything was so nearly ready. Malton knew the game now. He didn't know where it was coming from but he knew it was coming. She needed just one more day from Leon. One last tsunami of chaos to wash over Manchester. Enough to give her the chance to get into The Sentinel and spirit Emily away for the final part of her plan.

Leon groaned weakly beneath her. His clothes stuck to him with blood and sweat. The giant VICIOUS tattoo on his neck obscured by filth and gore.

'You can't die,' she told him.

Leon muttered something through a mouth of ruined yellow teeth.

'I know it hurts. You've been shot. But you're stronger than that. You're Leon Walker. I didn't bring you back to see you die now.'

He screwed his eyes up. The pain looked unbearable.

Keisha was losing him.

She slapped him hard across the face. Leon's eyes flared open.

'You feel that? That's pain. That's the pain that makes you angry. The pain that gets you back on your feet.'

'Fuck . . . you . . .' Leon seethed.

Keisha had come too far to let Leon Walker give up now.

'Fuck me?' she raged. Suddenly her voice was low and loud, the Moss Side in her rearing its head. She tore off her sunglasses and let Leon see the burning intensity in her eyes. 'You ungrateful piece of shit. I gave you a second chance. I gave you the thing you wanted more than anything. I gave you revenge.'

She loomed down over the far bigger man. For the first time that day, Leon looked scared.

Keisha reached over and grabbed one of the guns Leon had been carrying. It was a Glock 17. A long time ago it had belonged to a police firearms officer. Now the criminals were having their turn.

Keisha held it, the barrel pointing upwards, and addressed Leon, still in that assertive, clipped accent that placed her squarely in the M14 postcode.

'Do you want me to end it now?'

Leon squirmed but stayed silent.

'I could shoot you in the head and walk away and you'd rot here, undiscovered for months. A nothing. A no one. Leon Walker, used to be someone, found him in a squat, shot dead. Worthless junkie.'

Keisha noticed with satisfaction that tears had begun to form in Leon's eyes. His face screwed up like a scolded child. Beneath her she felt the tension go out of his body. He was nearly done.

'That's not you, is it? You're going to be a fucking legend. Came back from the dead. Killed Stevie Mitchum. Went on a rampage. Made the whole fucking city sit up and take notice. That's you, isn't it?'

Leon gave a loud sniff.

Keisha pointed the Glock at his forehead. 'Or am I wrong?'

She stared down into Leon's eyes. She knew if he wanted to he could easily overpower her. Even with his injuries he was a massively powerful man. Once more Keisha rolled the dice, knowing full well that one of these days her luck would run out.

'It's going to hurt, but I can fix you. I can put you back on your feet and get you back out there to finish this thing. Or I can end it now,' she said.

Keisha held the barrel against Leon's forehead. The gun slid over his skin. He was greasy with perspiration and filth. She pressed it in, feeling the hard bone beneath.

She was far too close to getting her second chance to go back now.

'Choose,' she said.

63

'I've worked with serial killers, rapists, gunmen, murderers and some of the most deranged people you could imagine. You think I'm going to go into hiding because you tell me I *might* be on your ex's shit list?'

This wasn't going how Malton had hoped it would. After the carnage he'd found at Danny Mitchum's place he'd driven as fast as he could back into town to Bea's office.

It was clear now that Keisha was hitting targets connected to him and that she was one step ahead. Emily's dad had told him she was somewhere safe. He hoped for her sake that was true.

Meanwhile back in Manchester, Bea was in imminent danger.

But when he'd finally reached her office and explained the situation he found her supremely unconcerned.

Now she sat behind her desk as she half listened, sorting through the day's paperwork.

'This is different,' said Malton.

Bea looked up. She was as close as she ever got to annoyed. Malton realised that despite seeing her for a couple of months now, their relationship comprised mostly of sex and a mutual professional curiosity. There had never been any conflict. No complication.

Now here he was telling her that her life was in danger and he wanted to help her. It was as close as either of them had got to a genuine expression of affection.

Bea gave a tight, impatient smile. 'What I do is dangerous. I represent the people no one else will. I get bad guys off.

Sometimes I don't. The kind of people I represent don't like it when things don't go their way. They like to blame someone. And that someone is usually me. Do you know how many death threats I've had?'

Malton didn't. He realised he didn't know much about Bea. He'd deliberately not looked too deeply. But when he thought she might be in trouble his first instinct was to rush to save her. It was what he did. It was how he first met Emily – on a job. It was how Keisha had blindsided him a few months back, making out that she was in danger when in reality she *was* the danger. And it was the only way he knew to show Bea Wallace that despite appearances he actually cared.

If Bea didn't need protecting then did that mean Bea also didn't need Malton? It had been fun up to now. Malton realised why that was. He had been postponing the moment when suddenly Bea meant something to him. The moment when everything would become difficult.

'People are dead,' said Malton.

Bea didn't even look up from her paperwork. 'I'm a criminal lawyer; dead people is what gets me work.'

She looked up and flashed a smile. Her accent was pure Geordie. 'If we're going to work together you're going to need to toughen up a bit.'

Malton smiled despite himself, turning away and making a show of looking out of the window so Bea wouldn't see.

Manchester was slipping into a lazy, summer evening. The rush of office workers had calmed down and now the streets were empty, the evening crowds yet to arrive. Somewhere out there was Leon Walker and behind him Keisha.

Dean had called to say he'd tracked down Waqar to above a kebab shop in Bolton. Malton couldn't be more impressed. True, Dean had kept things from him but now he sensed the boy pulling out all the stops to win back his approval. Though Malton knew better than to give it to him that easily. When Dean called with the news he'd held back on his praise. Just enough encouragement to keep him going, keep him hungry.

Malton didn't get where he was today by anyone ever telling him that he'd done a good job. Every moment of his life was a struggle to prove to the world he was good enough. It would never end.

Watching Bea continue with her paperwork he realised she was doing the same thing to him. Rejecting his offer of help and keeping him on his toes. Despite seeing the moving parts, Malton was still helpless in the face of her manipulation.

He didn't have time for this.

After the beating Leon Walker gave Waqar and his boys, Malton was sure that Waqar could wait. Dean had tracked him down and as far as he and Fauzia knew, a dangerous maniac called Galahad was still after them and the encrypted phone was still missing.

Malton knew exactly who Galahad was and he was willing to take the risk that he wouldn't be able to find Waqar for a little while yet. Enough time for him to deal with Keisha first – the biggest threat now.

Emily would have to wait. He was already spread dangerously thin.

Then there were the two bodies still in his house. That was a problem that he hoped Bea would be able to help him with later.

That left nothing to do but find Keisha's soldier, Leon Walker, and stop him dead.

'You could always call the police,' said Bea, not turning away from her paperwork.

Malton smiled. She was fucking with him. Despite everything she was still fucking with him. Maybe they did have a future after all.

Providing Keisha didn't kill her first.

64

Fauzia had made it in and out of the hospital without anyone stopping her. No one saw her sneaking into the storeroom and no one saw her emerging five minutes later with two bulging carrier bags.

She'd begged Waqar to come to the hospital or let her send an ambulance. But he'd refused. He told her that if she took him to a hospital he was as good as dead. According to Waqar, Galahad's men had already killed two of his friends. The hospital would be the first place he'd come looking to finish the job.

With no other option she was forced to improvise.

As she walked out of the hospital carrying the stolen medical supplies she marvelled at what her life had become.

She had helped her brother kill a man. Hired an underworld figure to trace a drug dealer's stolen phone. She'd faced down masked thugs and thanks to her, her political rival had been run over and nearly killed.

It was clear now, this never ended. There was no way out.

The car park was half empty. The staff who worked office hours packing up and going home for the day. A breeze was blowing down from off the hills. It soothed her throbbing head.

She was halfway across the car park when she saw Malton. He was standing by her rental car, waiting in the shadows. As if he knew she'd be there.

She couldn't stop now. Whatever Malton had to say, unless he was going to physically restrain her, Fauzia was getting in that car and going to Waqar's aid.

'I'm in a rush,' said Fauzia moving to open her car door. The only thing she cared about was getting to her brother.

'I've got good news,' said Malton.

Fauzia tossed the carrier bags onto the passenger seat. One opened, spilling syringes and bags of saline over the seat and into the footwell. She shut the door and hoped Malton hadn't noticed.

'What?' she asked brusquely.

Malton reached into his pocket and produced a matt-black phone. He held it out to her. 'This is what you hired me to do. Your brother's phone.'

Without thinking Fauzia took the phone. She looked down at the thing in her hands. The thing that had been the cause of so much chaos and death.

She suddenly felt very scared.

'You can't just give me it,' she said.

'That was the job,' said Malton plainly.

'But what about Galahad? What am I meant to do?'

Malton shrugged. 'You off somewhere?' he said, bending down and peering into the car.

'You've got to speak to Galahad, tell him it's over. Tell him to leave Waqar alone,' said Fauzia. 'Stay out of our lives.'

After all this time to now be holding the phone. It felt like a bomb waiting to go off.

'Your brother was at my house,' said Malton.

Fauzia was sure she must have misheard. She was more tired than she'd ever been in her entire life. Things were starting to sound different. Voices changing. Noises far away.

'What?'

'He came to my house with two other men. They had guns. Unfortunately for them they weren't the only ones looking for me.'

Fauzia's head spun. On the phone Waqar had simply told her that he'd been attacked by Galahad's men. He'd omitted to mention that he was in Malton's house when the attack happened.

It made no sense. Why would Waqar go after Malton? When he'd fled their parents' house after finding Dean in his room

293

she assumed he was simply embarrassed that once again his little sister was having to solve his problems. Her 'fucking up' was no different to every other time she had to be the one to save Waqar from himself. But what if there was more to it? What did he know about Malton that she didn't? Was it really Galahad who'd done that to him?

Malton was looking at her. Reading her reaction to the news. Luckily for Fauzia she was too tired to do anything except stare blankly back at him. He seemed so measured, so confident that he had every angle. Why would her brother not trust him?

Malton reminded Fauzia of Tahir. That night at the hustings. Tahir's confidence, his self-possession. His unshakeable belief that things would always be the way they were. That nothing would ever shake the status quo.

Then she thought how Tahir had looked the last time she saw him. Lying broken and scared on a hospital bed. Life-changing injuries. That was the current jargon.

As sick as it made her feel to see him there, just for a moment Fauzia had felt something else. A feeling so shameful that no sooner did she feel it than she put it as far from her mind as possible.

She had enjoyed the look of surprise on his face. Seeing the realisation that he had underestimated her.

Fauzia had seen that look many times before. Male students amazed she was ahead of them in their studies. Older white doctors shocked that this young Muslim woman had corrected them. Tahir when she had given her speech at the library. She also knew that usually what happened next was the backlash. The bruised male ego robbing her of her brief victory.

But not this time. Tahir had been utterly destroyed. Whatever Galahad had done to him he knew that not only had Fauzia bested him but also that there would be no rematch.

For the first time Fauzia saw a man accept fully that he had lost and she had won.

And so despite her horror at how she'd secured that victory, for as long as she allowed herself to, she had enjoyed it.

Looking at Malton she wanted to see that expression again. The job was done – she had the phone now, she had the power.

'I'm on the licensing committee. Did you know that?' she said.

Malton nodded. 'I looked into you. I look into all my clients.'

'Then you know that I'm responsible for monitoring everyone who applies for Security Industry Association certification?'

Malton said nothing so she continued.

'You don't have it. You're a CEO of a security firm and you don't have it. All those council jobs you do and you don't have the proper paperwork.'

'You don't need paperwork to do what I do,' he said a little too quickly.

'No. You don't. But if you don't have it you can get investigated. By the licensing committee. The committee I'm on. And if you do apply for it, then you can be scrutinised. By the licensing committee. The committee that I'm on.'

Malton grinned and looked away for a moment.

'So what is it you want?' he said.

Fauzia felt herself waver. It wasn't exactly fear. More the anticipation. It reminded her of the first time she'd assisted a surgeon. She had seen the fist sized incision leading to the patient's bowel. She'd been handed the tool to cauterise the exposed blood vessels. She had frozen. If she screwed up she could be thrown off her course. The patient might die. Everything in her world was in her hands at that one moment in time.

Then she remembered what she'd told herself – *you are Fauzia Malik. You can do this*. And she had.

She knew what she wanted from Malton and she knew just how much was at stake if she screwed up. But she also knew she was Fauzia Malik.

'I want to meet Galahad,' she said. 'And I want you to make it happen.'

65

'BYE, DEAN!' chorused a dozen young women standing at the bar dressed in nothing more than an assortment of very skimpy lingerie.

Dean stopped at the door, turned and, blushing bright red, waved goodbye to all the girls on duty that night at the Diamond Lounge Gentlemen's Club.

At the far end of the bar a couple of Malton Security staff were bent over, pissing themselves laughing.

Dean gave a gracious bow and – leaving behind the heavy curtains, dim lighting and ample flesh of the Diamond Lounge – stepped out into the night.

Whether or not Malton was impressed that he'd tracked down Waqar he couldn't say. No sooner had he told his boss over the phone that the man who'd stormed his house was hiding out above a kebab shop than Malton had told him about Stevie Mitchum.

That was why for the last few hours he'd been driving round the city centre dropping in on every premises currently watched over by Malton Security staff. He'd been fed Chinese food at the International Buffet, offered several drinks as he went round the bars and pubs of the gay village and worn himself out walking up and down the stairs of the dozens of office buildings Malton Security protected.

Everyone knew Dean. The only one in the office under fourteen stone, without tattoos or a neck thick enough to bend steel around. But everyone also knew he had Malton's absolute trust.. That was the kind of bona fides no amount of weightlifting and street fighting could earn you.

He was under instructions not to mention Leon Walker but to ensure that everyone was on full alert. Leon's name was still more than enough to cause the kind of panic Malton was keen to avoid.

Dean decided upon the story that Malton was planning a surprise inspection sometime in the next week and that he was doing them a favour, giving them a heads-up.

Everyone wanted to listen when they thought their boss might be dropping in on them unannounced.

The night wore on and Leon Walker was nowhere to be seen. One by one the bars and pubs closed. The offices locked their doors and gradually the lights went off as the city centre began to wind down.

It was nearly three in the morning. Aside from the Diamond Lounge there was only one other venue left open that was staffed by Malton Security personnel.

Bendicks Casino.

The casino was one of the few venues in the city that was truly open twenty-four hours a day. This time of night it was filled with a mixture of restaurant workers from Chinatown coming off shift and hardcore drinkers who'd sussed out one of the few remaining all-night venues left in the city.

Rather than the glamorous casinos of the movies, Bendicks was more like a dimly lit conference room at a regional hotel. Gambling tables were dotted across the floor and a bar at the end of the room provided nothing more exotic than you'd find in a local pub.

The air conditioning was always on, making the room freezing cold and keeping the gamblers awake and playing.

It was an engine to extract money from anyone unfortunate enough to have a taste for gambling and the last place on Dean's list.

Dean drove slowly through the empty streets. Aside from the occasional straggler it was deserted. Not so surprising given that it was midweek. In the time he'd spent briefing the guys in the Diamond Lounge only a single punter had wandered in.

He'd instantly been jumped on by five bored strippers, all of them offering him the chance to buy them a drink.

He deliberately drove slowly, peering down unlit side streets, driving with purpose towards dark figures in doorways. Hyper-alert for the presence of the towering monster who was still out there somewhere. And the woman who was pulling his strings.

Dean felt himself gripping the steering wheel tightly, his entire body tense in readiness.

Adam and Ed were the two guys on duty at Bendicks tonight. Both good guys. Adam was tough as boot leather. A pretty boy with a giant beard and hands beaten into clubs from a lifetime of scrapping. Ed was smaller and always smiling. Anyone who mistook that smile for weakness soon learned from their mistake.

After the awkwardness of the Diamond Lounge, Dean was looking forward to seeing them both, having a coffee and filling them in on just enough detail to get their eyes open and their radars up.

He was turning past Manchester Art Gallery when he heard the first shot. He wasn't sure at first but then it was quickly followed by dozens more. The unmistakable BRAP BRAP BRAP of a machine gun.

Dean's heart leapt into his mouth. He slammed his foot down.

He flung his Crossland around the corner. Bendicks was a few hundred metres ahead of him. He could see people running out of the front door. Screaming as they fled.

BRAP BRAP BRAP.

He saw Adam stagger out of the front of the casino clutching his chest. His Malton Security vest was red with blood. He got no more than a few steps before he fell, face down to the pavement. He didn't move after that.

There was no sign of Ed.

BRAP BRAP BRAP.

Dean hurtled towards the noise. It was then he saw the black Mercedes parked across the street. Its passenger door open. Waiting.

There behind the wheel was Keisha Bistacchi.

There wasn't any road left. No more time to think or plan. Dean did the first thing that came into his head.

He turned the wheel of his beloved Crossland, aimed his car at the black Mercedes and floored it.

66

For a few terrifying seconds Keisha's whole world exploded into noise and glass.

She had turned towards the sound of the accelerating car a split second before it had rammed into the front right-hand driver's side of her Mercedes.

Then the impact. The cacophony shaking all thoughts out of her head. Her seat belt holding her tight into her seat as her car spun round, before the back end smashed into the yellow car that had just hit her, the impact of the solidly heavy Mercedes flipping the lighter vehicle onto its roof.

And just like that it was over. Keisha sat in the driver's seat and wondered what she was meant to do now.

Without thinking, she went to open the driver's side door only to discover that the entire front right of the car was gone – crumpled in on itself.

The side impact cage had saved her life. Her head was ringing and her whole body screamed but she was moving. She lifted her hand to her face and felt broken glass in her hair. She crawled over and tumbled out of the passenger-side door. She managed to stand for a second and then felt her legs give way as she grabbed onto the car to stop herself falling to the tarmac.

Everything seemed brighter than before. She realised her sunglasses were missing.

She checked her clothes. The uniform. It was all still in one piece. That was good. She'd need it later.

People were still fleeing from the depths of Bendicks.

She saw a couple of bodies on the ground. Leon was back in business.

Keisha let go of the Mercedes and took a step, then another. She felt the earth solid beneath her feet and slowly some kind of order returned to the world.

A few feet away, the yellow car was on its roof. It had flipped and skidded into a communal bin at the entrance to the alley that ran down the side of the casino. The bin was heavily dented and the car a write-off.

There, hanging upside down and lifeless from his seat belt, she recognised a face she hadn't seen since the day she'd put a gun in it and pulled the trigger. Craig's lackey, Dean.

Keisha stopped dead.

She could smell petrol.

This was taking too much time. The crash. The gunfire. Police would be coming. She couldn't be caught. Not now. Not when she was so close to finishing this thing. Without her car she couldn't help Leon. He was on his own. She needed to run.

Keisha bent over, resting her hands on her knees. She breathed deeply, inhaling a huge draught of Manchester air. She felt the chill enter her lungs, slow down her thinking, bring everything back to an even keel.

This is why she always wore trainers. You never knew when you would have to run.

She turned and smelled it again. Petrol. It was leaking out of Dean's car, spilling down the side of the upturned vehicle and slowly pooling a few feet from where he limply hung.

BRAP BRAP BRAP.

Leon was still finding targets. Malton would have a blood-bath on his hands. Malton's connection to Leon's rampage might never make the papers, but the underworld would certainly put the pieces together. Danny Mitchum's father, Malton's house and now the casino he protected. Craig Malton's word would be good for nothing. He'd be finished.

Ready for Keisha's offer of salvation.

But she needed to make sure was he there to receive it.

The smell of petrol became even stronger as Keisha ran towards the upturned car. She could already hear sirens. It wouldn't be too late if she hurried.

She knelt down by the driver's side window. Dean wasn't moving.

Keisha whipped out the gun she'd been keeping in her bumbag and without hesitation flipped it around in her hand and used the handle to smash out the glass.

The sound of breaking glass stirred something in Dean. He moaned dimly, his eyes opening and closing but not focusing.

Keisha didn't care what state he was in. As long as he was alive he could pass on her message.

She leaned in and fumbled for the seat belt release. As she pressed the button with a click, Dean's full weight fell on her.

She was ready. She half caught, half dodged away as Dean awkwardly slumped down, landing on the ceiling of his upturned car.

Keisha wriggled out from under him and stood back up.

The sirens were getting louder. People were on the ground screaming for help. People with bullet wounds. People who wouldn't make it.

Keisha hoped Craig appreciated the lengths she'd go to just to make him sit up and take notice.

She bent her knees and hooked her own arms under Dean's. In one swift movement she hauled his skinny body through the empty window frame, over the broken glass and debris, and free of the car, dropping him a few feet away.

Dean started to stir. Keisha knelt over him, drew back a hand and slapped him hard across the face.

A shock went through Dean. He sat up and took a breath of air. Opening his eyes, he saw Keisha looking down on him.

'Now we're even,' she said.

She bent down and fixed Dean in the eye, making sure he clearly heard what she was about to say.

'Tell Craig we need to talk. I'll see him at home. Our home.'

Then she turned and ran.

67

The nearer they got to Rusholme the slower the progress they made. Fauzia didn't mind. Everyone she cared about was in the car with her. Her mum and dad but most of all her older brother Waqar. The brother who had forced his friends to let her join in playing cricket in the street. The brother who boasted to whoever would listen about how clever his sister was and how many books she'd read, even though she was still only seven years old. Waqar was Fauzia's world. There was no one who made her feel more happy and safe.

The family's car crawled through Longsight towards Dickenson Road and the parade of takeaways just off the main drag of the curry mile. Fauzia's father supplied half the takeaways in Rusholme so even on the busiest night of the year, they knew there would be a table for them – 2005 would be the best Eid ever.

It was less about the food. Whatever they wanted, no one could make it better than her mum. It was about being part of something, about seeing the roads packed full with smiling faces. The young men in hired sports cars revving their engines at each other. Families walking together through the darkness, laughing, talking and sharing the sense that Manchester was as much their city as anyone's.

They found themselves sitting in the window of the takeaway and Fauzia gazed out at the crowds passing by. For one night everyone on the pavement looked like her or her dad or her mum or her brother. Car horns and cheers filled the night air. The smell of spent fireworks made everything seem special.

Waqar had barely taken a mouthful when he started to have trouble breathing. At first no one noticed. Her mother and father were busy talking to the owner and Fauzia was smiling through the *glass at another little girl, holding her father's hand as he bought her a balloon.*

Then she felt her brother's hand on hers. Turning she saw the look of panic on his face. He was already going blue, the skin around his face bulging and swelling. Her screams brought the whole restaurant to a halt.

It was pure luck that Manchester Royal Infirmary was only a few hundred metres up the road. With the traffic like it was, an ambulance would never have reached them in time.

Fauzia hurried through the night holding her mother's hand as they followed behind Iffat. Her father ran, carrying his son as he struggled to breathe, the allergic reaction slowly closing his airways as Waqar's body flooded with antibodies and he went into anaphylactic shock.

Waqar was sleeping. After dressing his wounds and making sure he was hydrated and warm, Fauzia had put down the thin mattress she'd found propped up against a wall behind pizza boxes and laid her brother down to rest.

Watching him lying there she thought of the times she'd visited him in the hospital all those years ago. They'd put her brother in a medically induced coma and for two weeks the whole family made the daily trip from Bolton to Manchester to see him. Fauzia would take whatever book she was reading at the time and sit by Waqar's bed, reading aloud to him. Hoping that the sound of her voice would bring her brother back.

He came back but something had changed in him. Maybe it was the knowledge of his own mortality, maybe a misplaced sense of shame at suddenly discovering this fatal weakness in his previously strong body. The Waqar who returned from that fateful night was different. He was harder, colder. He seemed desperate to prove himself. Her thoughtful, generous brother became selfish and reckless.

Fauzia didn't know it at the time but looking back it was clear. Waqar hadn't woken up from the coma alone. Big Wacky had come back with him.

But he was still her brother and she would do everything she could to keep him safe.

The light was coming up when Waqar finally came to. Fauzia propped up his head and helped him drink.

She reached into her pocket and took out the encrypted phone. She held it up for him to see before laying it on the mattress beside Waqar.

Waqar's eyes widened. His mouth broke into a smile and he was about to reach over and hug Fauzia when he realised just how badly injured he was. He lay back down on the mattress and with great difficulty picked up the phone, examining it with a huge grin on his face.

'You did it! Fauz, you did it! My sister really *can* do anything.'

Fauzia blushed. She let herself enjoy the moment. But just for a moment. She had questions that needed answers. Questions that had kept her awake last night as well as any tablets could.

'Why did you attack Malton's house?' she asked.

Waqar huffed and looked away. 'How'd you know that?'

'Why did you do it?' repeated Fauzia, unwilling to be derailed.

Waqar's smile was gone. He glowered like a sullen teenager. 'You think someone like Malton is all neat and proper? Like getting someone in? It's not like that. You know who he works for?'

'Me. I hired him. It was him who got the phone back.'

Waqar turned to look at the phone in his hands. The colour drained from his face. 'He gave you this?'

'Yes.'

'Malton don't work for you. He takes your money and he smiles but he don't work for you.'

'He got the phone back.'

'That's what he does. He plays people. Both sides.'

Fauzia couldn't work out what her brother was saying. She was too tired, too emotional. She'd been running on empty for too long now. She needed it spelling out.

'Who *does* he work for?'

305

'Who do you think?' said Waqar impatiently. 'Galahad.'

Fauzia couldn't hide her shock.

'That's right, Fauz. This isn't your nice world of politics where people say nasty stuff and then you all go for a drink after. This is real. Everyone in my game knows about Malton. No one lasts as long as he has without throwing everyone else under the bus.'

'How do you know he's working for Galahad?' she asked, her voice trembling.

'When that phone went missing I knew it was only a matter of time before Galahad came asking why I'd gone quiet. That guy you helped me get rid of? He didn't want a quiet word. He had instructions to take an eye out. Make sure I knew how mad Galahad was. Before I got the drop on him he wanted me to know just how seriously Galahad was taking it.'

'More serious than losing an eye?' said Fauzia, amazed that even now she could be shocked by the brutal facts of her brother's world.

'He told me he'd got Craig Malton on the payroll,' said Waqar definitively.

Fauzia felt a thick, heavy blackness begin to swim at the edge of her vision. A distant dread on the horizon.

Seeing his sister's face, Waqar softened. He held up the phone with a grin. 'It don't matter now. You got the phone back. You can leave the rest to me. This is my mess. I'll do it my way.'

Fauzia was shaking her head. She looked at her brother, barely alive with his injuries. From the way he was moving it was clear that despite the medication she'd give him he was still in an enormous amount of pain.

'I can't,' she said. 'When he gave back the phone I asked him to do one more thing.'

Sensing the fear in his sister's voice, Waqar's smile faded. He licked his dry lips and asked, 'What thing, Fauz?'

'You've got to understand. I was trying to end this thing.'

'What did you do Fauz?' said Waqar urgently.

'I asked him to set up a meeting. Between me and Galahad.'

68

'He's awake!'

Dean opened his eyes to see half a dozen worried girls looking down at him. At first he didn't recognise them. They were wearing clothes.

He was laid out on one of the purple velvetcovered benches that filled the Diamond Lounge. Benches that had been designed to be big enough for two girls to put on a show, or when the card payment cleared, for a lucky punter to get himself a very strictly regulated private dance.

Dean sat up and looked around. He'd never been in the Diamond Lounge with the lights on. What, in the dark, appeared a salacious space full of unspoken pleasures, under strong strip lights looked nothing more than a slightly chintzy pub.

Suddenly it came back to him. The casino. Keisha. The crash.

'Adam . . .'

'He's dead,' said Malton as two girls stepped aside to let him through.

Dean could tell this was serious. Malton's face was unreadable. That meant something volcanic must be going on inside that shaved, scarred head. Something that wasn't for public consumption.

The girls drifted to the bar, where they sat throwing anxious looks Dean's way while Malton talked.

'Ed got out. Found you on the ground. Brought you here.'

Dean struggled to remember anything after the impact.

'What about Leon Walker?' he asked.

Malton shook his head. 'Gone. Six dead, another dozen injured. Adam rushed him, got shot for his troubles. But it gave Ed enough time to clear the place. I sent Ed back to the office. This thing has got too dangerous.'

Dean felt a lump in his throat. Before he started working for Malton Security he'd steered clear of men like Ed and Adam. Men who liked a fight, preferably with someone like Dean. But since working there he'd got to know the men behind the posturing and the bravado. Adam had a wife and kid. She was training to be a nurse and his job at Malton Security was paying for her college course.

He closed his eyes. He didn't want Malton to see him crying.

In the dark he felt a hand on his shoulder, huge and heavy. It was Malton reaching out to him.

'You should go home,' he said.

Home.

Tell Craig when he's ready I'll see him at home. Our home.

Suddenly it all came flooding back. Dean sat bolt upright. A couple of girls at the bar gasped at the suddenness of his movement.

'I remember now,' he said.

Malton removed his hand. He spoke slowly. 'Remember what?'

'Keisha, she was in the car and I saw her. I crashed my car into hers. I flipped it. My car. I flipped it. She got me out.'

Dean looked up at Malton questioningly. He couldn't quite believe what he was saying. Keisha had pulled him free from the wreck.

'Your car burned out,' said Malton. 'She saved your life. Why?'

Dean felt sick. Malton knew Keisha better than anyone. There was always an angle. He wasn't alive because Keisha wanted to make up for shooting him in the face. She needed someone to deliver her message.

'She told me to tell you. She wants to talk.'

308

Malton frowned. 'About what?'

'She didn't say. She just said she'd see you at home? Your home?'

'My home?' said Malton. 'The house in Didsbury?' He looked confused.

'No, that's not how she said it. She said . . .' Dean strained to remember Keisha's exact words. 'She said, "Tell Craig when he's ready I'll see him at home. *Our* home."'

Dean still wasn't sure what it meant but from the way Malton reacted, it clearly meant something to him.

'What else?' Malton demanded.

Dean wished he had something. The shock was wearing off and an aching pain was filling his body. His head felt like it was splitting in two.

He focused on the pain, tried to push himself to recall something. Anything. He saw Adam's body lying on the ground. He heard the gunfire from within the casino. He saw Keisha's black Mercedes rushing up to meet him.

The sound of someone hoovering the carpet broke the moment.

In the far corner of the room a cleaner had begun work. The night was long gone. It was morning.

Malton gave a look to one of the two Malton Security men still in the club and they went over to have a word.

Then it came to Dean. The detail was so slight it hadn't even seemed relevant until now.

'She was a cleaner,' he said.

'Don't worry about her, she can clean up later,' said Malton.

'No,' said Dean. 'Not the cleaner here. Keisha. She was in a tabard like a cleaner would wear.'

Suddenly Malton was listening. 'What else?'

'It had a logo. And a name. I think it said . . . The Sentinel?'

A look came over Malton's face. 'Lynne Harris wasn't on a four-month sabbatical. She was at The Sentinel,' said Malton, a faraway look in his eyes.

Dean looked confused. 'But what's The Sentinel?' he asked.

'The Sentinel is a private rehab facility. Very expensive. Very exclusive. That must be where Keisha met Lynne Harris. Lynne Harris wasn't on a sabbatical, she was in recovery. She was an addict . . .'

Malton tailed off. Dean saw his eyes goes dark. His features tighten. His mind running to some unspoken conclusion.

'I need you on your feet,' he said.

Dean struggled upright and swung his feet to the floor. It took a lot of effort but he did it. His fingers dug into the soft velvet of the seat and slowly the floor stopped moving.

'You need to find Bea,' ordered Malton. 'Find her and stick with her. Leon Walker's broken cover. After a mass shooting in a casino, the police will be looking for him. They'll flood the city to find him. He doesn't have long left.'

'Where are you going?' asked Dean.

'To stop Keisha killing Emily.'

69

The city centre was already crawling with police. A cordon had gone up around Bendicks Casino while armed officers were visibly patrolling the nearby streets.

As Malton sped away, the whole city was going into lockdown. The manhunt for Leon Walker was intensifying.

He put his foot down and felt the engine's deep growl beneath the hood. He let the car get all the way up to fifty before throwing it out of third and up into fourth.

Walker had hit three locations that Malton knew of, and he'd dropped bodies in all three. Big Wacky's men at Malton's house, Stevie Mitchum at his son's place and now one of Malton's own employees along with several customers at Bendicks Casino. It was an obscene body count. A grotesque rerun of all those years ago when Leon Walker went on his original rampage.

Leon had started small, robbing street dealers. Making a name for himself in the kind of circles that fell far below Malton's pay grade. It was when he escalated to openly robbing the men behind the dealers that Malton got involved.

It doesn't take much to track underworld money. The shop that never seems to sell anything. The bar that's always empty but never goes out of business. Endless cash-only car washes. It's complicated and messy but it's not so complex that a man like Leon Walker couldn't figure it out.

He wasn't just hitting businesses that were flush with pre-laundered drug money. He was sending out a message. Thumbing his nose at the established hierarchy.

Leon was unstoppable. Unnaturally strong, unhesitatingly violent and seemingly without fear.

After he brazenly walked into a Chinatown card game, beat up half a dozen men and walked out with over a hundred grand in cash, it was Malton who found himself tasked with pulling the brake on Leon Walker.

Malton still remembered how he'd felt walking into the city centre car park where he'd arranged to meet Leon. Malton's trade was negotiation. Brokering deals, fostering compromise. Letting everyone walk away feeling like they came out on top.

That wasn't how Leon Walker operated. Walking into that car park he knew what he was there to do. Put down Leon Walker or die trying.

Back then Leon only had his fists. Now he didn't just have Keisha's guns, he had her cunning too.

Malton could only imagine how long Keisha planned to string out the pain. How many other innocent people would die for her to prove her point. Whatever that point was. Over and over again he replayed their conversation at the awards ceremony. What had she said in those brief few moments they had together?

'You know where you belong.'

Where did he belong? Or at least where did Keisha think he belonged? Back with her? Was that all this madness came down to?

Whatever she was up to, thanks to Dean she was now on the run. Forced to accelerate her plan or risk everything being undone.

It was early enough that the drive out was clear. The morning traffic was all flowing in the opposite direction, commuters not yet aware that the city centre had become a no-go zone.

Malton gave them no thought as he tore up the road.

There was only one person he cared about who would be found in an exclusive, private rehab facility like The Sentinel: Emily.

She had been an addict when he met her. Emily's father had hired him to rescue her from the boyfriend who had first got her addicted. But in all the time that Malton had known her she'd been clean.

What had happened in those three months since he last saw her?

He'd only ever met one other person who saw the world like he did. One person who would take the clues he had and come to the same conclusions: Keisha.

This was why he had walked out all those years ago. As much as he loved Keisha he saw far too much of himself in her. That same violent drive, the complete lack of boundaries, the dark, unquenchable rage of those who'd realised that the deck is stacked against them.

Malton spent his whole life trying not to be that person. Keisha had gone the other way. She'd embraced all her damage and turned it into strength. In a way Malton envied her. But in another way he knew it made her impossibly dangerous.

Malton internalised his self-loathing. Keisha projected it.

If Emily was at The Sentinel there was no telling what Keisha had in mind for her.

Malton's jaw clenched as he sped through country lanes. He should have gone looking for Emily months ago.

All that time when he had no idea where she was.

But Keisha had known exactly where Emily was.

Malton blew past the gatehouse and on to main buildings of The Sentinel rehab facility. He pulled up directly in front of the main entrance, leapt out of his car and ran inside.

At the front desk a young woman looked up and upon seeing Malton got to her feet, her hand already on her walkie-talkie.

'I need to see Emily Haim now,' said Malton, doing his best to sound calm and measured.

The young woman hesitated for a moment. Malton could feel time slipping away from him.

'I'm her fiancé,' he lied.

The young woman looked just a fraction less worried.

'I wasn't meant to come here, not for the four months. I know what your regime is like. We decided it was best for her to be left alone. But I got a call.'

'Our guests aren't allowed phones,' said the young woman officiously.

'I know,' said Malton. 'That's why I was so worried. I just need to know that she's still here. That she's being looked after by professionals.'

Malton tried to forget the bloodbath he had just fled from and play the part of the over-concerned fiancé. He felt acutely his brown skin, the scar on his face. In somewhere like The Sentinel he was an unwelcome reminder of what the guests were paying to put behind them.

The receptionist picked up the phone, never once taking her eyes off Malton.

'Hi, it's front desk, just calling to check on a guest. Yes. Emily Haim. Right now? She should still be in her room. Yeah, thanks.' She cradled the receiver while she waited and smiled at Malton. 'I'll just check now.'

Malton stayed silent as someone came back on the other end. Suddenly confusion came over her face.

'What is it?' demanded Malton, dropping the act.

'Something's wrong. She's not in her room,' she said.

Malton knew that he was too late. Keisha had already been here.

Now he had no choice. He had to face Keisha and play her game.

He had to go home.

70

Beneath her sunglasses Keisha was bone-tired. She'd been awake all night and there was still so much left to do.

Emily sat quietly in the back seat. Getting her out of The Sentinel had been painless. The cleaner's uniform was enough to get her past the front desk and into the facility. From there she'd taken a wheelchair and loaded up a semi-sedated Emily. The plan was to wheel her out of the staff entrance and into a waiting car, all while she was still out of it.

Keisha's late husband Paul was a heavyweight dealer who kept half a dozen cars in permanent long-term parking around the city centre. Some he used to store drugs; others were simply getaway vehicles should the need ever arise. After her Mercedes had been totalled she knew she was only a couple of streets away from a multi-storey with a brand-new Audi ready and waiting. Thank god for the late Paul Bistacchi.

It was early morning at The Sentinel, with a skeleton staff, most of whom were minimum-wage cleaners just like Diane Okunkwe. They would much rather keep their jobs than risk challenging Keisha as she pushed a sleeping Emily out through the kitchens.

It was only outside the facility, in the fresh air that Emily had begun to stir. As Keisha gently slipped an arm round her to guide her to the car, her eyes had opened. Emily turned and looked Keisha full in the face.

Keisha was left in no doubt that Emily remembered her.

But there was no time for a reunion. Keisha bundled Emily onto the back seat, slammed the door behind her and took off, locking the car as she went.

Everything was still on track.

So why, as she drove through the weak morning sunlight, was Keisha suddenly so scared?

Looking at Emily sitting in the back seat, her hands cradling the first hints of a bump, Keisha wondered if she'd done enough to win Craig back.

Craig had rejected her twice before. Why would this time be different?

She felt nothing for the people Leon Walker had killed, even less for the final act of violence she had sent him on. Nor was she moved by the fear on Emily's face. But the thought of Craig turning her down yet again terrified her.

Her original plan had been months in the making. To take everything from Craig and feed him to the underworld. It was neat; it was poetic. It was safe.

But then the baby had changed everything.

Instead of leaving Craig to his fate she would offer him a future. A family. Craig, her and Emily's baby.

She would make that one final roll of the dice.

But before she made that gamble, Keisha would have one last chance to stack the odds. One final way to make sure that she didn't just humble Craig but that when he looked up for help he would see her. Take her hand and start over again.

She knew something Craig didn't. Something she'd kept to herself all these years. Locked away.

Her most precious secret.

The thought of speaking it out loud made Keisha feel sick to her stomach. But if it would bring Craig back to her she would do it.

Keisha gripped the wheel just a little tighter and put her foot down, keeping her gaze from wandering to the rear-view mirror and Emily, cowering in the back seat.

It was too late to go back now. Besides, maybe it would work? Maybe Craig would see the error of his ways and they would take the child inside Emily and become a family.

By now Craig would have got the message she gave to his underling. He would have worked out exactly where she was heading. He was clever, that one.

'Why are you doing this?' asked Emily from the back seat. She sounded scared.

Keisha ignored her and kept on driving.

'Was it you who gave me the heroin?'

Three months ago after her first attempt to reinsert herself into Craig's life had failed, Keisha had sent Emily, a recovering addict, a box full of high-grade heroin and everything she'd need to shoot it up. It had been petty, but thanks to that pettiness Emily had taken the bait and ended up in The Sentinel.

'I remember you. On the driveway. Outside Craig's house?'

Keisha wasn't used to hearing anyone but her use Malton's first name. It rankled. The last thing she was going to do was go on a trip down memory lane with Emily about the last time their paths crossed.

'How do you know Craig?' tried Emily, ignoring the pointed silence.

Finally Keisha broke. 'You don't know Craig,' she said. 'You know the version of him that he decided to show you. The big house, the business and those clothes he thinks make him look sophisticated. That's all you know.' She was surprised how bitter she sounded.

'Who do you know?' asked Emily.

Keisha thought about the Craig Malton who she met at the Hideaway Project all those years ago. The Hideaway was a local youth club. It was still standing to this day. The oldest youth club in Manchester. And it was a real club. They had dances, places to hang out, music and mentors who got what it was like growing up in Moss Side.

Keisha had found Craig hovering outside, unsure whether or not he should go in. She knew straight away what was wrong. The Hideaway was welcoming to anyone, but to an outsider it seemed like a foreign land. Keisha knew just about everyone there, knew Craig would be greeted like a brother.

But that first time she saw him, kicking his heels in the dirt and trying to look like he wasn't terrified of taking that initial step, she knew all she'd ever need to know about him. A young boy who wasn't black and wasn't white. Stuck in the middle waiting. In that moment she saw all his pain and all his fear and his desperate need to belong.

She fell in love with him right there and then.

'I know who Craig Malton is,' Keisha said, firmly ending the conversation.

However things were going to end, Keisha would never explain herself to someone like Emily. For all her middle-class, bleeding-heart sympathy, Keisha knew Emily and her kind would never quite be able to shake the idea that people like her and Craig were somehow broken. Projects for good, white people to save.

Keisha peeled off Princess Parkway and drove towards Hulme. To where once upon a time stood the Hulme Crescents.

In the Seventies the council had knocked down the old terraces of Hulme and in their place thrown up half a dozen giant, concrete tower blocks in the shape of long, curving waves. Streets in the sky. Modern living. A new start for Hulme.

Things went wrong almost immediately. The heating system failed. The flats were infested with rats and damp. It turned out the contractor had used asbestos in the internal walls. Everything that could go wrong went wrong.

The narrow walkways and alleys became home to muggers and drug dealers while the large open spaces intended for the leisure and relaxation of the residents became no-go zones filled with fly-tipped rubbish and gangs of youths.

The council abandoned the Crescents. They stopped collecting rent or charging utilities. The buildings filled up with junkies, anarchists, students, artists and anyone else eager to live off-grid in the ruins of Manchester City Council's failed housing project.

That was where Keisha had lived with her mum. First in the terraces, where her mum was a fierce local campaigner. She fought the council constantly, demanding that the people of Hulme be treated with the same dignity as anyone else.

When the council approached her about the Crescents they sold her on the new start. Recruited her to help persuade the community that everything would be better in this brave new future.

When things went south, Keisha watched her mother's heart break. The friends and neighbours who'd moved into this concrete hell on her word turned against her. She was dead long before the Crescents fell.

Alone, Keisha stayed in her mother's freezing, damp flat. With the rats and the asbestos.

Then Craig had come into her world and for just a while the Crescents had seemed like heaven.

But it was also in that flat some thirty years ago that Craig told her he was leaving her. Then a few months later everything changed.

If the night had been cold, the day was somehow colder. Now the flames had died down the air in the flat smelled of smoke. And under the smoke she could smell blood. Keisha had been awake all night. Despite the pain and the delirium she had clung to consciousness. Desperate to spend every moment awake. Make every second count.

Looking down at the child in her arms, she knew it was too late.

That was where Keisha was headed now. The place that held her darkest secret. The final and most devastating thing she had in her arsenal.

Keisha was going home.

As the familiar sights of Hulme passed by the windows, Keisha felt a cold calm descending over her.

She would stick to the plan. Offer Craig a second chance with her and their new child.

And if he turned her down? If that happened she would kill them all.

71

The door to Bea Wallace's office opened and Bea appeared wrapped in an elegant, knee-length, bright green overcoat, carrying an armful of papers.

Dean painfully rose to his feet, his body reminding him of the car crash he'd been in mere hours earlier.

When he'd got to Bea's offices he'd found them closed – unsurprising given how early in the morning it was. When Bea finally had turned up around seven Dean was half-frozen on her doorstep.

After being shown in, mothered and warmed up, he explained to her what had happened the night before. She listened as he detailed to her the shooting and the car crash. How Malton thought that Keisha would be making him choose between protecting Bea or his ex – Emily – and that Dean had been sent to keep her safe.

This last detail elicited a good deal of laughter from Bea. Her bright red lips peeling back to reveal her tiny, white teeth. Her blonde hair bouncing as she laughed a scandalous Geordie laugh.

She'd told Dean if he wanted he could hang around in her waiting room but that it would take more than a gunman on a killing spree to stop her going to work.

For the next hour Dean had hovered in her waiting room, wondering what exactly he'd do if Leon Walker marched in guns blazing.

Twice he'd called Vikki. Worried that maybe her father would come for her. She wasn't answering her phone. The entire city was crawling with armed police. The thought of

Leon Walker making it, on foot, all the way to Salford seemed far-fetched. Still, Dean wanted to know that she was safe, and not being able to get through to her was making him nervous.

Whenever she talked about her father, Vikki's eyes became impossibly sad. She recounted to Dean details of the most horrific neglect but still it was clear she loved Leon despite it all. It was to his flat that she fled after running away from her care home.

After all the death and carnage he'd seen the night before, it was Vikki who Dean found himself most worried about.

'Are you going out?' Dean asked Bea as she came out the office.

Bea rolled her eyes. 'I know he told you to watch me but you really don't have to follow me everywhere.'

'If you were me, would you tell Malton you decided to ignore what he told you and let his girlfriend wander about on her own?'

'If it was me, I'm sure I could bring him round.' She giggled. 'And I very much doubt he would refer to me as anything quite as cute as his girlfriend.'

Dean blushed.

Although Keisha and Bea were two very different people, Malton definitely did have a type.

'Sorry,' he said. 'I've got to come with you.'

Bea smiled sympathetically. 'Aren't you a good lad?'

'Where are we going?' asked Dean, making a move to stand up and instantly regretting it as several different parts of his body began to protest.

Bea's face lit up. 'I've got a new client. He's turned himself in to the police and asked for me by name.'

Dean felt a sense of mounting dread as he asked, 'What's his name?'

'Leon Walker.'

72

The grinding sound was overwhelming. It drowned out the words coming from the man's mouth as the conveyor belt tipped him down into the mincer. But for just a moment he was frozen in time, poised between life and death, his gaze locked on Fauzia's.

Fauzia's eyes shot open. She stood in her kitchen as her coffee machine ground out an espresso. She'd fallen asleep standing upright leaning on the counter.

After leaving Waqar above the kebab shop, unsure what else to do, she had returned to her flat to try and get some sleep. She planned to return to check on him before her shift.

She was too scared to sleep and having taken the last modafinil tablet just before she had bumped into Malton, she was forced to resort to coffee.

Waking from the maw of her nightmare brought no relief. Instead it carried with it the crushing knowledge that she had threatened Malton into leading her into a trap.

She bet he couldn't believe his luck when she had confidently demanded he take her to Galahad. The man she now knew was his boss.

He had told her to leave it with him. That he'd set the meeting up and be in touch. No time scale. No sense of when or where it was that he would deliver her into hands of the man who had been terrorising her and her family.

After getting Waqar's phone back she'd felt such a sense of elation. For just a moment all the terror had fallen away and she'd realised that the only way to stop running was to turn and face the danger.

But now she knew what the danger really was she felt sick.

The machine finished spitting the last of her espresso into the cup. Fauzia picked it up and blew on the hot, black liquid.

She turned to look over her flat. She had been so excited when she first started living here. It felt so liberating to be out on her own. Now it felt like someone else's home. The person who didn't ever imagine just how deep and dark the currents ran beneath the streets she called home.

Now she'd seen how the world really worked, all she wanted was her childhood bedroom, her mother's cooking and the feeling of safety and security that only her dad could provide.

She took a sip of the espresso. It was bitter and strong.

There on the kitchen counter sat the encrypted phone. When Waqar had passed out she had taken it back. After everything that had happened it felt cursed. A terrible artefact that brought its owner nothing but misfortune.

She couldn't leave it with her brother. Not in the state he was in.

While there was still some fight in him there was no telling what he might do. She was ashamed to think it but she hoped that when she checked on him next he would have got bad enough to realise what she'd been telling him all along. He needed to go to hospital.

By then she would have no choice in the matter. Whether he wanted to or not, she would have to call him an ambulance. That would mean having to call the police and warn them about the threat from Galahad. And that would mean the beginning of the end of everything.

If it was a choice between that and letting Waqar die then it was no choice at all. But that didn't make it any easier.

Fauzia drained the small cup and set it down. She walked over to the counter and picked up the phone. Her fingers tapped in the keycode Malton had given her and the phone turned on.

It many ways it was no different to a regular phone. There was the app that Waqar had used to communicate with his dealers and people working under him. It was called DLchat and was little more than WhatsApp with encryption on steroids. There too were all the messages from Galahad. She'd listened to a couple. Ranting voicemails threatening all manner of horrific consequences if the phone wasn't found.

Fauzia smiled. Galahad must have been desperate. It wasn't like leaving messages on a lost phone was going to make Waqar move any quicker.

Then it hit her. He *was* desperate.

Whatever was on that phone was worth waging war on Big Wacky. It was worth dragging her into the mix and terrorising her family. She had no doubt Galahad could have killed her by now. But he hadn't. Because if she was dead then he would never get that phone.

Whatever was on that phone was of vital importance to Galahad.

And for whatever reason, Malton had given it to her. Not Galahad. Whatever game Malton was playing, he clearly thought he'd already won.

He wouldn't be the first man to make that mistake.

73

Malton waited at the lights, gripping the wheel tightly, willing them to change.

Across the junction from him was what used to be the Corner House cinema. Malton remembered Keisha taking him there once to see a French film. He'd hated the film but loved the feeling of Keisha showing him a world he'd never seen. Letting him know that there was a city beyond Moss Side.

The lights went green and Malton took off up Whitworth Street. As he passed the Ritz where he had one of his very first jobs as a doorman, he remembered how Keisha used to come down and hang out with him on the door. Then at the end of the night they'd walk home together.

Home. Where he was going right now.

Malton tried to tell himself that he was racing to save Emily. That she was the reason he had taken off from the Diamond Lounge, raced to The Sentinel and was now tearing across the city centre.

He knew that was a lie. The reason he hit nearly fifty as he hurtled past the flats where the Hacienda nightclub once stood was because he was going to see Keisha. All the violence and bloodshed, that was just a tease. Their own little game played out against the canvas of Manchester.

Malton told himself that Keisha had to be stopped. That only he could do it. The truth was part of him never wanted it to stop. He never felt more alive than when Keisha was in his life. These thirty years she'd been gone had had their ups and downs but he'd never forgotten the girl who led him by the hand into the Hideaway Project and revealed to him who he could be.

Thirty years later and he was still torn. Half terrified of the darkness inside him to which she had such easy access and half enthralled with the idea of a world where the only person he had to answer to was Keisha.

It was a battle he was about to fight once more. In the place where it all began. Keisha's flat in the Crescents.

The flat had been on the ground floor of the building, facing out onto the vast, scruffy field of grass that had become a feral free-for-all as the Crescents slowly slid into anarchy. The Crescents had been torn down and consigned to history decades ago but Malton knew exactly where he was going.

Hulme might look different now but it hadn't changed. It couldn't change. As Malton drove over the arched bridge that linked the city centre to the south Manchester suburb, he felt the air change. While all around the city was growing upwards, Hulme was stuck in time.

It didn't matter what had been built since those days when he and Keisha lived together in that ground-floor flat. He knew the land, could feel the spaces forever marked out by their shared history.

There behind the Zion Centre, where once the Crescents sprawled in a concrete wasteland of abandoned flats and urban decay, now there was street after street of neat little houses. Homes that seemed to have been built with as little ambition as possible. Scared to repeat the disastrous consequences of the impossible folly that came before them.

Malton parked up and planted his feet. Beneath the tarmac he felt the energy coming up from the ground. A secret topography of times long past that only two people shared.

One of them was him. The other was waiting for him in the front room of one of those faceless houses. The house that had been built around the little portion of space that once housed Keisha's flat.

Through the front room window Malton could see Keisha waiting for him. The front door was already open.

He couldn't help but smile.

He was home.

74

Benton hadn't said a word to Dean. From the moment she saw him with Bea she had acted like she'd never met him before in her life. For his part, Dean played along, doing his best to look like Bea's paralegal, dutifully trotting behind, carrying her papers.

Walking behind Bea, Dean became aware of how much attention she attracted. The high heels with their red soles, the blonde hair and the seamed stockings. There wasn't a man she walked past who didn't risk snatching a look. Some more obviously than others.

The attention seemed to lift Bea. She wore it like armour. She knew that all eyes were on her, that she was dictating the pace of things. It reminded Dean of Malton, the way he simply sat in a space and let everything bend around him. Bea had that same energy, an immense, unspoken confidence in her ability to make the world exactly the way she wanted it to be.

Benton led Bea and Dean through Pendleton Police station. Greater Manchester Police had long ago closed all the holding cells in the city centre. When in the early hours a heavily armed Leon Walker had handed himself in to a twenty-four-hour inquiry desk, the PCSO manning it nearly had a fit. One frantic phone call later and dozens of armed police swarmed from all over Manchester. Leon was disarmed, cuffed and bundled off to the nearest holding cells – Pendleton Station at Salford Precinct.

The station was a giant modern fortress of policing. High, blue metal fences, search lights and CCTV. It made no bones about the role of the police in Salford. They were an occupying army deep in hostile enemy territory.

It was a stone's throw from Vikki's flat. Dean pictured Vikki looking out over Salford Precinct towards the station, unaware that her wayward dad was being held only a few hundred metres away in the cells.

Leon Walker had been away forever. Now he was very nearly home.

Benton led Bea and Dean into an interview room.

'He asked for you by name,' said Benton.

'I have a reputation,' replied Bea proudly.

'Yeah, you do.' Benton frowned. 'Due to the nature of the incident he's involved with, we are not prepared to remove your client's handcuffs.'

'I'm always glad to see Greater Manchester Police making my job easier.'

Benton started to laugh but caught herself.

'Love, and I say this with the utmost respect, no amount of legal bullshit is going to help this one.'

Bea smiled. 'But maybe a bit of basic competence might, eh pet? Not GMP's strong point in my experience,' she said in her thickest North East lilt.

Benton nodded. 'Cannot argue with you there. If anyone could fail to get a conviction against a man who turns up heavily armed at a police station and confesses to shooting half a dozen people dead, it's this lot.'

Dean was beginning to get it. The back and forth, the hostility. It was all for show. Benton and Bea knew exactly what they were doing. They knew exactly what they were up against. This was two old hands sizing each other up.

Benton was handing Bea the booking sheets as the door opened. Suddenly the doorframe was filled with the giant shape of Leon Walker. He'd been changed into a grey prison tracksuit. The top was far too small while the bottoms hung baggy around his waist. His hands were cuffed tightly in front of his body and two large police officers stood either side of him.

He was clean-shaven and Dean could clearly see the tattoo on his neck. The tribute to his daughter Vikki – VICIOUS.

'Here he is now,' said Benton, stepping aside to let Leon in. 'You've got half an hour. If anything goes wrong, these two are just outside.'

She indicated to the two officers. They were hands down the most brutal-looking policemen Dean had ever seen. If the police didn't work out, there'd definitely be a job for them at Malton Security.

Leon was sitting in one corner of the room, his long, ungainly legs splayed out in front of him. He kept his eyes down, moving his giant fingers to keep the blood flowing through the handcuffs.

Bea waited until Benton and the officers left before she began her job.

She pulled up a chair right next to Leon. Dean's heart leapt a little. She looked so tiny and fragile next to Walker. But it was Leon who seemed out of place. A lost little boy.

Malton had sent Dean to keep an eye on Bea but right now Bea was the one making Dean feel fractionally less terrified about being locked in a small room with a violent killer.

'How have they treated you, pet?' asked Bea, her voice gentle and enquiring.

'Can I see my paperwork?' said Leon quietly.

'Of course you can, love. It's your paperwork,' said Bea, handing him the sheets Benton had given her.

As far as Dean understood they were just formalities. Nothing of any interest as to why he was being kept here. Nevertheless Leon took the pages and began to carefully read them as Bea continued speaking.

'The most important thing is that you don't say anything. Nothing at all. "No comment" all the way. You turned yourself in, is that right?'

Walker nodded. He'd finished the papers and had started to slowly fold them lengthways, taking great care to smooth down each fold with his giant fingers.

'And you were armed when you did that?'

Walker nodded again. He'd folded the paper lengthways four times and now it was a thin strip about two inches wide and the length of an A4 page.

'That's not ideal but it's OK. In this sort of situation the best thing will be to stall until I can get a fuller picture of the situation. How did they treat you? Those two officers who brought you in?'

Leon shrugged. He had started to fold the strip of paper in on itself.

From where Dean was sitting it felt like Leon Walker's focus was elsewhere. Like he was simply waiting for something to happen. Dean began to feel intensely uneasy. He looked around the room for possible weapons. The police had had the same idea and the room was bare. There were the chairs Leon and Bea were sitting on and that was it. The biggest weapon in the room was sitting next to Bea Wallace, quietly folding a piece of paper.

'They're going to refuse bail. That's to be expected. But it also means that they've got to get moving. If they keep you in custody without progressing the case, that's something we can use.'

Bea finally took notice of what Leon was doing with his hands. He seemed distant.

Bea reached out a hand and rested it tenderly on his arm.

'I know this is a lot to take in, but you called me and that's the smartest thing you could have done. Can I ask, who recommended me?'

For the first time Leon Walker looked up. His eyes were bloodshot red. Dean noticed that he'd folded the paper into a kind of triangle shape, almost like an arrowhead.

His voice was dry and cracked. 'Keisha Bistacchi,' he said, getting to his feet.

Before Dean could do anything Leon strode across the narrow room, bent down and jammed the folded-up paper under the door, creating a wedge.

Bea calmly got to her feet and called out, 'We're done in here.' Her voice was controlled but with an unmistakable urgency.

The door unlocked but moved only a few centimetres, jamming the paper wedge beneath it. Through the crack Dean saw the look of confusion on the face of the officer trying and failing to get it open.

Leon turned to Bea. He looked resigned.

'It's not you,' he said. 'It's Malton.'

Dean did the only thing he could do. He stepped out and stood between Leon and Bea. Walker towered above him.

The officers were hammering on the door. It was opening but not fast enough.

Dean looked Leon Walker in the eye.

He thought how Leon's eyes were exactly the same as Vikki's. A dazzling blue.

Dean raised his skinny fists and said, 'You're going to have to go through me first.'

75

'Where is she?' demanded Malton.

The room looked like a rental property: a sofa, a chair and a space where a television would go. Marks on the walls and carpet spoke of previous occupants. Pictures and furniture were long gone.

Malton didn't see any of that. He saw the old flat. Its crumbling walls and broken windows. Those possessions of Keisha's mother that she couldn't bear to sell. The painting of Jesus, the sideboard that once had been polished daily but now bore cup marks and cigarette burns. The double bed where her mother had died. The bed that they had once shared.

He felt the past around him, as solid as any present.

Keisha leaned back in the chair. The smell of her perfume was overwhelming. It filled the room with memories. Malton wanted to give in to them but he told himself that wasn't the game.

He was here to save Emily.

Keisha had a gun. She didn't point it but kept it firmly in her hand. Like you might hold a cigarette or a wineglass. It was there for when she needed it and until then it was simply there.

'Sit down, Craig,' she invited.

Malton scanned the room. The door to the kitchen at the back of the house was open. Like the front room it seemed half stripped down. An empty space where a washing machine once stood. Now just pipes waiting to be reconnected. The blinds were down so he couldn't see into the back garden.

There was no sign of Emily but he hadn't expected Keisha to give her up that easily.

'You found me OK?' asked Keisha as Malton took a seat on the sofa across from where she sat.

Malton couldn't forget this place. Not the house. The house was just bricks and wood and plaster. But this spot was burned in his memory forever.

The sights and sounds of the Crescents. The constant noise. Music bleeding out of dozens of different speakers. The sound systems set up on the grass blasting all day and night. The air thick with cannabis smoke and conversations conducted at the top of angry voices.

There, anchoring then to now, sat Keisha. Not so different to the teenage girl he'd met all those years back. The curly, brown hair, the confident smile and the ever-present sunglasses.

Malton felt his heart race. The game was over. Thirty years had brought them right back here. It was just the two of them now. This was the dance they chose and both of them had a part to play.

'You can't keep doing this,' said Malton, staring into the dark lenses of Keisha's sunglasses.

'You have no idea what I'm doing,' said Keisha back.

'You turned Leon Walker into a weapon. Gave him the guns you stole from Danny Mitchum. Told him to go after me.'

Keisha nodded along. 'You're halfway there.'

'And now you've kidnapped Emily. Are you going to kill her too?'

Keisha smiled and tilted her head playfully. 'Almost. I was going to kill her. I was going to destroy everything you care about. Strip away everything that makes you who you are. But you know what? I changed my mind. You know a thing or two about that don't you, Craig?'

Malton felt the past all around him. He couldn't help but think about that last day he stood here. Just before he had walked out on her.

'If you harm her, you know what I'll do,' he said slowly.

'Oh I know what you *think* you'll do. And I know deep down you resent it. Resent what they all expect from you.

Resent having to prove to them you're worth keeping around.'

Malton didn't even try to pretend that Keisha was wrong. She knew him too well for him to ever fool her for long. Instead he forced himself to see the most dangerous woman he'd ever met. Not his first love. Not the girl who'd led him by the hand into the Hideaway Project. Not the girl who'd let him crash in the flat she had all to herself in the Crescents. That girl was long gone. This was Keisha Bistacchi and when she said she would kill, she meant it.

'But I'm not here to kill anyone,' Keisha said, reading his mind. She checked her watch. The same hand in which she held that gun.

'Besides, I know you don't care about dying. I've known that from the first moment I met you. Back then you had a death wish. It was me who taught you to use that. Make it a strength not a weakness.'

It was true, the moment you stopped worrying about dying then suddenly you became untouchable. The fear that kept others in check no longer had a hold on you. It was the only reason Malton could do the job he did. To walk through the sewers of the city and not once flinch or turn away. That had been just one of Keisha's gifts to him.

But it came at a high price. A lifetime apart. Never risking letting anyone get too close. He had let James into his heart and James had paid with his life. Then years later he'd dared to dream of a family with Emily and now she too was suffering for his weakness.

But Keisha was like him. Keisha lived her entire life to do and never be done to. She had never let anyone in ever. Except for Malton. They were two bodies falling through the darkness together.

Malton tried to focus on what had brought him here. He had to rescue Emily. Stop whatever it was Keisha was doing. He told himself that she was more dangerous than he could ever imagine. But still, he couldn't look away.

335

'What have you done to Emily?' he croaked.

Keisha smiled and let out a sigh of relief. 'You're so close to getting it. What all this is about. All those years ago I made you. I took all your fears and I taught you how to use them. Use all the pain and uncertainty. I made Craig Malton. But look at you now. You're lost, Craig.'

Malton shook his head. She sounded deranged. He had assumed this was about revenge. Breaking him down and then finally delivering the death blow herself. She'd tried to get him back months ago and failed – she could only want vengeance now.

But this felt different.

He still couldn't quite pin it down. She was standing right there in front of him but it was like staring at the sun. Her brilliance overwhelmed him and all he could make out were indistinct shadows. Something dark creeping around the periphery. He began to feel the unmistakable lightness in his body. The flight or fight kicking in.

He was in danger.

Malton rose to his feet. Keisha kept the gun trained on him but he didn't flinch. Everything she said was true. She had taught him not to fear death. No matter how beautiful it looked when it pointed a gun at your chest.

'I'm done,' he said. He couldn't say whether he was talking to Keisha or to himself. Either way he meant it.

'No you are not,' said Keisha, raising her voice. The hard, nasal Moss Side cut through. The edge of something rough and dangerous in her tone. 'You still don't get it, do you? What I'm trying to tell you. You are not the white knight here. You are not the saviour. You are not the person holding back the darkness. You tell yourself you are. When you go out and do the bidding of men like Danny Mitchum you tell yourself that you're not dealing with the devil, you're keeping him back from the rest of us. Craig Malton, up on his cross so that the rest of us poor souls stay safe.'

Malton felt his chest tighten. He tried to regain focus but his body betrayed him. Keisha's words were bypassing his conscious mind and talking to some deep, existential part of himself. The part that believed every word she was saying. Try as he might, he couldn't resist her pull.

'When I last reached out to you I made one terrible mistake. I thought you were the Craig Malton I knew before. I didn't realise that ever since you left me you've been running away from yourself.'

'I'm not running from anyone,' said Malton. He heard the words coming out of his mouth before he could stop himself. She was getting in his head.

'The Craig I knew did what he wanted. Went where he wanted. The Craig I knew didn't owe anyone anything. That Craig would have walked away with me in a heartbeat.'

'People change,' said Malton grimly.

Keisha smiled. 'And they can change back. You couldn't protect your home, or your clients. You can't protect Emily. You failed, Craig. The one thing you think gives you permission to be the hero in all of this. You fucked it up. And then there's poor Bea.'

Keisha tilted her head, waiting for a response.

Malton's head spun. He knew he should simply cross the floor and take the gun. Make her tell him everything. But he couldn't move a muscle. The weight of her words held him pinned to the spot.

It was all he could do to open his mouth and when he did his words came out deep and raw. 'What have you done to her?' he barked.

His whole body tensed. The muscles on his neck bulged, his battered fists clenched and throbbed as Keisha drew the darkness inside him rushing to the surface.

'You let them all down. And that's OK. You don't owe anyone anything. You don't have to apologise. To make them like you. To make them tolerate you. Because they never will.'

Keisha was on her feet now, gun hanging at her side, all her focus on Malton.

337

'They see what we are, Craig. Me and you. They see people who they can't control. People with the power to change the world. And they hate us for it.'

Malton tried to steady his breathing. It was like a thick curtain was lifting in his mind. Everything she said made awful sense and it terrified him to hear it. The truths that he fought so hard to bury deep inside. The endless expenditure of energy as he struggled against his true nature. His thoughts, his feelings, his desires. All subordinate to the fear that he didn't deserve any of them.

'People are dead,' was all he could think to say. It sounded utterly hollow.

Keisha snorted with laughter. 'And we're still here,' she said breezily. 'Now sit down.'

Malton was already sitting down before he realised it, his body reverting to that of his teenage self. Unsure, scared, eager to have someone strong like Keisha tell him how to be. Who to be.

Keisha took a step back to her own seat and sat down. Now the gun was trained firmly on Malton. 'You've been holding on so tight for so long that I know you can't believe a word I'm saying. But if you did it'd be the end of everything. A new beginning.'

'With you?' said Malton incredulously.

The smile faded from Keisha's face. She took a deep breath. 'I hoped after all this, it would be enough. But I can see there's only one thing left. One way to convince you that I'm telling you the truth. I've got to tell you about the first person you didn't save. The first person you let down. Someone you never even knew.'

Malton thought he saw Keisha's bottom lip wobble for just a moment.

'Who did I not save?' he asked, his mouth clenched tightly, his teeth pressing against each other.

'Your son,' said Keisha.

76

Dean clung on for dear life. Bea's and his own. He had his arms wrapped around Leon Walker's waist, his fingers interlinked and straining to hold on as Walker rained down blows on him. Each one felt like a sledgehammer, smashing the life out of him.

He could hear the police pushing the door open. Millimetre by painful millimetre, the paper wedge Leon slammed under the door soaking up precious seconds.

In the corner of the room he imagined Bea, standing cowering with fear as this monster of a man tried to shrug off Dean's twelve-stone frame.

Still he held on.

Leon raised a leg and hit Dean in the gut with a powerful knee. The air rushed out of Dean's lungs and he staggered back, bumping into Bea.

He looked up in time to see Leon's giant hands reaching out for him. The enormous fingers wrapped around his neck and he felt his feet leaving the floor as Leon lifted him off the ground and held him high in the air, choking the life out of him.

Dean kicked out, his legs flailing uselessly against Leon's mighty torso. Walker's eyes were crazed. The rage radiated off him like heat from a furnace.

Dean clawed at the vice-like grip to no avail. Those fingers like steel cables, firm around Dean's neck. Leon's face contorted with fury. Small flecks of white foam gathered at the corners of his mouth, his breath hot and fetid. His eyes clouded over. Wherever he was and whatever it was he thought he was doing, it no longer had anything to do with the events in this room.

Leon Walker was fighting the demons that had chased him his entire life. His horrific childhood, his violent career of crime, the broken back courtesy of Malton, the drug addiction, Keisha's manipulation. All the pain and hurt of his entire existence flowed through those hands, crushing Dean's neck.

Dean felt the lights start to dim. He tried to speak but nothing came out. His arms fell limp at his sides as the room fell away to blackness.

Then just like that the grip relaxed. Leon's eyes pulled focus and he dropped Dean.

Dean hit the floor and his legs collapsed underneath him. He had just about enough left in him to raise one arm against whatever was coming next.

Nothing came.

Blinking against the ceiling lights, he saw Leon Walker towering above him, a look of surprise on his face.

Blood was running down his chest.

His hands hung limply in front of him, still in the handcuffs. Leon turned his head to look with bewilderment at where one of Bea Wallace's stiletto heels was embedded in the side of his neck.

Dean felt Bea's arms under his shoulders dragging him back as the door finally burst open and the two officers rushed Leon, wrestling him to the floor.

Dean heard Bea ordering them to compress the wound. He heard the sound of gurgling blood coming from Leon. He heard the frantic shouts of the officers calling for medical assistance.

Then it all went black.

77

The Crescents were burning. From the window of her lonely ground-floor flat, Keisha looked out to see hundreds of people moving through the darkness. Bodies illuminated against the night by the flames.

Music blasted from somewhere. Echoing off the empty, concrete flats and bouncing back into the vast, open space towards which they all faced.

For days now Keisha had been dimly aware of dozens of people at work. Students, anarchists, artists. All the people who had taken over the Crescents in the past few years. When the dreams of people like her mother had died, they had moved in. Revelling in the chaos. Holidaying in other people's misery.

They'd been building something in the communal area. Whatever that thing was it was now ablaze.

Keisha staggered out of her front door and cried out for help. The cold wrapped itself tightly around her. Her voice disappeared in the cacophony of sounds filling the night air.

The smell of smoke and mud and the constant damp of the Crescents solidified in the freezing night air. Keisha felt like she was drowning.

A couple of students with a carrier bag full of cans barged past her. She cried out but they kept moving. It was as if they didn't even see her. The world was on fire and she was lost in the middle of it all.

She looked back to her flat. She was one of the very few original tenants left. After Craig had walked out, nearly six months had passed. She didn't know where else to go. She hadn't told him she was pregnant with his child. When he confessed to her he was gay, *she knew nothing she said would keep him there. The baby would be hers alone. A precious miracle that he had forfeited all rights to.*

Her front door hung open. The lights were still on. The reddish glow of the doorway alone in the darkness. Keisha had the thought that she ought to lock it. Stop the inevitable theft of what little she had left.

Every step back was agony. She could feel the baby inside her turning, moving, getting ready to be born.

As she reached the door a huge cry went up from the crowd. Her body tightened, the spasms of pain taking her breath away.

She turned to see what was happening.

It was then she saw it. It was magnificent.

A giant Viking longship. Built right there in the courtyard of the Crescents. It was huge and it was on fire. The sails had just gone up and the flames roared towards the night sky.

A terrible light filled the Crescents and Keisha realised it was too late. She was having her baby.

She staggered back into her flat alone, managing to close the front door behind her. The noise outside died back to a distant murmur.

Keisha made it as far as the bedroom before she toppled onto her dead mother's bed, heaved herself up onto all fours, giving in to her labour.

Maybe it was minutes, maybe it was hours. The pain made time meaningless. Waves of pulsating agony built to a crescendo. She writhed on sweat-soaked sheets. Blood came out of her, more blood than she'd ever seen. She pushed her face into the pillows, desperate for a scent of home. Of Malton, of her mother, of something that would stop her being so alone.

The light from the flames outside threw flickering shadows across the bedroom wall. The whole world was on fire and Keisha was right there at the heart of it all.

And then in one ear-splitting cry it was all over.

Keisha lay panting on the sheets. The radiant heat of the life inside her slowly began to dissipate into the stagnant air of the flat. Suddenly she felt very, very cold.

The noise outside sounded far away. Far louder was the sound of her own breath. Wet and hoarse.

But the baby was silent.

Keisha hauled herself up on her elbows. The pain between her legs was indescribable. She felt in among the sheets and the blood for the newborn. Her fingers came over it, wrapped around its tiny body. It was slick and wet.

He wasn't moving.

Keisha scooped the baby to her. She wiped his face. Desperately clearing his mouth with her fingers. Waiting for him to cry out and greet the world.

He was silent.

Keisha held him tightly against her chest. She already knew he was gone.

He wouldn't move again all through the night as Keisha held him and lay there waiting for the morning while outside the Viking longboat burned down to cold, black ash.

78

Keisha watched Malton closely as he processed what he'd just heard. She watched his face, his muscles clenched against the tears, his mind churning over her words.

For all these years Anthony had been hers and hers alone. A special angel who was by her side. Someone who saw her and forgave everything. She had never imagined ever sharing her angel with anyone until Craig was there in the room with her and she realised he still didn't get it.

He couldn't see that she was there to free him from himself. As much as she loved Anthony, she also loved Craig. If finally sharing her grief after all these years was the price to win Craig back, then she would do it. She would let Anthony finally meet his dad.

Across the room Malton was still silent.

She knew exactly what he was feeling. Despite carrying Anthony with her for all these years, this was the first time she had ever said his name out loud.

In doing so she had hoped it would free Craig from the crushing weight of responsibility he had wrapped himself in. Break his heart and set him free. She never thought for a moment what it would do to her.

But with every word she spoke it felt like suddenly her heart was swelling. The blinkers of rage and shame and hate that had given her such laser focus fell away and suddenly she became aware of just how big the world really was.

Bigger even than Craig Malton.

She had been dragged along for so many years by her anger and pain. It had given her permission to do whatever she wanted to whomever she wanted. But now she was free.

With the memory of Anthony finally spoken out loud into the world, she knew she could never take Emily's baby. Malton would never come with her. They would never be a family.

It was over.

For the first time she noticed how the morning light settled in the lines on Craig's face. The tiny cuts and scars. He looked old.

She saw him looking back at her. She wondered if he was thinking the same thing.

Finally he spoke. She could hear the effort it was taking to keep the emotion from his voice. 'I'm sorry.' He took a deep breath, grimaced. He wiped his eyes with the back of his hand and stood up.

Keisha put the gun in her belt, stood up and took off her sunglasses.

'He was beautiful,' she said and took a step across the room, throwing her arms around Craig.

As she held him tight she thought how strange life was. She had set out to free Craig and she had done just that. But in the process she had freed herself. Keeping Anthony a secret hadn't made her strong. It had made her impossibly weak. It had blinded her to the burden she was carrying. Turned that sadness into rage against the one man she had ever truly loved.

Malton was the first to break the embrace. His eyes were dry now.

'Why didn't you tell me?' he asked, his voice cracking.

A thousand different lies rushed through Keisha's head but none of them seemed worth the effort so she told the truth. 'After you left he was all I had. I knew you wouldn't come back. And even if you did, things wouldn't be the same. When he was inside me, I could feel him changing me. Making me question everything. If you had come back from Liverpool who would you have found waiting for you?'

'I would have been there for you. Both of you,' said Malton. He could hardly believe the words coming out of his mouth. It was as if after years of facing the world through raised fists,

345

both of them had finally let their guards down and truly saw each other for the first time.

'I know you would. I know you. You'd have been there for the same reason you get up every day and go out into this city. Because you can't ever get over that need to prove yourself. Again and again and again.'

'Maybe it would have been different with . . .' Malton stopped at Anthony's name. It didn't feel like his name to be saying out loud.

'Anthony?' said Keisha. 'Maybe it would have been. We'll never know. But I'm done with the past now.'

She sounded happy.

'Where is . . . he?' asked Malton.

'Cremated,' said Keisha. Maybe she *would* keep one last secret just for her.

Keisha looked Malton in the eye, searching his face for any signs he didn't believe the lie. But he just looked impossibly sad.

'Emily's upstairs. I'm sorry about Bea,' said Keisha.

Malton gave a small nod. For a moment Keisha thought he was about to say something but then without saying another word he turned and headed upstairs.

Keisha put her sunglasses back on and took one last look at the room.

It was raining. Between the rain and the Crescents the sun barely reached Keisha's ground-floor flat. She showered in cold water and dressed herself. Outside the last few stragglers were making their way home. The stench of burned wood was overpowering.

With the utmost delicacy she washed Anthony and dressed him in the only set of clothes he would ever have. Then for the next hour she sat on the bed and held him. Just the two of them.

346

79

When Fauzia returned to the room above the kebab shop, she found Waqar lying dead on the mattress.

After dealing with the encrypted phone she had come straight over, ready to drive him to the hospital herself or if need be pull rank to get an ambulance sent over as a matter of urgency.

She brought snacks, a book, a phone charger and her own iPad. She knew how long everything took in hospital and she wanted her brother to be as comfortable as possible.

But none of that mattered anymore.

Fauzia stood looking down at her brother, her hands full of all the supplies she had brought with her. She was still out of breath from the journey here. Running, giddy with excitement to have worked out a way for Waqar to receive the hospital treatment he desperately needed, safe from the reach of Galahad.

Waqar's eyes were open, staring up at the ceiling. There was a smile on his face.

Fauzia dropped her bags and took a faltering step forward, falling to her knees at her brother's side.

The doctor in her reached out to check the pulse in his neck. His skin was cold. She knew he was long gone.

Operating on instinct she turned to give instructions to a nurse who wasn't there. She wasn't in a hospital. She was in the scruffy room above a kebab shop, kneeling over her brother's dead body.

Fauzia grabbed her brother to her chest and let out a ragged howl.

Half crying, half screaming she held him, tears running down her face. Fauzia hugged his cold body tight to her own. Willing the heat and life to flow out of her and into Waqar.

At that moment she would have given up absolutely everything to get him back.

She'd let him down. Why didn't she insist he go to the hospital? She should have called the ambulance herself. Told the police everything. Got an armed guard. Made sure that her brother made it home.

But she didn't. She left him to die alone in this place. She was too scared to do the right thing and now Waqar was dead.

Minutes passed and Fauzia became hoarse with crying. Her tears ran dry. Waqar was still dead.

Finally she gently laid him back down on the mattress. He was still so handsome. Like a film star. Her big brother.

She closed his eyes and went to put his arms by his sides. That was when she realised he had his phone in his hand. Not the encrypted phone. That was safely hidden in her flat. This was just his own phone.

As she took it out of his hand the screen lit up. His lock screen was a photo of him next to a couple of sports cars. Holding a stack of notes in one hand and a Rolex in the other. Big Wacky leering at the camera. Taunting her.

What was he doing with his phone in his final moments? Had he tried to call her? Did he reach out and she simply ignored him?

With trembling fingers Fauzia opened up the phone with the same PIN code as the encrypted phone.

The lock screen vanished and was replaced with the home screen.

Fauzia gasped.

There, under a collection of apps was a photo of the two of them. Fauzia and Waqar. It was Fauzia's graduation. She was standing in front of the large, stone archway of Owens Hall on Oxford Road dressed in her cap and gown. There, next to her, smiling even wider than her was Waqar, his arm around his sister, his face bursting with happiness and pride.

Fauzia swallowed hard. That was always meant to be him standing there graduating. But when she got her medical degree he couldn't have been more pleased if it was him holding that roll of paper.

It could have been him. He could have done it all. Her beautiful, brilliant brother.

Fauzia would carry him with her for the rest of her life. Everything she achieved she would do it for him. Because it should have been him. She would never stop. Never doubt herself. Never pass up any opportunity. Waqar would live on in everything she did.

But Big Wacky died here. Alone in the squalid upstairs room of a kebab shop.

Fauzia had just got to the part where Harry was about to catch the train at Platform 9 ¾ when Waqar's hand moved. She nearly dropped her book. She looked round but there were no nurses nearby. She'd been left alone to read to her brother.

She leapt to her feet and grabbed his hand, squeezing it as tightly as she dared.

Waqar squeezed back and slowly, with immense effort his eyes opened. He smiled at his sister.

Fauzia couldn't help herself. She threw her arms around her brother and was still hugging him when the nurses rushed over.

Eventually the doctor convinced her to let them see to him, but even as she stepped back she swore to herself – she had nearly lost her big brother. She would never let him go again.

80

Malton had found Emily, just as Keisha said he would, upstairs, tied to a chair and gagged in an empty bedroom. Apart from the obvious immediate discomfort she seemed unharmed but when Malton pressed her all he could get out of her were 'yes'/'no' answers.

'Are you hurt?'

'No.'

'Does anyone else know you're here?'

'No.'

'Can you walk?'

'Yes.'

The whole time her voice was low and she avoided his gaze. Malton hardly noticed. He was on autopilot, still reeling from Keisha's revelation about his son. Emily may as well have been a complete stranger to him.

When he went back downstairs he found Keisha gone.

He rushed to the window but her car was also missing. Malton panicked. He ran to the kitchen, ignoring Emily. But the back door was locked. Keisha wasn't coming back. She had left him with a dead son, a thousand questions and no way to deal with any of it.

Malton remembered he wasn't alone. Emily was standing watching him. From the look on her face he could tell she knew something had changed in him.

All she said was, 'Take me back to The Sentinel.'

They drove in silence. Emily looked out of the window, shuffling her body to the far edge of the seat. Putting as much distance between Malton and herself as the Volvo would allow.

At every opportunity Malton stole glances across at his passenger. She looked well. As well as could be expected. Her hair was longer and she looked like she'd put on a little weight, but whatever had led her to The Sentinel it looked like she was on top of it.

Alone in the car with Emily all he could think about was Keisha.

They had just passed by Hindley when Malton realised in all the chaos he'd forgotten something.

He took a breath and broke the silence.

'I got a call from your dad. He said you wanted to talk?'

Emily kept looking out the window. She didn't speak.

'I'm sorry for all this,' he said.

Emily turned to face Malton. He did his best to keep his eyes on the road.

'She loves you,' she said.

Malton felt something stir inside him. He kept it to himself.

'The way she speaks about you. Not the "you" I knew. Someone else. Someone you were once. Someone I think you probably still are.'

Malton wanted to argue. To tell her that everyone had a past. That he shouldn't be judged on who he was. But the events of the past twenty-four hours made that argument seem self-serving and hollow. He kept quiet and let Emily fill the silence.

'Dad said you came round his new place. To be honest I thought you'd have found me at The Sentinel. Then I realised, you can find anyone, wherever they go. That's what you do. If you hadn't found me it was because you weren't looking.'

Her voice cracked a bit. Malton knew what she said was true. He hadn't gone looking until it was far too late. He'd let Emily drift out of his life. Whether it was grief at losing her or the suspicion that she was better off without him didn't matter. He'd dragged her into this and then he'd left her vulnerable for Keisha to find.

'That's why I wasn't going to tell you. But then Dad said you showed up. I felt guilty. Thought you should know.'

A sudden thought lodged in Malton's mind. Why Keisha hadn't killed Emily, when he knew she was more than capable. What she was doing bringing him back to the flat, telling him about the baby. Their baby.

Keeping his eyes on the road he let Emily continue.

Emily's hands instinctively went to her belly as she struggled to find the words.

'What we talked about? Starting a family together?' She laughed. 'All that agonising about IVF? Then it just happens.'

She looked across the car at Malton.

'I'm pregnant.'

Malton looked over at Emily. His eyes flitted down to her belly and back to her face. He meant to say something. Maybe reassurance. Maybe congratulations. Instead he found himself turning away in silence.

An unfamiliar feeling crept over Malton. Something that took him a moment to identity. Then he had it. He felt scared.

To anyone else the news of a child would have been a cause for celebration. For Malton it meant he could never let go now. Never be safe.

Back when he and Emily had decided to start a family he'd managed to hold the fear at bay. Tell himself that if he was strong enough and smart enough that it would be OK. As long as he never once faltered then maybe he too could enjoy a little happiness.

But the past few days had showed him that no matter what he did he couldn't protect the ones he loved. He couldn't protect anyone against someone determined to bring him down.

Someone like Keisha.

Malton had seen too much to take any joy in knowing that he was bringing another life into this world. He had spent so long in the dark currents of the Manchester underworld that he no longer related to anything approaching normality.

Everywhere he saw danger. In everyone he suspected secret vices and barely repressed malice.

What use could he be to someone like Emily if not to keep her from the darkness? But who was it who brought that darkness into her world in the first place if not him?

He had been living trapped in the contradiction of it all. When Bea had shrugged off his offers of protection he had assumed it was over. That she had no further use for him. It had never occurred to him that all she wanted from him was who he was. He hoped she was OK. 'Sorry about Bea' is all Keisha had said before she left. Something told Malton that she would be harder to kill than Keisha imagined.

He realised his mind was wandering. Emily had just told him he was going to be a father and all he could think about was Keisha and Bea.

They were approaching the gatehouse to The Sentinel when Emily said, 'I don't want to see you again.'

Malton let the words sink in. He felt a deep sense of relief. They both knew he could never be a father. The best thing he could do for his unborn child was to stay as far away as possible.

'Keisha's gone. She won't be coming back,' he said.

'Until the next time?' said Emily turning on him. She had a sharp look in her eyes. He'd never seen her angry before.

Malton killed the engine. He was exhausted. He'd barely slept the past few days. The physical and emotional toll was finally sinking in. Keisha's parting words stripping away whatever resilience he had left.

He wanted to tell Emily that if things were different he would have done anything to be part of his child's life. Let her know that he wouldn't make the same mistakes his dad had made. He'd make their baby the centre of his world. Bring them up happy, secure and loved.

He wanted to tell her all those things but he knew they were all lies. History was repeating itself. When his dad had been drunk he was full of lachrymose sentiment about how much

353

he loved his son, the light of his life. How he would do anything for his son. Somewhere in his pickled heart his dad knew what a good father was and part of him desperately wanted to be one.

At best his father was absent; at worst he was a terrifying alcoholic who made sure Malton grew up knowing he was unwanted.

'I'll help with the money,' he said. The words sounding hollow and cheap. From the look Emily gave him back, he knew she felt exactly the same.

All Malton could do was watch in silence as Emily undid her seat belt and got out of the car.

In one morning he'd lost not one but two children. As if somehow fate knew that the idea of Malton as a father was an obscene joke.

Malton hung back as Emily walked into The Sentinel, the doors closing behind her. Inside her the future that could never be.

81

When Benton finally tracked Dean down she found him propped up in a hospital bed doing his best to ignore the crushing pain he felt every time he swallowed anything more than a few sips of water.

It had been a week now since Leon Walker had tried to kill him. A week since Bea Wallace had saved his life. Since then he'd been holed up in a private hospital while Bea did everything in her power to keep the police at bay.

But even Bea Wallace couldn't stop Benton.

First her face appeared at the window of his private room and before he could say a word she was in the doorway holding up a greasy bag of McDonald's, which she dumped on the bed with a smile.

'Whatever he's paying you, I hope it's worth it,' she said.

Dean wondered how on earth Benton had found him, much less managed to get all the way into his room. Benton was in a permanent state of dishevelment. Whether it was trouser suits or jeans and jumpers, everything she wore ended up looking like she'd slept in it. Add to that her bright purple anorak and complete lack of an inside voice and she wasn't hard to miss.

'You mind?' asked Benton, diving into the McDonald's bag.

She didn't wait for Dean to answer before she started on a congealed Quarter Pounder with Cheese.

After she'd inhaled several mouthfuls of her burger she paused and pushed a hand to her chest. Dean wondered if she got heartburn. Eating the way she did couldn't be good for her.

Benton swallowed hard and forced out a smile and a thumbs-up.

She took a look round the room and whistled.

'Big-screen telly; private en-suite. Is that a minibar? Malton paying for this? Or is it Bea?'

Dean had no idea. He gave a shrug and Benton nodded, uninterested.

'They tell you much in here?'

The truth was Dean had no idea what had happened this past week. After his run-in with Leon Walker he woke up in the hospital with Bea briefing him not to talk to anyone. Especially the police.

He'd asked Bea to check on Vikki. Since he'd been in here he'd not heard from her. From Bea he knew the full extent of Leon Walker's killing spree. The nearest Walker had got to Vikki's flat was the inside of Pendleton Police station. Dean hoped that she didn't hold what happened between him and her dad against him.

Benton stuffed the rest of the burger in her mouth and reached into her anorak pocket. She pulled out a tattered copy of the *Manchester Evening News* and spread it out before Dean.

The headline read 'Lawyer Brings Gunman to Heel' and there were three photos. On the left a blurry photo of Leon Walker taken from a CCTV camera. On the right was a posed shot of Bea Wallace. She looked very glamorous but stern with it. In the middle was a product shot of a Louboutin high-heeled shoe. Just like the one Bea had lodged in Leon's neck.

'You're lucky it wasn't me in there with you – don't reckon I'd get far with these,' said Benton, lifting up her own foot. She wore the kind of bulky, rubber-soled boots favoured by bouncers and warehouse workers. Anyone who had to spend a lot of time on their feet.

Dean smiled. He couldn't help it.

Benton took the newspaper away, folded it up and put it back in her pocket.

'Lot been happening since then. Leon Walker's alive. Nine people dead. Stevie Mitchum being one of them. Couple of

Walker's victims found in the home of one Craig Malton. Who knows, maybe he even killed Danny?'

Dean gasped and then immediately winced at the pain.

'I know,' said Benton sympathetically. 'Of course Malton's nowhere to be seen. Which is a problem.'

Dean kept silent.

'Not seen him then?' said Benton. 'How about Keisha?'

Dean shrugged.

'Fair enough. Don't know if it's even her I'm looking for. Nothing to connect her to Leon Walker. And he's not talking. Not a whole lot to go on. I suppose I've got you.'

She let that hang.

'Soon as you-know-who gives you a bell, you know where to find me. Loyalty's a great thing. Just make sure you're being loyal to the right man. Or woman.'

Benton patted the bag of McDonald's with a grin, dropped her card beside it and wandered out of the room and away down the corridor.

A few minutes after she'd gone, the door to the en-suite bathroom opened and Malton walked out with a big grin on his face.

'Good lad. Didn't tell her a thing,' said Malton.

Any lingering doubts about whether or not Malton had forgiven him had long since gone. After he'd nearly died not once but twice in the one day, even Malton had been moved to tell him he'd done a good job.

'I don't know a thing,' said Dean.

'Time to change that,' said Malton. 'Time to wrap this all up.'

He peered into the bag of McDonald's Benton had left on the bed, grimaced and then looked back to Dean.

'How'd you like to meet the man who killed Danny Mitchum?'

82

When Malton finally called Fauzi to tell her that Galahad was ready to meet it came as an immense relief.

The past week had been unbearable. Waqar's death had devasted Fauzia's parents. She had done her best to keep the police at bay. Iffat had wanted to bury Waqar as soon as possible, but due to Waqar's violent death his body was currently in a morgue in Manchester pending the conclusion of police inquiries.

As Fauzia did her best to support her parents, the full extent of what had been unfolding around him had become clear.

The gunman who had attacked Waqar in Malton's house had killed nine people in total and injured dozens more. He'd then tried to kill his own lawyer, beaten a paralegal half to death and only been stopped when his lawyer stabbed him in the neck with a stiletto heel.

This was the world of the man in whom Fauzia had put her trust. The man who had called her early that morning and told her Galahad was ready to meet.

That was why she now found herself on the very edge of Manchester. Parked up in a hangar at Barton Aerodrome.

Barton Aerodrome was hidden beneath the outer ring road, beyond the Trafford Centre as the city surrendered to the countryside. It was the very definition of remote.

Manchester's first ever airport, it was little more than a control tower with a single runway and a collection of hangars housing the light aircraft of flight schools and wealthy hobbyists. The only sign of life was a forlorn pub in the middle of it all, providing shelter to the long-suffering families of plane spotters.

The hangar itself was a large metal building with a curved roof made from corrugated iron. Three aircraft were lined up under tarpaulin and waiting for her at the far end of the hangar were Malton and Dean.

Once Fauzia got out of the car there would be no going back. With no other choice, she opened her door and stepped out. Her heels echoing off the hard, concrete floor.

Malton was as unreadable as ever but next to him Dean looked in a bad way. His face and neck black with bruises. Whatever had happened to him he'd got off lighter than Waqar.

'So where is he?' Fauzia demanded, her voice echoing off the vaulted, metal roof. She hoped she sounded more confident than she felt.

'Late,' said Malton. 'As usual.'

Almost on cue the sound of a car being ground through its paces filled the air. It sounded distant but was getting closer.

'That'll be him now,' said Malton. 'The man of the moment. Galahad.'

Fauzia pressed against her car as a familiar blue VW Golf screeched into the hangar at speed.

The car barely slowed down as the driver pulled into a turn bringing it to a dead stop with the stink of burning rubber.

The windows were all tinted black, the cheap film starting to curl around the edges.

Fauzia wondered, if Galahad was so big and powerful, why did he only have the one beat-up car?

The front doors opened and two men all in black, wearing balaclavas over their faces got out of the car. It was impossible to tell whether or not they were the same men who had threatened her at her father's wedding venue, who'd stolen her car and her bloody clothes.

'Are you Galahad?' said Fauzia, determined to take the lead.

Neither man answered.

A second later the back door opened and nasal voice came from within. It sounded muffled. Like the speaker was covering up their mouth. But still, it was unmistakably Mancunian.

'Barton fucking Aerodrome? Love a bit of drama don't you Malton?'

Fauzia stifled a gasp as a skinny young white guy in overalls got out of the car.

He didn't have a balaclava covering his face. He didn't have a face.

He turned to Fauzia and grinned. His teeth bared through surgically reconstructed lips.

'Malton here says you got something of mine,' he said.

'Fauzia Khan, meet Galahad,' said Malton.

For just a moment Fauzia faltered. The sight of the man before her was nightmarish. Scrambling for a way to process what was happening, she fell back on to what she knew best. She forced herself to look at Galahad as a patient. Not a monster but someone in need of her help.

Severe fourth-degree burns to the eyes, mouth and nose. Third degree burns to the soft tissue of the face as well as signs of necrosis from failed skin grafts.

She wondered what had happened to him to leave him like this. How she would have dealt with him if he were her patient.

'What you fucking looking at?' spat Galahad.

'I have your phone,' said Fauzia, refusing to look away.

A smile broke out over Galahad's ruined mouth.

'Before I give you it, I need you to know. The entire phone has been uploaded to the cloud,' said Fauzia.

Galahad turned to Malton and frowned.

'Fuck she on about? You didn't mention any fucking clouds?'

'Online storage. I saved everything on the phone to an online hard drive,' interrupted Fauzia.

Galahad shook his head. His tongue darted in and out between his teeth. It reminded Fauzia of a dog getting ready to attack.

'Your fucking brother. You have no idea how much aggro he's caused me. First he loses the phone bad enough. Then you get this one here to find it,' he said gesturing to Malton.

Malton shrugged to Fauzia and kept quiet.

'He's dead,' said Fauzia defiantly.

Galahad grinned and clapped. 'One less job for me.'

Fauzia looked to Malton for some sort of lead. Malton stared back blankly. She was on her own.

'I'd have thought you'd be a little bit more grateful. Especially after I made sure you get to be an MP,' said Galahad.

Tahir was still in hospital. Fauzia had been keeping her distance but making sure to stay updated on his condition. The deadline to register to stand in the Farnworth and Great Lever byelection had been and gone. Tahir wasn't going to run.

'I never asked for your help,' she said.

Galahad shook his head wearily. 'Or I could kill you now,' he said, pulling a long blade out of his overalls and lazily waving it about.

He didn't move, as if trying to sense her reaction.

Fauzia wondered if he had any idea that Malton was quietly shaking his head in her direction. Willing her to hold her nerve.

She looked more closely at Galahad.

Deep tissue nerve damage. Severe respiratory complications and a heighted risk of sinus infections.

Galahad sensed the lack of reaction he was getting and stopped swinging the blade. 'Fuck it,' he said. 'Wacky's dead. What's on that phone means fuck all to you. But you forgot a third option.'

'What's that?' asked Fauzia, picturing the various scars from skin grafts all over the thighs and buttocks of the man in front of her.

'One night I visit you and fucking take you to bits,' he said, his tongue shooting out and licking what approximated his lips.

Fauzia held herself tightly against the instinctive terror his words provoked.

'At which point the software I set up will distribute the information that was on the phone to the police and the press. If there's a single day that goes by that I don't log in and give the password, that's what happens. A dead man's trigger,' she said.

She felt her heart racing. It had been tricky setting it up. She couldn't ask for help and had spent several hours downloading and configuring the software. But now as she stood in front of the man who on Waqar's encrypted phone called himself Galahad she knew it had been worth it.

Impaired sense of taste due to massive sinus damage. Potential deep-tissue nerve damage to the neck and ears. Potential post-traumatic stress and associated psychological complications.

Galahad burst out laughing. Spit flew from his mouth and he shook his head.

'Fuck me, Malton, you like your women mardy don't you? Fuck it. Done. Give me the phone and get the fuck out of my hangar. Don't want to see you again. Ever again. I know you don't want to see me. So you make sure you keep logging in every day. Or else you might just get a visit. Now get back in your car and fuck off.'

Malton turned to Fauzia.

'I'd say that's a result,' he said.

After handing the phone to Galahad Fauzia was about to get back in her car when Malton walked across the hangar and out of Galahad's earshot explained to her his own price for setting up this meeting.

83

There wasn't much to keep Keisha in Harpurhey. In need of quick money, she had sold the rest of the guns to an underworld dealer out in the Peak District, keeping a pistol for herself.

Now she had packed up what little she felt was worth keeping and, with the money from the guns, she was ready to get moving.

The problem was she had no idea where to move to.

The plan had failed but she had her second chance. Not with Craig or a new family. But with a new Keisha.

She felt alive. Like something toxic had been purged from her body. She felt light.

Now there was nothing to keep her in Manchester. The thought of starting again excited her. Her dead husband's business meant that she knew people all over the world. Anywhere someone was involved in making, smuggling and selling drugs Keisha could find a warm welcome.

But that had been the last thirty years. What had started as a way to show the world what she was made of had overnight become dull to her. She had done it all. Why retread old ground?

She had the money and the brains to do whatever she wanted. To become something new. Someone else entirely. Maybe someone who didn't feel the need to do these things anymore.

The past that had held her down for so long suddenly felt like a distant dream. Vignettes that happened to someone else entirely. A place that she could never go back to.

Back there in Hulme as they embraced, Keisha could feel Craig's grief as it mirrored her own. There was a catharsis in the sharing of it.

Now they had both lost a child. It wasn't flowers and romance. But it was something.

Wheeling her suitcase into the hallway there was only one thing left to do.

Keisha took a step into the second locked room.

There was the small white coffin, lying in the crib where she'd set it down all those months ago. The wood was disintegrating, the white finish yellowed. The small brass plate on its lid pitted and worn.

Keisha closed her eyes, her lips moving in a wordless prayer.

She opened her eyes and placed a hand on the coffin, holding it there a moment.

Satisfied, she bent down and from underneath the crib picked up a plastic jerry can that had been waiting, concealed beneath the white lace skirts of the crib.

Without ceremony or hesitation she walked around the room, emptying the jerry can over the floor, saving the last third of the petrol it contained for the crib and the coffin.

The house was well ablaze by the time she pulled out of the driveway.

Keisha felt the baby move inside her. But she lingered outside a second more, her eyes fixed on the burning longboat. All around her was the damp and decay of the Crescents. But against the night sky the fire burned bright and hopeful. A furiously radiant god who spoke directly to her – there's nothing so fixed in this world that it can't be burned down and started over again.

For the last thirty years she had been fighting the past. Now the past was well and truly behind her. It was going up in flames.

All that was left was the future.

Whatever future Keisha wanted.

364

84

'You got the right fucking idea, meeting somewhere like this. Still all a bit new to me, this low-key shit.'

Danny Mitchum and Malton walked along the far end of the airstrip. Away from the prying eyes of the plane spotters and maintenance staff. Danny was wearing dirty overalls and had a trucker cap pulled down over his head. With his collar up, at a distance you might even mistake him for just another skinny, thirty-year-old scally. Not the most instantly recognisable gangland figure in all of Manchester.

Every so often Danny's hand would shoot out to Malton's shoulder, gaining his bearings before stuffing it back into his overalls. Neither of them mentioned it.

Fauzia had left half an hour ago. Malton had been genuinely impressed. She'd made the exact same move he'd have made and in the process, for a moment at least, outmanoeuvred both him and Danny. There was nothing to harm Malton on the phone, but it meant that Danny would be behaving himself in the foreseeable.

It was Danny's bad luck that Fauzia had asked Malton to find the phone. Otherwise he just might have managed to fake his own death and start over as Galahad.

Danny turned to face the M60 flyover, the giant bridge that took the motorway hundreds of feet into the air and over the Ship Canal. Under the arches they could see the sloped building of the indoor ski slope and nestled beside it a dinosaur-themed crazy golf course. As Manchester dissolved into the countryside it gradually gave up trying to be a coherent urban space and devolved into random buildings, thrown up against each other, surrounded by the brown field land that even the developers didn't want to touch.

'How did you work it all out?'

'The phone,' said Malton.

Danny shook his head and swore.

'You're the only one on it who leaves voice messages. Everyone else texts.'

'Fucking hate text,' spat Danny.

'When I saw the messages left after you'd died. I knew it must have been you who set the whole thing up. But why?'

'You spent the last three months meeting my lot – what do you reckon?'

Malton thought back over the past few months of trawling through Danny Mitchum's associates.

'They're unreliable, unstable, prone to violence, drug addicts, thieves, criminal bottom feeders, opportunists and worse.'

'Stop, you're making me blush,' said Danny.

'But without you holding it together, there was nothing there.'

'Exactly!' said Danny with pride. 'That's why it was such a fucking great plan. Kill myself off, let my old operation burn itself out and then start again. Get some professionals to storm the warehouse where you were keeping me. Shoot the place up. Dump a corpse they'd prepared earlier and then incinerate the place. Fuck me, the amount of effort I put into it all. Best of all, I got you to back it all up. Get killed on your watch and now I got Craig Malton to stand by my story. And then that fucking idiot goes and loses his phone. Worse still his sister comes to you.'

'If you'd have asked first I would have found it for you. Only you were dead.'

Danny cackled. 'I nearly fucking had you. So fucking nearly.'

Malton had to admit if it wasn't for bad luck Danny would be a ghost now. And Stevie would still be alive. It had cost Malton a lot of time, aggro and blood but those were the commodities he dealt in. He knew the game he was playing.

366

'I'm sorry about your dad,' said Malton.

For a moment Danny went quiet. He gazed out across the horizon and then muttered to himself, 'Should never have left him in charge. Fucking idiot.'

They stood in silence for a moment.

Finally Malton spoke. 'But why? You were on top. Untouchable.'

Danny took off walking again, talking over his shoulder to Malton.

'This city, fuck me, used to be I could remember it all. Every street, every skyline. It was all in here.' Danny aggressively tapped the side of his head, his eyeless gaze fixed on Malton. He continued, 'That was ten years ago. I know that city's not there anymore. I can hear it changing. The cranes and diggers. I can feel it closing in. It's changing around me. I fucking hate it, but if I don't change with it then I'm fucked.'

Even monsters like Danny Mitchum grew up eventually. If they lived that long.

'So what now?' asked Malton.

Danny rubbed his hands together. 'Proper drugs,' he said proudly. 'None of this cocaine, heroin, ecstasy shit. That's a flashing light. Cops know that shit. Let Callum Hester and those dickheads out in Oldham and Bradford fight over that. I've seen the future. Synthetics.'

So that was why he'd stopped buying from Hester. Danny hadn't found a new supplier, he'd found a new game.

'The amount of Chinese money going into this city. Turning it into something else. I thought why not see if the Chinese fancy taking over the Manchester you don't see? The Manchester of Crumpsall and Blackley and Moston and Moss Side and Cheetham Hill. All the places that still remember what this fucking city is about.'

Malton had to admit he was impressed. But Danny wasn't finished. He stopped and turned to face Malton.

'This city's not buildings and fucking glass and fucking money. It's people. People like you and me. That's why we're not Leeds, or fucking Birmingham, or fuck me, Liverpool. Manchester is a million mad scally bastards running around up to no fucking good. Time one of them reminded this city who it belongs to.'

Danny stomped off around the edge of the airstrip. Malton hurried to catch up.

'I need to know you're going to leave Fauzia Malik alone,' he said.

'You not been listening to a fucking word? This is low-key shit. This is off-the-radar shit. She keeps her mouth shut, I won't have to shut it for her. Easy as that.'

'I got one last question,' said Malton.

Danny looked impatient. 'Hurry it up. I've got investors to meet. They own a fucking factory out in China. Just makes synthetics, tons and tons. Totally legal. Stronger than fucking heroin. Love the Chinese, me. They do not give a fuck. They're all about getting shit done.'

'Why Galahad?'

For a moment Danny's face went slack. He slowed his pace. The manic energy left him and he stared out towards the motorway, deep in thought.

'You tell a soul this, I'll fucking bury you,' said Danny turning to Malton.

Malton raised his hands in surrender and Danny continued.

'Right after those cunts did this to my face yeah? I was done. Fucking done. Lying in hospital all woe is fucking me. Everything's fucked. It's over. I asked a mate to get me some pills. Fucking pills. Utter cunt.'

Danny seemed to have gone into himself. Malton had never seen him like this. As if he were arguing with some internal interlocutor and Malton was merely a spectator.

'So there I was. Blind and ready to fucking do myself in. When this nurse tells me she's going to play me a documentary on the telly. I fucking told her, what fucking good is that to me? I can't see a fucking thing. But fuck her, she stuck it on anyway. It was about this bloke, this soldier yeah? Went off to war, got blown to shit, burned his face off. You know what he did? He fucking kept going. Lad was a fucking trouper about it. None of that self-pity bullshit.'

Danny gritted his teeth and swallowed. The mood seemed to pass.

'So I thought fuck it. If that cunt can make a go of it then so can I. I'm going to get better, get out of hospital and fucking kill every last bastard who did this to me.'

Having returned to the familiar territory of senseless violence Danny seemed back to his old self. From under his trucker cap he broke into a broad, rictus grin.

'The ship that bloke was on when they blew it up? *Galahad.*'

Danny turned and started walking back to the hangar. Malton had no idea if Danny had ever been here before. But as Malton watched him walk at a pace back towards where they'd come from, he didn't once falter or miss a step.

Malton waited for just a moment. He took one last look out towards the city. The new skyscrapers on the horizon looked like what they were: latecomers. Clumsy additions to a city of over five million souls. A city built on dirt and greed and suffering.

The city into which Emily would be bringing his child. A child who would never meet its father or get lost in the grief that he brought in his wake.

He looked over at Danny Mitchum as he made his way over broken concrete and potholes back to the hangar. This was where Malton belonged. Talking shop with psychopaths. Trawling the edges of the city. Making moves in the corners where no one was looking.

Malton couldn't change who he was. He saw that now. He could no more be a father than he could erase the forty years that had brought him to this point. All he could do was what he always did – keep one step ahead.

Whatever it was she had set out to do originally, Keisha had ended up doing something neither of them had expected. She'd set him free from the past.

Malton looked up at the sky. It was clear and bright, stretching all the way down to the horizon. Somewhere out there was his son. Anthony.

He started off after Danny while above his head a light aircraft climbed upwards into the deep blue beyond.

85

Yes was the kind of place that made Dean feel glad to be in Manchester. What had once been a nondescript warehouse near where the old BBC building previously stood, was now three floors of bars and music venues. Night after night, bands Dean had never heard of played in a room painted floor-to-ceiling pink while in the basement DJs played music that if he was honest he didn't really enjoy all that much. If that wasn't enough it had its own takeaway inside the ground-floor bar serving vegan fried chicken as well as a staff comprised almost entirely of aloof hipsters.

Dean loved it.

It was where Manchester was going. Young people who didn't give a shit about the old Manchester. This was his Manchester. A place where nostalgia was a dirty word. It was the future. The perfect place to meet Vikki for their first date.

She didn't know it was a date and he hadn't sold it to her as a date but once he'd told her everything about the past few weeks she had insisted on taking him out to thank him. Her dad was in prison but he had the best lawyer in the city and thanks to Dean he didn't have the murder of that lawyer as yet another charge against him.

Leon Walker was going to spend the rest of his life behind bars, but at least he was alive, and thanks to Bea, aware that despite his atrocious neglect his daughter had made something of her life.

But more than that, Dean had kept his word and found Olivia. Malton had told him about what had happened and why Olivia couldn't risk meeting up with Vikki. At least not until her adoption was formalised. He'd also given Dean something from Olivia to pass on. A gift to show that she hadn't forgotten Vikki.

Dean sipped his beer and nodded along to the music. At the far end of the bar, decks had been set up and a couple of girls danced away behind them as they rifled through boxes of seven-inches.

Danny Mitchum was alive too. It was a lot to process. He'd watched in shock as Danny had been reborn in the hangar at Barton Aerodrome as Galahad.

Dean still didn't know what exactly had happened with Keisha. All Malton would say on the matter was that she was gone and wouldn't be coming back.

After being shot in the face by her, there would always be a part of him that would rather know where Keisha was than take Malton's word that she was out of the picture for good. But for now Malton's word would have to do.

At least the scar on his face was healing nicely, thanks to the antibiotics Fauzia had suggested.

Dean's neck was still a mess of bruises, but between Bea and Malton the only thing he had to worry about now was getting better.

That and the girl who'd just walked in the door.

Vikki waved to Dean from across the bar. She was wearing a short denim skirt and a band T-shirt paired with Doc Marten boots and a tracksuit top. She looked totally at home among the trendy set at Yes.

He reached into his pocket and his fingers felt the uncut diamond Malton had given him from Olivia. On his way to Yes he'd stopped at a small jeweller's in the Northern Quarter to get it valued. They were a client of Malton Security and the owner was happy to give a no-questions-asked valuation. Nearly fifty thousand pounds. A life-changing sum for someone like Vikki.

As Vikki walked towards him half smiling, half hiding the look of concern at the state of his injuries, he smiled back at her.

Manchester was changing and so was he. And if he was lucky he wouldn't be doing it alone.

86

'Waqar Malik was a business owner, a worker, a son, my brother. If this can happen to him, it can happen to anyone.'

Fauzia looked out over the die-hard hangers-on who had stayed for the final count. Even though the by-election had been a foregone conclusion, it had been fought like every vote counted.

Galahad had made sure that Tahir dropped out before it even began. The local press could barely show an interest beyond a couple of puff pieces in the *Manchester Evening News*. After the events of a few weeks ago it felt like an anticlimax.

Fauzia could see Iffat and Samia standing watching in the crowd. Her mother had made sure to feed her entire team these past few weeks. Tonight was no different. She'd brought several boxes full of snacks and made sure no one went without. Even the slightly sad-looking, older gentleman from Chorley who the Conservatives were forced to field for want of a local candidate, would be going home tonight with a belly full of home cooking.

'I was told to keep quiet about my brother. To sweep it under the rug. And for the sake of my family I almost did. But I can't. Because I loved him more than anyone. He was my hero growing up and I owe it to him to make sure that what happened to him never happens again.'

When her election team had told her to play down her brother, what they didn't know and what she didn't tell them was the deal she had struck with Malton.

He had wanted access to Big Wacky's network and in exchange had promised to bury anything and everything connecting Fauzia to her brother's final days. He had ensured the return of the rest of her bloody clothes and assured her that Galahad would no longer be an issue.

Having met face to face, Fauzia was less certain that she had heard the end of Galahad. After what he did to Tahir it was clear he felt she still owed him. But for now she would be able to fight the election without having to look over her shoulder. She could make sure that Waqar's legacy was his own. Not Big Wacky's. She couldn't save her brother in life but in death she would make sure that no one could hurt him.

And, if she ever needed a favour, something that was so far beyond the boundaries of what a public servant ought to do, if that day ever came she had Malton's number.

'I'd like to thank my mother and father, my election team and most of all my brother. Waqar Malik.'

A few of her team were mopping their eyes. Fatigue and emotion overcoming them.

The hall burst into applause. Even the elderly gentleman with his forlorn blue rosette still pinned hopefully to his grey suit was cheering.

Fauzia looked out over the hall. She'd done it. She breathed it in. Savouring the moment. All the faces upturned, looking to her smiling.

And then she saw him. Alone in the middle of them all. The face she'd never forget. The look of terror as the conveyor belt dragged him closer.

Suddenly the hall was empty. The applause silent.

It was just her and him. His face a bloody mask of horror. He opened his mouth to scream but all that came out was the meat grinder's hollow, metallic roar.

Fauzia staggered back and he was gone. The hall was full of cheering supporters. The lights were bright and she'd just become MP for Farnworth and Great Lever.

87

'Let me get this straight, you're offering me Big Wacky's entire operation?'

Benton had forgone Malton's offer of a pint in favour of three packets of crisps. She was already on her second packet.

Across the table Malton nodded. After the business with Leon Walker he'd expected to find Benton knee-deep in the investigation. But when he'd called she'd asked him to meet her out in Gorton where she'd been assigned to a far from high-profile murder case.

'That is, if you're still into that sort of thing,' said Malton.

The Vulcan pub was quiet at this time in the afternoon. The barmaid had looked slightly disappointed when neither Malton nor Benton had bought anything stronger than a Diet Coke.

'You promised me Galahad,' said Benton through a mouthful of crisps.

'I know. And for reasons I can't go into, that's going to have to wait. So this is my way of making it up to you while you do. Giving you a million-pound organised crime gang, top to bottom. Every last piece.'

Malton let his offer hang while Benton slowly folded her empty crisp packet into a neat bow.

'Thing with Greater Manchester Police, you're never really forgiven. The boys at the top with the rolled-up trouser legs have got long memories,' said Benton.

She wiped her greasy hands on her anorak.

'I thought I was bang in the middle of things and then some poor lad gets killed out near Belle Vue and suddenly someone at the top thinks we're overstaffed on the Leon Walker case. Everyone else getting ready to say they worked on a once-in-a-lifetime case while I'm here with another dead boy.'

She sounded callous but there was something in what she said. Malton was always shocked how little of the violence that stalked the streets of Manchester ever made it into the local press, much less the nationals.

Stabbings, gun fights and murder, the likes of which would be front-page news if they happened down south, all quietly passed without comment. Leon Walker's rampage was a career maker. Unlike the poor boy who was found cold and dead behind the cement works.

Malton knew that he was the third such body in the past two years. He always kept track of such things. Young men turning up brutally slain always reminded him of James. His killers were still out there somewhere.

Benton tore open the third packet of crisps, scattering shards over the table.

Malton brushed some off his black, raw denim jeans and waited for Benton's response.

'You got me the encrypted phone?' said Benton hopefully.

Malton shook his head. 'I can't give you that. But what I can give you is everything off that phone that relates to Big Wacky and the Bolton crew.'

'You know I can't do fuck all with that. I need the originals.'

'Not true. With what I give you you'll have names, dates, shipments, prices. You'll have enough information to wind up the whole thing. I can point you in the right direction. All you have to do is follow.'

Benton laughed. 'That all?'

Malton shrugged. 'Take it or leave it. A few hours ago Farnworth and Great Lever's new MP just gave a speech about how she's going to clean up Bolton. I told her about an ambitious detective who'd love to help her do it.'

Benton smiled and shook her head. 'So where have you been hiding?' she asked, changing the subject.

'Leon Walker shot six people dead in the city centre. Killed another couple in my house. It felt like as good a time as any to lie low.'

Benton paused. Her eyes shot round the empty pub. 'I was worried,' she said.

Malton smiled. Underneath all the banter and bullshit he knew Benton would do anything for him. The feeling was mutual.

'I'm a big boy,' he said.

'Manchester's bigger,' said Benton as she rose to her feet. 'I'll take what you've got. Let them take it off me most likely. Leave me with the stuff no one else wants.'

Benton was on her way out of the door when she turned back. 'You ever work out what Keisha was up to?'

Malton shook his head. Benton raised an eyebrow but left it at that and returned to her crime scene.

He lingered in the Vulcan. It was a traditional pub. A taste of how Manchester was. The speedway and the dog track. Back when the coal mine out towards Ashton was still in living memory.

As he walked out into the afternoon sunshine he could see the city centre less than a mile away. Looking back he saw Benton talking to forensic officers. A tent erected around the final resting place of a body. Down a cobbled street behind a factory.

Malton smiled.

This was his Manchester. And it would never change.

Epilogue

Bea sat naked astride Malton, the two of them in the middle of her vast bed.

She faced away from him, her back arched and her hands on his thighs as she writhed atop him.

Malton held her tight to him, gripping her hips, his fingers framing the recently embellished tattoo of a bee on her lower back. It now mirrored the new logo she'd had commissioned for her law firm.

After being first attacked by Leon Walker and then nearly killing him with a high-heeled shoe, she had gone on to defend him in court and in the process became a household name in Manchester. The badass blonde lawyer who not only represented hardcore criminals but could also go toe to toe with them.

Bea had milked it for all it was worth. That included a corporate rebrand, prominently featuring her new bee logo.

Malton watched the tattoo move in time with Bea's hips. Her soft, warm body pouring itself over him.

Bea's flat had no curtains. It was high up enough to look down on the rest of the city. With the blackness of the night outside the floor-to-ceiling windows looked like polished black obsidian. Malton wondered if anyone could see them. If Bea would care if they could.

What he didn't think about was Keisha or Emily or Danny Mitchum or any of them. The past couple of months had been a return to normal.

If occasionally he found himself thinking about Anthony or the unborn child in Emily's belly, he had more than enough going on in his life to shuffle them to the distant recesses of his mind and move on.

Between Bea's lawyering and Fauzia's eagerness to keep her brother's legacy away from her political career, Malton Security was in the clear. He'd slipped back into the quiet anonymity that his line of work required. Things were almost boring.

His mind blank, he felt himself reaching climax. Bea felt it too. She gripped his thighs as he began to tense.

A phone rang out through the flat.

Before Malton knew what had happened Bea had rolled off him and crawled across the expanse of the mattress to retrieve it.

She was about to answer when she saw Malton's look of disappointment.

'Sorry, special clients phone. VIP clients.'

She stuck her tongue out playfully, turned away and stood by the window, naked as she took the call. Her white body stark against the black of the night.

With nowhere better to be, Malton sat on the bed and watched her talk, catching snatched phrases, trying to figure out what could possibly be so important.

Finally Bea hung up and turned to him. She was smiling from ear to ear. 'That was Nate Alquist,' she said.

Malton knew Alquist. He was in property. Owned half the terraces in Moss Side while he and his family lived in a grade two listed mansion out in Worsley. He also knew that Bea had just helped get his son Zak acquitted of the murder of Zak's girlfriend. Only his father's money had kept Zak out of prison.

'I didn't know you were on his son's case,' said Malton.

'I'm not,' said Bea, as she got back on the bed and crawled over to Malton. 'No one is anymore.'

She sat cross-legged in front of him, tapping away on the phone screen. Whatever the outcome of the call was, Bea's mind was already racing.

'His son's just been found murdered,' she said, looking up from her phone.

Malton knew Bea saw the look on his face. They were both still naked, they had nothing to hide.

'You know how badly Greater Manchester Police wanted this one,' said Bea, putting her phone down and kneeling in front of Malton, a look of excitement on her face.

She continued. 'Rich kid at a posh school accused of murdering his girlfriend. A girlfriend who's there on a scholarship. They got him on body camera confessing to it. If they can't get Zak then who can they get?'

'And now he's dead?'

Bea nodded. She seemed delighted about this turn of events. She put her arms around Malton's neck. He felt her breasts press up against him. She spoke inches from his face, like a lover sharing a confidence.

'Nate asked for my help. He doesn't trust GMP to investigate it properly. Thinks they're going to fudge it, let everyone feel like justice was done one way or another.'

Malton already knew what was coming next. He felt his heart race like it hadn't for weeks now. Not with fear or confusion or rage but with the prospect of diving back into the world he knew so well. The world of death and violence and secrets and lies.

'What did you tell him?' asked Malton.

Bea leaned in and kissed Malton full on the mouth. She savoured him, taking her time before she finally pulled away.

'I said I'd put my best man on it.'

Acknowledgements

Sam Tobin would like to thank the following people for their help, advice, suggestions, patience and encouragement in putting together *Pay the Price*:

Sam's agents Gordon Wise and Michael McCoy. A great combination of professional advice and heartfelt enthusiasm. Dr Anne-Marie Hughes for helping make Fauzia and Keisha every bit as able, ruthless and moreish as she is. Sam's editor Bethany Wickington for her brilliantly thoughtful, constructive and insightful suggestions. Eddie for walking me around the best bits of beautiful Bolton. And not forgetting Fenchurch, Mansool, Helena, Vince, Waleed, Tommy, Mayer, Mum and Dad and everyone who has listened at length as Sam unspooled all this madness. On to book 3...

Read on for a sneak peek of the third book in Sam Tobin's gritty Manchester Underworld series.

Out June 2023.

Prologue

The lights were on in the small, ground floor flat on the edge of Moss Side. The man standing outside in the darkness looking through the window was as good as invisible. He was free to take in the scene. Bide his time. Wait for just the right moment to make his move.

What he saw disgusted him.

The sofa was missing all the cushions. A filthy duvet had been thrown over the bare base to try to give some impression of domesticity. All it achieved was to make the room look even more squalid.

The floor was covered in burn marks and debris. Takeaway wrappers, cigarette butts and drugs paraphernalia.

People had defaced the magnolia walls with marker pens, blood and what looked like faeces.

The man turned and silently spat on the floor. He hated junkies.

When he looked back up, for just a moment before his eyes adjusted to the light levels, he caught a glimpse of his own reflection in the glass. A broad, white face, hair shaved to reveal the ridges of his skull at the sides and swept back on top. There was an unrelenting motion to his eyes, never at rest, always alert. His nostrils wide and flared, sucking in the night air.

His eyes reacquainted themselves and he saw a mattress in one corner of the room that seemed to have been slept on recently and the door to the living room which was open. Through the poorly insulated glass he could hear movement. The person he was waiting for.

A young black teenager walked into living room, his face glued to his phone. He had the height of an older man but his soft features betrayed every one of his sixteen years. Even if he had looked up he wouldn't have seen the man outside standing in the darkness. But the man saw him and smiled. It was nearly time.

He felt his heart began to race. Not with fear but with excitement. This is what he lived for. Savouring the moments of quiet before the storm. His mouth tasted dry with the anticipation of what he was about to do. His heavy fists clenched and unclenched, he jogged from foot to foot as the adrenaline built up in him. He looked like a professional athlete gearing up to play.

In a way he was. He'd made his living turning his innate love of extreme violence into a profitable career.

In the flat the teenager turned and walked back out of the room oblivious.

The man outside ran his tongue around his dry lips, licking the empty gap in his gums where his front teeth once were. Then he slowly pushed open the ground floor window and hauled his short, squat body into the flat.

It smelt worse that it looked. Stale body odour and smoke. The marks on the wall definitely were shit. Human shit by the looks of it. The man felt not a glimmer of doubt about what he was about to do as he walked through the living room and into the hallway where the teenager was still on his phone.

The man was breathing heavily now, ready for action. The sound of his breath whistled through the gap in his teeth. It was the first indication the teenager had that he was not alone in the hallway.

The boy turned and had just enough time to register the appropriate reaction of fear before the man was on him.

The first blow knocked the teenager clean out, his body falling awkwardly against the wall and down to the floor.

But one punch wouldn't be enough. Not by a long shot.

It was only a matter of seconds but what followed was a blur of fists and feet. Blows struck without any regard for their target.

All the while the man hissed softly to himself, 'Fuckin'... fuckin'... fuckin'...' His own private hymn to his frenzied brutality.

Then as soon as it had started it was over. The man opened his toothless mouth and sucked in a lungful of air. He felt his head clear and the painfully tight knot in his guts ease just a little.

On the floor the teenager was making wet, groaning sounds.

The man was about to pick up the body when the door to the bathroom opened and he found himself face to face with a wretched-looking man in his thirties; lank hair, blotchy, ulcerated skin and the rheumy red eyes of a junkie.

The knot in the man's guts pulled itself tight once more and he pounced.

1

Malton was late for a murder. It was a warm Saturday night in May and thousands of bodies filled Manchester city centre, blocking his way as Mancunians and visitors alike spilled out of the bars, restaurants and clubs over the pavement and into the road.

Sat behind the wheel of his vintage, green Volvo Estate Malton watched packs of middle-aged men from out of town, their bellies hanging over skinny jeans, their sunburned arms dangling from shirt sleeves as they shouted and swaggered their way across the city centre. He saw endless groups of hens; from the women all dressed as superheroes to the party wearing T-shirts with the mortified hen's face on them. They all moved with purpose. Determined to squeeze as much fun as possible out of their night in Manchester.

He had got the call ten minutes ago. A boy called Zak Alquist had turned up dead. Slaughtered in his own flat. Because of who his father was, soon enough the whole of the Greater Manchester Police would be mobilised to find the killer.

Malton's job was to beat them to it.

A drunk banged his hands on the roof of Malton's car. A red-faced man, his shirt untucked, sweat pouring off him. As he came level with Malton's side window the smile left his face. Looking back at him from inside the car was an eighteen-stone, shaved headed man with deep scar running down one side of his face. His features were unmistakably mixed race. His expression unmistakably hostile.

The drunk held his hands up in surrender. Stammered something that Malton didn't have time to hear. He needed to get to Zak's flat.

Malton wasn't police. Not even close. He owned Malton Security. A firm that ran doors, protected property and provided security to high net-worth individuals. But that was just the tip of the iceberg.

Craig Malton was the man who Manchester's criminal fraternity turned to when they needed to get to the bottom of something and would rather not get the law involved. He solved crimes for criminals.

Malton finally managed to weave through the bodies and turn off the inner ring road into the newly minted neighbourhood of Ancoats. Towering mills had been filled with flats, their ground floors a carefully curated selection of international cuisine, themed bars and artisanal eateries. What had been a no-go area just a decade ago was now teeming with life.

One of the men responsible for this miraculous change was Nate Alquist. Nate was as close as it came to Mancunian royalty. A property developer with the council's ear, Nate owned half of Moss Side as well as several tower blocks in the city centre. He had spent the last decade remaking Manchester in his image, cheered on all the way with generous government grants and glowing press coverage.

But now his son was lying dead in one of the flats he himself had built. But it wasn't the police who Nate turned to. It was Malton.

Manchester had long since shed its image of post-industrial deprivation. But just under the surface the grime and filth were still there. Nate Alquist knew that as well as anyone. Greater Manchester Police would get their turn but Nate had the money and connections to reach out to someone like Malton. Someone who saw how Manchester really worked.

Malton knew every criminal in the city. The families out east involved in the wholesale importation of drugs. The gangs that clustered around the deprived northern edge of the city centre selling those drugs. The various firms around Salford and Chorlton whose criminal exploits ebbed and flowed across multiple generations. Malton could talk to people who would never speak to the police on pain of death. He could go places the police would be scared to even think about treading. And he could do things the police would never dream of doing. Whatever it took to get answers.

Malton parked his car down a cobbled backstreet and walked through the shadows cast by the towering Ancoats mills. His footsteps echoed on the same streets that hundreds of years ago workers would have trodden as they poured out of their slums ready to break their bodies on the wheels of industry. Manchester used to make cotton. Now it sold flats and men like Nate Alquist had made their fortune doing it.

Malton emerged from the canyons of converted mills and out into what was left of the evening sun. Ahead of him lay the last remaining patch of green space in Ancoats. An empty field threatened on all sides by development. The tram ran across the far end of the field and beyond the tram stop lay dozens of newly constructed blocks of flats. It had been twenty minutes since he got the phone call telling him that in one of those flats he would find the body of Zak Alquist.

As Malton picked his way between the groups of people sat on the grass, drinking in the evening light, a tram pulled in from East Manchester and disgorged dozens of clubbers. Everyone was too excited with thoughts of the night ahead to pay much attention to the solid, mixed-race man stalking towards Zak Alquist's canal-side apartment block.

Malton noted with satisfaction that there were no police around. He could hear only the distant, ambient sirens of a Saturday night in Manchester. He had made it clear that if Nate wanted his services he needed to be the first one to see Zak's body. The crime scene would be his and his alone.

He walked through the lobby and slipped into the stairwell. By the time Malton reached Zak's floor he was jogging. He didn't want to spend any longer than he had to in the building.

The door to flat 304 was ajar. Malton paused briefly to slip on a pair of blue latex gloves and a facemask. He was walking into a crime scene; he didn't want to leave anything of himself behind. Looking left and right to make sure the coast was clear he took a breath and stepped into the apartment.

He was greeted by an abattoir.

The lights were off but in the glow thrown from the flats across the canal he saw a body sprawled on the floor of the small, open plan apartment. But only the body. The neck ended in a ragged gash of flesh. Where the head used to be was little more than a nauseating, wet pulp. Meat and jelly and bone. Malton recognised the round, indentations of a hammer beaten into the laminate flooring. Whoever had been wielding the weapon hadn't stopped until there was nothing left. Extreme overkill. Looking up at the ceiling confirmed it – the wild blood splatter of a frenzied attack.

The unmistakable smell of viscera filled the flat. A hollow, salty stench.

A large pool of blood was spreading out from the body, across the wooden flooring and soaking into the nearby rug. Zak Alquist hadn't stood a chance.

Malton took a step back and looked around. Aside from the gore the flat was immaculate. High end appliances, hard wood floors, elegant, Scandinavian furniture and brash, modern art hanging on softly pastel walls. A flat like this would easily cost a couple of thousand a month.

But the body wasn't the only thing out of place. All round the flat lay scattered piles and piles of money. Paper money. Tens of thousands of pounds. Some in bundles, some loose notes. All of it covered in blood.

In the distance Malton heard a single, determined siren. He froze. It was getting closer.

Malton bent down over the human remains. Something caught his eye and he gently lifted the tracksuit top. The torso was naked underneath. There on the right breast a tattoo that read – CARRIE 4EVA. The stylishly modern font contrasted with the ironically old school text.

He was getting up when he saw something he'd missed. Leaning in closer, amongst the cash he instantly recognised what he was looking at. Bright and white in the half light. A kilo brick of cocaine. A dealer's amount. And something else, a mark on top of the brick.

The siren was definitely getting louder now. Other sirens joined it. A murder would be a top priority. Police all over the city centre racing to get a piece of the action.

Malton squinted through the gloom at the brick of cocaine. There on the top was an imprint. A signature. The stamp branded into it by whoever was selling it on. In drugs as in most things nowadays, branding was everything.

As his eyes adjusted to the light he made out the marking. It was a circle inside of which was the outline of a hand grenade. Whoever had pressed the cocaine into a brick had also imprinted their logo onto the top of it.

By the time the police stormed Zak Alquist's flat Malton was already walking out the underground car park and taking the long way round to his car.

Whoever had killed Zak Alquist had done so with such a high level of violence that there was only one thing Malton could say for sure. It wouldn't be long before they did it again.

Go back to where it all started with
book one in the series!
There's only room for one boss in this city...

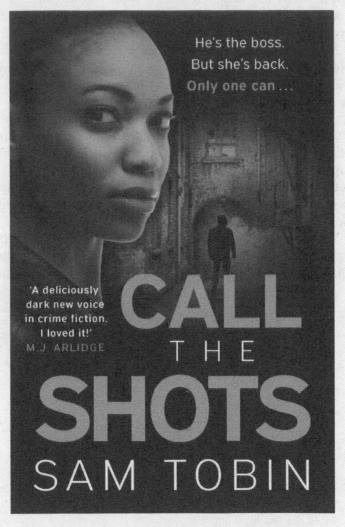

He's the boss.
But she's back.
Only one can...

'A deliciously
dark new voice
in crime fiction.
I loved it!'
M.J. ARLIDGE

CALL
THE
SHOTS
SAM TOBIN

Meet Craig Malton and Keisha Bistacchi in the first book
in Sam Tobin's Manchester Underworld series.
Available now.